## Praise for Michael Moorcock and the Elric Series

"A mythological cycle . . . highly relevant to the twentieth century . . . The figure of Elric often resembles many purely contemporary figureheads from Charles Manson to James Dean."
—*Time Out*

"Elric is back! Herald the event!"
—*Los Angeles Daily News* on *The Fortress of the Pearl*

"[The Elric] novels are totally enthralling."
—*Midwest Book Review*

"Among the most memorable characters in fantasy literature."
—*Science Fiction Chronicle*

"A work of powerful and sustained imagination . . . The vast, tragic symbols by which Mr. Moorcock continually illuminates the metaphysical quest of his hero are a measure of the author's remarkable talents."
—J. G. Ballard, author of *Crash*

"If you are at all interested in fantastic fiction, you must read Michael Moorcock. He changed the field single-handedly: He is a giant."
—Tad Williams

"A giant of fantasy."
—*Kirkus Reviews*

"A superb writer."
—*Locus*

# ELRIC
## The Stealer of Souls

# ELRIC
# The Stealer of Souls

## CHRONICLES OF THE LAST EMPEROR OF MELNIBONÉ

— VOLUME I —

MICHAEL MOORCOCK

ILLUSTRATED BY JOHN PICACIO

BALLANTINE BOOKS • NEW YORK

A Del Rey Trade Paperback Original



Published in the United States by Del Rey Books, an imprint of The Random House Publishing Group, a division of Random House, Inc., New York.



The stories contained in this work originally appeared in various science fiction magazines.

Library of Congress Cataloging-in-Publication Data

Moorcock, Michael.
Elric the stealer of souls / Michael Moorcock.
p. cm. — (Chronicles of the Last Emperor of Melniboné ; vol. 1)
The first of a series of six volumes collecting Michael Moorcock's Elric stories. Included in this volume: "The Dreaming City," "While the Gods Laugh," "The Stealer of Souls," "Kings of Darkness," and "The Flamebringers" (formerly collected as The Stealer of Souls) and "Dead God's Homecoming," "Black Sword's Brothers," "Sad Giant's Shield," and "Doomed Lord's Passing" (formerly collected as Stormbringer).
ISBN 978-0-345-49862-5 (pbk. : acid-free paper)
1. Elric of Melniboné (Fictitious character)—Fiction. 2. Albinos and albinism—Fiction. 3. Swordsmen—Fiction. 4. Fantasy fiction, English. I. Title.
PR6063.O59E47 2008
823'.914—dc22 2007033639

Printed in the United States of America on acid-free paper

www.delreybooks.com

9 8 7 6 5 4 3 2 1

*Book design by Julie Schroeder*

All the stories in *The Stealer of Souls* and *Stormbringer* first appeared in *Science Fantasy* magazine from June 1961 to April 1964.

"Putting a Tag on It" first appeared in *Amra,* vol. 2, no. 15, edited by George Scithers, May 1961.

"Mission to Asno!" first appeared in *Tarzan Adventures,* vol. 7, no. 25, September 1957.

"Elric" first appeared in *Niekas,* no. 8, edited by Ed Meskys, March 1964.

"The Secret Life of Elric of Melniboné" first appeared in *Camber,* no. 14, edited by Alan Dodd, June 1964.

"Final Judgement" (under a different title), by Alan Forrest, first appeared in *New Worlds,* no. 147, February 1965.

"The Zenith Letter," 1924, first appeared in *Monsieur Zenith the Albino,* by Anthony Skene, Savoy Books, 2001.

Cover artwork for *Sexton Blake Library,* 3rd series, no. 49, by Eric Parker, June 1943.

Cover artwork for *Science Fantasy* magazine by Brian Lewis, no. 47, June 1961, and James Cawthorn, nos. 55 and 63, October 1962 and February 1964.

"The Age of the Young Kingdoms" map, by James Cawthorn, 1962, first appeared in *The Fantastic Swordsmen,* edited by L. Sprague de Camp, Pyramid Books, 1967.

*Stormbringer* cover artwork by James Cawthorn, Herbert Jenkins, 1965.

James Cawthorn's "The Adventures of Sojan" illustration first appeared in *Tarzan Adventures,* vol. 7, no. 25, September 1957.

ALSO BY MICHAEL MOORCOCK

Behold the Man
Breakfast in the Ruins
Gloriana
The Metatemporal Detective

THE CORNELIUS QUARTET

The Final Program
A Cure for Cancer
The English Assassin
The Condition of Muzak

BETWEEN THE WARS: THE PYAT QUARTET

Byzantium Endures
The Laughter of Carthage
Jerusalem Commands
The Vengeance of Rome

*And many more*

To the memory of E. J. Carnell,
who originally asked for these stories,
and for Betsy Mitchell and John Davey,
who created this edition

CONTENTS

## FOREWORD

# THE RETURN OF THE THIN WHITE DUKE

by Alan Moore

I remember Melniboné. Not the empire, obviously, but its aftermath, its debris: mangled scraps of silver filigree from brooch or breastplate, tatters of checked silk accumulating in the gutters of the Tottenham Court Road. Exquisite and depraved, Melnibonéan culture had been shattered by a grand catastrophe before recorded history began—probably some time during the mid-1940s—but its shards and relics and survivors were still evident in London's tangled streets as late as 1968. You could still find reasonably priced bronze effigies of Arioch amongst the stalls on Portobello Road, and when I interviewed Dave Brock of Hawkwind for the English music paper *Sounds* in 1981 he showed me the black runesword fragment he'd been using as a plectrum since the band's first album. Though the cruel and glorious civilization of Melniboné was by then vanished as if it had never been, its flavours and its atmospheres endured, a perfume lingering for decades in the basements and back alleys of the capital. Even the empire's laid-off gods and demons were effectively absorbed into the ordinary British social structure; its Law Lords rapidly became a cornerstone of the judicial system while its Chaos Lords went, for the most part, into industry or government. Former Melnibonéan Lord of Chaos Sir Giles Pyaray, for instance, currently occupies a seat at the Department of Trade and Industry, while his company Pyaray Holdings has been recently awarded major contracts as a part of the ongoing reconstruction of Iraq.

Despite Melniboné's pervasive influence, however, you will find few public figures ready to acknowledge their huge debt to this all-but-forgotten world, perhaps because the willful decadence and tortured romance that Melniboné exemplified has fallen out of favour with the resolutely medieval world-view we embrace today throughout the globe's foremost neoconservative theocracies. Just as with the visitor's centres serving the Grand Canyon that have been instructed to remove all reference to the canyon's geologic age lest they offend creationists, so too has any evidence for the existence of Melniboné apparently been stricken from the record. With its central governmental district renamed Marylebone and its distinctive azure ceremonial tartans sold off in job lots to boutiques in the King's Road, it's entirely possible that those of my own post-war generation might have never heard about Melniboné were it not for allusions found in the supposedly fictitious works of the great London writer Michael Moorcock.

My own entry to the Moorcock oeuvre came, if I recall correctly, by way of a Pyramid Books science fantasy anthology entitled *The Fantastic Swordsmen*, edited by the ubiquitous L. Sprague de Camp and purchased from the first science fiction, fantasy and comics bookshop, Dark They Were And Golden Eyed, itself a strikingly neo-Melnibonéan establishment. The paperback, touchingly small and underfed to modern eyes, had pages edged a brilliant Naples yellow and came with the uninviting cover image of a blond barbarian engaged in butchering some sort of octopus, clearly an off day from the usually inspired Jack Gaughan. The contents, likewise, while initially attractive to an undiscriminating fourteen-year-old boy, turned out upon inspection to be widely varied in their quality, a motley armful of fantastic tales swept up under the loose rubric of sword and sorcery, ranging from a pedestrian early outing by potboiler king John Jakes through more accomplished works by the tormented, would-be cowboy Robert Howard to a dreamlike early Lovecraft piece, or one by Lovecraft's early model, Lord Dunsany, to a genuinely stylish and more noticeably modern offering from Fritz Leiber. Every story had a map appended to it, showing the geographies of the distinct imaginary worlds in which the various narratives were set. All in all it was a decent and commendable collection for its genre for its time.

And then, clearly standing aloof and apart from the surrounding mighty-thewed pulp and Dunsanian fairy tales, there was the Elric yarn by Michael Moorcock.

Now, at almost forty years' remove, I can't even recall which one it was—one of the precious handful from *The Stealer of Souls*, no doubt, and thus included elsewhere in this current volume—but I still remember vividly its impact. Its alabaster hero Elric, decadent, hallucinatory and feverish, battled with his howling, parasitic blade against a paranoiac back-drop that made other fantasy environments seem lazy and anaemic in their Chinese-takeaway cod orientalism or their snug Arcadian idylls. Unlike every other sword-wielding protagonist in the anthology, it was apparent that Moorcock's wan, drug-addicted champion would not be stigmatized by a dismaying jacket blurb declaring him to be in the tradition of J.R.R. Tolkien. The Melnibonéan landscape—seething, mutable, warped by the touch of fractal horrors—was an anti-matter antidote to Middle Earth, a toxic and fluorescing elf repellent. Elric's world churned with a fierce and unself-conscious poetry, churned with the breakneck energies of its own furious pulp-deadline composition. Not content to stand there, shuffling uneasily beneath its threadbare sword and sorcery banner, Moorcock's prose instead took the whole stagnant genre by its throat and pummeled it into a different shape, transmuted Howard's blustering overcompensation and the relatively tired and bloodless efforts of Howard's competitors into a new form, a delirious romance with different capabilities, delivered in a language that was adequate to all the tumult and upheaval of its times, a voice that we could recognize.

Moorcock was evidently writing from experience, with the extravagance and sheer exhilaration of his stories marking him as from a different stock than the majority of his contemporaries. The breadth and richness of his influences hinted that he was himself some kind of a Melnibonéan expat, nurtured by the cultural traditions of his homeland, drawing from a more exotic pool of reference than that available to those who worked within the often stultifying literary conventions found in post-war England. When Moorcock commenced his long career while in his teens he showed no interest in the leading authors of the day, the former Angry Young Men—who were in truth far more petulant than angry and had never been that young—cleaving instead to sombre, thoughtful voices such as that of Angus Wilson or to marvelous, baroque outsiders such as Mervyn Peake. After solid apprentice work on his conventional blade-swinging hero Sojan in the weekly Tarzan comic book or in the Sexton Blake adventures that he penned alongside notables such as the wonderful Jack Trevor Story (and, as rumour has it, even Irish genius Flann O'Brien), Moorcock emerged as a formidable rare beast with an extensive reach, as capable of championing the then-unpublished *Naked Lunch* by Burroughs (W. S.) as he was of appreciating the wild colour and invention that was to be found in Burroughs (E. R.). Whether by virtue of his possibly Melnibonéan heritage or by some other means, Moorcock was consummately hip and brought the sensibilities of a progressive and much wider world of art and literature into a field that was, despite the unrestrained imagination promised by its sales pitch, for the most part both conservative and inward looking.

Growing out of a mid-1950's correspondence between the young writer and his long-serving artist confederate James Cawthorn, the first Elric stories were an aromatic broth of Abraham Merritt and Jack Kerouac, of Bertolt Brecht and Anthony Skene's Monsieur Zenith, the albino drug-dependent foe of Sexton Blake who'd turned out to have more charisma than his shrewd detective adversary. With the series finally seeing daylight in Carnell's *Science Fantasy* in 1961, it was immediately quite clear that a dangerous mutation had occurred within the narrow gene pool of heroic fantasy, a mutation just as elegant and threatening as Elvis Presley had turned out to be in the popular music of this decade or that James Dean represented in its cinema. Most noticeably, Elric in no way conformed to the then-current definition of a hero, being instead a pink-eyed necromaniac invalid, a traitor to his kind and slayer of his wife, a sickly and yet terrifying spiritual vampire living without hope at the frayed limits of his own debatable humanity. Bad like Gene Vincent, sick like Lenny Bruce and haunted by addiction like Bill Burroughs, though Elric ostensibly existed in a dawn world of antiquity this was belied by his being so obviously a creature of his Cold War brothel-creeper times, albeit one whose languid decadence placed him slightly ahead of them and presciently made his pallid, well-outfitted figure just as emblematic of the psychedelic sixties yet to come.

By 1963, when the character first appeared in book form, Britain was beginning to show healthy signs of energetic uproar and a glorious peacock-feathered blossoming, against which setting Elric would seem even more appropriate. The Beatles had, significantly, changed the rules of English culture by erupting from a background of the popular and vulgar to make art more vital and transformative than anything produced by the polite society-approved and -vetted artistic establishment. The wrought-iron and forbidding gates had been thrown open so that artists, writers and musicians could storm in to explore subjects that seemed genuinely relevant to the eventful and uncertain world in which they found themselves; could define the acceptable according to their own rules. Within five years, when I first belatedly discovered Elric sometime during 1968, provincial English life had been transmuted into a phantasmagoric territory, at least psychologically, so that the exploits of this fated, chalk-white aesthete somehow struck the perfect resonance, made Moorcock's anti-hero just as much a symbol of the times as demonstrations at the U.S. embassy in Grosvenor Square or Jimi Hendrix or the *OZ* trial.

Naturally by then Moorcock himself had moved on and was editing *New Worlds*, the last and the best of traditional science fiction magazines published in England. Under Moorcock's guidance, the magazine became a vehicle for modernist experiment, gleefully reimagining the SF genre as a field elastic enough to include the pathological and alienated "condensed novels" of J. G. Ballard, the brilliantly skewed and subverted conventional science fiction tropes of Barrington Bayley and even the black urban comedies dished up by old Sexton Blake mucker Jack Trevor Story. Moorcock's own main contribution to the magazine—aside from his task as commander of the entire risky, improbable venture—came in the form of his Jerry Cornelius stories.

Cornelius, a multiphasic modern Pierrot with his doings catalogued by most of Moorcock's *New Worlds* writing stable at one time or other, rapidly became an edgy mascot for the magazine and also for the entire movement that the magazine was spear-heading, an icon of the fractured moral wasteland England would become after the wild, fluorescent brush-fire of the 1960s had burned out. His debut, starting in the pages of *New Worlds* in 1965 and culminating in Avon Books' publication of *The Final Programme* during 1968 was a spectacular affair—"Michael Moorcock's savagely satirical breakthrough in speculative fiction, *The Final Programme*, a breathtaking vivid, rapid-fire novel of tomorrow that says things you may not want to hear today!"—and a mind-bending apparent change of tack for those readers who thought that they knew Moorcock from his Elric or his Dorian Hawkmoon fantasies. Even its dedication, "To Jimmy Ballard, Bill Burroughs, and the Beatles, who are pointing the way through," seemed dangerously avant-garde within the cosy rocket-robot-ray-gun comfort zone of early sixties science fiction. As disorienting as *The Final Programme* was, however, its relentless novelty was undercut by a peculiar familiarity: Cornelius's exploits mirrored those of Elric of Melniboné almost exactly, blow for blow. Even a minor character like the Melnibonéan servant Tanglebones could turn up anagrammatized as the Cornelius family's retainer John Gnatbeelson. It became clear that, far from abandoning his haunted and anaemic prince of ruins, Moorcock had in some way cleverly refracted that persona through a different glass until it looked and spoke and acted differently, became a different creature fit for different times, while still retaining all the fascinating, cryptic charge of the original.

As Moorcock's work evolved into progressively more radical and startling forms over the coming decades, this process of refracting light and ideas through a prototypical Melnibonéan gemstone would continue. Even in the soaring majesty of *Mother London* or the dark symphony of Moorcock's Pyat quartet, it is still possible to hear the music of Tarkesh, the Boiling Sea, or Old Hrolmar. With these later works and with Moorcock's ascent to literary landmark, it has become fashionable to assert that only in such offerings as the exquisite *Vengeance of Rome* are we seeing the real Moorcock; that the staggering sweep of glittering fantasy trilogies that preceded these admitted masterpieces are in some way minor works, safely excluded from the author's serious canon. This is to misunderstand, I think, the intertextual and organic whole of Moorcock's writings. All the blood and passion that informs his work has the genetic markers of Melniboné stamped clearly on each paragraph, each line. No matter where the various strands of Moorcock's sprawling opera ended up, or in what lofty climes, the bloodline started out with Elric. All the narratives have his mysterious, apocalyptic eyes.

The tales included in this current volume are the first rush of that blood, the first pure spurts from what would prove to be a deep and never-ending fountain. Messy, uncontrolled and beautiful, the stories here are the raw heart of Michael Moorcock, the spells that first drew me and all the numerous admirers of his work with whom I am acquainted into Moorcock's luminous and captivating web. Read them and remember the frenetic, fiery world and times that gave them birth. Read them and recall the days when all of us were living in Melniboné.

Alan Moore
Northampton
31 January 2007

## INTRODUCTION

The past is a script we are constantly rewriting. Experience changes over the years to suit whatever story we believe we are telling about ourselves and our friends. It's why the police and the courts are forever questioning accounts offered by honest people.

If proof of this were needed, it is in the stories I have told over the years about how Elric came into being. Nothing crucial hangs on my slightly varying versions of my hero's conception; and in reprinting those versions I've made no attempt to make them coherent, so readers will discover some inconsistencies here which, were I interested in promoting a particular version of events, I would have edited out. They are what I believed to be truthful accounts when I wrote them or else I was arguing within a specific context, as in a letter I wrote to the fanzine *Niekas* some short while before the four-part serial published as *Stormbringer* came out in 1963–1964. In such arguments, where I was defending myself against criticism, I gave more emphasis to certain experience than I would have done ordinarily. Like much of my fiction, which nowadays seems so solidly a part of a genre's history, when the Elric stories first appeared there were some readers who found them offensive or otherwise infuriating. Then, as now, some readers seemed to be uncomfortable with their ironic tone. They were probably the first "interventions" into the fantasy canon, such as it was. Later, writers like Stephen Donaldson, Steven Erikson, and Scott Bakker would be similarly criticized. The criticism I received in letters or in fanzine reviews at the time made me far more defensive than I would be these days. I've always known that fanzine critics prepared you for the worst any mainstream critics could say about you. They weren't unlike some aspects of the web. It's interesting to note in these pieces (which I've placed so as to avoid spoilers) the evident strength of my feelings when Elric was still, as it were, newborn and in need of his parent's protection!

I notice, for instance, that I claimed to be the product of a particular form of Christian mysticism. While it is true that for a short time (at around the age of seven) I attended Michael Hall School in Sussex, which was run on the rather attractive mystical Christian principles of Rudolf Steiner (in turn a break-away from Madame Blavatsky's brand of spiritualism), it is not really true to suggest, as I did in one of the pieces reprinted here, that I was "brought up" according to Steiner's ideas. In fact, my background was almost wholly secular, much of my immediate circle was Jewish and I was only briefly interested, as a young adult, in Steiner's ideas, which had influenced my mentor, Ernst Jelinek. These, however, *did* influence the cosmology of the Elric stories. Poul Anderson's marvelous fantasies *The Broken Sword* and *Three Hearts and Three Lions* were probably of equal influence, as was my fascination with Norse, Celtic, Hindu, and Zoroastrian mythology.

I had begun my professional career as a contributor to a British weekly juvenile magazine called *Tarzan Adventures*, which was a mixture of reprinted newspaper strips and original text. My first regular commission was a series of articles on Edgar Rice Burroughs and his characters, but I was soon writing fiction, some, like Sojan, adapted from the stories that first appeared in my fanzine *Burroughsania*, which I had founded in my last year at school (I left at the age of fifteen). These first stories were fantasy adventures bearing, not surprisingly, a strong ERB influence, and I have reprinted one here to give a flavour of what I was doing a few years before I created Elric. More of my early ups and downs in publishing can be found in the various departments of www.multiverse.org. Warts and all, they don't show as much promise as I sometimes like to think. They do offer, I hope, some encouragement to writers who are yet to publish professionally! Rereading these stories, however, I think they do show a fairly marked improvement as it began to dawn on me that there was a readership for that kind of fiction and that I was no longer—as I had been when I worked as a journalist and for the comics—anonymous.

Over a period of time following almost exactly the period in which I was writing the first Elric stories, I was inclined to distance myself from the work of Robert E. Howard, even though he had been an important influence (unlike Lovecraft, for whom I had no taste). Over the years I have seen many other writers put space between themselves and their main sources of inspiration and have come to understand it as an important, if not particularly admirable, part of the process of trying to make one's individual mark. I soon began giving Anthony Skene the credit he deserved for Zenith the Albino. Eventually I was instrumental in helping get Skene's only Zenith hardback novel, *Monsieur Zenith the Albino*, republished in a particularly fine edition by Savoy Books (www.savoy.abel.co.uk/HTML/zenith.html). Until then, there were only three copies of the book known, one of which was in the British Library. In recent times, of course, I have also given Howard due credit and even by the early 1960s was perfectly happy to announce him as an important influence. Tolkien, although my dislike for *The Lord of the Rings* became exaggerated in argument, was never an influence. As with Lovecraft, I think I came to him too late. Neither author needed any help from me to get the readership he deserved. I am proud, however, of my part in getting Skene republished and helping, in a small way, to make so many of his old magazine stories available online. From being a hero of my youth Monsieur Zenith appears to have become the friend of my seniority. As well as helping Savoy to reprint their extraordinarily lavish version of *Monsieur Zenith*, I have written a number of stories designed to return Elric to his roots. By linking Zenith (or Zodiac as he's sometimes called) and Elric, I hope I show how they were almost certainly the same person! Sexton Blake is "disguised" by my use of the detective's real name (Seaton Begg) from his days as a Home Office investigator. These stories were recently published as *The Metatemporal Detective* (Pyr, 2007). Zenith, rumoured to be a Yugoslavian aristocrat, disappeared during the intensity of World War II, making his last Sexton Blake appearance in a story called "The Affair of the Bronze Basilisk." Another version of his return can be found at the Sexton Blake web site written by Mark Hodder (Blakiana.com).

Looking back through the non-fiction pieces of the 1950s and early 1960s, I seem to have been consistent in my admiration for Fritz Leiber. My dislike of *The Lord of the Rings* has, as I say, been exaggerated. I do, I must admit, dislike the religiosity exhibited by the work's nuttier fans but had, in fact, every reason to like Professor Tolkien. When I was young and *The Lord of the Rings* was seen as one idiosyncratic book among others—like William Morris's pseudo-sagas, E. R. Eddison's *The Worm Ouroboros*, Lord Dunsany's *The Gods of Pegana* or David Lindsay's *A Voyage to Arcturus*—Tolkien and C. S. Lewis were both very kind to me, as were writers I admired rather more, like T. H. White, author of *The Sword in the Stone*, and Mervyn Peake, author of *Titus Groan*. Peake in particular was a more direct influence on the Elric stories. I came to know Leiber and take as much pleasure from his company as I did from his fine, precise prose which in my view is superior to that of every English fantast of his generation. I don't think I was alone as a boy in preferring, for well-written escapism at least, the work of American writers. And not just for escapism, of course. Faulkner—though not most of Hemingway or Fitzgerald—was a huge enthusiasm, and I had others, including Twain, of course, together with Sinclair Lewis and his generation of realists. There were many I found in the pulps. I had loved the full-blooded science fantasies of Leigh Brackett and the work of the young writer she had befriended, Ray Bradbury, who often appeared in the same issues of *Planet Stories* and *Thrilling Wonder Stories*. It only occurred to me later how so much that was good about Anglophone fiction came out of California. It wasn't just the great movies being made there from the beginning of the twentieth century. Edgar Rice Burroughs's Mars wasn't too far away in the deserts beyond Tarzana, and both Brackett and Bradbury grew up there, making of Burroughs's Mars what others made of Dickens's London. Like his Vermilion Sands, Ballard's Mars is as Californian as the language that influenced the likes of Chandler, Hammett, Cain and all those other Americans whose tone can still be heard, faintly perhaps in English literary fiction, to this day.

Before I came to write the first Elric stories I was already absorbing the kind of literature which influenced my generation, including that of the great French Existentialist writers and film-makers. I made my first trip to Paris at the age of fifteen. I went to see Sartre's *Huis Clos* and Camus's *Caligula*. I read their novels. I became an enthusiast for the likes of Henry Miller, Samuel Beckett, Boris Vian, Blaise Cendrars and William Burroughs. Although no great fan of most of the Beats, I had met some of them in Paris and had friends who were huge admirers. Later, I did come to know and like Burroughs. I absorbed the ideas of the time as much through conversation as by reading and, when I had gone from editing *Tarzan Adventures* to becoming an editor at Sexton Blake Library (a pulp series that had begun before World War I and that had published many of those Zenith stories before World War II), I had lost my taste for most fantasy fiction. SBL publishers, Amalgamated Press, at that time the largest periodical producers in the world, were horribly overstaffed in those easy years. Editorial offices were full of young men like me who came to journalism through juvenile publishing but who were huge enthusiasts for surrealism and the situationalists, for Brecht and Beckett and Ionesco. They would go on to do great things, not always as journalists.

We went to Paris every chance we had. At George Whitman's Paris bookstore (then called Mistral but now known as Shakespeare & Company) I would busk with my guitar, seated on a chair outside the shop (George didn't mind since he knew all the money went back to him), and then as soon as I had enough, buy a couple of paperbacks for the rest of the day. It was there, in the shadow of Notre Dame, that I read my first true SF story, Alfred Bester's *The Stars My Destination*, and wondered what I'd been missing. As it turned out, Bester was one of the few SF writers of his day that I enjoyed. He was a sophisticated, much-traveled man. He was associated with a group who published primarily in *Galaxy* magazine and included Frederik Pohl and C. M. Kornbluth, Philip K. Dick and Robert Sheckley. During the shame of McCarthyism, they were amongst the earliest to raise literary voices to examine modern times often far more rigorously and amusingly than literary writers had done. There were a few brave voices who, like their Russian counterparts, found places to publish and speak to a public who mourned what was going on.

I wasn't the only one to see some sort of literary salvation in science fiction. That Kingsley Amis, Robert Conquest and Edmund Crispin shared enthusiasm for certain kinds of SF is well-known, but many of us found it sketchy and condescending (Amis hated Burroughs and the Ballard of *Atrocity Exhibition*). But less obvious people, including Doris Lessing (then known only as a realist), were keen SF readers. Considered by many to be the finest literary writer of his day (and a prescient SF writer, as in his *The Old Men at the Zoo*) Angus Wilson had recommended that Sidgwick & Jackson in the UK publish *Tiger! Tiger!*, the original title of *The Stars My Destination*. Wilson, Elizabeth Bowen and an increasing number of writers of social fiction, as well as a surprising bunch of well-known philosophers, were discriminating readers of SF and other kinds of imaginative fiction. They sometimes even wrote it. Although the Amis camp demanded that SF remain a kind of literary ghetto, the rest of us wondered if it was possible, through the genre, for popular fiction and literary fiction to find common ground. At some point in the nineteenth century, perhaps even the early twentieth century, fiction had become the victim of a random kind of snobbery which denied a public to many highly accessible writers of equal ambition and artistic success and thus also discouraged a popular public from reading the established canon ("too highbrow"). My friends—Ballard, Bayley and Aldiss especially—believed much as I did. Quite a bit of our late-1950s and early-1960s conversation envisaged a magazine that would combine the values of the best SF and the best contemporary literature as well as features about what was happening in the arts and sciences.

You can imagine—with all these glorious ideas of reuniting the values of popular and literary fiction, which we shared with composers and visual artists as well as film-makers—the last kind of fiction I imagined myself writing was what Leiber had christened both heroic fantasy and sword and sorcery but which I had, it appeared, already termed epic fantasy (see "Putting a Tag on It"). By some strange twist of fate I was telling tales that had more in common with the nineteenth century than the twentieth in order to help support an avant-garde movement which looked forward to the twenty-first.

Though Tolkien had been published, he was still relatively obscure, and his kind of fantasy fiction was never published in the mainstream (Tolkien's primarily academic publisher, George Allen &

Unwin, was better known as Jung's). Hard as it is to believe now, *The Lord of the Rings* was considered as some kind of post-nuclear allegory, too risky to chance in a paperback edition (which Tolkien, anyway, regarded as a bit vulgar). Both Burroughs and Howard were thoroughly out of fashion in the United States (though not so much in Britain), and there was no longer any kind of market for supernatural adventure fiction. The eagerness with which the public embraced the fantasts when they were finally released, an uncaged flock, upon the world, is a good lesson for publishers and for politicians.

I mention elsewhere how E. J. Carnell, editor of the three surviving British SF magazines, commissioned the first Elric stories. It was in *Science Fantasy* and *Science Fiction Adventures* and *New Worlds* that the likes of Clarke, Aldiss, Ballard, Brunner and even Terry Pratchett published their early work. Philip K. Dick's first significant novel, *Time Out of Joint*, was serialized in *New Worlds*. Carnell's taste was broader than that of his American contemporaries. Although unintentionally, he was without doubt the father of what became a significant literary renaissance whose influence would spread throughout Anglophone fiction. In our different ways, he and I were as much an instrument of the Zeitgeist as anyone. By the time I took over the magazine (see my introduction to *New Worlds: An Anthology*, Thunder's Mouth Press, 2004) I had a clear agenda: to merge generic SF and literary fiction. *New Worlds* not only ran an exclusive interview with Tolkien, when he was refusing everyone else but also was the first to judge Philip K. Dick as an important writer, and I was able to persuade Tom Maschler of Jonathan Cape to publish his best work in hardback simply as literary fiction. Meanwhile we ran work by Disch, Pynchon, Zoline, D. M. Thomas, Peake and a good many other ambitious writers, artists and scientists, until we at last began to see our hopes fulfilled. Now some of our finest living writers turn increasingly to the methods of SF—and, the insistent Ms. Atwood aside, I need name only Lessing, Rushdie, Roth, McCarthy, Mosley and Pynchon to support my understanding that we are at last all happily wallowing in the same pond, no longer able to distinguish by subject matter or even language what is art and what is not, choosing the techniques that best suit our current subject.

Which is not to say that everything *is* art! These stories, for instance, are escapism, however intensely imagined and felt. They were written quickly by a young man who was still throwing everything he had into whatever he did and still getting rejected, whether by editors or girls, enough to hurt. So it's all in here. All the angst that's fit to print and maybe a little more that isn't. I describe somewhere in here how one period of my life was marked by broken glass (and a sequence of small, though happily not especially destructive, fires, miscellaneous victimless hurlings of typewriters and so on) as the elemental agony of my existence, coupled with an indulgence in some good clarets and single malts, overwhelmed me. Elric could not confront many of the contemporary concerns, however, which is how by 1965 I came to re-invent him in the person of Jerry Cornelius, rewriting "The Dreaming City" as the beginning of *The Final Programme*.

In those years I was a bit self-destructive, I think. I was tall, speedy, with a Fleet Street journalist's capacity for drink and a habit of knocking stuff over or breaking it by accident. Luckily, I was also for the most part pretty amiable. Although not as a rule quarrelsome, I was also eloquent enough, it seems, to wound people, which I never did intentionally. I was self-dramatizing, as my mother had been before me, and I had learned a lot about the melodramatic gesture. I hated that in myself, however, and set about getting rid of it. As a result I sometimes had a grimmer, narrower notion of the truth, which perhaps compensated for having something of a Baron Munchausen at the family home.

Early on I became a very conscious as well as a very rapid writer, pouring my life pretty much as it happened into my work. Emotional, visual, intellectual, it was all thrown into the pot. Like most writers I know, I wasted nothing. Many of the fantastic landscapes in my early stories were versions of those around where I lived in Notting Hill, when I would take my children out to the park and write while they snoozed or played. Holland Park had been blitzed, but though the house itself had been consumed by incendiary bombs, the outbuildings and the wonderful botanical gardens had been preserved pretty much intact. The already exotic plants and birds of that park, in particular, deserve credit for their inspiration of early books such as *The Fireclown* and *The Shores of Death*. The Blitz proved an excellent experience for the chaotic landscapes I wrote about in *Stormbringer*.

It took me a decade or so to realize that my stories are notable for their absence of fathers. Whether the character is Elric, Jerry Cornelius (his modern avatar), Gloriana or Colonel Pyat, fathers are rarely around for their offspring. My father's decision to leave my mother at the end of European hostilities was a blessing in so many ways but had clearly made something of an unconscious emotional impact on me. So what else is Elric looking for? You'll have to forgive me the odd reference to Freud or Jung because I began producing these stories at the time I was writing essays about the psychological roots of fantasy fiction. Although, of course, it was not my business to jam these ideas down the throats of readers of fiction, a glance at *Wizardry & Wild Romance* (MonkeyBrain Books, rep. rev. 2004), a version of those early essays, will show that they were not, at pretty much any level, unconsciously written. I was certainly aware of the Freudian interpretations of black swords or the Jungian interpretation of incubi and succubi.

While Mervyn Peake's fiction soon became my favourite fantasy (ironically, it contains no real supernatural elements), I had also read a great deal of Gothic fiction and other, harder-going stuff, like Southey's *Palmerin of England* and the few available translations of Peninsula Romances a kid like me would be likely to find. I'd shuddered at *The Monk*, skipped a bit through the longueurs of *The Mysteries of Udolpho*, loved the imagery of *Vathek*. As many of us do, who develop an enthusiasm, I had gone back as far as it was possible to go and met another early influence on the way—John Bunyan's *The Pilgrim's Progress*, together, of course, with Milton's *Paradise Lost*. Cornerstones of Puritan literature? But they worked for me. Bunyan taught me that you could tell more than one story in a single narrative. Milton taught me that Satan can be excessive attractive. To this day I advise people who want to write fantastic fiction for a living to stop reading generic fantasy and to go back to the roots of the genre as deeply as possible, the way anyone might who takes his craft seriously. One avoids becoming a

Tolkien clone precisely by returning to the same roots that inspired *The Lord of the Rings*.

And so Elric himself figuratively went back to those wellsprings increasingly as I told his story. But it is here, in what became the first two books, I think you'll find the psychological roots, the essence, if you like, of Elric, before I understood that we were as locked together as firmly as Conan Doyle and Holmes and that my creations would engulf me in a tidal wave of imitations or inspirations. Poor Bob Howard, distraught over the death of his mother, took a shotgun to himself and at least avoided the Conan clones, just as Tolkien never had to see Gandalf bobbleheads or gaming companies lifting and vulgarizing aspects of his work wholesale. I'm sure Howard would have learned how to deal with anything, had he survived, and I still enjoy a fantasy of him as an old guy in a rocking chair, sitting on his front porch and swapping technical tips with his visitors while sometimes privately confiding that the fire's gone out of the stuff since he first started doing it. Except, of course—and then he'd reel off a list of names crossing a spectrum as wide as the state. Howard could not predict the success of his character any more than I could guess Elric's future. Unaware of the coming influence of Dungeons & Dragons and others, I cheerfully permitted free use of my ideas and cosmology until I had the peculiar experience of watching different companies going to law over characters and cosmologies I had created, which is why the Elric gods and demons appeared in the original D&D book but were later dropped.

We've come a long way since 1957, when it was still possible to order the set of *The Lord of the Rings* and wait a week before receiving the first editions at, as I recall, a guinea apiece. Tolkien's phenomenal story was still considered as much an expensive rarity as Arkham House Lovecrafts, luxuriously illustrated limited editions of Dunsany or the Gnome Press editions of the Conan books. Ironically, none was as widely published as Anderson's second novel (his first was a mystery) *The Broken Sword*, which was done in an ordinary commercial edition by Abelard-Schuman. This was long before Lin Carter's rediscovery series of fantasy classics, which provided a rich education for those interested in what was still a pretty disparate bunch of books! Before

Carter's series, the fantasy canon was an expensive prospect, even if you could find the book in print. *Weird Tales* of the magazine's golden age were, however, still relatively cheap in the second-hand bookstores, especially those that specialized in giving you half price on any title you brought back in good condition. This meant that all my copies had big purple rubber stamps on the inside pages. I think I'd miss that purple if I saw the magazines in any other state! That's where I was introduced to the likes of Seabury Quinn, Clark Ashton Smith and other exotically named individuals, good writers who could find no commercial publication save in the marginal pulps, which, like *Black Mask*, had their own specific readerships. Some, like Frank Owen, loved couching their stories in styles influenced by Chinese tale-tellers. Other *Weird Tales* writers even pretended to be translating from Far Eastern sources. I remember coming across a story by Tennessee Williams which purported to be, as I recall, a previously untranslated Greek scroll. *Weird Tales*, which had published almost every major fantasist including Lovecraft, Howard, and Bradbury, inspired Carnell. He always saw *Science Fantasy* as the most literary of his magazines (though *Science Fiction Adventures* published *The Drowned World* and several other Ballard or Aldiss classics) and ran the best of John Brunner's Society of Time stories; Thomas Burnett Swann's tales of the Greek gods and demigods; together with stories by H. K. Bulmer, John Phillifent, Keith Roberts, E. C. Tubb and a few others, all at the top of their form. *Science Fantasy* also published some Mervyn Peake stories for the first time as well as some beautifully done covers by Gerard Quinn, Brian Lewis and James Cawthorn. Admittedly, Lewis's hefty Elric was painted before the story was completed. There was worse to come. Jack Gaughan's illustrations for the first U.S. Elric paperbacks of *The Stealer of Souls* and *Stormbringer*, with their strange, spiky hats, influenced Barry Windsor-Smith's depiction for a later Conan-meets-Elric comic story drafted by Jim Cawthorn and myself. I'm never sure where Jack got those conical hats, which looked like dunce caps to me, but he seemed very proud of them and I never liked to complain too much, at least until it couldn't hurt him. Soon after the British edition of *Stormbringer* appeared there came a number of other creations called "Stormbringer." At least two music albums (by John Martyn and by Deep Purple), a band, some comics and even TV shows have borrowed it. Other bands around the world have also referenced the sword. That Stormbringer failed to appear in the movie *Red Sonja* was thanks to some swift footwork by lawyers. While I've watched as people lift stuff like the Chaos symbol, created as the opposite of Law's single arrow, and murmured "be my guest" as the multiverse term and concept is cheerfully appropriated, I've always felt especially proprietorial when people rip off my big black sword. The fully-loaded Raven Armoury version has to be kept in a gun cupboard, just in case. . . .

I'm often asked who my favourite Elric artist is. There have been so many good ones from Cawthorn in England to Phillippe Druillet in France (both have also done graphic novel versions), to Michael Whelan and Robert Gould in the United States. Frank Brunner, Howard Chaykin, Walter Simonson. Rodney Matthews, Jim Burns, Chris Achilleos and, of course, the great Yoshitaka Amano. And now it's John Picacio's turn. It might be worth mentioning here that Elric does not, of course, exhibit human albinism but an alien condition that occasionally produces a "Silverskin" of Melnibonéan royal blood. He has no real equivalent amongst the races of the Young Kingdoms, with whom we have much more in common. That human albinos have had something of a bad press in our world, frequently cast as villains (cf. *The Da Vinci Code*) is demonstrated in Anthony Skene's description, also reprinted here, of how he was inspired to create Zenith. Monsieur Zenith came into existence less than a decade after Gaston Leroux's *Phantom of the Opera*, but over a half century before him came Jean Blanc in *Le Loup Blanc*, creation of Paul Féval, the prolific feuilletonist who supplied the French public with a considerable amount of its popular fiction in the middle of the nineteenth century. It came as something of a shock to realize Elric had such a long pedigree. I am indebted to Jess Nevins's extraordinary *Encyclopedia of Fantastic Victoriana* and to Jean-Marc Lofficier, of The Black Coat Press, for details of *Le Loup Blanc*. Anyone who would like to investigate this wonderful world any further can do so by reading Lofficier's *Tales of the Shadowmen* series. I might feel a little astonishment at the title, *Stormbringer,* being used by others so frequently, but Terry Pratchett believes that fiction is a huge cauldron which one helps fill and from which one takes. He and I are sardonically agreed about the number of writers who tend to take out rather more than they put in. . . .

Over the years, in Elric's translations into French, Japanese, Portuguese, Spanish, Hebrew, Italian, Greek, Albanian, Serbian, German, Dutch, Danish, Swedish, Finnish, Latvian, Lithuanian, Estonian, Russian and so on, many variant maps have been published, and I thought it would be of some interest to readers of this edition if I included the occasional map of Elric's world, beginning with Cawthorn's first-ever map. As Elric explored more and more of the world of the Young Kingdoms, Jim was able to add an increasing amount of information. We intend to publish further maps in subsequent volumes.

To give something of the flavour of the time in which the stories were published, we have reprinted the introductory material Carnell attached to them when they appeared for the first time. There are no "early drafts," I fear, since all the stories were first draft and the only carbon copies were given away to various charity auctions soon after they were published. I have no idea who owns these manuscripts. In a subsequent volume, however, I shall be publishing Elric's first appearance in the guise of Jerry Cornelius.

It is still a little strange for me to accept that Elric has become part of the pantheon of epic fantasy. I suppose I hoped for something of the sort when I was sixteen or thereabouts, but my ambitions changed. Or so I thought. I have been extraordinarily lucky in doing pretty much all I ever dreamed of doing as a teenager. Indeed, various ambitions came together in the late 1980s when Hawkwind, the band with which I frequently performed, staged a rock version of *The Stealer of Souls* and *Stormbringer*, put out as *The Chronicle of the Black Sword*, complete with a mime troupe enacting the story. I also had a great time collaborating with Eric Bloom on Blue Öyster Cult's version of "Black Blade," which I first performed in a different form with my own band the Deep Fix at Dingwalls in the late 1970s.

It seems Elric will, like the Eternal Champion he is, keep coming back in various incarnations, but this version is without doubt my favourite and probably the last I shall produce. I must thank Betsy Mitchell for her commitment to this project. And finally I thank my friend John Picacio who, by coincidence, began his professional illustrating career with my *Behold the Man* and followed it with a representation of Elric in *Tales from the Texas Woods*. If you are familiar with Elric, I trust you enjoy revisiting him in this present form. If you are new to him, I hope you find him good, rather dangerous company.

Michael Moorcock
Rue Amélie, Paris/Lost Pines, Texas
October/December 2006

# ELRIC
# The Stealer of Souls

# AT THE BEGINNING

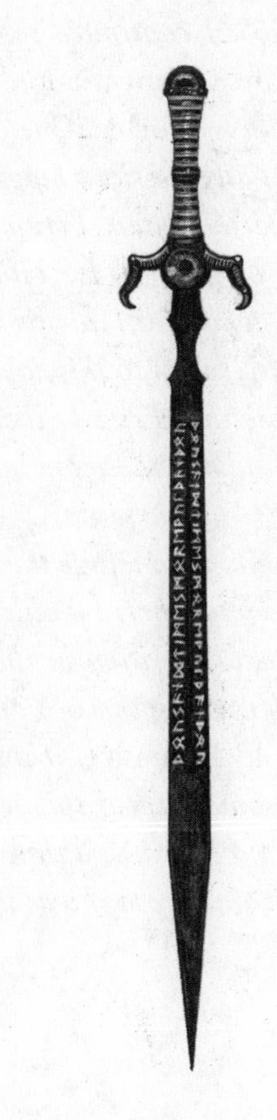

*I'm inclined to forget how many contributions I made to fanzines between, say, 1955 and 1965. I continued to contribute to them while I was editor of* Tarzan Adventures *and even wrote the odd letter while I was editing* New Worlds. *One of the finest of these fanzines was* AMRA, *essentially a serious magazine for that handful of people then interested in fantasy fiction and specifically—thus the title—the work of Robert E. Howard. Run by an enthusiast, George Scithers, who is still involved in enthusiast publishing (most recently* Weird Tales*) to this day. By the evidence of my approach, I must suppose that Fritz Leiber had not yet taken part in the correspondence and had therefore not come up with the terms "sword and sorcery" or "heroic fantasy." Actually, I still prefer my own suggestion. I would not include the Peake books in that list anymore, and there are a few others I would mention if writing the piece today. It was probably written in the middle of 1960. I reprint it here because, with my "Aspects of Fantasy" essays, which became* Wizardry and Wild Romance, *it immediately precedes the Elric stories and gives some idea of the atmosphere in which "The Dreaming City" was published, at a time when supernatural adventure fantasy (to give it another tag) was thought to have only a very limited readership. . . .*

## PUTTING A TAG ON IT

(1961)

I'VE ALWAYS KIDDED myself, and until recently had convinced myself, that names were of no importance and that what really mattered was the Thing Concerned, not the tag which was put on said Thing. Although in principle I still agree with the idea, I am having to admit to myself that names are convenient and save an awful lot of wordage. Thus with "Science Fiction": a much disputed tag, agreed, but one which at least helps us to visualize roughly what someone who uses the words means.

We have two tags, really—SF and "Fantasy"—but I feel that we should have another general name to include the sub-genre of books which deal with Middle Earths and lands and worlds based on this planet, worlds which exist only in some author's vivid imagination. In this sub-genre I would classify books like *The Worm Ouroboros*, *Jurgen*, *The Lord of the Rings*, *The Once and Future King*, the Gray Mouser/Fafhrd series, the Conan series, *The Broken Sword*, *The Well of the Unicorn*, etc.

Now all these stories have several things in common—they are fantasy stories which could hardly be classified as SF, and they are stories of high adventure, generally featuring a central hero very easy to identify oneself with. For the most part they *are* works of escapism, anything else usually being secondary (exceptions, I would agree, are *Jurgen* and *The Once and Future King*). But all of them are tales told for the tale's sake, and the authors have obviously thoroughly enjoyed the telling.

The roots of most of these stories are in legendry, classic romance, mythology, folklore, and dubious ancient works of "History."

In a recent letter, Sprague de Camp called this stuff Prehistoric-Adventure-Fantasy and this name, although somewhat unwieldy, could apply to much of the material I have listed. PAF? Then again, you could call it Saga-Fantasy or Fantastic-Romance (in the sense of the Chivalric Romances).

What we want is a name which might not, on analysis, include every book in this category, but which, like "Science Fiction," would give readers some idea what you're talking about when you're doing articles, reviews, etc., on books in this genre. Or for that matter it would be useful to use just in conversation or when forming clubs, launching magazines, etc.

*Epic Fantasy* is the name which appeals most to me as one which includes many of these stories—certainly all of the ones I have mentioned.

Most of the tales listed have a basic general formula. They are "quest" stories. The necessary sense of conflict in a book designed to hold the reader's interest from start to finish is supplied by the simple formula:

A) Hero must get or do something;
B) Villains disapprove;
C) Hero sets out to get what he wants anyway;
D) Villains thwart him one or more times (according to length of story); and finally
E) Hero, in the face of all odds, does what the reader expects of him.

Of course E) often has a twist of some kind, to it but in most cases the other four parts are there. This is not so in *Jurgen* nor in White's tetralogy admittedly, but then *Jurgen* is definitely an allegory, while in *The Sword in the Stone* and its sequels it is the characters which are of main importance to the author. *Jurgen* only just manages to squeeze into the category anyway.

Also, it can be argued that this basic plotline can apply to most stories. Agreed, but the point is that here the plotline tends to dominate both theme and hero, and is easily spotted for what it is.

Conan and the Gray Mouser generally have to start at point A), pass wicked points B) and D), and eventually win through to goal—point E). Anything else, in the meantime, is extra—in fact, the extra is that which puts these stories above many others. The Ringbearers in Tolkien's magnificent saga do this also.

Now, the point is that every one of these tales, almost without exception, follows the pattern of the old Heroic Sagas and Epic Romances. Basically, Conan and Beowulf have much in common; Ragnar Lodbrok and Fafhrd also; Gandalf and Merlin; Amadis of Gaul and Airar (of *The Well of the Unicorn*). And I'm sure many of the unhuman characters (elves, orcs, wizards, and such) and monsters these heroes encounter can trace their ancestry right back to the Sidhe; Lord Soulis; Urganda the Unknown; Grendel; Siegfried's dragon; Cerberus; and the various hippogriffs, firedrakes, and serpents of legend and mythology.

As de Camp showed in his "Exegesis of Howard's Hyborian Tales" and as I did in my earlier and not nearly so complete article "Historical Fact and Fiction in Connection with the Conan Series" (*Burroughsania*, vol. 2, no. 16, August 1957), the names for characters and backgrounds in Howard's wonderful series were nearly all culled from legendry. Most of Howard's sources are easily traced, for he did not even change names. The same goes for *The Broken Sword*; and the Ring tetralogy is obviously based (only *based*, mind you) on Anglo-Saxon foundations.

This, of course, does not detract one iota from the stories themselves. In fact all the authors have done much, much more than simply rehash old folk literature—they have taken crudely formed and paradoxical tales as their bases and written new, subtler stories which are often far better than the ones which undoubtedly influenced them. Also, when I compare Conan with Beowulf and so on, I am not saying that these characters were the originals upon which Howard, Leiber, Tolkien, and the others based their own heroes and villains—I am simply trying to point out that the *influence* was there.

So, all in all, I would say that *Epic Fantasy* is about the best name for the sub-genre, considering its general form and roots. Obviously, Epic Fantasy includes the Conan, Kull, and Bran Mak Morn stories of

R. E. Howard; the Gray Mouser/Fafhrd stories by Fritz Leiber; the Arthurian tetralogy by T. H. White; the Middle Earth stories of J.R.R. Tolkien; *The Worm Ouroboros* by E. R. Eddison; the Zothique stories of Clark Ashton Smith; some of the works of Abraham Merritt (*The Ship of Ishtar*, etc.); some of H. Rider Haggard's stories (*Allan and the Ice Gods*, etc.); *The Broken Sword* by Poul Anderson; the Gormenghast trilogy of Mervyn Peake (it just gets in, I think); the Poictesme stories of James Branch Cabell (including *Jurgen*, *The Silver Stallion*, and others); and *The Well of the Unicorn* by Fletcher Pratt.

I would appreciate other suggestions for possible inclusions. *Titus Groan* and its sequels by Mervyn Peake actually do not have the form nor roots I have described but they have the general atmosphere and are certainly set outside of our own space-time Earth.

The question might be raised as to whether or not to include Alternate Space-Time Continuum stories such as de Camp's and Pratt's Harold Shea tales, Anderson's *Three Hearts and Three Lions*, Mark Twain's *A Connecticut Yankee at the Court of King Arthur* (obviously the main influence for many subsequent stories), L. Ron Hubbard's *Masters and Slaves of Sleep*, etc., in which present day heroes enter worlds of legend and myth and don't take the idea altogether seriously. The basic difference is in the treatment, I think. In the Epic Fantasy group the author more or less asks you to accept the background and so on as *important* because his characters consider it important, then take the story from there, respecting the laws and logic which are to be taken for what they are, and taken seriously.

In the AS-TC group the treatment is often humorous, the author having the attitude of a teller of tall stories who doesn't expect to be believed but knows that he is entertaining his hearers—which is all that is required of him. Thus, although several of the AS-TC group could just about fall into the Epic Fantasy group, I consider it best to describe them as simply "Fantasy" (which I usually interpret to mean the kind of stuff which filled the majority of *Unknown*'s pages).

What do you think?

# THE STEALER OF SOULS

For my mother.

---

*This is the first of a new series of stories by a new author to our pages. Unlike many central characters, Elric is puny on his own, but as a wanderer in another place and time he has the power of sorcery to boost his strength.*

*—John Carnell, SCIENCE FANTASY No. 47, June 1961*

# THE DREAMING CITY

## Introduction

FOR TEN THOUSAND years did the Bright Empire of Melniboné flourish—ruling the world. Ten thousand years before history was recorded—or ten thousand years after history had ceased to be chronicled. For that span of time, reckon it how you will, the Bright Empire had thrived. Be hopeful, if you like, and think of the dreadful past the Earth has known, or brood upon the future. But if you would believe the unholy truth—then Time is an agony of Now, and so it will always be.

Ravaged, at last, by the formless terror called Time, Melniboné fell and newer nations succeeded her: Ilmiora, Sheegoth, Maidahk, S'aaleem. Then memory began: Ur, India, China, Egypt, Assyria, Persia, Greece, and Rome—all these came after Melniboné. But none lasted ten thousand years.

And none dealt in the terrible mysteries, the secret sorceries of old Melniboné. None used such power or knew how. Only Melniboné ruled the Earth for one hundred centuries—and then she, shaken by the casting of frightful runes, attacked by powers greater than men; powers who decided that Melniboné's span of ruling had been overlong—then she crumbled and her sons were scattered. They became wanderers across an Earth which hated and feared them, siring few offspring, slowly dying, slowly forgetting the secrets of their mighty ancestors. Such a one was the cynical, laughing Elric, a man of bitter brooding and gusty humour, proud prince of ruins, lord of a lost and humbled people; last son of Melniboné's sundered line of kings.

Elric, the moody-eyed wanderer—a lonely man who fought a world, living by his wits and his runesword Stormbringer. Elric, last

Lord of Melniboné, last worshipper of its grotesque and beautiful gods—reckless reaver and cynical slayer—torn by great griefs and with knowledge locked in his skull which would turn lesser men to babbling idiots. Elric, moulder of madnesses, dabbler in wild delights . . .

## Chapter One

"What's the hour?" The black-bearded man wrenched off his gilded helmet and flung it from him, careless of where it fell. He drew off his leathern gauntlets and moved closer to the roaring fire, letting the heat soak into his frozen bones.

"Midnight is long past," growled one of the other armoured men who gathered around the blaze. "Are you still sure he'll come?"

"It's said that he's a man of his word, if that comforts you."

It was a tall, pale-faced youth who spoke. His thin lips formed the words and spat them out maliciously. He grinned a wolf-grin and stared the new arrival in the eyes, mocking him.

The newcomer turned away with a shrug. "That's so—for all your irony, Yaris. He'll come." He spoke as a man does when he wishes to reassure himself.

There were six men, now, around the fire. The sixth was Smiorgan—Count Smiorgan Baldhead of the Purple Towns. He was a short, stocky man of fifty years with a scarred face partially covered with a thick, black growth of hair. His morose eyes smouldered and his lumpy fingers plucked nervously at his rich-hilted longsword. His pate was hairless, giving him his name, and over his ornate, gilded armour hung a loose woolen cloak, dyed purple.

Smiorgan said thickly, "He has no love for his cousin. He has become bitter. Yyrkoon sits on the Ruby Throne in his place and has proclaimed him an outlaw and a traitor. Elric needs us if he would take his throne and his bride back. We can trust him."

"You're full of trust tonight, count," Yaris smiled thinly, "a rare thing to find in these troubled times. I say this—" He paused and took a long breath, staring at his comrades, summing them up. His gaze flicked from lean-faced Dharmit of Jharkor to Fadan of Lormyr who pursed his podgy lips and looked into the fire.

"Speak up, Yaris," petulantly urged the patrician-featured Vilmirian, Naclon. "Let's hear what you have to say, lad, if it's worth hearing."

Yaris looked towards Jiku the dandy, who yawned impolitely and scratched his long nose.

"Well!" Smiorgan was impatient. "What d'you say, Yaris?"

"I say that we should start now and waste no more time waiting on Elric's pleasure! He's laughing at us in some tavern a hundred miles from here—or else plotting with the Dragon Princes to trap us. For years we have planned this raid. We have little time in which to strike—our fleet is too big, too noticeable. Even if Elric has not betrayed us, then spies will soon be running eastwards to warn the Dragons that there is a fleet massed against them. We stand to win a fantastic fortune—to vanquish the greatest merchant city in the world—to reap immeasurable riches—or horrible death at the hands of the Dragon Princes, if we wait overlong. Let's bide our time no more and set sail before our prize hears of our plan and brings up reinforcements!"

"You always were too ready to mistrust a man, Yaris." King Naclon of Vilmir spoke slowly, carefully—distastefully eyeing the taut-featured youth. "We could not reach Imrryr without Elric's knowledge of the maze-channels which lead to its secret ports. If Elric will not join us—then our endeavour will be fruitless—hopeless. We need him. We must wait for him—or else give up our plans and return to our homelands."

"At least I'm willing to take a risk," yelled Yaris, anger lancing from his slanting eyes. "You're getting old—all of you. Treasures are not won by care and forethought but by swift slaying and reckless attack."

"Fool!" Dharmit's voice rumbled around the fire-flooded hall. He laughed wearily. "I spoke thus in my youth—and lost a fine fleet soon after. Cunning and Elric's knowledge will win us Imrryr—that and the mightiest fleet to sail the Dragon Sea since Melniboné's banners fluttered over all the nations of the Earth. Here we are—the most powerful sea-lords in the world, masters, every one of us, of more than a hundred swift vessels. Our names are feared and famous—our fleets ravage the coasts of a score of lesser nations. We hold *power*!" He clenched his great fist and shook it in Yaris's face. His tone became more level and he smiled viciously, glaring at the youth and choosing his words with precision.

"But all this is worthless—meaningless—without the power which Elric has. That is the power of knowledge—of dream-learned sorcery, if I must use the cursed word. His fathers knew of the maze which guards Imrryr from sea-attack. And his fathers passed that secret on to him. Imrryr, the Dreaming City, dreams in peace—and will continue to do so unless we have a guide to help us steer a course through the treacherous waterways which lead to her harbours. We *need* Elric—we know it, and he knows it. That's the truth!"

"Such confidence, gentlemen, is warming to the heart." There was irony in the heavy voice which came from the entrance to the hall. The heads of the six sea-lords jerked towards the doorway.

Yaris's confidence fled from him as he met the eyes of Elric of Melniboné. They were old eyes in a fine featured, youthful face. Yaris shuddered, turned his back on Elric, preferring to look into the bright glare of the fire.

Elric smiled warmly as Count Smiorgan gripped his shoulder. There was a certain friendship between the two. He nodded condescendingly to the other four and walked with lithe grace towards the fire. Yaris stood aside and let him pass. Elric was tall, broad-shouldered and slim-hipped. He wore his long hair bunched and pinned at the nape of his neck and, for an obscure reason, affected the dress of a southern barbarian. He had long, knee-length boots of soft doe-leather, a breastplate of strangely wrought silver, a jerkin of chequered blue and white linen, britches of scarlet wool and a cloak of rustling green velvet. At his hip rested his runesword of black iron—the feared Stormbringer, forged by ancient and alien sorcery.

His bizarre dress was tasteless and gaudy, and did not match his sensitive face and long-fingered, almost delicate hands, yet he flaunted it since it emphasized the fact that he did not belong in any company—that he was an outsider and an outcast. But, in reality, he had little need to wear such outlandish gear—for his eyes and skin were enough to mark him.

Elric, Last Lord of Melniboné, was a pure albino who drew his power from a secret and terrible source.

Smiorgan sighed. "Well, Elric, when do we raid Imrryr?"

Elric shrugged. "As soon as you like; I care not. Give me a little time in which to do certain things."

"Tomorrow? Shall we sail tomorrow?" Yaris said hesitantly, conscious of the strange power dormant in the man he had earlier accused of treachery.

Elric smiled, dismissing the youth's statement. "Three days' time," he said, "Three—or more."

"Three days! But Imrryr will be warned of our presence by then!" Fat, cautious Fadan spoke.

"I'll see that your fleet's not found," Elric promised. "I have to go to Imrryr first—and return."

"You won't do the journey in three days—the fastest ship could not make it." Smiorgan gaped.

"I'll be in the Dreaming City in less than a day," Elric said softly, with finality.

Smiorgan shrugged. "If you say so, I'll believe it—but why this necessity to visit the city ahead of the raid?"

"I have my own compunctions, Count Smiorgan. But worry not—I shan't betray you. I'll lead the raid myself, be sure of that." His dead-white face was lighted eerily by the fire and his red eyes smouldered. One lean hand firmly gripped the hilt of his runesword and he appeared to breathe more heavily. "Imrryr fell, in spirit, five hundred years ago—she will fall completely soon—for ever! I have a little debt to settle. This is my sole reason for aiding you. As you know I have made only a few conditions—that you raze the city to the ground and a certain man and woman are not harmed. I refer to my cousin Yyrkoon and his sister Cymoril . . ."

Yaris's thin lips felt uncomfortably dry. Much of his blustering manner resulted from the early death of his father. The old sea-king had died—leaving the youthful Yaris as the new ruler of his lands and his fleets. Yaris was not at all certain that he was capable of commanding such a vast kingdom—and tried to appear more confident than he actually felt. Now he said: "How shall we hide the fleet, Lord Elric?"

The Melnibonéan acknowledged the question. "I'll hide it for you," he promised. "I go now to do this—but make sure all your men are off the ships first—will you see to it, Smiorgan?"

"Aye," rumbled the stocky count.

He and Elric departed from the hall together, leaving five men behind; five men who sensed an air of icy doom hanging about the overheated hall.

"How could he hide such a mighty fleet when we, who know this fjord better than any, found nowhere?" Dharmit of Jharkor said bewilderedly.

None answered him.

They waited, tensed and nervous, while the fire flickered and died untended. Eventually Smiorgan returned, stamping noisily on the boarded floor. There was a haunted haze of fear surrounding him; an almost tangible aura, and he was shivering, terribly. Tremendous, racking undulations swept up his body and his breath came short.

"Well? Did Elric hide the fleet—all at once? What did he do?" Dharmit spoke impatiently, choosing not to heed Smiorgan's ominous condition.

"He has hidden it." That was all Smiorgan said, and his voice was thin, like that of a sick man, weak from fever.

Yaris went to the entrance and tried to stare beyond the fjord slopes where many campfires burned, tried to make out the outlines of ships' masts and rigging, but he could see nothing.

"The night mist's too thick," he murmured, "I can't tell whether our ships are anchored in the fjord or not." Then he gasped involuntarily as a white face loomed out of the clinging fog. "Greetings, Lord Elric," he stuttered, noting the sweat on the Melnibonéan's strained features.

Elric staggered past him, into the hall. "Wine," he mumbled, "I've done what's needed and it's cost me hard."

Dharmit fetched a jug of strong Cadsandrian wine and with a shaking hand poured some into a carved wooden goblet. Wordlessly he passed the cup to Elric who quickly drained it. "Now I will sleep," he said, stretching himself into a chair and wrapping his green cloak around him. He closed his disconcerting crimson eyes and fell into a slumber born of utter weariness.

Fadan scurried to the door, closed it and pulled the heavy iron bar down.

None of the six slept much that night and, in the morning, the door was unbarred and Elric was missing from the chair. When they went outside, the mist was so heavy that they soon lost sight of one another, though scarcely two feet separated any of them.

Elric stood with his legs astride on the shingle of the narrow beach. He looked back at the entrance to the fjord and saw, with satisfaction, that the mist was still thickening, though it lay only over the fjord itself, hiding the mighty fleet. Elsewhere, the weather was clear and overhead a pale winter sun shone sharply on the black rocks of the rugged cliffs which dominated the coastline. Ahead of him the sea rose and fell monotonously, like the chest of a sleeping water-giant, grey and pure, glinting in the cold sunlight. Elric fingered the raised runes on the hilt of his black broadsword and a steady north wind blew into the voluminous folds of his dark green cloak, swirling it around his tall, lean frame.

The albino felt fitter than he had done on the previous night when he had expended all his strength in conjuring the mist. He was well-versed in the arts of nature-wizardry, but he did not have the reserves of power which the Sorcerer Emperors of Melniboné had possessed when they had ruled the world. His ancestors had passed their knowledge down to him—but not their mystic vitality and many of the spells and secrets that he had were unusable, since he did not have the reservoir of strength, either of soul or of body, to work them. But for all that, Elric knew of only one other man who matched his knowledge—his cousin Yyrkoon. His hand gripped the hilt tighter as he thought of the cousin who had twice betrayed his trust, and he forced himself to concentrate on his present task—the speaking of spells to aid him on his voyage to the Isle of the Dragon Masters whose only city, Imrryr the Beautiful, was the object of the sea-lords' massing.

Drawn up on the beach, a tiny sailing-boat lay. Elric's own small craft, sturdy, oddly wrought and far stronger, far older, than it appeared. The brooding sea flung surf around its timbers as the tide withdrew, and Elric realized that he had little time in which to work his helpful sorcery.

His body tensed and he blanked his conscious mind, summoning secrets from the dark depths of his dreaming soul. Swaying, his eyes staring unseeingly, his arms jerking out ahead of him and making unholy signs in the air, he began to speak in a sibilant monotone. Slowly the pitch of his voice rose, resembling the scarcely heard shriek of a distant gale as it comes closer—then, quite suddenly, the voice rose higher until it was howling wildly to the skies and the air began to tremble and quiver. Shadow-shapes began slowly to form and they were never still but darted around Elric's body as, stiff-legged, he started forward towards his boat.

His voice was inhuman as it howled insistently, summoning the wind elementals—the *sylphs* of the breeze; the *sharnahs*, makers of gales; the *h'Haarshanns*, builders of whirlwinds—hazy and formless, they eddied around him as he summoned their aid with the alien words of his forefathers who had, in dream-quests taken ages before, made impossible, unthinkable pacts with the elementals in order to procure their services.

Still stiff-limbed, Elric entered the boat and, like an automaton, ran his fingers up the sail and set its ropes, binding himself to his tiller. Then a great wave erupted out of the placid sea, rising higher and higher until it towered over the vessel. With a surging crash, the water smashed down on the boat, lifted it and bore it out to sea. Sitting blank-eyed in the stern, Elric still crooned his hideous song of sorcery as the spirits of the air plucked at the sail and sent the boat flying over the water faster than any mortal ship could speed. And all the while, the deafening, unholy shriek of the released elementals filled the air about the boat as the shore vanished and open sea was all that was visible.

## Chapter Two

So it was, with wind-demons for shipmates, that Elric, last Prince of the royal line of Melniboné, returned to the last city still ruled by his own race—the last city and the final remnant of extant Melnibonéan architecture. All the other great cities lay in ruins, abandoned save for hermits and solitaries. The cloudy pink and subtle yellow tints of the old city's nearer towers came into sight within a few hours of Elric's leaving the fjord and just off-shore of the Isle of the Dragon Masters the elementals left the boat and fled back to their secret haunts among the peaks of the highest mountains in the world. Elric awoke, then, from his trance, and regarded with fresh wonder the beauty of his own birthplace's delicate towers which were visible even so far away, guarded still by the formidable sea wall with its great gate, the five-doored maze and the twisting, high-walled channels, of which only one led to the inner harbour of Imrryr.

Elric knew that he dare not risk entering the harbour by the maze, though he understood the route perfectly. He decided, instead, to land the boat further up the coast in a small inlet of which he had knowledge. With sure, capable hands, he guided the little craft towards the hidden inlet which was obscured by a growth of shrubs loaded with ghastly blue berries of a type decidedly poisonous to men since their juice first turned one blind and then slowly mad. This berry, the *noidel*, grew only on Melniboné, as did other rare and deadly plants whose mixture sustained the frail prince.

Light, low-hanging cloud wisps streamed slowly across the sun-painted sky, like fine cobwebs caught by a sudden breeze. All the world seemed blue and gold and green and white, and Elric, pulling his boat up on the beach, breathed the clean, sharp air of winter and savoured the scent of decaying leaves and rotting undergrowth. Somewhere a bitch-fox barked her pleasure to her mate and Elric regretted the fact that his depleted race no longer appreciated natural beauty, preferring to stay close to their city and spend many of their days in drugged slumber; in study. It was not the city which dreamed, but its overcivilized inhabitants. Or had they become one and the same? Elric, smelling the rich, clean winter-scents, was wholly glad that he had renounced his birthright and no longer ruled the city as he had been born to do.

Instead, Yyrkoon, his cousin, sprawled on the Ruby Throne of Imrryr the Beautiful and hated Elric because he knew that the albino, for all his disgust with crowns and rulership, was still the rightful king of the Dragon Isle and that he, Yyrkoon, was an usurper, not elected by Elric to the throne, as Melnibonéan tradition demanded.

But Elric had better reasons for hating his cousin. For those reasons the ancient capital would fall in all its magnificent splendour and the last fragment of a glorious empire would be obliterated as the pink, the yellow, the purple and white towers crumbled—if Elric had his vengeful way and the sea-lords were successful.

On foot, Elric strode inland, towards Imrryr, and as he covered the miles of soft turf, the sun cast an ochre pall over the land and sank, giving way to a dark and moonless night, brooding and full of evil portent.

At last he came to the city. It stood out in stark black silhouette, a city of fantastic magnificence, in conception and in execution. It was the oldest city in the world, built by artists and conceived as a work of art rather than a functional dwelling place, but Elric knew that squalor lurked in many narrow streets and that the Lords of Imrryr left many of the towers empty and uninhabited rather than let the bastard population of the city dwell therein. There were few Dragon Masters left; few who would claim Melnibonéan blood.

Built to follow the shape of the ground, the city had an organic appearance, with winding lanes spiraling to the crest of the hill where stood the castle, tall and proud and many-spired, the final, crowning masterpiece of the ancient, forgotten artist who had built it. But there was no life-sound emanating from Imrryr the Beautiful, only a sense of soporific desolation. The city slept—and the Dragon Masters and their ladies and their special slaves dreamed drug-induced dreams of grandeur and incredible horror, learning unusable skills, while the rest of the population, ordered by curfew, tossed on straw-strewn stone and tried not to dream at all.

Elric, his hand ever near his sword-hilt, slipped through an unguarded gate in the city wall and began to walk cautiously through the ill-lit streets, moving upwards, through the winding lanes, towards Yyrkoon's great palace.

Wind sighed through the empty rooms of the Dragon towers and sometimes Elric would have to withdraw into places where the shadows were deeper when he heard the tramp of feet and a group of guards would pass, their duty being to see that the curfew was rigidly obeyed. Often he would hear wild laughter echoing from one of the towers, still ablaze with bright torchlight which flung strange, disturbing shadows on the walls; often, too, he would hear a chilling scream and a frenzied, idiot's yell as some wretch of a slave died in obscene agony to please his master.

Elric was not appalled by the sounds and the dim sights. He appreciated them. He was still a Melnibonéan—their rightful leader if he chose to regain his powers of kingship—and though he had an obscure urge to wander and sample the less sophisticated pleasures of the outside world, ten thousand years of a cruel, brilliant and malicious culture was behind him, its wisdom gained as he slept, and the pulse of his ancestry beat strongly in his deficient veins.

Elric knocked impatiently upon the heavy, blackwood door. He had reached the palace and now stood by a small back entrance, glancing cautiously around him, for he knew that Yyrkoon had given the guards orders to slay him if he entered Imrryr.

A bolt squealed on the other side of the door and it moved silently inwards. A thin, seamed face confronted Elric.

"Is it the king?" whispered the man, peering out into the night. He was a tall, extremely thin individual with long, gnarled limbs which shifted awkwardly as he moved nearer, straining his beady eyes to get a glimpse of Elric.

"It's Prince Elric," the albino said. "But you forget, Tanglebones, my friend, that a new king sits on the Ruby Throne."

Tanglebones shook his head and his sparse hair fell over his face. With a jerking movement he brushed it back and stood aside for Elric to enter. "The Dragon Isle has but one king—and his name is Elric, whatever usurper would have it otherwise."

Elric ignored this statement, but he smiled thinly and waited for the man to push the bolt back into place.

"She still sleeps, sire," Tanglebones murmured as he climbed unlit stairs, Elric behind him.

"I guessed that," Elric said. "I do not underestimate my good cousin's powers of sorcery."

Upwards, now, in silence, the two men climbed until at last they reached a corridor which was aflare with dancing torchlight. The marble walls reflected the flames and showed Elric, crouching with Tanglebones behind a pillar, that the room in which he was interested was guarded by a massive archer—a eunuch by the look of him—who was alert and wakeful. The man was hairless and fat, his blue-black gleaming armour tight on his flesh, but his fingers were curled round the string of his short, bone bow and there was a slim arrow resting on the string. Elric guessed that this man was one of the crack eunuch archers, a member of the Silent Guard, Elric's finest company of warriors.

Tanglebones, who had taught the young Elric the arts of fencing and archery, had known of the guard's presence and had prepared for it. Earlier he had placed a bow behind the pillar. Silently he picked it up and, bending it against his knee, strung it. He fitted an arrow to the string, aimed it at the right eye of the guard and let fly—just as the eunuch turned to face him. The shaft missed. It clattered against the man's helmet and fell harmlessly to the reed-strewn stones of the floor.

So Elric acted swiftly, leaping forward, his runesword drawn and its alien power surging through him. It howled in a searing arc of black steel and cut through the bone bow which the eunuch had hoped would deflect it. The guard was panting and his thick lips were wet as he drew breath to yell. As he opened his mouth, Elric saw what he had expected, the man was tongueless and was a mute. His own shortsword came out and he just managed to parry Elric's next thrust. Sparks flew from the iron and Stormbringer bit into the eunuch's finely edged blade; he staggered and fell back before the nigromantic sword which appeared to be endowed with a life of its own. The clatter of metal echoed loudly up and down the short corridor and Elric cursed the fate which had made the man turn at the crucial moment. Grimly, silently, he broke down the eunuch's clumsy guard.

The eunuch saw only a dim glimpse of his opponent behind the black, whirling blade which appeared to be so light and which was twice the length of his own stabbing sword. He wondered, frenziedly, who his attacker could be and he thought he recognized the face. Then a scarlet eruption obscured his vision, he felt searing agony at his face and then, philosophically, for eunuchs are necessarily given to a certain fatalism, he realized that he was to die.

Elric stood over the eunuch's bloated body and tugged his sword from the corpse's skull, wiping the mixture of blood and brains on his late opponent's cloak. Tanglebones had wisely vanished. Elric could hear the clatter of sandaled feet rushing up the stairs. He pushed the door open and entered the room which was lit by two small candles placed at either end of a wide, richly tapestried bed. He went to the bed and looked down at the raven-haired girl who lay there.

Elric's mouth twitched and bright tears leapt into his strange red eyes. He was trembling as he turned back to the door, sheathed his sword and pulled the bolts into place. He returned to the bedside and knelt down beside the sleeping girl.

Her features were as delicate and of a similar mould as Elric's own, but she had an added, exquisite beauty. She was breathing shallowly, in a sleep induced not by natural weariness but by her own brother's evil sorcery.

Elric reached out and tenderly took one fine-fingered hand in his. He put it to his lips and kissed it.

"Cymoril," he murmured, and an agony of longing throbbed in that name. "Cymoril—wake up."

The girl did not stir, her breathing remained shallow and her eyes remained shut. Elric's white features twisted and his red eyes blazed as he shook in terrible and passionate rage. He gripped the hand, so limp and nerveless, like the hand of a corpse; gripped it until he had to stop himself for fear that he would crush the delicate fingers.

A shouting soldier began to beat at the door.

Elric replaced the hand on the girl's breast and stood up. He glanced uncomprehendingly at the door.

A sharper, colder voice interrupted the soldier's yelling.

"What is happening? Who disturbs my poor sleeping sister?"

"Yyrkoon, the black hellspawn," said Elric to himself.

Confused babblings from the soldier and Yyrkoon's voice raised as he shouted through the door. "Whoever is in there—you will be destroyed a thousand times when you are caught. You cannot escape. If my good sister is harmed in any way—then you will never die, I promise you that. But you will pray to your gods that you could!"

"Yyrkoon, you paltry bombast—you cannot threaten one who is your equal in the dark arts. It is I, Elric—your rightful master. Return to your rabbit hole before I call down every power upon, above, and under the earth to blast you!"

Yyrkoon laughed hesitantly. "So you have returned again to try to waken my sister. Any such attempt will not only slay her—it will send her soul into the deepest hell—where you may join it, willingly!"

"By Arnara's six breasts—you it will be who samples the thousand deaths before long."

"Enough of this." Yyrkoon raised his voice. "Soldiers—I command you to break this door down—and take that traitor alive. Elric—there are two things you will never again have—my sister's love and the Ruby Throne. Make what you can of the little time available to you, for soon you will be groveling to me and praying for release from your soul's agony!"

Elric ignored Yyrkoon's threats and looked at the narrow window to the room. It was just large enough for a man's body to pass through. He bent down and kissed Cymoril upon the lips, then he went to the door and silently withdrew the bolts.

There came a crash as a soldier flung his weight against the door. It swung open, pitching the man forward to stumble and fall on his face. Elric drew his sword, lifted it high and chopped at the warrior's neck. The head sprang from its shoulders and Elric yelled loudly in a deep, rolling voice.

"*Arioch! Arioch!* I give you blood and souls—only aid me now! This man I give you, mighty Duke of Hell—aid your servant, Elric of Melniboné!"

Three soldiers entered the room in a bunch. Elric struck at one and sheared off half his face. The man screamed horribly.

"Arioch, Lord of the Darks—I give you blood and souls. Aid me, great one!"

In the far corner of the gloomy room, a blacker mist began slowly to form. But the soldiers pressed closer and Elric was hard put to hold them back.

He was screaming the name of Arioch, Lord of the Higher Hell, incessantly, almost unconsciously as he was pressed back further by the weight of the warriors' numbers. Behind them, Yyrkoon mouthed in rage and frustration, urging his men, still, to take Elric alive. This gave Elric some small advantage. The runesword was glowing with a strange black light and its shrill howling grated in the ears of those who heard it. Two more corpses now littered the carpeted floor of the chamber, their blood soaking into the fine fabric.

"*Blood and souls for my lord Arioch!*"

The dark mist heaved and began to take shape, Elric spared a look towards the corner and shuddered despite his inurement to hell-born horror. The warriors now had their backs to the thing in the corner and

Elric was by the window. The amorphous mass, that was a less than pleasant manifestation of Elric's fickle patron god, heaved again and Elric made out its intolerably alien shape. Bile flooded into his mouth and, as he drove the soldiers towards the thing which was sinuously flooding forward, he fought against madness.

Suddenly, the soldiers seemed to sense that there was something behind them. They turned, four of them, and each screamed insanely as the black horror made one final rush to engulf them. Arioch crouched over them, sucking out their souls. Then, slowly, their bones began to give and snap and still shrieking bestially the men flopped like obnoxious invertebrates upon the floor: their spines broken, they still lived. Elric turned away, thankful for once that Cymoril slept, and leapt to the window ledge. He looked down and realized with despair that he was not going to escape by that route after all. Several hundred feet lay between him and the ground. He rushed to the door where Yyrkoon, his eyes wide with fear, was trying to drive Arioch back. Arioch was already fading.

Elric pushed past his cousin, spared a final glance at Cymoril, then ran the way he had come, his feet slipping on blood. Tanglebones met him at the head of the dark stairway.

"What has happened, King Elric—what's in there?"

Elric seized Tanglebones by his lean shoulder and made him descend the stairs. "No time," he panted, "but we must hurry while Yyrkoon is still engaged with his current problem. In five days' time Imrryr will experience a new phase in her history—perhaps the last. I want you to make sure that Cymoril is safe. Is that clear?"

"Aye, Lord, but . . ."

They reached the door and Tanglebones shot the bolts and opened it.

"There is no time for me to say anything else. I must escape while I can. I will return in five days—with companions. You will realize what I mean when that time comes. Take Cymoril to the Tower of D'a'rputna—and await me there."

Then Elric was gone, soft-footed, running into the night with the shrieks of the dying still ringing through the blackness after him.

## Chapter Three

Elric stood unsmiling in the prow of Count Smiorgan's flagship. Since his return to the fjord and the fleet's subsequent sailing for open sea, he had spoken only orders, and those in the tersest of terms. The sea-lords muttered that a great hate lay in him, that it festered his soul and made him a dangerous man to have as comrade or enemy; and even Count Smiorgan avoided the moody albino.

The reaver prows struck eastward and the sea was black with light ships dancing on the bright water in all directions; they looked like the shadow of some enormous sea-bird flung on the water. Over half a thousand fighting ships stained the ocean—all of them of similar form, long and slim and built for speed rather than battle, since they were for coast-raiding and trading. Sails were caught by the pale sun; bright colours of fresh canvas—orange, blue, black, purple, red, yellow, light green or white. And every ship had sixteen or more rowers—each rower a fighting man. The crews of the ships were also the warriors who would attack Imrryr—there was no wastage of good manpower since the sea-nations were underpopulated, losing hundreds of men each year in their regular raids.

In the centre of the great fleet, certain larger vessels sailed. These carried massive catapults on their decks and were to be used for storming the sea wall of Imrryr. Count Smiorgan and the other lords looked at their ships with pride, but Elric only stared ahead of him, never sleeping, rarely moving, his white face lashed by salt spray and wind, his white hand tight upon his sword-hilt.

The reaver ships ploughed steadily eastwards—forging towards the Dragon Isle and fantastic wealth—or hellish horror. Relentlessly, doom-driven, they beat onwards, their oars splashing in unison, their sails bellying taut with a good wind.

Onwards they sailed, towards Imrryr the Beautiful, to rape and plunder the world's oldest city.

Two days after the fleet had set sail, the coastline of the Dragon Isle was sighted and the rattle of arms replaced the sound of oars as the mighty fleet hove to and prepared to accomplish what sane men thought impossible.

Orders were bellowed from ship to ship and the fleet began to mass into battle formation, then the oars creaked in their grooves and ponderously, with sails now furled, the fleet moved forward again.

It was a clear day, cold and fresh, and there was a tense excitement about all the men, from sea-lord to galley hand, as they considered the immediate future and what it might bring. Serpent prows bent towards the great stone wall which blocked off the first entrance to the harbour. It was nearly a hundred feet high and towers were built upon it—more functional than the lacelike spires of the city which shimmered in the distance, behind them. The ships of Imrryr were the only vessels allowed to pass through the great gate in the centre of the wall, and the route through the maze—the exact entrance even—was a well-kept secret from outsiders.

On the sea wall, which now loomed tall above the fleet, amazed guards scrambled frantically to their posts. To them, threat of attack was well-nigh unthinkable, yet here it was—a great fleet, the greatest they had ever seen—come against Imrryr the Beautiful! They took to their posts, their yellow cloaks and kilts rustling, their bronze armour rattling, but they moved with bewildered reluctance as if refusing to accept what they saw. And they went to their posts with desperate fatalism, knowing that even if the ships never entered the maze itself, they would not be alive to witness the reavers' failure.

Dyvim Tarkan, Commander of the Wall, was a sensitive man who loved life and its pleasures. He was high-browed and handsome, with a thin wisp of beard and a tiny moustache. He looked well in the bronze armour and high-plumed helmet; he did not want to die. He issued terse orders to his men and, with well-ordered precision, they obeyed him. He listened with concern to the distant shouts from the ships and he wondered what the first move of the reavers would be. He did not wait long for his answer.

A catapult on one of the leading vessels twanged throatily and its throwing arm rushed up, releasing a great rock which sailed, with every appearance of leisurely grace, towards the wall. It fell short and splashed into the sea which frothed against the stones of the wall.

Swallowing hard and trying to control the shake in his voice, Dyvim Tarkan ordered his own catapult to discharge. With a thudding crash the release rope was cut and a retaliatory iron ball went hurtling towards the enemy fleet. So tight-packed were the ships that the ball could not miss—it struck full on the deck of the flagship of Dharmit of Jharkor and crushed the timbers in. Within seconds, accompanied by the cries of maimed and drowning men, the ship had sunk and Dharmit with it. Some of the crew were taken aboard other vessels but the wounded were left to drown.

Another catapult sounded and this time a tower full of archers was squarely hit. Masonry erupted outwards and those who still lived fell sickeningly to die in the foam-tipped sea lashing the wall. This time, angered by the deaths of their comrades, Imrryrian archers sent back a stream of slim arrows into the enemy's midst. Reavers howled as red-fletched shafts buried themselves thirstily in flesh. But reavers returned the arrows liberally and soon only a handful of men were left on the wall as further catapult rocks smashed into towers and men, destroying their only war-machine and part of the wall besides.

Dyvim Tarkan still lived, though red blood stained his yellow tunic and an arrow shaft protruded from his left shoulder. He still lived when the first ram-ship moved intractably towards the great wooden gate and smashed against it, weakening it. A second ship sailed in beside it and, between them, they stove in the gate and glided through the entrance. Perhaps it was outraged horror that tradition had been broken which caused poor Dyvim Tarkan to lose his footing at the edge of the wall and fall screaming down to break his neck on the deck of Count Smiorgan's flagship as it sailed triumphantly through the gate.

Now the ram-ships made way for Count Smiorgan's craft, for Elric had to lead the way through the maze. Ahead of them loomed five tall entrances, black gaping maws all alike in shape and size. Elric pointed to the second from the left and with short strokes the oarsmen began to paddle the ship into the dark mouth of the entrance. For some minutes, they sailed in darkness.

"Flares!" shouted Elric. "Light the flares!"

Torches had already been prepared and these were now lighted. The men saw that they were in a vast tunnel hewn out of natural rock which twisted in all directions.

"Keep close," Elric ordered and his voice was magnified a score of times in the echoing cavern. Torchlight blazed and Elric's face was a mask of shadow and frisking light as the torches threw up long tongues of flame to the bleak roof. Behind him, men could be heard muttering in awe and, as more craft entered the maze and lit their own torches, Elric could see some torches waver as their bearers trembled in superstitious fear. Elric felt some discomfort as he glanced through the flickering shadows and his eyes, caught by torchflare, gleamed fever-bright.

With dreadful monotony, the oars splashed onwards as the tunnel widened and several more cave-mouths came into sight. "The middle entrance," Elric ordered. The steersman in the stern nodded and guided the ship towards the entrance Elric had indicated. Apart from the muted murmur of some men and the splash of oars, there was a grim and ominous silence in the towering cavern.

Elric stared down at the cold, dark water and shuddered.

Eventually they moved once again into bright sunlight and the men looked upwards, marveling at the height of the great walls above them. Upon those walls squatted more yellow-clad, bronze-armoured archers and as Count Smiorgan's vessel led the way out of the black caverns, the torches still burning in the cool winter air, arrows began to hurtle down into the narrow canyon, biting into throats and limbs.

"Faster!" howled Elric. "Row faster—speed is our only weapon now."

With frantic energy the oarsmen bent to their sweeps and the ships began to pick up speed even though Imrryrian arrows took heavy toll of the reaver crewmen. Now the high-walled channel ran straight and Elric saw the quays of Imrryr ahead of him.

"*Faster! Faster! Our prize is in sight!*"

Then, suddenly, the ship broke past the walls and was in the calm waters of the harbour, facing the warriors drawn up on the quay. The ship halted, waiting for reinforcements to plunge out of the channel and join them. When twenty ships were through, Elric gave the command to attack the quay and now Stormbringer howled from its scabbard. The flagship's port side thudded against the quay as arrows rained down upon it. Shafts whistled all around Elric but, miraculously, he was unscathed as he led a bunch of yelling reavers on to land. Imrryrian axe-men bunched forward and confronted the reavers, but it was plain that they had little spirit for the fight—they were too disconcerted by the course which events had taken.

Elric's black blade struck with frenzied force at the throat of the leading axe-man and sheared off his head. Howling demoniacally now that it had again tasted blood, the sword began to writhe in Elric's grasp, seeking fresh flesh in which to bite. There was a hard, grim smile on the albino's colourless lips and his eyes were narrowed as he struck without discrimination at the warriors.

He planned to leave the fighting to those he had led to Imrryr, for he had other things to do—and quickly. Behind the yellow-garbed soldiers, the tall towers of Imrryr rose, beautiful in their soft and scintillating colours of coral pink and powdery blue, of gold and pale yellow, white and subtle green. One such tower was Elric's objective—the tower of D'a'rputna where he had ordered Tanglebones to take Cymoril, knowing that in the confusion this would be possible.

Elric hacked a blood-drenched path through those who attempted to halt him and men fell back, screaming horribly as the runesword drank their souls.

Now Elric was past them, leaving them to the bright blades of the reavers who poured on to the quayside, and was running up through the twisting streets, his sword slaying anyone who attempted to stop him. Like a white-faced ghoul he was, his clothing tattered and bloody, his armour chipped and scratched, but he ran speedily over the cobblestones of the twisting streets and came at last to the slender tower of hazy blue and soft gold—the Tower of D'a'rputna. Its door was open, showing that someone was inside, and Elric rushed through it and entered the large ground-floor chamber. No-one greeted him.

"Tanglebones!" he yelled, his voice roaring loudly even in his own ears. "Tanglebones—are you here?" He leapt up the stairs in great bounds, calling his servant's name. On the third floor he stopped suddenly, hearing a low groan from one of the rooms. "Tanglebones—is that you?" Elric strode towards the room, hearing a strangled gasping. He pushed open the door and his stomach seemed to twist within him as he saw the old man lying upon the bare floor of the chamber, striving vainly to stop the flow of blood which gouted from a great wound in his side.

"What's happened man—where's Cymoril?"

Tanglebones's old face twisted in pain and grief. "She—I—I brought her here, master, as you ordered. But—" he coughed and blood dribbled down his wizened chin, "but—Prince Yyrkoon—he—he apprehended me—must have followed us here. He—struck me down and took Cymoril back with him—said she'd be—safe in the Tower of B'aal'nezbett. Master—I'm sorry . . ."

"So you should be," Elric retorted savagely. Then his tone softened. "Do not worry, old friend—I'll avenge you and myself. I can still reach Cymoril now I know where Yyrkoon has taken her. Thank you for trying, Tanglebones—may your long journey down the last river be uneventful."

He turned abruptly on his heel and left the chamber, running down the stairs and out into the street again.

The Tower of B'aal'nezbett was the highest tower in the Royal Palace. Elric knew it well, for it was there that his ancestors had studied their dark sorceries and conducted frightful experiments. He shuddered as he thought what Yyrkoon might be doing to his own sister.

The streets of the city seemed hushed and strangely deserted, but Elric had no time to ponder why this should be so. Instead he dashed towards the palace, found the main gate unguarded and the main entrance to the building deserted. This too was unique, but it constituted luck for Elric as he made his way upwards, climbing familiar ways towards the topmost tower.

Finally, he reached a door of shimmering black crystal which had no bolt or handle to it. Frenziedly, Elric struck at the crystal with his sorcerous blade but the crystal appeared only to flow and re-form. His blows had no effect.

Elric racked his mind, seeking to remember the single alien word which would make the door open. He dared not put himself in the trance which would have, in time, brought the word to his lips, instead he had to dredge his subconscious and bring the word forth. It was dangerous but there was little else he could do. His whole frame trembled as his face twisted and his brain began to shake. The word was coming as his vocal chords jerked in his throat and his chest heaved.

He ripped the word from his throat and his whole mind and body ached with the strain. Then he cried:

"I command thee—open!"

He knew that once the door opened, his cousin would be aware of his presence, but he had to risk it. The crystal expanded, pulsating and seething, and then began to flow *out*. It flowed into nothingness, into something beyond the physical universe, beyond time. Elric breathed thankfully and passed into the Tower of B'aal'nezbett. But now an eerie fire, chilling and mind-shattering, was licking around Elric as he struggled up the steps towards the central chamber. There was a strange music surrounding him, uncanny music which throbbed and sobbed and pounded in his head.

Above him he saw a leering Yyrkoon, a black runesword also in his hand, the mate of the one in Elric's own grasp.

"Hellspawn!" Elric said thickly, weakly, "I see you have recovered Mournblade—well, test its powers against its brother if you dare. I have come to destroy you, cousin."

Stormbringer was giving forth a peculiar moaning sound which sighed over the shrieking, unearthly music accompanying the licking, chilling fire. The runesword writhed in Elric's fist and he had difficulty in controlling it. Summoning all his strength he plunged up the last few steps and aimed a wild blow at Yyrkoon. Beyond the eerie fire bubbled yellow-green lava, on all sides, above and beneath. The two men were surrounded only by the misty fire and the lava which lurked beyond it—they were outside the Earth and facing one another for a final battle. The lava seethed and began to ooze inwards, dispersing the fire.

The two blades met and a terrible shrieking roar went up. Elric felt his whole arm go numb and it tingled sickeningly. Elric felt like a puppet. He was no longer his own master—the blade was deciding his actions for him. The blade, with Elric behind it, roared past its brother sword and cut a deep wound in Yyrkoon's left arm. He howled and his eyes widened in agony. Mournblade struck back at Stormbringer, catching Elric in the very place he had wounded his cousin. He sobbed in pain, but continued to move upwards, now wounding Yyrkoon in the right side with a blow strong enough to have killed any other man. Yyrkoon laughed then—laughed like a gibbering demon from the foulest depths of hell. His sanity had broken at last and Elric now had the advantage. But the great sorcery which his cousin had conjured was still in evidence and Elric felt as if a giant had grasped him, was crushing him as he pressed his advantage, Yyrkoon's blood spouting from the wound and covering Elric, also. The lava was slowly withdrawing and now Elric saw the entrance to the central chamber. Behind his cousin another form moved. Elric gasped. Cymoril had awakened and, with horror on her face, was shrieking at him.

The sword still swung in a black arc, cutting down Yyrkoon's brother blade and breaking the usurper's guard.

"Elric!" cried Cymoril desperately. "Save me—save me now, else we are doomed for eternity."

Elric was puzzled by the girl's words. He could not understand the sense of them. Savagely he drove Yyrkoon upwards towards the chamber.

"Elric—put Stormbringer away. Sheathe your sword or we shall part again."

But even if he could have controlled the whistling blade, Elric would not have sheathed it. Hate dominated his being and he would sheathe it in his cousin's evil heart before he put it aside.

Cymoril was weeping, now, pleading with him. But Elric could do nothing. The drooling, idiot thing which had been Yyrkoon of Imrryr, turned at its sister's cries and stared leeringly at her. It cackled and reached out one shaking hand to seize the girl by her shoulder. She struggled to escape, but Yyrkoon still had his evil strength. Taking advantage of his opponent's distraction Elric cut deep through his body, almost severing the trunk from the waist.

And yet, incredibly, Yyrkoon remained alive, drawing his vitality from the blade which still clashed against Elric's own rune-carved sword. With a final push he flung Cymoril forward and she died screaming on the point of Stormbringer.

Then Yyrkoon laughed one final cackling shriek and his black soul went howling down to hell.

The tower resumed its former proportions, all fire and lava gone. Elric was dazed—unable to marshal his thoughts. He looked down at the dead bodies of the brother and the sister. He saw them, at first, only as corpses—a man's and a woman's.

Dark truth dawned on his clearing brain and he moaned in grief, like an animal. He had slain the girl he loved. The runesword fell from his grasp, stained by Cymoril's lifeblood, and clattered unheeded down the stairs. Sobbing now, Elric dropped beside the dead girl and lifted her in his arms.

"Cymoril," he moaned, his whole body throbbing. "Cymoril—I have slain you."

## Chapter Four

Elric looked back at the roaring, crumbling, tumbling, flame-spewing ruins of Imrryr and drove his sweating oarsmen faster. The ship, sail still unfurled, bucked as a contrary current of wind caught it and Elric was forced to cling to the ship's side lest he be tossed overboard. He looked back at Imrryr and felt a tightness in his throat as he realized that he was truly rootless, now; a renegade and a woman-slayer, though involuntarily the latter. He had lost the only woman he had loved in his blind lust for revenge. Now it was finished—everything was finished. He could envisage no future, for his future had been bound up with his past and now, effectively, that past was flaming in ruins behind him. Dry sobs eddied in his chest and he gripped the ship's rail yet more firmly.

His mind reluctantly brooded on Cymoril. He had laid her corpse upon a couch and had set fire to the tower. Then he had gone back to find the reavers successful, straggling back to their ships loaded with loot and girl-slaves, jubilantly firing the tall and beautiful buildings as they went.

He had caused to be destroyed the last tangible sign that the grandiose, magnificent Bright Empire had ever existed. He felt that most of himself was gone with it.

Elric looked back at Imrryr and suddenly a greater sadness overwhelmed him as a tower, as delicate and as beautiful as fine lace, cracked and toppled with flames leaping about it.

He had shattered the last great monument to the earlier race—his own race. Men might have learned again, one day, to build strong, slender towers like those of Imrryr, but now the knowledge was dying with the thundering chaos of the fall of the Dreaming City and the fast-diminishing race of Melniboné.

But what of the Dragon Masters? Neither they nor their golden ships had met the attacking reavers—only their foot-soldiers had been there to defend the city. Had they hidden their ships in some secret waterway and fled inland when the reavers overran the city? They had put up too short a fight to be truly beaten. It had been far too easy. Now that the ships were retreating, were they planning some sudden retaliation? Elric felt that they might have such a plan—perhaps a plan concerning dragons. He shuddered. He had told the others nothing of the beasts which Melnibonéans had controlled for centuries. Even now, someone might be unlocking the gates of the underground Dragon Caves. He turned his mind away from the unnerving prospect.

As the fleet headed towards open sea, Elric's eyes were still looking sadly towards Imrryr as he paid silent homage to the city of his forefathers and the dead Cymoril. He felt hot bitterness sweep over him again as the memory of her death upon his own sword-point came sharply to him. He recalled her warning, when he had left her to go adventuring in the Young Kingdoms, that by putting Yyrkoon on the Ruby Throne as regent, by relinquishing his power for a year, he doomed them both. He cursed himself. Then a muttering, like a roll of distant thunder, spread through the fleet and he wheeled sharply, intent on discovering the cause of the consternation.

Thirty golden-sailed Melnibonéan battle-barges had appeared on both sides of the harbour, issuing from two mouths of the maze. Elric realized that they must have hidden in the other channels, waiting to attack the fleet when they returned, satiated and depleted. Great war-galleys they were, the last ships of Melniboné and the secret of their building was unknown. They had a sense of age and slumbering might about them as they rowed swiftly, each with four or five banks of great sweeping oars, to encircle the raven ships.

Elric's fleet seemed to shrink before his eyes as though it were a bobbing collection of wood-shavings against the towering splendour of the shimmering battle-barges. They were well-equipped and fresh for a fight, whereas the weary reavers were intensely battle-tired. There was only one way to save a small part of the fleet, Elric knew. He would have to conjure a witch-wind for sailpower. Most of the flagships were around him and he now occupied that of Yaris, for the youth had got himself wildly drunk and had died by the knife of a Melnibonéan slave wench. Next to Elric's ship was Count Smiorgan's and the stocky sea-lord was frowning, knowing full well that he and his ships, for all their superior numbers, would not stand up to a sea-fight.

But the conjuring of winds great enough to move many vessels was a dangerous thing, for it released colossal power and the elementals who controlled the winds were apt to turn upon the sorcerer himself if he was not more than careful. But it was the only chance, otherwise the rams which sent ripples from the golden prows would smash the reaver ships to driftwood.

Steeling himself, Elric began to speak the ancient and terrible, many-voweled names of the beings who existed in the air. Again, he could not risk the trance-state, for he had to watch for signs of the elementals turning upon him. He called to them in a speech that was sometimes high like the cry of a gannet, sometimes rolling like the roar of shore-bound surf, and the dim shapes of the Powers of the Wind began to flit before his blurred gaze. His heart throbbed horribly in his ribs and his legs felt weak. He summoned all his strength and conjured a wind which shrieked wildly and chaotically about him, rocking even the huge Melnibonéan ships back and forth. Then he directed the wind and sent it into the sails of some forty of the reaver ships. Many he could not save for they lay outside even his wide range.

But forty of the craft escaped the smashing rams and, amidst the sound of howling wind and sundered timbers, leapt on the waves, their masts creaking as the wind cracked into their sails. Oars were torn from the hands of the rowers, leaving a wake of broken wood on the white salt trail which boiled behind each of the reaver ships.

Quite suddenly, they were beyond the slowly closing circle of Melnibonéan ships and careering madly across the open sea, while all the crews sensed a difference in the air and caught glimpses of strange, soft-shaped forms around them. There was a discomforting sense of evil about the beings which aided them, an awesome alienness.

Smiorgan waved to Elric and grinned thankfully.

"We're safe, thanks to you, Elric!" he yelled across the water. "I knew you'd bring us luck!"

Elric ignored him.

Now the Dragon Lords, vengeance-bent, gave chase. Almost as fast as the magic-aided reaver fleet were the golden barges of Imrryr, and some reaver galleys, whose masts cracked and split beneath the force of the wind driving them, were caught.

Elric saw mighty grappling hooks of dully gleaming metal swing out from the decks of the Imrryrian galleys and thud with a moan of wrenched timber into those of the fleet which lay broken and powerless behind him. Fire leapt from catapults upon the Dragon Lords' ships and careered towards many a fleeing reaver craft. Searing, foul-stinking flame hissed like lava across the decks and ate into planks like vitriol into paper. Men shrieked, beating vainly at brightly burning clothes, some leaping into water which would not extinguish the fire. Some sank beneath the sea and it was possible to trace their descent as, flaming even below the surface, men and ships fluttered to the bottom like blazing, tired moths.

Reaver decks, untouched by fire, ran red with reaver blood as the enraged Imrryrian warriors swung down the grappling ropes and dropped among the raiders, wielding great swords and battle-axes and wreaking terrible havoc amongst the sea-ravens. Imrryrian arrows and Imrryrian javelins swooped from the towering decks of Imrryrian galleys and tore into the panicky men on the smaller ships.

All this Elric saw as he and his vessels began slowly to overhaul the leading Imrryrian ship, flag-galley of Admiral Magum Colim, commander of the Melnibonéan fleet.

Now Elric spared a word for Count Smiorgan. "We've outrun them!" he shouted above the howling wind to the next ship where Smiorgan stood staring wide-eyed at the sky. "But keep your ships heading westwards or we're finished!"

Smiorgan did not reply. He still looked skyward and there was horror in his eyes; in the eyes of a man who, before this, had never known the quivering bite of fear. Uneasily, Elric let his own eyes follow the gaze of Smiorgan. Then he saw them.

They were dragons, without doubt! The great reptiles were some miles away, but Elric knew the stamp of the huge flying beasts. The average wingspan of these near-extinct monsters was some thirty feet across. Their snakelike bodies, beginning in a narrow-snouted head and terminating in a dreadful whip of a tail, were forty feet long and although they did not breathe the legendary fire and smoke, Elric knew that their venom was combustible and could set fire to wood or fabric on contact.

Imrryrian warriors rode the dragon backs. Armed with long, spearlike goads, they blew strangely shaped horns which sang out curious notes over the turbulent sea and calm blue sky. Nearing the golden fleet, now half-a-league away, the leading dragon sailed down and circled towards the huge golden flag-galley, its wings making a sound like the crack of lightning as they beat through the air.

The grey-green, scaled monster hovered over the golden ship as it heaved in the white-foamed turbulent sea. Framed against the cloudless sky, the dragon was in sharp perspective and it was possible for Elric to get a clear view of it. The goad which the Dragon Master waved to Admiral Magum Colim was a long, slim spear upon which the strange pennant of black and yellow zig-zag lines was, even at this distance, noticeable. Elric recognized the insignia on the pennant.

Dyvim Tvar, friend of Elric's youth, Lord of the Dragon Caves, was leading his charges to claim vengeance for Imrryr the Beautiful.

Elric howled across the water to Smiorgan. "These are your main danger, now. Do what you can to stave them off!" There was a rattle of iron as the men prepared, near-hopelessly, to repel the new menace. Witch-wind would give little advantage over the fast-flying dragons. Now Dyvim Tvar had evidently conferred with Magum Colim and his goad lashed out at the dragon throat. The huge reptile jerked upwards and began to gain altitude. Eleven other dragons were behind it, joining it now.

With seeming slowness, the dragons began to beat relentlessly towards the reaver fleet as the crewmen prayed to their own gods for a miracle.

They were doomed. There was no escaping the fact. Every reaver ship was doomed and the raid had been fruitless.

Elric could see the despair in the faces of the men as the masts of the reaver ships continued to bend under the strain of the shrieking witch-wind. They could do nothing, now, but die . . .

Elric fought to rid his mind of the swirling uncertainty which filled it. He drew his sword and felt the pulsating, evil power which lurked in rune-carved Stormbringer. But he hated that power now—for it had caused him to kill the only human he had cherished. He realized how much of his strength he owed to the black-iron sword of his fathers and how weak he might be without it. He was an albino and that meant that he lacked the vitality of a normal human being. Savagely, futilely, as the mist in his mind was replaced by red fear, he cursed the pretensions of revenge he had held, cursed the day when he had agreed to lead the raid on Imrryr and most of all he bitterly vilified dead Yyrkoon and his twisted envy which had been the cause of the whole doom-ridden course of events.

But it was too late now for curses of any kind. The loud slapping of beating dragon wings filled the air and the monsters loomed over the fleeing reaver craft. He had to make some kind of decision—though he had no love for life, he refused to die by the hands of his own people. When he died, he promised himself, it would be by his hand. He made his decision, hating himself.

He called off the witch-wind as the dragon venom seared down and struck the last ship in line.

He put all his powers into sending a stronger wind into the sails of his own boat while his bewildered comrades in the suddenly becalmed ships called over the water, enquiring desperately the reason for his act. Elric's ship was moving fast, now, and might just escape the dragons. He hoped so.

He deserted the man who had trusted him, Count Smiorgan, and watched as venom poured from the sky and engulfed him in blazing green and scarlet flame. Elric fled, keeping his mind from thoughts of the future, and sobbed aloud, that proud prince of ruins; and he cursed the malevolent gods for the black day when idly, for their amusement, they had spawned sentient creatures like himself.

Behind him, the last reaver ships flared into sudden appalling brightness and, although half-thankful that they had escaped the fate of their comrades, the crew looked at Elric accusingly. He sobbed on, not heeding them, great griefs racking his soul.

A night later, off the coast of an island called Pan Tang, when the ship was safe from the dreadful recriminations of the Dragon Masters and their beasts, Elric stood brooding in the stern while the men eyed him with fear and hatred, muttering betrayal and heartless cowardice. They appeared to have forgotten their own fear and subsequent safety.

Elric brooded and he held the black runesword in his two hands. Stormbringer was more than an ordinary battle-blade, this he had known for years, but now he realized that it was possessed of more sentience than he had imagined. Yet he was horribly dependent upon it; he realized this with soul-rending certainty. But he feared and resented the sword's power—hated it bitterly for the chaos it had wrought in his brain and spirit. In an agony of uncertainty he held the blade in his hands and forced himself to weigh the factors involved. Without the sinister sword, he would lose pride—perhaps even life—but he might know the soothing tranquility of pure rest; with it he would have power and strength—but the sword would guide him into a doom-racked future. He would savour power—but never peace.

He drew a great, sobbing breath and, blind misgiving influencing him, threw the sword into the moon-drenched sea.

Incredibly, it did not sink. It did not even float on the water. It fell point forwards into the sea and *stuck* there, quivering as if it were embedded in timber. It remained throbbing in the water, six inches of its blade immersed, and began to give off a weird devil-scream—a howl of horrible malevolence.

With a choking curse Elric stretched out his slim, white, gleaming hand, trying to recover the sentient hellblade. He stretched further, leaning far out over the rail. He could not grasp it—it lay some feet from him, still. Gasping, a sickening sense of defeat overwhelming him, he dropped over the side and plunged into the bone-chilling water, striking out with strained, grotesque strokes, towards the hovering sword. He was beaten—the sword had won.

He reached it and put his fingers around the hilt. At once it settled in his hand and Elric felt strength seep slowly back into his aching body. Then he realized that he and the sword were interdependent, for though he needed the blade, Stormbringer, parasitic, required a user—without a man to wield it, the blade was also powerless.

"We must be bound to one another then," Elric murmured despairingly. "Bound by hell-forged chains and fate-haunted circumstance. Well, then—let it be thus so—and men will have cause to tremble and flee when they hear the names of Elric of Melniboné and Stormbringer, his sword. We are two of a kind—produced by an age which has deserted us. Let us give this age *cause* to hate us!"

Strong again, Elric sheathed Stormbringer and the sword settled against his side; then, with powerful strokes, he began to swim towards the island while the men he left on the ship breathed with relief and speculated whether he would live or perish in the bleak waters of that strange and nameless sea . . .

*The first Elric story, "The Dreaming City," appeared in No. 47 and mainly set the stage for the colourful backcloth Michael Moorcock is beginning to weave in this series.*

*—John Carnell, SCIENCE FANTASY No. 49, October 1961*

# WHILE THE GODS LAUGH

I, while the gods laugh, the world's vortex am;
Maelstrom of passions in that hidden sea
Whose waves of all-time lap the coasts of me,
And in small compass the dark waters cram.

—*Mervyn Peake, "Shapes and Sounds," 1941*

## Chapter One

One night, as Elric sat moodily drinking alone in a tavern, a wingless woman of Myyrrhn came gliding out of the storm and rested her lithe body against him.

Her face was thin and frail-boned, almost as white as Elric's own albino skin, and she wore flimsy pale-green robes which contrasted well with her dark red hair.

The tavern was ablaze with candle-flame and alive with droning argument and gusty laughter, but the words of the woman of Myyrrhn came clear and liquid, carrying over the zesty din.

"I have sought you twenty days," she said to Elric who regarded her insolently through hooded crimson eyes and lazed in a high-backed chair, a silver wine-cup in his long-fingered right hand and his left on the pommel of his sorcerous runesword Stormbringer.

"Twenty days," murmured the Melnibonéan softly, speaking as if to himself, mockingly rude. "A long time for a beautiful and lonely woman to be wandering the world." He opened his eyes a trifle wider and spoke to her directly: "I am Elric of Melniboné, as you evidently know. I grant no favours and ask none. Bearing this in mind, tell me why you have sought me for twenty days."

Equably, the woman replied, undaunted by the albino's supercilious tone. "You are a bitter man, Elric; I know this also—and you are grief-haunted for reasons which are already legend. I ask you no favours—but bring you myself and a proposition. What do you desire most in the world?"

"Peace," Elric told her simply. Then he smiled ironically and said: "I am an evil man, lady, and my destiny is hell-doomed, but I am not unwise, nor unfair. Let me remind you a little of the truth. Call this legend if you prefer—I do not care.

"A woman died a year ago, on the blade of my trusty sword." He patted the blade sharply and his eyes were suddenly hard and self-mocking. "Since then I have courted no woman and desired none. Why should I break such secure habits? If asked, I grant you that I could speak poetry to you, and that you have a grace and beauty which moves me to interesting speculation, but I would not load any part of my dark burden upon one as exquisite as you. Any relationship be-

tween us, other than formal, would necessitate my unwilling shifting of part of that burden." He paused for an instant and then said slowly: "I should admit that I scream in my sleep sometimes and am often tortured by incommunicable self-loathing. Go while you can, lady, and forget Elric for he can bring only grief to your soul."

With a quick movement he turned his gaze from her and lifted the silver wine-cup, draining it and replenishing it from a jug at his side.

"No," said the wingless woman of Myyrrhn calmly, "I will not. Come with me."

She rose and gently took Elric's hand. Without knowing why, Elric allowed himself to be led from the tavern and out into the wild, rainless storm which howled around the Filkharian city of Raschil. A protective and cynical smile hovered about his mouth as she drew him towards the sea-lashed quayside where she told him her name. Shaarilla of the Dancing Mist, wingless daughter of a dead necromancer—a cripple in her own strange land, and an outcast.

Elric felt uncomfortably drawn to this calm-eyed woman who wasted few words. He felt a great surge of emotion well within him, emotion he had never thought to experience again, and he wanted to take her finely moulded shoulders and press her slim body to his. But he quelled the urge and studied her marble delicacy and her wild hair which flowed in the wind about her head.

Silence rested comfortably between them while the chaotic wind howled mournfully over the sea. Here, Elric could ignore the warm stink of the city and he felt almost relaxed. At last, looking away from him towards the swirling sea, her green robe curling in the wind, she said: "You have heard, of course, of the Dead Gods' Book?"

Elric nodded. He was interested, despite the need he felt to disassociate himself as much as possible from his fellows. The mythical book was believed to contain knowledge which could solve many problems that had plagued men for centuries—it held a holy and mighty wisdom which every sorcerer desired to sample. But it was believed destroyed, hurled into the sun when the Old Gods were dying in the cosmic wastes which lay beyond the outer reaches of the solar system. Another legend, apparently of later origin, spoke vaguely of the dark ones who had interrupted the Book's sunward coursing and had stolen it before it could be destroyed. Most scholars discounted this legend, arguing that, by this time, the Book would have come to light if it did still exist.

Elric made himself speak flatly so that he appeared to be uninterested when he answered Shaarilla. "Why do you mention the Book?"

"I know that it exists," Shaarilla replied intensely, "and I know where it is. My father acquired the knowledge just before he died. Myself—and the Book—you may have if you will help me get it."

Could the secret of peace be contained in the Book? Elric wondered. Would he, if he found it, be able to dispense with Stormbringer?

"If you want it so badly that you seek my help," he said eventually, "why do you not wish to keep it?"

"Because I would be afraid to have such a thing perpetually in my custody—it is not a book for an ordinary mortal to own, but you are possibly the last mighty nigromancer left in the world and it is fitting that you should have it. Besides, you might kill me to obtain it—I would never be safe with such a volume in my hands. I need only one small part of its wisdom."

"What is that?" Elric enquired, studying her patrician beauty with a new pulse stirring within him.

Her mouth set and the lids fell over her eyes. "When we have the Book in our hands—then you will have your answer. Not before."

"This answer is good enough," Elric remarked quickly, seeing that he would gain no more information at that stage. "And the answer appeals to me." Then, half before he realized it, he seized her shoulders in his slim, pale hands and pressed his colourless lips to her scarlet mouth.

Elric and Shaarilla rode westwards, towards the Silent Land, across the lush plains of Shazaar where their ship had berthed two days earlier. The border country between Shazaar and the Silent Land was a lonely stretch of territory, unoccupied even by peasant dwellings; a no-man's land, though fertile and rich in natural wealth. The inhabitants of

Shazaar had deliberately refrained from extending their borders further, for though the dwellers in the Silent Land rarely ventured beyond the Marshes of the Mist, the natural borderline between the two lands, the inhabitants of Shazaar held their unknown neighbours in almost superstitious fear.

The journey had been clean and swift, though ominous, with several persons who should have known nothing of their purpose warning the travelers of nearing danger. Elric brooded, recognizing the signs of doom but choosing to ignore them and communicate nothing to Shaarilla who, for her part, seemed content with Elric's silence. They spoke little in the day and so saved their breath for the wild love-play of the night.

The thud of the two horses' hoofs on the soft turf, the muted creak and clatter of Elric's harness and sword, were the only sounds to break the stillness of the clear winter day as the pair rode steadily, nearing the quaking, treacherous trails of the Marshes of the Mist.

One gloomy night, they reached the borders of the Silent Land, marked by the marsh, and they halted and made camp, pitching their silk tent on a hill overlooking the mist-shrouded wastes.

Banked like black pillows against the horizon, the clouds were ominous. The moon lurked behind them, sometimes piercing them sufficiently to send a pale tentative beam down on to the glistening marsh or its ragged, grassy frontiers. Once, a moonbeam glanced off silver, illuminating the dark silhouette of Elric, but, as if repelled by the sight of a living creature on that bleak hill, the moon once again slunk behind its cloud-shield, leaving Elric thinking deeply. Leaving Elric in the darkness he desired.

Thunder rumbled over distant mountains, sounding like the laughter of far-off gods. Elric shivered, pulled his blue cloak more tightly about him, and continued to stare over the misted lowlands.

Shaarilla came to him soon, and she stood beside him, swathed in a thick woolen cloak which could not keep out all the damp chill in the air.

"The Silent Land," she murmured. "Are all the stories true, Elric? Did they teach you of it in old Melniboné?"

Elric frowned, annoyed that she had disturbed his thoughts. He turned abruptly to look at her, staring blankly out of crimson-irised eyes for a moment and then saying flatly:

"The inhabitants are unhuman and feared. This I know. Few men ventured into their territory, ever. None have returned, to my knowledge. Even in the days when Melniboné was a powerful empire, this was one nation my ancestors never ruled—nor did they desire to do so. Nor did they make a treaty. The denizens of the Silent Land are said to be a dying race, far more selfish than my ancestors ever were, who enjoyed dominion over the Earth long before Melnibonéans gained any sort of power. They rarely venture beyond the confines of their territory, nowadays, encompassed as it is by marshland and mountains."

Shaarilla laughed, then, with little humour. "So they are unhuman are they, Elric? Then what of my people, who are related to them? What of me, Elric?"

"You're unhuman enough for me," replied Elric insouciantly, looking her in the eyes. She smiled.

"A compliment? I'll take it for one—until your glib tongue finds a better."

That night they slept restlessly and, as he had predicted, Elric screamed agonizingly in his turbulent, terror-filled sleep and he called a name which made Shaarilla's eyes fill with pain and jealousy. Wide-eyed in his grim sleep, Elric seemed to be staring at the one he named, speaking other words in a sibilant language which made Shaarilla block her ears and shudder.

The next morning, as they broke camp, folding the rustling fabric of the yellow silk tent between them, Shaarilla avoided looking at Elric directly but later, since he made no move to speak, she asked him, in a voice which shook somewhat, a question.

It was a question which she needed to ask, but one which came hard to her lips. "Why do you desire the Dead Gods' Book, Elric? What do you believe you will find in it?"

Elric shrugged, dismissing the question, but she repeated her words less slowly, with more insistence.

"Very well then," he said eventually. "But it is not easy to answer you in a few sentences. I desire, if you like, to know one of two things."

"And what is that, Elric?"

The tall albino dropped the folded tent to the grass and sighed. His fingers played nervously with the pommel of his runesword. "Can an ultimate god exist—or not? That is what I need to know, Shaarilla, if my life is to have any direction at all.

"The Lords of Law and Chaos now govern our lives. But is there some being greater than them?"

Shaarilla put a hand on Elric's arm. "Why must you know?" she said.

"Despairingly, sometimes, I seek the comfort of a benign god, Shaarilla. My mind goes out, lying awake at night, searching through black barrenness for something—anything—which will take me to it, warm me, protect me, tell me that there is order in the chaotic tumble of the universe; that it is consistent, this precision of the planets, not simply a brief, bright spark of sanity in an eternity of malevolent anarchy."

Elric sighed and his quiet tones were tinged with hopelessness. "Without some confirmation of the order of things, my only comfort is to accept anarchy. This way, I can revel in chaos and know, without fear, that we are all doomed from the start—that our brief existence is both meaningless and damned. I can accept, then, that we are more than forsaken, because there was never anything there to forsake us. I have weighed the proof, Shaarilla, and must believe that anarchy prevails, in spite of all the laws which seemingly govern our actions, our sorcery, our logic. I see only chaos in the world. If the book we seek tells me otherwise, then I shall gladly believe it. Until then, I will put my trust only in my sword and myself."

Shaarilla stared at Elric strangely. "Could not this philosophy of yours have been influenced by recent events in your past? Do you fear the consequences of your murder and treachery? Is it not more comforting for you to believe in deserts which are rarely just?"

Elric turned on her, crimson eyes blazing in anger, but even as he made to speak, the anger fled him and he dropped his eyes towards the ground, hooding them from her gaze.

"Perhaps," he said lamely. "I do not know. That is the only *real* truth, Shaarilla. *I do not know*."

Shaarilla nodded, her face lit by an enigmatic sympathy; but Elric did not see the look she gave him, for his own eyes were full of crystal tears which flowed down his lean, white face and took his strength and will momentarily from him.

"I am a man possessed," he groaned, "and without this devil-blade I carry I would not be a man at all."

## Chapter Two

They mounted their swift, black horses and spurred them with abandoned savagery down the hillside towards the marsh, their cloaks whipping behind them as the wind caught them, lashing them high into the air. Both rode with set, hard faces, refusing to acknowledge the aching uncertainty which lurked within them.

And the horses' hoofs had splashed into quaking bogland before they could halt.

Cursing, Elric tugged hard on his reins, pulling his horse back on to firm ground. Shaarilla, too, fought her own panicky stallion and guided the beast to the safety of the turf.

"How do we cross?" Elric asked her impatiently.

"There was a map—" Shaarilla began hesitantly.

"*Where is it?*"

"It—it was lost. I lost it. But I tried hard to memorize it. I think I'll be able to get us safely across."

"How did you lose it—and why didn't you tell me of this before?" Elric stormed.

"I'm sorry, Elric—but for a whole day, just before I found you in that tavern, my memory was gone. Somehow, I lived through a day without knowing it—and when I awoke, the map was missing."

Elric frowned. "There is some force working against us, I am sure," he muttered, "but what it is, I do not know." He raised his voice and said to her: "Let us hope that your memory is not too faulty, now. These marshes are infamous the world over, but by all accounts, only natural hazards wait for us." He grimaced and put his fingers around the hilt of his runesword. "Best go first, Shaarilla, but stay close. Lead the way."

She nodded, dumbly, and turned her horse's head towards the north, galloping along the bank until she came to a place where a great, tapering rock loomed. Here, a grassy path, four feet or so across, led out into the misty marsh. They could only see a little distance ahead, because of the clinging mist, but it seemed that the trail remained firm for some way. Shaarilla walked her horse on to the path and jolted forward at a slow trot, Elric following immediately behind her.

Through the swirling, heavy mist which shone whitely, the horses moved hesitantly and their riders had to keep them on short, tight rein. The mist padded the marsh with silence and the gleaming, watery fens around them stank with foul putrescence. No animal scurried, no bird shrieked above them. Everywhere was a haunting, fear-laden silence which made both horses and riders uneasy.

With panic in their throats, Elric and Shaarilla rode on, deeper and deeper into the unnatural Marshes of the Mist, their eyes wary and even their nostrils quivering for scent of danger in the stinking morass.

Hours later, when the sun was long past its zenith, Shaarilla's horse reared, screaming and whinnying. She shouted for Elric, her exquisite features twisted in fear as she stared into the mist. He spurred his own bucking horse forwards and joined her.

Something moved, slowly, menacingly in the clinging whiteness. Elric's right hand whipped over to his left side and grasped the hilt of Stormbringer.

The blade shrieked out of its scabbard, a black fire gleaming along its length and alien power flowing from it into Elric's arm and through his body. A weird, unholy light leapt into Elric's crimson eyes and his mouth was wrenched into a hideous grin as he forced the frightened horse further into the skulking mist.

"Arioch, Lord of the Seven Darks, be with me now!" Elric yelled as he made out the shifting shape ahead of him. It was white, like the mist, yet somehow *darker*. It stretched high above Elric's head. It was nearly ten feet tall and almost as broad. But it was still only an outline, seeming to have no face or limbs—only movement: darting, malevolent movement! But Arioch, his patron god, chose not to hear.

Elric could feel his horse's great heart beating between his legs as the beast plunged forward under its rider's iron control. Shaarilla was screaming something behind him, but he could not hear the words. Elric hacked at the white shape, but his sword met only mist and it howled angrily. The fear-crazed horse would go no further and Elric was forced to dismount.

"Keep hold of the steed," he shouted behind him to Shaarilla and moved on light feet towards the darting shape which hovered ahead of him, blocking his path.

Now he could make out some of its saliencies. Two eyes, the colour of thin, yellow wine, were set high in the thing's body, though it had no separate head. A mouthing, obscene slit, filled with fangs, lay just beneath the eyes. It had no nose or ears that Elric could see. Four appendages sprang from its upper parts and its lower body slithered along the ground, unsupported by any limbs. Elric's eyes ached as he looked at it. It was incredibly disgusting to behold and its amorphous body gave off a stench of death and decay. Fighting down his fear, the albino inched forward warily, his sword held high to parry any thrust the thing might make with its arms. Elric recognized it from a description in one of his grimoires. It was a Mist Giant—possibly the only Mist Giant, Bellbane. Even the wisest wizards were uncertain how many existed—one or many. It was a ghoul of the swamp-lands which fed off the souls and the blood of men and beasts. But the Marshes of this Mist were far to the east of Bellbane's reputed haunts.

Elric ceased to wonder why so few animals inhabited that stretch of the swamp. Overhead the sky was beginning to darken.

Stormbringer throbbed in Elric's grasp as he called the names of the ancient demon-gods of his people. The nauseous ghoul obviously recognized the names. For an instant, it wavered backwards. Elric made his legs move towards the thing. Now he saw that the ghoul was not white at all. But it had no colour to it that Elric could recognize. There was a suggestion of orangeness dashed with sickening greenish yellow, but he did not see the colours with his eyes—he only *sensed* the alien, unholy tinctures.

Then Elric rushed towards the thing, shouting the names which now had no meaning to his surface consciousness. "*Balaan—Marthim! Aesma! Alastor! Saebos! Verdelet! Nizilfkm! Haborym!* Haborym of the Fires Which Destroy!" His whole mind was torn in two. Part of him wanted to run, to hide, but he had no control over the power which now gripped him and pushed him to meet the horror. His sword blade hacked and slashed at the shape. It was like trying to cut through water—sentient, pulsating water. But Stormbringer had effect. The whole shape of the ghoul quivered as if in dreadful pain. Elric felt himself plucked into the air and his vision went. He could see nothing—do nothing but hack and cut at the thing which now held him.

Sweat poured from him as, blindly, he fought on.

Pain which was hardly physical—a deeper, horrifying pain, filled his being as he howled now in agony and struck continually at the yielding bulk which embraced him and was pulling him slowly towards its gaping maw. He struggled and writhed in the obscene grasp of the thing. With powerful arms, it was holding him, almost lasciviously, drawing him closer as a rough lover would draw a girl. Even the mighty power intrinsic in the runesword did not seem enough to kill the monster. Though its efforts were somewhat weaker than earlier, it still drew Elric nearer to the gnashing, slavering mouth-slit.

Elric cried the names again, while Stormbringer danced and sang an evil song in his right hand. In agony, Elric writhed, praying, begging and promising, but still he was drawn inch by inch towards the grinning maw.

Savagely, grimly, he fought and again he screamed for Arioch. A mind touched his—sardonic, powerful, evil—and he knew Arioch responded at last! Almost imperceptibly, the Mist Giant weakened. Elric pressed his advantage and the knowledge that the ghoul was losing its strength gave him more power. Blindly, agony piercing every nerve of his body, he struck and struck.

Then, quite suddenly, he was falling.

He seemed to fall for hours, slowly, weightlessly until he landed upon a surface which yielded beneath him. He began to sink.

Far off, beyond time and space, he heard a distant voice calling to him. He did not want to hear it; he was content to lie where he was as the cold, comforting stuff in which he lay dragged him slowly into itself.

Then, some sixth sense made him realize that it was Shaarilla's voice calling him and he forced himself to make sense out of her words.

"*Elric—the marsh! You're in the marsh. Don't move!*"

He smiled to himself. Why should he move? Down he was sinking, slowly, calmly—down into the welcoming marsh . . . *Had there been another time like this; another marsh?*

With a mental jolt, full awareness of the situation came back to him and he jerked his eyes open. Above him was mist. To one side a pool of unnamable colouring was slowly evaporating, giving off a foul odour. On the other side he could just make out a human form, gesticulating wildly. Beyond the human form were the barely discernible shapes of two horses. Shaarilla was there. Beneath him—

Beneath him was the marsh.

Thick, stinking slime was sucking him downwards as he lay spreadeagled upon it, half-submerged already. Stormbringer was still in his right hand. He could just see it if he turned his head. Carefully, he tried to lift the top half of his body from the sucking morass. He succeeded, only to feel his legs sink deeper. Sitting upright, he shouted to the girl.

"Shaarilla! Quickly—a rope!"

"There is no rope, Elric!" She was ripping off her top garment, frantically tearing it into strips.

Still Elric sank, his feet finding no purchase beneath them.

Shaarilla hastily knotted the strips of cloth. She flung the makeshift rope inexpertly towards the sinking albino. It fell short. Fumbling in her haste, she threw it again. This time his groping left hand found it. The girl began to haul on the fabric. Elric felt himself rise a little and then stop.

"It's no good, Elric—I haven't the strength."

Cursing her, Elric shouted: "The horse—tie it to the horse!"

She ran towards one of the horses and looped the cloth around the pommel of the saddle. Then she tugged at the beast's reins and began to walk it away.

Swiftly, Elric was dragged from the sucking bog and, still gripping Stormbringer, was pulled to the inadequate safety of the strip of turf.

Gasping, he tried to stand, but found his legs incredibly weak beneath him. He rose, staggered, and fell. Shaarilla knelt down beside him.

"Are you hurt?"

Elric smiled in spite of his weakness. "I don't think so."

"It was dreadful. I couldn't see properly what was happening. You seemed to disappear and then—then you screamed that—that name!" She was trembling, her face pale and taut.

"What name?" Elric was genuinely puzzled. "What name did I scream?"

She shook her head. "It doesn't matter—but whatever it was—it saved you. You reappeared soon afterwards and fell into the marsh . . ."

Stormbringer's power was still flowing into the albino. He already felt stronger.

With an effort, he got up and stumbled unsteadily towards his horse.

"I'm sure that the Mist Giant does not usually haunt this marsh—it was sent here. By what—or whom—I don't know, but we must get to firmer ground while we can."

Shaarilla said: "Which way—back or forward?"

Elric frowned. "Why, forward, of course. Why do you ask?"

She swallowed and shook her head. "Let's hurry, then," she said.

They mounted their horses and rode with little caution until the marsh and its cloak of mist was behind them.

Now the journey took on a new urgency as Elric realized that some force was attempting to put obstacles in their way. They rested little and savagely rode their powerful horses to a virtual standstill.

On the fifth day they were riding through barren, rocky country and a light rain was falling.

The hard ground was slippery so that they were forced to ride more slowly, huddled over the sodden necks of their horses, muffled in cloaks which only inadequately kept out the drizzling rain. They had ridden in silence for some time before they heard a ghastly cackling baying ahead of them and the rattle of hoofs.

Elric motioned towards a large rock looming to their right. "Shelter there," he said. "Something comes towards us—possibly more enemies. With luck, they'll pass us." Shaarilla mutely obeyed him and together they waited as the hideous baying grew nearer.

"One rider—several other beasts," Elric said, listening intently. "The beasts either follow or pursue the rider."

Then they were in sight—racing through the rain. A man frantically spurring an equally frightened horse—and behind him, the distance decreasing, a pack of what at first appeared to be dogs. But these were not dogs—they were half-dog and half-bird, with the lean, shaggy bodies and legs of dogs but possessing birdlike talons in place of paws and savagely curved beaks which snapped where muzzles should have been.

"The hunting dogs of the Dharzi!" gasped Shaarilla. "I thought that they, like their masters, were long extinct!"

"I, also," Elric said. "What are they doing in these parts? There was never contact between the Dharzi and the dwellers of this land."

"Brought here—by *something*," Shaarilla whispered. "Those devil-dogs will scent us to be sure."

Elric reached for his runesword. "Then we can lose nothing by aiding their quarry," he said, urging his mount forward. "Wait here, Shaarilla."

By this time, the devil-pack and the man they pursued were rushing past the sheltering rock, speeding down a narrow defile. Elric spurred his horse down the slope.

"Ho there!" he shouted to the frantic rider. "Turn and stand, my friend—I'm here to aid you!"

His moaning runesword lifted high, Elric thundered towards the snapping, howling devil-dogs and his horse's hoofs struck one with an impact which broke the unnatural beast's spine. There were some five or six of the weird dogs left. The rider turned his horse and drew a long sabre from a scabbard at his waist. He was a small man, with a broad ugly mouth. He grinned in relief.

"A lucky chance, this meeting, good master."

This was all he had time to remark before two of the dogs were leaping at him and he was forced to give his whole attention to defending himself from their slashing talons and snapping beaks.

The other three dogs concentrated their vicious attention upon Elric. One leapt high, its beak aimed at Elric's throat. He felt foul breath on his face and hastily brought Stormbringer round in an arc which chopped the dog in two. Filthy blood spattered Elric and his horse and the scent of it seemed to increase the fury of the other dogs' attack. But the blood made the dancing black runesword sing an almost ecstatic tune and Elric felt it writhe in his grasp and stab at another of the hideous dogs. The point caught the beast just below its breastbone as it reared up at the albino. It screamed in terrible agony and turned its beak to seize the blade. As the beak connected with the lambent black metal of the sword, a foul stench, akin to the smell of burning, struck Elric's nostrils and the beast's scream broke off sharply.

Engaged with the remaining devil-dog, Elric caught a fleeting glimpse of the charred corpse. His horse was rearing high, lashing at the last alien animal with flailing hoofs. The dog avoided the horse's attack and came at Elric's unguarded left side. The albino swung in the saddle and brought his sword hurtling down to slice into the dog's skull and spill brains and blood on the wet and gleaming ground. Still somehow alive, the dog snapped feebly at Elric, but the Melnibonéan ignored its futile attack and turned his attention to the little man who had dispensed with one of his adversaries, but was having difficulty with the second. The dog had grasped the sabre with its beak, gripping the sword near the hilt.

Talons raked towards the little man's throat as he strove to shake the dog's grip. Elric charged forward, his runesword aimed like a lance to where the devil-dog dangled in mid-air, its talons slashing, trying to reach the flesh of its former quarry. Stormbringer caught the beast in its lower abdomen and ripped upwards, slitting the thing's underparts from crutch to throat. It released its hold on the small man's sabre and fell writhing to the ground. Elric's horse trampled it into the rocky ground. Breathing heavily, the albino sheathed Stormbringer and warily regarded the man he had saved. He disliked unnecessary contact with anyone and did not wish to be embarrassed by a display of emotion on the little man's part.

He was not disappointed, for the wide, ugly mouth split into a cheerful grin and the man bowed in the saddle as he returned his own curved blade to its scabbard.

"Thanks, good sir," he said lightly. "Without your help, the battle might have lasted longer. You deprived me of good sport, but you meant well. Moonglum is my name."

"Elric of Melniboné, I," replied the albino, but saw no reaction on the little man's face. This was strange, for the name of Elric was now infamous throughout most of the world. The story of his treachery and the slaying of his cousin Cymoril had been told and elaborated upon in taverns throughout the Young Kingdoms. Much as he hated it, he was used to receiving some indication of recognition from those he met. His albinism was enough to mark him.

Intrigued by Moonglum's ignorance, and feeling strangely drawn towards the cocky little rider, Elric studied him in an effort to discover from what land he came. Moonglum wore no armour and his clothes were of faded blue material, travel-stained and worn. A stout leather belt carried the sabre, a dirk and a woolen purse. Upon his feet, Moonglum wore ankle-length boots of cracked leather. His horse-furniture was much used but of obviously good quality. The man himself, seated high in the saddle, was barely more than five feet tall, with legs too long in proportion to the rest of his slight body. His nose was short and uptilted, beneath grey-green eyes, large and innocent-seeming. A mop of vivid red hair fell over his forehead and down his neck, unrestrained. He sat his horse comfortably, still grinning but looking now behind Elric to where Shaarilla rode to join them.

Moonglum bowed elaborately as the girl pulled her horse to a halt.

Elric said coldly, "The Lady Shaarilla—Master Moonglum of—?"

"Of Elwher," Moonglum supplied, "the mercantile capital of the East—the finest city in the world."

Elric recognized the name. "So you are from Elwher, Master Moonglum. I have heard of the place. A new city, is it not? Some few centuries old. You have ridden far."

"Indeed I have, sir. Without knowledge of the language used in these parts, the journey would have been harder, but luckily the slave who inspired me with tales of his homeland taught me the speech thoroughly."

"But why do you travel these parts—have you not heard the legends?" Shaarilla spoke incredulously.

"Those very legends were what brought me hence—and I'd begun to discount them, until those unpleasant pups set upon me. For what reason they decided to give chase, I will not know, for I gave them no cause to take a dislike to me. This is, indeed, a barbarous land."

Elric was uncomfortable. Light talk of the kind which Moonglum seemed to enjoy was contrary to his own brooding nature. But in spite of this, he found that he was liking the man more and more.

It was Moonglum who suggested that they travel together for a while. Shaarilla objected, giving Elric a warning glance, but he ignored it.

"Very well then, friend Moonglum, since three are stronger than two, we'd appreciate your company. We ride towards the mountains." Elric, himself, was feeling in a more cheerful mood.

"And what do you seek there?" Moonglum enquired.

"A secret," Elric said, and his new-found companion was discreet enough to drop the question.

## Chapter Three

So they rode, while the rainfall increased and splashed and sang among the rocks with a sky like dull steel above them and the wind crooning a dirge about their ears. Three small figures riding swiftly towards the black mountain barrier which rose over the world like a brooding god. And perhaps it was a god that laughed sometimes as they neared the foothills of the range, or perhaps it was the wind whistling through the dark mystery of canyons and precipices and the tumble of basalt and granite which climbed towards lonely peaks. Thunder clouds formed around those peaks and lightning smashed downwards like a monster finger searching the earth for grubs. Thunder rattled over the range and Shaarilla spoke her thoughts at last to Elric; spoke them as the mountains came in sight.

"Elric—let us go back, I beg you. Forget the Book—there are too many forces working against us. Take heed of the signs, Elric, or we are doomed!"

But Elric was grimly silent, for he had long been aware that the girl was losing her enthusiasm for the quest she had started.

"Elric—please. We will never reach the Book. Elric, turn back."

She rode beside him, pulling at his garments until impatiently he shrugged himself clear of her grasp and said:

"I am intrigued too much to stop now. Either continue to lead the way—or tell me what you know and stay here. You desired to sample the Book's wisdom once—but now a few minor pitfalls on our journey have frightened you. What was it you needed to learn, Shaarilla?"

She did not answer him, but said instead: "And what was it you desired, Elric? Peace, you told me. Well, I warn you, you'll find no peace in those grim mountains—if we reach them at all."

"You have not been frank with me, Shaarilla," Elric said coldly, still looking ahead of him at the black peaks. "You know something of the forces seeking to stop us."

She shrugged. "It matters not—I know little. My father spoke a few vague warnings before he died, that is all."

"What did he say?"

"He said that He who guards the Book would use all his power to stop mankind from using its wisdom."

"What else?"

"Nothing else. But it is enough, now that I see that my father's warning was truly spoken. It was this guardian who killed him, Elric—or one of the guardian's minions. I do not wish to suffer that fate, in spite of what the Book might do for me. I had thought you powerful enough to aid me—but now I doubt it."

"I have protected you so far," Elric said simply. "Now tell me what you seek from the Book?"

"I am too ashamed."

Elric did not press the question, but eventually she spoke softly, almost whispering. "I sought my wings," she said.

"Your wings—you mean the Book might give you a spell so that you could grow wings!" Elric smiled ironically. "And that is why you seek the vessel of the world's mightiest wisdom!"

"If you were thought deformed in your own land—it would seem important enough to you," she shouted defiantly.

Elric turned his face towards her, his crimson-irised eyes burning with a strange emotion. He put a hand to his dead white skin and a crooked smile twisted his lips. "I, too, have felt as you do," he said quietly. That was all he said and Shaarilla dropped behind him again, shamed.

They rode on in silence until Moonglum, who had been riding

discreetly ahead, cocked his overlarge skull on one side and suddenly drew rein.

Elric joined him. "What is it, Moonglum?"

"I hear horses coming this way," the little man said. "And voices which are disturbingly familiar. More of those devil-dogs, Elric—and this time accompanied by riders!"

Elric, too, heard the sounds, now, and shouted a warning to Shaarilla.

"Perhaps you were right," he called. "More trouble comes towards us."

"What now?" Moonglum said, frowning.

"Ride for the mountains," Elric replied, "and we may yet outdistance them."

They spurred their steeds into a fast gallop and sped towards the hills.

But their flight was hopeless. Soon a black pack was visible on the horizon and the sharp birdlike baying of the devil-dogs drew nearer. Elric stared backwards at their pursuers. Night was beginning to fall, and visibility was decreasing with every passing moment but he had a vague impression of the riders who raced behind the pack. They were swathed in dark cloaks and carried long spears. Their faces were invisible, lost in the shadow of the hoods which covered their heads.

Now Elric and his companions were forcing their horses up a steep incline, seeking the shelter of the rocks which lay above.

"We'll halt here," Elric ordered, "and try to hold them off. In the open they could easily surround us."

Moonglum nodded affirmatively, agreeing with the good sense contained in Elric's words. They pulled their sweating steeds to a standstill and prepared to join battle with the howling pack and their dark-cloaked masters.

Soon the first of the devil-dogs were rushing up the incline, their beak-jaws slavering and their talons rattling on stone. Standing between two rocks, blocking the way between with their bodies, Elric and Moonglum met the first attack and quickly dispatched three of the animals. Several more took the place of the dead and the first of the riders was visible behind them as night crept closer.

"Arioch!" swore Elric, suddenly recognizing the riders. "These are the Lords of Dharzi—dead these ten centuries. We're fighting dead men, Moonglum, and the too-tangible ghosts of their dogs. Unless I can think of a sorcerous means to defeat them, we're doomed!"

The zombie-men appeared to have no intention of taking part in the attack for the moment. They waited, their dead eyes eerily luminous, as the devil-dogs attempted to break through the swinging network of steel with which Elric and his companion defended themselves. Elric was racking his brains—trying to dredge a spoken spell from his memory which would dismiss these living dead. Then it came to him, and hoping that the forces he had to invoke would decide to aid him, he began to chant:

> "Let the Laws which govern all things
> Not so lightly be dismissed;
> Let the Ones who flaunt the Earth Kings
> With a fresher death be kissed."

Nothing happened. "I've failed." Elric muttered hopelessly as he met the attack of a snapping devil-dog and spitted the thing on his sword.

But then—the ground rocked and seemed to *seethe* beneath the feet of the horses upon whose backs the dead men sat. The tremor lasted a few seconds and then subsided.

"The spell was not powerful enough," Elric sighed.

The earth trembled again and small craters formed in the ground of the hillside upon which the dead Lords of Dharzi impassively waited. Stones crumbled and the horses stamped nervously. Then the earth rumbled.

"Back!" yelled Elric warningly. "Back—or we'll go with them!" They retreated—backing towards Shaarilla and their waiting horses as the ground sagged beneath their feet. The Dharzi mounts were rearing and snorting and the remaining dogs turned nervously to regard their masters with puzzled, uncertain eyes. A low moan was coming from the lips of the living dead. Suddenly, a whole area of the surrounding hillside split into cracks, and yawning crannies appeared in the surface. Elric and his companions swung themselves on to their horses as, with a frightful multivoiced scream, the dead lords were swallowed by the earth, returning to the depths from which they had been summoned.

A deep unholy chuckle arose from the shattered pit. It was the mocking laughter of the earth elemental King Grome, taking his rightful subjects back into his keeping. Whining, the devil-dogs slunk towards the edge of the pit, sniffing around it. Then, with one accord, the black pack hurled itself down into the chasm, following its masters to whatever unholy doom awaited it.

Moonglum shuddered. "You are on familiar terms with the strangest people, friend Elric," he said shakily and turned his horse towards the mountains again.

They reached the black mountains on the following day and nervously Shaarilla led them along the rocky route she had memorized. She no longer pleaded with Elric to return—she was resigned to whatever fate awaited them. Elric's obsession was burning within him and he was filled with impatience—certain that he would find, at last, the ultimate truth of existence in the Dead Gods' Book. Moonglum was cheerfully skeptical, while Shaarilla was consumed with foreboding.

Rain still fell and the storm growled and crackled above them. But, as the driving rainfall increased with fresh insistence, they came, at last, to the black, gaping mouth of a huge cave.

"I can lead you no further," Shaarilla said wearily. "The Book lies somewhere beyond the entrance to this cave."

Elric and Moonglum looked uncertainly at one another, neither of them sure what move to make next. To have reached their goal seemed somehow anti-climactic—for nothing blocked the cave entrance—and nothing appeared to guard it.

"It is inconceivable," said Elric, "that the dangers which beset us were not engineered by something, yet here we are—and no-one seeks to stop us entering. Are you sure that this is the *right* cave, Shaarilla?"

The girl pointed upwards to the rock above the entrance. Engraved in it was a curious symbol which Elric instantly recognized.

"The sign of Chaos!" Elric exclaimed. "Perhaps I should have guessed."

"What does it mean, Elric?" Moonglum asked.

"That is the symbol of everlasting disruption and anarchy," Elric told him. "We are standing in territory presided over by the Lords of Entropy or one of their minions. So that is who our enemy is! This can only mean one thing—the Book is of extreme importance to the order of things on this plane—possibly all the myriad planes of the multiverse. It was why Arioch was reluctant to aid me—he, too, is a Lord of Chaos!"

Moonglum stared at him in puzzlement. "What do you mean, Elric?"

"Know you not that two forces govern the world—fighting an eternal battle?" Elric replied. "Law and Chaos. The upholders of Chaos state that in such a world as they rule, all things are possible. Opponents of Chaos—those who ally themselves with the forces of Law—say that without Law *nothing* material is possible.

"Some stand apart, believing that a balance between the two is the proper state of things, but we cannot. We have become embroiled in a dispute between the two forces. The Book is valuable to either faction, obviously, and I could guess that the minions of Entropy are worried what power we might release if we obtain this book. Law and Chaos rarely interfere directly in Men's lives—that is why only adepts are fully aware of their presence. Now perhaps, I will discover at last the answer to the one question which concerns me—does an ultimate force rule over the opposing factions of Law and Chaos?"

Elric stepped through the cave entrance, peering into the gloom while the others hesitantly followed him.

"The cave stretches back a long way. All we can do is press on until we find its far wall," Elric said.

"Let's hope that its far wall lies not *downwards*," Moonglum said ironically as he motioned Elric to lead on.

They stumbled forward as the cave grew darker and darker. Their voices were magnified and hollow to their own ears as the floor of the cave slanted sharply down.

"This is no cave," Elric whispered, "it's a *tunnel*—but I cannot guess where it leads."

For several hours they pressed onwards in pitch darkness, clinging to one another as they reeled forward, uncertain of their footing and still aware that they were moving down a gradual incline. They lost all sense of time and Elric began to feel as if he were living through a dream. Events seemed to have become so unpredictable and beyond his control that he could no longer cope with thinking about them in ordinary terms. The tunnel was long and dark and wide and cold. It offered no comfort and the floor eventually became the only thing which had any reality. It was firmly beneath his feet. He began to feel that possibly he was not moving—that the floor, after all, was moving and he was remaining stationary. His companions clung to him but he was not aware of them. He was lost and his brain was numb. Sometimes he swayed and felt that he was on the edge of a precipice. Sometimes he fell and his groaning body met hard stone, disproving the proximity of the gulf down which he half-expected to fall.

All the while he made his legs perform walking motions, even though he was not at all sure whether he was actually moving forward. And time meant nothing—became a meaningless concept with relation to nothing.

Until, at last, he was aware of a faint, blue glow ahead of him and he knew that he had been moving forward. He began to run down the incline, but found that he was going too fast and had to check his speed. There was a scent of alien strangeness in the cool air of the cave tunnel and fear was a fluid force which surged over him, something separate from himself.

The others obviously felt it, too, for though they said nothing, Elric could sense it. Slowly they moved downward, drawn like automatons towards the pale blue glow below them.

And then they were out of the tunnel, staring awe-struck at the unearthly vision which confronted them. Above them, the very air seemed of the strange blue colour which had originally attracted them. They were standing on a jutting slab of rock and, although it was still somehow *dark*, the eerie blue glow illuminated a stretch of glinting silver beach beneath them. And the beach was lapped by a surging dark sea which moved restlessly like a liquid giant in disturbed slumber. Scattered along the silver beach were the dim shapes of wrecks—the bones of peculiarly designed boats, each of a different pattern from the rest. The sea surged away into darkness and there was no horizon—only blackness. Behind them, they could see a sheer cliff which was also lost in darkness beyond a certain point. And it was cold—bitterly cold, with an unbelievable sharpness. For though the sea threshed beneath them, there was no dampness in the air—no smell of salt. It was a bleak and awesome sight and, apart from the sea, they were the only things that moved—the only things to make sound, for the sea was horribly silent in its restless movement.

"What now, Elric?" whispered Moonglum, shivering.

Elric shook his head and they continued to stand there for a long time until the albino—his white face and hands ghastly in the alien light said: "Since it is impracticable to return—we shall venture over the sea."

His voice was hollow and he spoke as one who was unaware of his words.

Steps, cut into the living rock, led down towards the beach and now Elric began to descend them. Staring around them, their eyes lit by a terrible fascination, the others allowed him to lead them.

## Chapter Four

Their feet profaned the silence as they reached the silver beach of crystalline stones and crunched across it. Elric's crimson eyes fixed upon one of the objects littering the beach and he smiled. He shook his head savagely from side to side, as if to clear it. Trembling, he pointed to one of the boats, and the pair saw that it was intact, unlike the others. It was yellow and red—vulgarly gay in this environment and nearing it they observed that it was made of wood, yet unlike any wood they had seen. Moonglum ran his stubby fingers along its length.

"Hard as iron," he breathed. "No wonder it has not rotted as the others have." He peered inside and shuddered. "Well the owner won't argue if we take it," he said wryly.

Elric and Shaarilla understood him when they saw the unnaturally twisted skeleton which lay at the bottom of the boat. Elric reached inside and pulled the thing out, hurling it on the stones. It rattled and rolled over the gleaming shingle, disintegrating as it did so, scattering bones over a wide area. The skull came to rest by the edge of the beach, seeming to stare sightlessly out over the disturbing ocean.

As Elric and Moonglum strove to push and pull the boat down the beach towards the sea, Shaarilla moved ahead of them and squatted down, putting her hand into the wetness. She stood up sharply, shaking the stuff from her hand.

"This is not water as I know it," she said. They heard her, but said nothing.

"We'll need a sail," Elric murmured. The cold breeze was moving out over the ocean. "A cloak should serve." He stripped off his cloak and knotted it to the mast of the vessel. "Two of us will have to hold this at either edge," he said. "That way we'll have some slight control over the direction the boat takes. It's makeshift—but the best we can manage."

They shoved off, taking care not to get their feet in the sea.

The wind caught the sail and pushed the boat out over the ocean, moving at a faster pace than Elric had at first reckoned. The boat began to hurtle forward as if possessed of its own volition and Elric's and Moonglum's muscles ached as they clung to the bottom ends of the sail.

Soon the silver beach was out of sight and they could see little—the pale blue light above them scarcely penetrating the blackness. It was then that they heard the dry flap of wings over their heads and looked up.

Silently descending were three massive apelike creatures, borne on great leathery wings. Shaarilla recognized them and gasped.

"*Clakars!*"

Moonglum shrugged as he hurriedly drew his sword—"A name only—what are they?" But he received no answer for the leading winged ape descended with a rush, mouthing and gibbering, showing long fangs in a slavering snout. Moonglum dropped his portion of the sail and slashed at the beast but it veered away, its huge wings beating, and sailed upwards again.

Elric unsheathed Stormbringer—and was astounded. The blade remained silent, its familiar howl of glee muted. The blade shuddered in his hand and instead of the rush of power which usually flowed up his arm, he felt only a slight tingling. He was panic-stricken for a moment—without the sword, he would soon lose all vitality. Grimly fighting down his fear, he used the sword to protect himself from the rushing attack of one of the winged apes.

The ape gripped the blade, bowling Elric over, but it yelled in pain as the blade cut through one knotted hand, severing fingers which lay twitching and bloody on the narrow deck. Elric held tight to the side of the boat and hauled himself upright once more. Shrilling its agony, the winged ape attacked again, but this time with more caution. Elric summoned all his strength and swung the heavy sword in a two-handed grip, ripping off one of the leathery wings so that the mutilated beast flopped about the deck. Judging the place where its heart should be, Elric drove the blade in under the breast-bone. The ape's movements subsided.

Moonglum was lashing wildly at two of the winged apes which were attacking him from both sides. He was down on one knee, vainly hacking at random. He had opened up the whole side of a beast's head but, though in pain, it still came at him. Elric hurled Stormbringer through the darkness and it struck the wounded beast in the throat, point first. The ape clutched with clawing fingers at the steel and fell overboard. Its corpse floated on the liquid but slowly began to sink. Elric grabbed with frantic fingers at the hilt of his sword, reaching far over the side of the boat. Incredibly, the blade was sinking with the beast; knowing Stormbringer's properties as he did, Elric was amazed. Now it was being dragged beneath the surface as any ordinary blade would be dragged. He gripped the hilt and hauled the sword out of the winged ape's carcass.

His strength was seeping swiftly from him. It was incredible. What alien laws governed this cavern world? He could not guess—and all he was concerned with was regaining his waning strength. Without the runesword's power, that was impossible!

Moonglum's curved blade had disemboweled the remaining beast and the little man was busily tossing the dead thing over the side. He turned, grinning triumphantly, to Elric.

"A good fight," he said.

Elric shook his head. "We must cross this sea speedily," he replied, "else we're lost—finished. My power is gone."

"How? Why?"

"I know not—unless the forces of Entropy rule more strongly here. Make haste—there is no time for speculation."

Moonglum's eyes were disturbed. He could do nothing but act as Elric said.

Elric was trembling in his weakness, holding the billowing sail with draining strength. Shaarilla moved to help him, her thin hands close to his, her deep-set eyes bright with sympathy.

"What *were* those things?" Moonglum gasped, his teeth naked and white beneath his back-drawn lips, his breath coming short.

"Clakars," Shaarilla replied. "They are the primeval ancestors of my people, older in origin than recorded time. My people are thought the oldest inhabitants of this planet."

"Whoever seeks to stop us in this quest of yours had best find some—original means." Moonglum grinned. "The old methods don't work." But the other two did not smile, for Elric was half-fainting and the woman was concerned only with his plight. Moonglum shrugged, staring ahead.

When he spoke again, sometime later, his voice was excited. "We're nearing land!"

Land it was, and they were traveling fast towards it. Too fast. Elric heaved himself upright and spoke heavily and with difficulty. "Drop the sail!" Moonglum obeyed him. The boat sped on, struck another stretch of silver beach and ground up it, the prow ploughing a dark scar through the glinting shingle. It stopped suddenly, tilting violently to one side so that the three were tumbled against the boat's rail.

Shaarilla and Moonglum pulled themselves upright and dragged the limp and nerveless albino on to the beach. Carrying him between them, they struggled up the beach until the crystalline shingle gave way to thick, fluffy moss, padding their footfalls. They laid the albino down and stared at him worriedly, uncertain of their next actions.

Elric strained to rise, but was unable to do so. "Give me time," he gasped. "I won't die—but already my eyesight is fading. I can only hope that the blade's power will return on dry land."

With a mighty effort, he pulled Stormbringer from its scabbard and he smiled in relief as the evil runesword moaned faintly and then, slowly, its song increased in power as black flame flickered along its length. Already the power was flowing into Elric's body, giving him renewed vitality. But even as strength returned, Elric's crimson eyes flared with terrible misery.

"Without this black blade," he groaned, "I am nothing, as you see. But what is it making of me? Am I to be bound to it for ever?"

The others did not answer him and they were both moved by an emotion they could not define—an emotion blended of fear, hate and pity—linked with something else . . .

Eventually, Elric rose, trembling, and silently led them up the mossy hillside towards a more natural light which filtered from above. They could see that it came from a wide chimney, leading apparently to the upper air. By means of the light, they could soon make out a dark, irregular shape which towered in the shadow of the gap.

As they neared the shape, they saw that it was a castle of black stone—a sprawling pile covered with dark green crawling lichen which curled over its ancient bulk with an almost sentient protectiveness. Towers appeared to spring at random from it and it covered a vast area. There seemed to be no windows in any part of it and the only orifice was a rearing doorway blocked by thick bars of a metal which glowed with dull redness, but without heat. Above this gate, in flaring amber, was the sign of the Lords of Entropy, representing eight arrows radiating from a central hub in all directions. It appeared to hang in the air without touching the black, lichen-covered stone.

"I think our quest ends here," Elric said grimly. "Here, or nowhere."

"Before I go further, Elric, I'd like to know what it is you seek," Moonglum murmured. "I think I've earned the right."

"A book," Elric said carelessly. "The Dead Gods' Book. It lies within those castle walls—of that I'm certain. We have reached the end of our journey."

Moonglum shrugged. "I might not have asked," he smiled, "for all your words mean to me. I hope that I will be allowed some small share of whatever treasure it represents."

Elric grinned, in spite of the coldness which gripped his bowels, but he did not answer Moonglum.

"We need to enter the castle, first," he said instead.

As if the gates had heard him, the metal bars flared to a pale green and then their glow faded back to red and finally dulled into non-existence. The entrance was unbarred and their way apparently clear.

"I like not *that*," growled Moonglum. "Too easy. A trap awaits us—are we to spring it at the pleasure of whoever dwells within the castle confines?"

"What else can we do?" Elric spoke quietly.

"Go back—or forward. Avoid the castle—do not tempt He who guards the Book!" Shaarilla was gripping the albino's right arm, her whole face moving with fear, her eyes pleading. "Forget the Book, Elric!"

"*Now?*" Elric laughed humourlessly. "Now—after this journey? No, Shaarilla, not when the truth is so close. Better to die than never to have tried to secure the wisdom in the Book when it lies so near."

Shaarilla's clutching fingers relaxed their grip and her shoulders slumped in hopelessness. "We cannot do battle with the minions of Entropy . . ."

"Perhaps we will not have to." Elric did not believe his own words but his mouth was twisted with some dark emotion, intense and terrible. Moonglum glanced at Shaarilla.

"Shaarilla is right," he said with conviction. "You'll find nothing but bitterness, possibly death, inside those castle walls. Let us, instead, climb yonder steps and attempt to reach the surface." He pointed to some twisting steps which led towards the yawning rent in the cavern roof.

Elric shook his head. "No. You go if you like."

Moonglum grimaced in perplexity. "You're a stubborn one, friend Elric. Well, if it's all or nothing—then I'm with you. But personally, I have always preferred compromise."

Elric began to walk slowly forward towards the dark entrance of the bleak and towering castle.

In a wide, shadowy courtyard a tall figure, wreathed in scarlet fire, stood awaiting them.

Elric marched on, passing the gateway. Moonglum and Shaarilla nervously followed.

Gusty laughter roared from the mouth of the giant and the scarlet fire fluttered about him. He was naked and unarmed, but the power which flowed from him almost forced the three back. His skin was scaly and of smoky purple colouring. His massive body was alive with rippling muscle as he rested lightly on the balls of his feet. His skull was long, slanting sharply backwards at the forehead and his eyes were like slivers of blue steel, showing no pupil. His whole body shook with mighty, malicious joy.

"*Greetings to you, Lord Elric of Melniboné—I congratulate you for your remarkable tenacity!*"

"Who are you?" Elric growled, his hand on his sword.

"*My name is Orunlu the Keeper and this is a stronghold of the Lords of Entropy.*" The giant smiled cynically. "*You need not finger your puny blade so nervously, for you should know that I cannot harm you now. I gained power to remain in your realm only by making a vow.*"

Elric's voice betrayed his mounting excitement. "You cannot stop us?"

"*I do not dare to—since my oblique efforts have failed. But your foolish endeavours perplex me somewhat, I'll admit. The Book is of importance to us—but what can it mean to you? I have guarded it for three hundred centuries and have never been curious enough to seek to discover why my Masters place so much importance upon it—why they bothered to rescue it on its sunward course and incarcerate it on this boring ball of earth populated by the capering, briefly lived clowns called Men.*"

"I seek in it the Truth," Elric said guardedly.

"*There is no Truth but that of Eternal struggle*," the scarlet-flamed giant said with conviction.

"What rules above the forces of Law and Chaos?" Elric asked. "What controls your destinies as it controls mine?"

The giant frowned.

"*That question, I cannot answer. I do not know. There is only the Balance.*"

"Then perhaps the Book will tell us who holds it," Elric said purposely. "Let me pass—tell me where it lies."

The giant moved back, smiling ironically. "*It lies in a small chamber in the central tower. I have sworn never to venture there, otherwise I might even lead the way. Go if you like—my duty is over.*"

Elric, Moonglum and Shaarilla stepped towards the entrance of the castle, but before they entered, the giant spoke warningly from behind them.

"*I have been told that the knowledge contained in the Book could swing the balance on the side of the forces of Law. This disturbs me—but, it appears, there is another possibility which disturbs me even more.*"

"What is that?" Elric said.

"*It could create such a tremendous impact on the multiverse that complete entropy would result. My Masters do not desire that—for it could mean the destruction of all matter in the end. We exist only to fight—not to win, but to preserve the eternal struggle.*"

"I care not," Elric told him. "I have little to lose, Orunlu the Keeper."

"*Then go.*" The giant strode across the courtyard into blackness.

Inside the tower, light of a pale quality illuminated winding steps leading upwards. Elric began to climb them in silence, moved by his own doom-filled purpose. Hesitantly, Moonglum and Shaarilla followed in his path, their faces set in hopeless acceptance.

On and upward the steps mounted, twisting tortuously towards their goal, until at last they came to the chamber, full of blinding light, many-coloured and scintillating, which did not penetrate outwards at all but remained confined to the room which housed it.

Blinking, shielding his red eyes with his arm, Elric pressed forward and, through slitted pupils saw the source of the light lying on a small stone dais in the centre of the room.

Equally troubled by the bright light, Shaarilla and Moonglum followed him into the room and stood in awe at what they saw.

It was a huge book—the Dead Gods' Book, its covers encrusted with alien gems from which the light sprang. It gleamed, it *throbbed* with light and brilliant colour.

"At last," Elric breathed. "At last—the Truth!"

He stumbled forward like a man made stupid with drink, his pale hands reaching for the thing he had sought with such savage bitterness. His hands touched the pulsating cover of the Book and, trembling, turned it back.

"Now, I shall learn," he said, half-gloatingly.

With a crash, the cover fell to the floor, sending the bright gems skipping and dancing over the paving stones.

Beneath Elric's twitching hands lay nothing but a pile of yellowish dust.

"No!" His scream was anguished, unbelieving. "No!" Tears flowed down his contorted face as he ran his hands through the fine dust. With a groan which racked his whole being, he fell forward, his face hitting the disintegrated parchment. Time had destroyed the Book—untouched, possibly forgotten, for three hundred centuries. Even the wise and powerful gods who had created it had perished—and now its knowledge followed them into oblivion.

They stood on the slopes of the high mountain, staring down into the green valleys below them. The sun shone and the sky was clear and blue. Behind them lay the gaping hole which led into the stronghold of the Lords of Entropy.

Elric looked with sad eyes across the world and his head was lowered beneath a weight of weariness and dark despair. He had not spoken since his companions had dragged him sobbing from the chamber of the Book. Now he raised his pale face and spoke in a voice tinged with self-mockery, sharp with bitterness—a lonely voice: the calling of hungry seabirds circling cold skies above bleak shores.

"Now," he said, "I will live my life without ever knowing why I live it—whether it has purpose or not. Perhaps the Book could have told me. But would I have believed it, even then? I am the eternal skeptic—never *sure* that my actions are my own, never certain that an ultimate entity is not guiding me.

"I envy those who know. All I can do now is to continue my quest and hope, without hope, that before my span is ended, the truth will be presented to me."

Shaarilla took his limp hands in hers and her eyes were wet.

"Elric—let me comfort you."

The albino sneered bitterly. "Would that we'd never met, Shaarilla of the Dancing Mist. For a while, you gave me hope—I had thought to be at last at peace with myself. But, because of you, I am left more hopeless than before. There is no salvation in this world—only malevolent doom. Goodbye."

He took his hands away from her grasp and set off down the mountainside.

Moonglum darted a glance at Shaarilla and then at Elric. He took something from his purse and put it in the girl's hand.

"Good luck," he said, and then he was running after Elric until he caught him up.

Still striding, Elric turned at Moonglum's approach and despite his brooding misery said: "What is it, friend Moonglum? Why do you follow me?"

"I've followed you thus far, Master Elric, and I see no reason to stop," grinned the little man. "Besides, unlike yourself, I'm a materialist. We'll need to eat, you know."

Elric frowned, feeling a warmth growing within him. "What do you mean, Moonglum?"

Moonglum chuckled. "I take advantage of situations of any kind, where I may," he answered. He reached into his purse and displayed something on his outstretched hand which shone with a dazzling brilliancy. It was one of the jewels from the cover of the Book. "There are more in my purse," he said, "And each one worth a fortune." He took Elric's arm.

"Come Elric—what new lands shall we visit so that we may change these baubles into wine and pleasant company?"

Behind them, standing stock still on the hillside, Shaarilla stared miserably after them until they were no longer visible. The jewel Moonglum had given her dropped from her fingers and fell, bouncing and bright, until it was lost amongst the heather. Then she turned—and the dark mouth of the cavern yawned before her.

*In this third Elric story the forces of Wind and Fire meet on opposing sides in a cataclysmic battle to decide the fate of one particular sorcerer. The previous stories in this series were "The Dreaming City" (No. 47), and "While the Gods Laugh" (No. 49).*

*—John Carnell, SCIENCE FANTASY No. 51, February 1962*

# THE STEALER OF SOULS

## Chapter One

IN A CITY called Bakshaan, which was rich enough to make all other cities of the north-east seem poor, in a tall-towered tavern one night, Elric, Lord of the smoking ruins of Melniboné, smiled like a shark and dryly jested with four powerful merchant princes whom, in a day or so, he intended to pauperize.

Moonglum the Outlander, Elric's companion, viewed the tall albino with admiration and concern. For Elric to laugh and joke was rare—but that he should share his good humour with men of the merchant stamp, that was unprecedented. Moonglum congratulated himself that he was Elric's friend and wondered upon the outcome of the meeting. Elric had, as usual, elaborated little of his plan to Moonglum.

"We need your particular qualities as swordsman and sorcerer, Lord Elric, and will, of course, pay well for them." Pilarmo, overdressed, intense and scrawny, was main spokesman for the four.

"And how shall you pay, gentlemen?" enquired Elric politely, still smiling.

Pilarmo's colleagues raised their eyebrows and even their spokesman was slightly taken aback. He waved his hand through the smoky air of the tavern-room which was occupied only by the six men.

"In gold—in gems," answered Pilarmo.

"In chains," said Elric. "We free travelers need no chains of that sort."

Moonglum bent forward out of the shadows where he sat, his expression showing that he strongly disapproved of Elric's statement.

Pilarmo and the other merchants were plainly astonished, too. "Then how shall we pay you?"

"I will decide that later," Elric smiled. "But why talk of such things until the time—what do you wish me to do?"

Pilarmo coughed and exchanged glances with his peers. They nodded. Pilarmo dropped his tone and spoke slowly:

"You are aware that trade is highly competitive in this city, Lord Elric. Many merchants vie with one another to secure the custom of the people. Bakshaan is a rich city and its populace is comfortably off, in the main."

"This is well known," Elric agreed; he was privately likening the well-to-do citizens of Bakshaan to sheep and himself to the wolf who would rob the fold. Because of these thoughts, his scarlet eyes were full of a humour which Moonglum knew to be malevolent and ironic.

"There is one merchant in this city who controls more warehouses and shops than any other," Pilarmo continued. "Because of the size and strength of his caravans, he can afford to import greater quantities of goods into Bakshaan and thus sell them for lower prices. He is virtually a thief—he will ruin us with his unfair methods." Pilarmo was genuinely hurt and aggrieved.

"You refer to Nikorn of Ilmar?" Moonglum spoke from behind Elric.

Pilarmo nodded mutely.

Elric frowned. "This man heads his own caravans—braves the dangers of the desert, forest and mountain. He has earned his position."

"That is hardly the point," snapped fat Tormiel, beringed and powdered, his flesh aquiver.

"No, of course not." Smooth-tongued Kelos patted his colleague's arm consolingly. "But we all admire bravery, I hope." His friends nodded. Silent Deinstaf, the last of the four, also coughed and wagged his hairy head. He put his unhealthy fingers on the jeweled hilt of an ornate but virtually useless poignard and squared his shoulders. "But," Kelos went on, glancing at Deinstaf with approval, "Nikorn takes no risks selling his goods cheaply—he's killing us with his low prices."

"Nikorn is a thorn in our flesh," Pilarmo elaborated unnecessarily.

"And you gentlemen require myself and my companion to remove this thorn," Elric stated.

"In a nutshell, yes." Pilarmo was sweating. He seemed more than a trifle wary of the smiling albino. Legends referring to Elric and his dreadful, doom-filled exploits were many and elaborately detailed. It was only because of their desperation that they had sought his help in this matter. They needed one who could deal in the nigromantic arts as well as wield a useful blade. Elric's arrival in Bakshaan was potential salvation for them.

"We wish to destroy Nikorn's power," Pilarmo continued. "And if this means destroying Nikorn, then—" He shrugged and half-smiled, watching Elric's face.

"Common assassins are easily employed, particularly in Bakshaan," Elric pointed out softly.

"Uh—true," Pilarmo agreed. "But Nikorn employs a sorcerer—and a private army. The sorcerer protects him and his palace by means of magic. And a guard of desert men serve to ensure that if magic fails, then natural methods can be used for the purpose. Assassins have attempted to eliminate the trader, but unfortunately, they were not lucky."

Elric laughed. "How disappointing, my friends. Still, assassins are the most dispensable members of the community—are they not? And their souls probably went to placate some demon who would otherwise have plagued more honest folk."

The merchants laughed half-heartedly and, at this, Moonglum grinned, enjoying himself from his seat in the shadows.

Elric poured wine for the other five. It was of a vintage which the law in Bakshaan forbade the populace to drink. Too much drove the imbiber mad, yet Elric had already quaffed great quantities and showed no ill effects. He raised a cup of the yellow wine to his lips and drained it, breathing deeply and with satisfaction as the stuff entered his system. The others sipped theirs cautiously. The merchants were already regretting their haste in contacting the albino. They had a feeling that not only were the legends true—but they did not do justice to the strange-eyed man they wished to employ.

Elric poured more yellow wine into his goblet and his hand trembled slightly and his dry tongue moved over his lips quickly. His breathing increased as he allowed the beverage to trickle down his throat. He had taken more than enough to make other men into mewling idiots, but those few signs were the only indication that the wine had any effect upon him at all.

This was a wine for those who wished to dream of different and less tangible worlds. Elric drank it in the hope that he would, for a night or so, cease to dream.

Now he asked: "And who is this mighty sorcerer, Master Pilarmo?"

"His name is Theleb K'aarna," Pilarmo answered nervously.

Elric's scarlet eyes narrowed. "The sorcerer of Pan Tang?"

"Aye—he comes from that island."

Elric put his cup down upon the table and rose, fingering his blade of black iron, the runesword Stormbringer.

He said with conviction: "I will help you, gentlemen." He had made up his mind not to rob them, after all. A new and more important plan was forming in his brain.

*Theleb K'aarna*, he thought. *So you have made Bakshaan your bolthole, eh?*

Theleb K'aarna tittered. It was an obscene sound, coming as it did from the throat of a sorcerer of no mean skill. It did not fit with his sombre, black-bearded countenance, his tall, scarlet-robed frame. It was not a sound suited to one of his extreme wisdom.

Theleb K'aarna tittered and stared with dreamy eyes at the woman who lolled on the couch beside him. He whispered clumsy words of endearment into her ear and she smiled indulgently, stroking his long, black hair as she would stroke the coat of a dog.

"You're a fool, for all your learning, Theleb K'aarna," she murmured, her hooded eyes staring beyond him at the bright green and orange tapestries which decorated the stone walls of her bed-chamber. She reflected lazily that a woman could not but help take advantage of any man who put himself so fully into her power.

"Yishana, you are a bitch," Theleb K'aarna breathed foolishly, "and all the learning in the world cannot combat love. I love you." He spoke simply, directly, not understanding the woman who lay beside him. He had seen into the black bowels of hell and had returned sane, he knew secrets which would turn any ordinary man's mind into quivering, jumbled jelly. But in certain arts he was as unversed as his youngest acolyte. The art of love was one of those. "I love you," he repeated, and wondered why she ignored him.

Yishana, Queen of Jharkor, pushed the sorcerer away from her and rose abruptly, swinging bare, well-formed legs off the divan. She was a handsome woman, with hair as black as her soul; though her youth was fading, she had a strange quality about her which both repelled and attracted men. She wore her multicoloured silks well and they swirled about her as, with light grace, she strode to the barred window of the chamber and stared out into the dark and turbulent night. The sorcerer watched her through narrow, puzzled eyes, disappointed at this halt to their love-making.

"What's wrong?"

The queen continued to stare out at the night. Great banks of black cloud moved like predatory monsters, swiftly across the wind-torn sky. The night was raucous and angry about Bakshaan; full of ominous portent.

Theleb K'aarna repeated his question and again received no answer. He stood up angrily, then, and joined her at the window.

"Let us leave now, Yishana, before it is too late. If Elric learns of our presence in Bakshaan, we shall both suffer." She did not reply, but her breasts heaved beneath the flimsy fabric and her mouth tightened.

The sorcerer growled, gripping her arm. "Forget your renegade freebooter, Elric—you have me now, and I can do much more for you than any sword-swinging medicine-man from a broken and senile empire!"

Yishana laughed unpleasantly and turned on her lover. "You are a fool, Theleb K'aarna, and you're much less of a man than Elric. Three aching years have passed since he deserted me, skulking off into the night on your trail and leaving me to pine for him! But I still remember his savage kisses and his wild love-making. Gods! I wish he had an equal. Since he left, I've never found one to match him—though many have tried and proved better than you—until you came skulking back and your spells drove them off or destroyed them." She sneered, mocking and taunting him. "You've been too long among your parchments to be much good to me!"

The sorcerer's face muscles tautened beneath his tanned skin and he scowled. "Then why do you let me remain? I could make you my slave with a potion—you know that!"

"But you wouldn't—and are thus *my* slave, mighty wizard. When Elric threatened to displace you in my affections, you conjured that demon and Elric was forced to fight it. He won you'll remember—but in his pride refused to compromise. You fled into hiding and he went in search of you—leaving me! That is what you did. You're in *love*, Theleb K'aarna . . ." she laughed in his face. "And your love won't let you use your arts against me—only my other lovers. I put up with you because you are often useful, but if Elric were to return . . ."

Theleb K'aarna turned away, pettishly picking at his long black beard. Yishana said: "I half hate Elric, aye! But that is better than half loving you!"

The sorcerer snarled: "Then why did you join me in Bakshaan? Why did you leave your brother's son upon your throne as regent and come here? I sent word and you came—you must have some affection for me to do that!"

Yishana laughed again. "I heard that a pale-faced sorcerer with crimson eyes and a howling runesword was traveling in the north-east. That is why I came, Theleb K'aarna."

Theleb K'aarna's face twisted with anger as he bent forward and gripped the woman's shoulder in his taloned hand.

"You'll remember that this same pale-faced sorcerer was responsible for your own brother's death," he spat. "You lay with a man who was a slayer of his kin and yours. He deserted the fleet, which he had led to pillage in his own land, when the Dragon Masters retaliated. Dharmit, your brother, was aboard one of those ships and he now lies scorched and rotting on the ocean bed."

Yishana shook her head wearily. "You always mention this and hope to shame me. Yes, I entertained one who was virtually my brother's murderer—but Elric had ghastlier crimes on his conscience and I still loved him, in spite or because of them. Your words do not have the effect you require, Theleb K'aarna. Now leave me, I wish to sleep alone."

The sorcerer's nails were still biting into Yishana's cool flesh. He relaxed his grip. "I am sorry," he said, his voice breaking. "Let me stay."

"Go," she said softly. And, tortured by his own weakness, Theleb K'aarna, sorcerer of Pan Tang, left. Elric of Melniboné was in Bakshaan—and Elric had sworn several oaths of vengeance upon Theleb K'aarna on several separate occasions—in Lormyr, Nadsokor and Tanelorn, as well as in Jharkor. In his heart, the black-bearded sorcerer knew who would win any duel which might take place.

## Chapter Two

The four merchants had left swathed in dark cloaks. They had not deemed it wise for anyone to be aware of their association with Elric. Now, Elric brooded over a fresh cup of yellow wine. He knew that he would need help of a particular and powerful kind, if he were going to capture Nikorn's castle. It was virtually unstormable and, with Theleb K'aarna's nigromantic protection, a particularly potent sorcery would have to be used. He knew that he was Theleb K'aarna's match and more when it came to wizardry, but if all his energy were expended on fighting the other magician, he would have none left to effect an entry past the crack guard of desert warriors employed by the merchant prince.

He needed help. In the forests which lay to the south of Bakshaan, he knew he would find men whose aid would be useful. But would they help him? He discussed the problem with Moonglum.

"I have heard that a band of my countrymen have recently come north from Vilmir where they have pillaged several large towns," he informed the Eastlander. "Since the great battle of Imrryr four years ago, the men of Melniboné have spread outwards from the Dragon Isle, becoming mercenaries and freebooters. It was because of me that Imrryr fell—and this they know, but if I offer them rich loot, they might aid me."

Moonglum smiled wryly. "I would not count on it, Elric," he said. "Such an act as yours can hardly be forgotten, if you'll forgive my frankness. Your countrymen are now unwilling wanderers, citizens of a razed city—the oldest and greatest the world has known. When Imrryr the Beautiful fell, there must have been many who wished great suffering upon you."

Elric emitted a short laugh. "Possibly," he agreed, "but these *are* my people and I know them. We Melnibonéans are an old and sophisticated race—we rarely allow emotions to interfere with our general well-being."

Moonglum raised his eyebrows in an ironic grimace and Elric interpreted the expression rightly. "I was an exception for a short while," he said. "But now Cymoril and my cousin lie in the ruins of Imrryr and my own torment will avenge any ill I have done. I think my countrymen will realize this."

Moonglum sighed. "I hope you are right, Elric. Who leads this band?"

"An old friend," Elric answered. "He was Dragon Master and led the attack upon the reaver ships after they had looted Imrryr. His name is Dyvim Tvar, once Lord of the Dragon Caves."

"And what of his beasts, where are they?"

"Asleep in the caves again. They can be roused only rarely—they need years to recuperate while their venom is re-distilled and their energy revitalized. If it were not for this, the Dragon Masters would rule the world."

"Lucky for you that they don't," Moonglum commented.

Elric said slowly: "Who knows? With me to lead them, they might yet. At least, we could carve a new empire from this world, just as our forefathers did."

Moonglum said nothing. He thought, privately, that the Young Kingdoms would not be so easily vanquished. Melniboné and her people were ancient, cruel and wise—but even their cruelty was tempered with the soft disease which comes with age. They lacked the vitality of the barbarian race who had been the ancestors of the builders of Imrryr and her long-forgotten sister cities. Vitality was often replaced by tolerance—the tolerance of the aged, the ones who have known past glory but whose day is done.

"In the morning," said Elric, "we will make contact with Dyvim Tvar and hope that what he did to the reaver fleet, coupled with the conscience-pangs which I have personally suffered, will serve to give him a properly objective attitude to my scheme."

"And now, sleep, I think," Moonglum said. "I need it, anyway—and the wench who awaits me might be growing impatient."

Elric shrugged. "As you will. I'll drink a little more wine and seek my bed later."

* * *

The black clouds which had huddled over Bakshaan on the previous night, were still there in the morning. The sun rose behind them, but the inhabitants were unaware of it. It rose unheralded, but in the fresh, rain-splashed dawn, Elric and Moonglum rode the narrow streets of the city, heading for the south gate and the forests beyond.

Elric had discarded his usual garb for a simple jerkin of green-dyed leather which bore the insignia of the royal line of Melniboné: a scarlet dragon, rampant on a gold field. On his finger was the Ring of Kings, the single rare Actorios stone set in a ring of rune-carved silver. This was the ring that Elric's mighty forefathers had worn; it was many centuries old. A short cloak hung from his shoulders and his hose was blue, tucked into high black riding boots. At his side hung Stormbringer.

A symbiosis existed between man and sword. The man without the sword could become a cripple, lacking sight and energy—the sword without the man could not drink the blood and the souls it needed for its existence. They rode together, sword and man, and none could tell which was master.

Moonglum, more conscious of the inclement weather than his friend, hugged a high-collared cloak around him and cursed the elements occasionally.

It took them an hour's hard riding to reach the outskirts of the forest. As yet, in Bakshaan, there were only rumours of the Imrryrian freebooters' coming. Once or twice, a tall stranger had been seen in obscure taverns near the southern wall, and this had been remarked upon but the citizens of Bakshaan felt secure in their wealth and power and had reasoned, with a certain truth in their conviction, that Bakshaan could withstand a raid far more ferocious than those raids which had taken weaker Vilmirian towns. Elric had no idea why his countrymen had driven northwards to Bakshaan. Possibly they had come only to rest and turn their loot into food supplies in the bazaars.

The smoke of several large campfires told Elric and Moonglum where the Melnibonéans were entrenched. With a slackening of pace, they guided their horses in that direction while wet branches brushed their faces and the scents of the forest, released by the life-bringing rain, impinged sweetly upon their nostrils. It was with a feeling akin to relaxation that Elric met the outguard who suddenly appeared from the undergrowth to bar their way along the forest trail.

The Imrryrian guard was swathed in furs and steel. Beneath the visor of an intricately worked helmet he peered at Elric with wary eyes. His vision was slightly impaired by the visor and the rain which dripped from it so that he did not immediately recognize Elric.

"Halt. What do you in these parts?"

Elric said impatiently, "Let me pass—it is Elric, your lord and your emperor."

The guard gasped and lowered the long-bladed spear he carried. He pushed back his helmet and gazed at the man before him with a myriad of different emotions passing across his face. Among these were amazement, reverence and hate.

He bowed stiffly. "This is no place for you, my liege. You renounced and betrayed your people four years ago and while I acknowledge the blood of kings which flows in your veins, I cannot obey you or do you the homage which it would otherwise be your right to expect."

"Of course," said Elric proudly, sitting his horse straight-backed. "But let your leader—my boyhood friend Dyvim Tvar—be the judge of how to deal with me. Take me to him at once and remember that my companion has done you no ill, but treat him with respect as befits the chosen friend of an emperor of Melniboné."

The guard bowed again and took hold of the reins of Elric's mount. He led the pair down the trail and into a large clearing wherein were pitched the tents of the men of Imrryr. Cooking fires flared in the centre of the great circle of pavilions and the fine-featured warriors of Melniboné sat talking softly around them. Even in the light of the gloomy day, the fabrics of the tents were bright and gay. The soft tones were wholly Melnibonéan in texture. Deep, smoky greens, azure, ochre, gold, dark blue. The colours did not clash—they blended. Elric felt sad nostalgia for the sundered, multicoloured towers of Imrryr the Beautiful.

As the two companions and their guide drew nearer, men looked up in astonishment and a low muttering replaced the sounds of ordinary conversation.

"Please remain here," the guard said to Elric. "I will inform Lord Dyvim Tvar of your coming." Elric nodded his acquiescence and sat firmly in his saddle conscious of the gaze of the gathered warriors. None approached him and some, whom Elric had known personally in the old days, were openly embarrassed. They were the ones who did not stare but rather averted their eyes, tending to the cooking fires or taking a sudden interest in the polish of their finely wrought longswords and dirks. A few growled angrily, but they were in a definite minority. Most of the men were simply shocked—and also inquisitive. Why had this man, their king and their betrayer, come to their camp?

The largest pavilion, of gold and scarlet, had at its peak a banner upon which was emblazoned a dormant dragon, blue upon white. This was the tent of Dyvim Tvar and from it the Dragon Master hurried, buckling on his sword belt, his intelligent eyes puzzled and wary.

Dyvim Tvar was a man a little older than Elric and he bore the stamp of Melnibonéan nobility. His mother had been a princess, a cousin to Elric's own mother. His cheek-bones were high and delicate, his eyes slightly slanting while his skull was narrow, tapering at the jaw. Like Elric, his ears were thin, near lobeless and coming almost to a point. His hands, the left one now folded around the hilt of his sword, were long-fingered and, like the rest of his skin, pale, though not nearly so pale as the dead white of the albino's. He strode towards the mounted emperor of Melniboné and now his emotions were controlled. When he was five feet away from Elric, Dyvim Tvar bowed slowly, his head bent and his face hidden. When he looked up again, his eyes met those of Elric and remained fixed.

"Dyvim Tvar, Lord of the Dragon Caves, greets Elric, Master of Melniboné, Exponent of her Secret Arts." The Dragon Master spoke gravely the age-old ritual greeting.

Elric was not as confident as he seemed as he replied: "Elric, Master of Melniboné, greets his loyal subject and demands that he give audience to Dyvim Tvar." It was not fitting, by ancient Melnibonéan standards, that the king should *request* an audience with one of his subjects and the Dragon Master understood this. He now said:

"I would be honoured if my liege would allow me to accompany him to my pavilion."

Elric dismounted and led the way towards Dyvim Tvar's pavilion. Moonglum also dismounted and made to follow, but Elric waved him back. The two Imrryrian noblemen entered the tent.

Inside, the small oil lamp augmented the gloomy daylight which filtered through the colourful fabric. The tent was simply furnished, possessing only a soldier's hard bed, a table and several carved wooden stools. Dyvim Tvar bowed and silently indicated one of these stools. Elric sat down.

For several moments, the two men said nothing. Neither allowed emotion to register on their controlled features. They simply sat and stared at one another. Eventually Elric said:

"You know me for a betrayer, a thief, a murderer of my own kin and a slayer of my countrymen, Dragon Master."

Dyvim Tvar nodded. "With my liege's permission, I will agree with him."

"We were never so formal in the old days, when alone," Elric said. "Let us forget ritual and tradition—Melniboné is broken and her sons are wanderers. We meet, as we used to, as equals—only, now, this is wholly true. We *are* equals. The Ruby Throne crashed in the ashes of Imrryr and now no emperor may sit in state.

Dyvim Tvar sighed. "This is true, Elric—but why have you come here? We were content to forget you. Even while thoughts of vengeance were fresh, we made no move to seek you out. Have you come to mock?"

"You know I would never do that, Dyvim Tvar. I rarely sleep, in these days, and when I do I have such dreams that I would rather be awake. You know that Yyrkoon forced me to do what I did when he usurped the throne for the second time, after I had trusted him as regent, when, again for the second time, he put his sister, whom I loved, into a sorcerous slumber. To aid that reaver fleet was my only hope of forcing him to undo his work and release Cymoril from the spell. I was moved by vengeance but it was Stormbringer, my sword, which slew Cymoril, not I."

"Of this, I am aware." Dyvim Tvar sighed again and rubbed one jeweled hand across his face. "But it does not explain why you came here. There should be no contact between you and your people. We are wary of you, Elric. Even if we allowed you to lead us again you would take your own doomed path and us with you. There is no future here for myself and my men."

"Agreed. But I need your help for this one time—then our ways can part again."

"We should kill you, Elric. But which would be the greater crime? Failure to do justice and slay our betrayer—or regicide? You have given me a problem at a time when there are too many problems already. Should I attempt to solve it?"

"I but played a part in history," Elric said earnestly. "Time would have done what I did, eventually. I but brought the day nearer—and brought it when you and our people were still resilient enough to combat it and turn to a new way of life."

Dyvim Tvar smiled ironically. "That is one point of view, Elric—and it has truth in it, I grant you. But tell it to the men who lost their kin and their homes because of you. Tell it to warriors who had to tend maimed comrades, to brothers, fathers and husbands whose wives, daughters and sisters—proud Melnibonéan women—were used to pleasure the barbarian pillagers."

"Aye." Elric dropped his eyes. When he next spoke it was quietly. "I can do nothing to replace what our people have lost—would that I could. I yearn for Imrryr often, and her women, and her wines and entertainments. But I can offer plunder. I can offer you the richest palace in Bakshaan. Forget the old wounds and follow me this once."

"Do you seek the riches of Bakshaan, Elric? You were never one for jewels and precious metal! Why, Elric?"

Elric ran his hands through his white hair. His red eyes were troubled. "For vengeance, once again, Dyvim Tvar. I owe a debt to a sorcerer from Pan Tang—Theleb K'aarna. You may have heard of him—he is fairly powerful for one of a comparatively young race."

"Then we're joined in this, Elric," Dyvim Tvar spoke grimly. "You are not the only Melnibonéan who owes Theleb K'aarna a debt! Because of that bitch-queen Yishana of Jharkor, one of our men was done to death a year ago in a most foul and horrible manner. Killed by Theleb K'aarna because he gave his embraces to Yishana who sought a substitute for you. We can unite to avenge that blood, King Elric, and it will be a fitting excuse for those who would rather have your blood on their knives."

Elric was not glad. He had a sudden premonition that this fortunate coincidence was to have grave and unpredictable outcomings. But he smiled.

## Chapter Three

In a smoking pit, somewhere beyond the limitations of space and time, a creature stirred. All around it, shadows moved. They were the shadows of the souls of men and these shadows which moved through the bright darkness were the masters of the creature. It allowed them to master it—so long as they paid its price. In the speech of men, this creature had a name. It was called Quaolnargn and would answer to this name if called.

Now it stirred. It heard its name carrying over the barriers which normally blocked its way to the Earth. The calling of the name effected a temporary pathway through those intangible barriers. It stirred again, as its name was called for the second time. It was unaware of why it was called or to what it was called. It was only muzzily conscious of one fact. When the pathway was opened to it, it could *feed*. It did not eat flesh and it did not drink blood. It fed on the minds and the souls of adult men and women. Occasionally, as an appetizer, it enjoyed the morsels, the sweetmeats as it were, of the innocent life-force which it sucked from children. It ignored animals since there was not enough *awareness* in an animal to savour. The creature was, for all its alien stupidity, a gourmet and a connoisseur.

Now its name was called for the third time. It stirred again and flowed forward. The time was approaching when it could, once again, *feed* . . .

Theleb K'aarna shuddered. He was, basically, he felt, a man of peace. It was not his fault that his avaricious love for Yishana had turned him mad. It was not his fault that, because of her, he now controlled several powerful and malevolent demons who, in return for the slaves and enemies he fed them, protected the palace of Nikorn the merchant. He felt, very strongly, that none of it was his fault. It was circumstance which had damned him. He wished sadly that he had never met Yishana, never returned to her after that unfortunate episode outside the walls of Tanelorn. He shuddered again as he stood within the pentacle and summoned Quaolnargn. His embryonic talent for precognition had shown him a little of the near-future and he knew that Elric was preparing to do battle with him. Theleb K'aarna was taking the opportunity of summoning all the aid he could control. Quaolnargn must be sent to destroy Elric, if it could, before the albino reached the castle. Theleb K'aarna congratulated himself that he still retained the lock of white hair which had enabled him, in the past, to send another, now deceased, demon against Elric.

Quaolnargn knew that it was reaching its master. It propelled itself sluggishly forward and felt a stinging pain as it entered the alien continuum. It knew that its master's soul hovered before it but, for some reason, was disappointingly unattainable. Something was dropped in front of it. Quaolnargn scented at it and knew what it must do. This was part of its new *feed*. It flowed gratefully away, intent on finding its prey before the pain which was endemic of a prolonged stay in the strange place grew too much.

Elric rode at the head of his countrymen. On his right was Dyvim Tvar, the Dragon Master, on his left, Moonglum of Elwher. Behind him rode two hundred fighting men and behind them the wagons containing their loot, their war-machines and their slaves.

The caravan was resplendent with proud banners and the gleaming, long-bladed lances of Imrryr. They were clad in steel, with tapering greaves, helmets and shoulder-pieces. Their breastplates were polished and glinted where their long fur jerkins were open. Over the jerkins were flung bright cloaks of Imrryrian fabrics, scintillating in the watery sunshine. The archers were immediately close to Elric and his companions. They carried unstrung bone bows of tremendous power, which only they could use. On their backs were quivers crammed with black-fletched arrows. Then came the lancers, with their shining lances at a tilt to avoid the low branches of the trees. Behind these rode the main strength—the Imrryrian swordsmen carrying longswords and shorter stabbing weapons which were too short to be real swords and too long to be named as knives. They rode, skirting Bakshaan, for the palace of Nikorn which lay to the north of Bakshaan. They rode, these men, in silence. They could think of nothing to say while Elric, their liege, led them to battle for the first time in five years.

Stormbringer, the black hellblade, tingled under Elric's hand, anticipating a new sword-quenching. Moonglum fidgeted in his saddle, nervous of the forthcoming fight which he knew would involve dark sorcery. Moonglum had no liking for the sorcerous arts or for the creatures they spawned. To his mind, men should fight their own battles without help. They rode on, nervous and tense.

Stormbringer shook against Elric's side. A faint moan emanated from the metal and the tone was one of warning. Elric raised a hand and the cavalcade reined to a halt.

"There is something coming near which only I can deal with," he informed the men. "I will ride on ahead."

He spurred his horse into a wary canter, keeping his eyes before him. Stormbringer's voice was louder, sharper—a muted shriek. The horse trembled and Elric's own nerves were tense. He had not expected trouble so soon and he prayed that whatever evil was lurking in the forest was not directed against him.

"Arioch, be with me," he breathed. "Aid me now, and I'll dedicate a score of warriors to you. Aid me, Arioch."

A foul odour forced itself into Elric's nostrils. He coughed and covered his mouth with his hands, his eyes seeking the source of the stink. The horse whinnied. Elric jumped from the saddle and slapped his mount on the rump, sending it back along the trail. He crouched warily, Stormbringer now in his grasp, the black metal quivering from point to pommel.

He sensed it with the witch-sight of his forefathers before he saw it with his eyes. And he recognized its shape. He, himself, was one of its masters. But this time he had no control over Quaolnargn—he was standing in no pentacle and his only protection was his blade and his wits. He knew, also, of the power of Quaolnargn and shuddered. Could he overcome such a horror single-handedly?

"*Arioch! Arioch! Aid me!*" It was a scream, high and desperate.

"*Arioch!*"

There was no time to conjure a spell. Quaolnargn was before him, a great green reptilian thing which hopped along the trail obscenely, moaning to itself in its Earth-fostered pain. It towered over Elric so that the albino was in its shadow before it was ten feet away from him. Elric breathed quickly and screamed once more: "*Arioch! Blood and souls, if you aid me, now!*"

Suddenly, the reptile-demon leapt.

Elric sprang to one side, but was caught by a long-nailed foot which sent him flying into the undergrowth. Quaolnargn turned clumsily and its filthy mouth opened hungrily, displaying a deep toothless cavity from which a foul odour poured.

"*Arioch!*"

In its evil and alien insensitivity, the reptile-thing did not even recognize the name of so powerful a demon-god. It could not be frightened—it had to be fought.

And as it approached Elric for the second time, the clouds belched rain from their bowels and a downpour lashed the forest.

Half-blinded by the rain smashing against his face, Elric backed behind a tree, his runesword ready. In ordinary terms, Quaolnargn was

blind. It could not see Elric or the forest. It could not feel the rain. It could only see and smell men's souls—its *feed*. The reptile-demon blundered past him and, as it did so, Elric leapt high, holding his blade with both hands, and plunged it to the hilt into the demon's soft and quivering back. Flesh—or whatever Earth-bound stuff formed the demon's body—squelched nauseatingly. Elric pulled at Stormbringer's hilt as the sorcerous sword seared into the hell-beast's back, cutting down where the spine should be but where no spine was. Quaolnargn piped its pain. Its voice was thin and reedy, even in such extreme agony. It retaliated.

Elric felt his mind go numb and then his head was filled with a pain which was not natural in any sense. He could not even shriek. His eyes widened in horror as he realized what was happening to him. His soul was being drawn from his body. He knew it. He felt no physical weakness, he was only aware of looking out into . . .

But even that awareness was fading. Everything was fading, even the pain, even the dreadful hell-spawned pain.

"Arioch!" he croaked.

Savagely, he summoned strength from somewhere. Not from himself, not even from Stormbringer—from somewhere. Something was aiding him at last, giving him strength—enough strength to do what he must.

He wrenched the blade from the demon's back. He stood over Quaolnargn. Above him. He was floating somewhere, not in the air of Earth. Just floating over the demon. With thoughtful deliberation he selected a spot on the demon's skull which he somehow knew to be the only spot on his body where Stormbringer might slay. Slowly and carefully, he lowered Stormbringer and twisted the runesword through Quaolnargn's skull.

The reptilian thing whimpered, dropped—and vanished.

Elric lay sprawled in the undergrowth, trembling the length of his aching body. He picked himself up slowly. All his energy had been drained from him. Stormbringer, too, seemed to have lost its vitality, but that, Elric knew would return and, in returning, bring him new strength.

But then he felt his whole frame tugged rigid. He was astounded. What was happening? His senses began to blank out. He had the feeling that he was staring down a long, black tunnel which stretched into nowhere. Everything was vague. He was aware of motion. He was traveling. How—or where, he could not tell.

For brief seconds he traveled, conscious only of an unearthly feeling of motion and the fact that Stormbringer, his life, was clutched in his right hand.

Then he felt hard stone beneath him and he opened his eyes—or was it, he wondered, that his vision returned?—and looked up at the gloating face above him.

"Theleb K'aarna," he whispered hoarsely, "how did you effect this?"

The sorcerer bent down and, with gloved hands, tugged Stormbringer from Elric's enfeebled grasp. He sneered. "I followed your commendable battle with my messenger, Lord Elric. When it was obvious that somehow you had summoned aid—I quickly conjured another spell and brought you here. Now I have your sword and your strength. I know that without it you are nothing. You are in my power, Elric of Melniboné."

Elric gasped air into his lungs. His whole body was pain-racked. He tried to smile, but he could not. It was not in his nature to smile when he was beaten. "Give me back my sword."

Theleb K'aarna gave a self-satisfied smirk. He chuckled. "Who talks of vengeance, now, Elric?"

"Give me my sword!" Elric tried to rise but he was too weak. His vision blurred until he could hardly see the gloating sorcerer.

"And what kind of bargain do you offer?" Theleb K'aarna asked. "You are not a well man, Lord Elric—and sick men do not bargain. They beg."

Elric trembled in impotent anger. He tightened his mouth. He would not beg—neither would he bargain. In silence, he glowered at the sorcerer.

"I think that first," Theleb K'aarna said, smiling, "I shall lock this away." He hefted Stormbringer, which he had now sheathed, in his hand and turned towards a cupboard behind him. From his robes he produced a key with which he unlocked the cupboard and placed the runesword inside, carefully locking the door again when he had done so. "Then, I think, I'll show our virile hero to his ex-mistress—the sister of the man he betrayed four years ago."

Elric said nothing.

"After that," Theleb K'aarna continued, "my employer Nikorn shall be shown the assassin who thought he could do what others failed to achieve." He smiled. "What a day," he chuckled. "What a day! So full. So rich with pleasure."

Theleb K'aarna tittered and picked up a hand-bell. He rang it. A door behind Elric opened and two tall desert warriors strode in. They glanced at Elric and then at Theleb K'aarna. They were evidently amazed.

"No questions," Theleb K'aarna snapped. "Take this refuse to the chambers of Queen Yishana."

Elric fumed as he was hefted up between the two. The men were dark-skinned, bearded and their eyes were deep-set beneath shaggy brows. They wore the heavy wool-trimmed metal caps of their race, and their armour was not of iron but of thick, leather-covered wood. Down a long corridor they lugged Elric's weakened body and one of them rapped sharply on a door.

Elric recognized Yishana's voice bid them enter. Behind the desert men and their burden came a tittering, fussing sorcerer. "A present for you, Yishana," he called.

The desert men entered. Elric could not see Yishana but he heard her gasp. "On the couch," directed the sorcerer. Elric was deposited on yielding fabric. He lay completely exhausted on the couch, staring up at a bright, lewd mural which had been painted on the ceiling.

Yishana bent over him. Elric could smell her erotic perfume. He said hoarsely: "An unprecedented reunion, queen." Yishana's eyes were, for a moment, concerned, then they hardened and she laughed cynically.

"Oh—my hero has returned to me at last. But I'd rather he'd come at his own volition, not dragged here by the back of his neck like a puppy. The wolf's teeth have all been drawn and there's no-one to savage me at nights." She turned away, disgust on her painted face. "Take him away, Theleb K'aarna. You have proved your point."

The sorcerer nodded.

"And now," he said, "to visit Nikorn—I think he should be expecting us by this time . . ."

## Chapter Four

Nikorn of Ilmar was not a young man. He was well past fifty but had preserved his youth. His face was that of a peasant, firm-boned but not fleshy. His eyes were keen and hard as he stared at Elric who had been mockingly propped in a chair.

"So you are Elric of Melniboné, the Wolf of the Snarling Sea, spoiler, reaver and woman-slayer. I think that you could hardly slay a child now. However, I will say that it discomforts me to see any man in such a position—particularly one who has been so active as you. Is it true what the spell-maker says? Were you sent here by my enemies to assassinate me?"

Elric was concerned for his men. What would they do? Wait—or go on. If they stormed the palace now they were doomed—and so was he.

"Is it true?" Nikorn was insistent.

"No," whispered Elric. "My quarrel was with Theleb K'aarna. I have an old score to settle with him."

"I am not interested in old scores, my friend," Nikorn said, not unkindly. "I *am* interested in preserving my life. Who sent you here?"

"Theleb K'aarna speaks falsely if he told you I was sent," Elric lied. "I was interested only in paying my debt."

"It is not only the sorcerer who told me, I'm afraid," Nikorn said. "I have many spies in the city and two of them independently informed me of a plot by local merchants to employ you to kill me."

Elric smiled faintly. "Very well," he agreed. "It was true, but I had no intention of doing what they asked."

Nikorn said: "I might believe you, Elric of Melniboné. But now I do not know what to do with you. I would not turn anyone over to Theleb K'aarna's mercies. May I have your word that you will not make an attempt on my life again?"

"Are we bargaining, Master Nikorn?" Elric said faintly.

"We are."

"Then what do I give my word in return for, sir?"

"Your life and freedom, Lord Elric."

"And my sword?"

Nikorn shrugged regretfully. "I'm sorry—not your sword."

"Then take my life," said Elric brokenly.

"Come now—my bargain's good. Have your life and freedom and give your word that you will not plague me again."

Elric breathed deeply. "Very well."

Nikorn moved away. Theleb K'aarna who had been standing in the shadows put a hand on the merchant's arm. "You're going to release him?"

"Aye," Nikorn said. "He's no threat to either of us now."

Elric was aware of a certain feeling of friendship in Nikorn's attitude towards him. He, too, felt something of the same. Here was a man both courageous and clever. But—Elric fought madness—without Stormbringer, what could he do to fight back?

The two hundred Imrryrian warriors lay hidden in the undergrowth as dusk gave way to night. They watched and wondered. What had happened to Elric? Was he now in the castle as Dyvim Tvar thought? The Dragon Master knew something of the art of divining, as did all members of the royal line of Melniboné. From what small spells he had conjured, it seemed that Elric now lay within the castle walls.

But without Elric to battle Theleb K'aarna's power, how could they take it?

Nikorn's palace was also a fortress, bleak and unlovely. It was surrounded by a deep moat of dark, stagnant water. It stood high above the surrounding forest, built into rather than onto the rock. Much of it had been carved out of the living stone. It was sprawling and rambling and covered a large area, surrounded by natural buttresses. The rock was porous in places, and slimy water ran down the walls of the lower parts, spreading through dark moss. It was not a pleasant place, judging from the outside, but it was almost certainly impregnable. Two hundred men could not take it, without the aid of magic.

Some of the Melnibonéan warriors were becoming impatient. There were a few who muttered that Elric had, once again, betrayed them. Dyvim Tvar and Moonglum did not believe this. They had seen the signs of conflict—and heard them—in the forest.

They waited, hoping for a signal from the castle itself.

They watched the castle's great main gate—and their patience at last proved of value. The huge wood and metal gate swung inwards on chains and a white-faced man in the tattered regalia of Melniboné appeared between two desert warriors. They were supporting him, it seemed. They pushed him forward—he staggered a few yards along the causeway of slimy stone which bridged the moat.

Then he fell. He began to crawl wearily, painfully, forward.

Moonglum growled. "What have they done to him? I must help him." But Dyvim Tvar held him back.

"No—it would not do to betray our presence here. Let him reach the forest first, then we can help him."

Even those who had cursed Elric, now felt pity for the albino as, staggering and crawling alternately, he dragged his body slowly towards them. From the battlements of the fortress a tittering laugh was borne down to the ears of those below. They also caught a few words.

"*What now, wolf?*" said the voice. "*What now?*"

Moonglum clenched his hands and trembled with rage, hating to see his proud friend so mocked in his weakness. "What's happened to him? What have they done?"

"Patience," Dyvim Tvar said. "We'll find out in a short while."

It was an agony to wait until Elric finally crawled on his knees into the undergrowth.

Moonglum went forward to aid his friend. He put a supporting arm around Elric's shoulders but the albino snarled and shook it off, his whole countenance aflame with terrible hate—made more terrible because it was impotent. Elric could do nothing to destroy that which he hated. Nothing.

Dyvim Tvar said urgently: "Elric, you must tell us what happened. If we're to help you—we must know what happened."

Elric breathed heavily and nodded his agreement. His face partially cleared of the emotion he felt and weakly he stuttered out the story.

"So," Moonglum growled, "our plans come to nothing—and you have lost your strength for ever."

Elric shook his head. "There must be a way," he gasped. "There must!"

"What? How? If you have a plan, Elric—let me hear it now."

Elric swallowed thickly and mumbled. "Very well, Moonglum, you shall hear it. But listen carefully, for I have not the strength to repeat it."

Moonglum was a lover of the night, but only when it was lit by the torches found in cities. He did not like the night when it came to open countryside and he was not fond of it when it surrounded a castle such as Nikorn's, but he pressed on and hoped for the best.

If Elric had been right in his interpretation, then the battle might yet be won and Nikorn's palace taken. But it still meant danger for Moonglum and he was not one deliberately to put himself into danger.

As he viewed the stagnant waters of the moat with distaste he reflected that this was enough to test any friendship to the utmost. Philosophically, he lowered himself down into the water and began to swim across it.

The moss on the fortress offered a flimsy handhold, but it led to ivy which gave a better grip. Moonglum slowly clambered up the wall. He hoped that Elric had been right and that Theleb K'aarna would need to rest for a while before he could work more sorcery. That was why Elric had suggested he make haste. Moonglum clambered on, and eventually reached the small unbarred window he sought. A normal-size man could not have entered, but Moonglum's small frame was proving useful.

He wriggled through the gap, shivering with cold, and landed on the hard stone of a narrow staircase which ran both up and down the interior wall of the fortress. Moonglum frowned, and then took the steps leading upwards. Elric had given him a rough idea of how to reach his destination.

Expecting the worst, he went soft-footed up the stone steps. He went towards the chambers of Yishana, Queen of Jharkor.

In an hour, Moonglum was back, shivering with cold and dripping with water. In his hands he carried Stormbringer. He carried the runesword with cautious care—nervous of its sentient evil. It was alive again; alive with black, pulsating life.

"Thank the gods I was right," Elric murmured weakly from where he lay surrounded by two or three Imrryrians, including Dyvim Tvar who was staring at the albino with concern. "I prayed that I was correct in my assumption and Theleb K'aarna was resting after his earlier exertions on my behalf . . ."

He stirred, and Dyvim Tvar helped him to sit upright. Elric reached out a long white hand—reached like an addict of some terrible drug towards the sword. "Did you give her my message?" he asked as he gratefully seized the pommel.

"Aye," Moonglum said shakily, "and she agreed. You were also right in your other interpretation, Elric. It did not take her long to inveigle the key out of a weary Theleb K'aarna. The sorcerer was tremendously tired and Nikorn was becoming nervous wondering if an attack of any kind would take place while Theleb K'aarna was incapable of action. She went herself to the cupboard and got me the blade."

"Women can sometimes be useful," said Dyvim Tvar dryly. "Though usually, in matters like these, they're a hindrance." It was possible to see that something other than immediate problems of taking the castle was worrying Dyvim Tvar, but no-one thought to ask him what it was that bothered him. It seemed a personal thing.

"I agree, Dragon Master," Elric said, almost gaily. The gathered men were aware of the strength which poured swiftly back into the albino's deficient veins, imbuing him with a new hellborn vitality. "It is time for our vengeance. But remember—no harm to Nikorn. I gave him my word."

He folded his right hand firmly around Stormbringer's hilt. "Now for a sword-quenching. I believe I can obtain the help of just the allies we need to keep the sorcerer occupied while we storm the castle. I'll need no pentacle to summon my friends of the air!"

Moonglum licked his long lips. "So it's sorcery again. In truth, Elric, this whole country is beginning to stink of wizardry and the minions of hell."

Elric murmured for his friend's ears: "No hell-beings these—but

honest elementals, equally powerful in many ways. Curb your belly-fear, Moonglum—a little more simple conjuring and Theleb K'aarna will have no desire to retaliate."

The albino frowned, remembering the secret pacts of his forefathers. He took a deep breath and closed his pain-filled scarlet eyes. He swayed, the runesword half-loose in his grip. His chant was low, like the far-off moaning of the wind itself. His chest moved quickly up and down, and some of the younger warriors, those who had never been fully initiated into the ancient lore of Melniboné, stirred with discomfort. Elric's voice was not addressing human folk—his words were for the invisible, the intangible—the supernatural. An old and ancient rhyme began the casting of word-runes . . .

"Hear the doomed one's dark decision,
Let the Wind Giant's wail be heard,
Graoll and Misha's mighty moaning
Send my enemy like a bird.

By the sultry scarlet stones,
By the bane of my black blade,
By the Lasshaar's lonely mewling,
Let a mighty wind be made.

Speed of sunbeams from their homeland,
Swifter than the sundering storm,
Speed of arrow deerwards shooting,
Let the sorcerer so be borne."

His voice broke and he called high and clear:

"*Misha! Misha! In the name of my fathers I summon thee, Lord of the Winds!*"

Almost at once, the trees of the forest suddenly bent as if some great hand had brushed them aside. A terrible soughing voice swam from nowhere. And all but Elric, deep in his trance, shivered.

"ELRIC OF MELNIBONÉ," the voice roared like a distant storm,

"WE KNEW YOUR FATHERS. I KNOW THEE. THE DEBT WE OWE THE LINE OF ELRIC IS FORGOTTEN BY MORTALS BUT GRAOLL AND MISHA, KINGS OF THE WIND, REMEMBER. HOW MAY THE LASSHAAR AID THEE?"

The voice seemed almost friendly—but proud and aloof and awe-inspiring.

Elric, completely in a state of trance now, jerked his whole body in convulsions. His voice shrieked piercingly from his throat—and the words were alien, unhuman, violently disturbing to the ears and nerves of the human listeners. Elric spoke briefly and then the invisible Wind Giant's great voice roared and sighed:

"I WILL DO AS YOU DESIRE." Then the trees bent once more and the forest was still and muted.

Somewhere in the gathered ranks, a man sneezed sharply and this was a sign for others to start talking—speculating.

For many moments, Elric remained in his trance and then, quite suddenly, he opened his enigmatic eyes and looked gravely around him, puzzled for a second. Then he clasped Stormbringer more firmly and leaned forward, speaking to the men of Imrryr. "Soon Theleb K'aarna will be in our power, my friends, and so also will we possess the loot of Nikorn's palace!"

But Dyvim Tvar shuddered then. "I'm not so skilled in the esoteric arts as you, Elric," he said quietly. "But in my soul I see three wolves leading a pack to slaughter and one of those wolves must die. My doom is near me, I think."

Elric said uncomfortably: "Worry not, Dragon Master. You'll live to mock the ravens and spend the spoils of Bakshaan." But his voice was not convincing.

## Chapter Five

In his bed of silk and ermine, Theleb K'aarna stirred and awoke. He had a brooding inkling of coming trouble and he remembered that earlier in his tiredness he had given more to Yishana than had been wise. He could not remember what it was and now he had a presentiment of danger—the closeness of which overshadowed thoughts of any past indiscretion. He arose hurriedly and pulled his robe over his head, shrugging into it as he walked towards a strangely silvered mirror which was set on one wall of his chamber and reflected no image.

With bleary eyes and trembling hands he began preparations. From one of the many earthenware jars resting on a bench near the window, he poured a substance which seemed like dried blood mottled with the hardened blue venom of the black serpent whose homeland was in far Dorel which lay on the edge of the world. Over this, he muttered a swift incantation, scooped the stuff into a crucible and hurled it at the mirror, one arm shielding his eyes. A crack sounded, hard and sharp to his ears, and bright green light erupted suddenly and was gone. The mirror flickered deep within itself, the silvering seemed to undulate and flicker and flash and then a picture began to form.

Theleb K'aarna knew that the sight he witnessed had taken place in the recent past. It showed him Elric's summoning of the Wind Giants.

Theleb K'aarna's dark features grinned with a terrible fear. His hands jerked as spasms shook him. Half-gibbering, he rushed back to his bench and, leaning his hands upon it, stared out of the window into the deep night. He knew what to expect.

A great and dreadful storm was blowing—and he was the object of the Lasshaar's attack. He *had* to retaliate, else his own soul would be wrenched from him by the Giants of the Wind and flung to the air spirits, to be borne for eternity on the winds of the world. Then his voice would moan like a banshee around the cold peaks of high ice-clothed mountains for ever—lost and lonely. His soul would be damned to travel with the four winds wherever their caprice might bear it, knowing no rest.

Theleb K'aarna had a respect born of fear for the powers of the aeromancer, the rare wizard who could control the wind elementals—and aeromancy was only one of the arts which Elric and his ancestors possessed. Then Theleb K'aarna realized what he was battling—ten thousand years and hundreds of generations of sorcerers who had gleaned knowledge from the Earth and beyond it and passed it down to the albino whom he, Theleb K'aarna, had sought to destroy. Then Theleb K'aarna fully regretted his actions. Then—it was too late.

The sorcerer had no control over the powerful Wind Giants as Elric had. His only hope was to combat one element with another. The fire-spirits must be summoned, and quickly. All of Theleb K'aarna's pyromantic powers would be required to hold off the ravening supernatural winds which were soon to shake the air and the earth. Even hell would shake to the sound and the thunder of the Wind Giants' wrath.

Quickly, Theleb K'aarna marshaled his thoughts and, with trembling hands, began to make strange passes in the air and promise unhealthy pacts with whichever of the powerful fire elementals would help him this once. He promised himself to eternal death for the sake of a few more years of life.

With the gathering of the Wind Giants came the thunder and the rain. The lightning flashed sporadically, but not lethally. It never touched the earth. Elric, Moonglum, and the men of Imrryr were aware of disturbing movements in the atmosphere, but only Elric with his witch-sight could see a little of what was happening. The Lasshaar Giants were invisible to other eyes.

The war-engines which the Imrryrians were even now constructing from pre-fashioned parts were puny things compared to the Wind Giants' might. But victory depended upon these engines since the Lasshaar's fight would be with the supernatural not the natural.

Battle-rams and siege ladders were slowly taking shape as the warriors worked with frantic speed. The hour of the storming came closer as the wind rose and thunder rattled. The moon was blanked out by huge billowings of black cloud, and the men worked by the light of torches. Surprise was no great asset in an attack of the kind planned.

Two hours before dawn, they were ready.

At last the men of Imrryr, Elric, Dyvim Tvar and Moonglum riding high at their head, moved towards the castle of Nikorn. As they did so, Elric raised his voice in an unholy shout—and thunder rumbled in answer to him. A great gout of lightning seared out of the sky towards the palace and the whole place shook and trembled as a ball of mauve and orange fire suddenly appeared over the castle and *absorbed* the lightning! The battle between fire and air had begun.

The surrounding countryside was alive with a weird and malignant shrieking and moaning, deafening to the ears of the marching men. They sensed conflict all round them, and only a little was visible.

Over most of the castle an unearthly glow hung, waxing and waning, defending a gibbering wretch of a sorcerer who knew that he was doomed if once the Lords of the Flame gave way to the roaring Wind Giants.

Elric smiled without humour as he observed the war. On the supernatural plane, he now had little to fear. But there was still the castle and he had no extra supernatural aid to help him take that. Swordplay and skill in battle were the only hope against the ferocious desert warriors who now crowded the battlements, preparing to destroy the two hundred men who came against them.

Up rose the Dragon Standards, their cloth-of-gold fabric flashing in the eerie glow. Spread out, walking slowly, the sons of Imrryr moved forward to do battle. Up, also, rose the siege ladders as captains directed

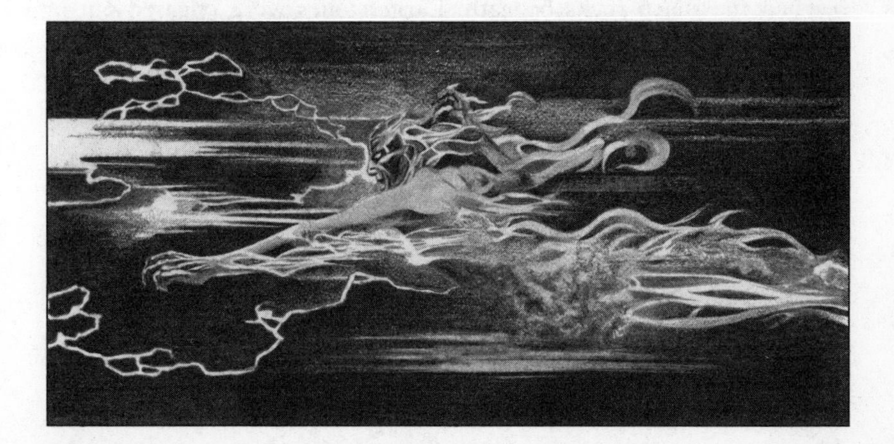

warriors to begin the assault. The defenders' faces were pale spots against the dark stone and thin shouts came from them; but it was impossible to catch their words.

Two great battle-rams, fashioned the day before, were brought to the vanguard of the approaching warriors. The narrow causeway was a dangerous one to pass over, but it was the only means of crossing the moat at ground level. Twenty men carried each of the great iron-tipped rams and now they began to run forward while arrows hailed downwards. Their shields protecting them from most of the shafts, the warriors reached the causeway and rushed across it. Now the first ram connected with the gate. It seemed to Elric as he watched this operation that nothing of wood and iron could withstand the vicious impact of the ram, but the gates shivered almost imperceptibly—and held!

Like vampires, hungry for blood, the men howled and staggered aside crabwise to let pass the log held by their comrades. Again the gates shivered, more easily noticed this time, but they yet held.

Dyvim Tvar roared encouragement to those now scaling the siege ladders. These were brave, almost desperate men, for few of the first climbers would reach the top and even if they were successful, they would be hard pressed to stay alive until their comrades arrived.

Boiling lead hissed from great cauldrons set on spindles so that they could be easily emptied and filled quickly. Many a brave Imrryrian warrior fell earthwards, dead from the searing metal before he reached the sharp rocks beneath. Large stones were released out of leather bags hanging from rotating pulleys which could swing out beyond the battlements and rain bone-crushing death on the besiegers. But still the invaders advanced, voicing half-a-hundred war-shouts and steadily scaling their long ladders, whilst their comrades, using a shield barrier still, to protect their heads, concentrated on breaking down the gates.

Elric and his two companions could do little to help the scalers or the rammers at that stage. All three were hand-to-hand fighters, leaving even the archery to their rear ranks of bowmen who stood in rows and shot their shafts high into the castle defenders.

The gates were beginning to give. Cracks and splits appeared in them, ever widening. Then, all at once, when hardly expected, the right gate creaked on tortured hinges and fell. A triumphant roar erupted from the throats of the invaders and, dropping their hold on the logs, they led their companions through the breach, axes and maces swinging like scythes and flails before them—and enemy heads springing from necks like wheat from the stalk.

"The castle is ours!" shouted Moonglum, running forward and upward towards the gap in the archway. "The castle's taken."

"Speak not too hastily of victory," replied Dyvim Tvar, but he laughed as he spoke and ran as fast as the others to reach the castle.

"And where is your doom, now?" Elric called to his fellow Melnibonéan, then broke off sharply when Dyvim Tvar's face clouded and his mouth set grimly. For a moment there was tension between them, even as they ran, then Dyvim Tvar laughed loud and made a joke of it. "It lies somewhere, Elric, it lies somewhere—but let us not worry about such things, for if my doom hangs over me, I cannot stop its descent when my hour arrives!" He slapped Elric's shoulder, feeling for the albino's uncharacteristic confusion.

Then they were under the mighty archway and in the courtyard of the castle where savage fighting had developed almost into single duels, enemy choosing enemy and fighting him to the death.

Stormbringer was the first of the three men's blades to take blood and send a desert man's soul to hell. The song it sang as it was lashed through the air in strong strokes was an evil one—evil and triumphant.

The dark-faced desert warriors were famous for their courage and skill with swords. Their curved blades were reaping havoc in the Imrryrian ranks for, at that stage, the desert men far outnumbered the Melnibonéan force.

Somewhere above, the inspired scalers had got a firm foothold on the battlements and were closing with the men of Nikorn, driving them back, forcing many over the unrailed edges of the parapets. A falling, still-screaming warrior plummeted down, to land almost on Elric, knocking his shoulder and causing him to fall heavily to the blood-and-rain-slick cobbles. A badly scarred desert man, quick to see his chance, moved forward with a gloating look on his travesty of a face. His scimitar moved up, poised to hack Elric's neck from his shoulders, and then his helmet split open and his forehead spurted a sudden gout of blood.

Dyvim Tvar wrenched a captured axe from the skull of the slain warrior and grinned at Elric as the albino rose.

"We'll both live to see victory, yet," he shouted over the din of the warring elementals above them and the sound of clashing arms. "My doom, I will escape until—" He broke off, a look of surprise on his fine-boned face, and Elric's stomach twisted inside him as he saw a steel point appear in Dyvim Tvar's right side. Behind the Dragon Master, a maliciously smiling desert warrior pulled his blade from Dyvim Tvar's body. Elric cursed and rushed forward. The man put up his blade to defend himself, backing hurriedly away from the infuriated albino. Stormbringer swung up and then down, it howled a death-song and sheared right through the curved steel of Elric's opponent—and it kept on going, straight through the man's shoulder blade, splitting him half in two. Elric turned back to Dyvim Tvar who was still standing up, but was pale and strained. His blood dripped from his wound and seeped through his garments.

"How badly are you hurt?" Elric said anxiously. "Can you tell?"

"That trollspawn's sword passed through my ribs, I think—no vitals were harmed." Dyvim Tvar gasped and tried to smile. "I'm sure I'd know if he'd made more of the wound."

Then he fell. And when Elric turned him, he looked into a dead and staring face. The Dragon Master, Lord of the Dragon Caves, would never tend his beasts again.

Elric felt sick and weary as he got up, standing over the body of his kinsman. Because of me, he thought, another fine man has died. But this was the only conscious thought he allowed himself for the meantime. He was forced to defend himself from the slashing swords of a couple of desert men who came at him in a rush.

The archers, their work done outside, came running through the breach in the gate and their arrows poured into the enemy ranks.

Elric shouted loudly: "My kinsman Dyvim Tvar lies dead, stabbed in the back by a desert warrior—avenge him brethren. Avenge the Dragon Master of Imrryr!"

A low moaning came from the throats of the Melnibonéans and their attack was even more ferocious than before. Elric called to a bunch of axemen who ran down from the battlements, their victory assured.

"You men, follow me. We can avenge the blood that Theleb K'aarna took!" He had a good idea of the geography of the castle.

Moonglum shouted from somewhere. "One moment, Elric, and I'll join you!" A desert warrior fell, his back to Elric, and from behind him emerged a grinning Moonglum, his sword covered in blood from point to pommel.

Elric led the way to a small door, set into the main tower of the castle. He pointed at it and spoke to the axemen. "Set to with your axes, lads, and hurry!"

Grimly, the axemen began to hack at the tough timber. Impatiently, Elric watched as the wood chips started to fly.

The conflict was appalling. Theleb K'aarna sobbed in frustration. Kakatal, the Fire Lord, and his minions were having little effect on the Wind Giants. Their power appeared to be increasing if anything. The sorcerer gnawed his knuckles and quaked in his chamber while below him the human warriors fought, bled and died. Theleb K'aarna made himself concentrate on one thing only—total destruction of the Lasshaar forces. But he knew, somehow, even then, that sooner or later, in one way or another, he was doomed.

The axes drove deeper and deeper into the stout timber. At last it gave. "We're through, my lord," one of the axemen indicated the gaping hole they'd made.

Elric reached his arm through the gap and prised up the bar which secured the door. The bar moved upwards and then fell with a clatter to the stone flagging. Elric put his shoulder to the door and pushed.

Above them, now, two huge, almost-human figures had appeared in the sky, outlined against the night. One was golden and glowing like the sun and seemed to wield a great sword of fire. The other was dark blue and silver, writhing, smokelike, with a flickering spear of restless orange in his hand.

Misha and Kakatal clashed. The outcome of their mighty struggle might well decide Theleb K'aarna's fate.

"Quickly," Elric said. "Upwards!"

They ran up the stairs. The stairs which led to Theleb K'aarna's chamber.

Suddenly the men were forced to stop as they came to a door of jet-black, studded with crimson iron. It had no keyhole, no bolts, no bars, but it was quite secure. Elric directed the axemen to begin hewing at it. All six struck at the door in unison.

In unison, they screamed and vanished. Not even a wisp of smoke remained to mark where they had disappeared.

Moonglum staggered backwards, eyes wide in fear. He was backing away from Elric who remained firmly by the door, Stormbringer throbbing in his hand. "Get out, Elric—this is a sorcery of terrible power. Let your friends of the air finish the wizard!"

Elric shouted half-hysterically: "Magic is best fought by magic!" He hurled his whole body behind the blow which he struck at the black door. Stormbringer whined into it, shrieked as if in victory and howled like a soul-hungry demon. There was a blinding flash, a roaring in Elric's ears, a sense of weightlessness; and then the door had crashed inwards. Moonglum witnessed this—he had remained against his will.

"Stormbringer has rarely failed me, Moonglum," cried Elric as he leapt through the aperture. "Come, we have reached Theleb K'aarna's den—" He broke off, staring at the gibbering thing on the floor. It had been a man. It had been Theleb K'aarna. Now it was hunched and twisted—sitting in the middle of a broken pentacle and tittering to itself.

Suddenly, intelligence came into its eyes. "Too late for vengeance, Lord Elric," it said. "I have won, you see—I have claimed your vengeance as my own."

Grim-faced and speechless, Elric stepped forward, lifted Stormbringer and brought the moaning runesword down into the sorcerer's skull. He left it there for several moments.

"Drink your fill, hell-blade," he murmured. "We have earned it, you and I."

Overhead, there was a sudden silence.

## Chapter Six

"It's untrue! You lie!" screamed the frightened man. "We were not responsible." Pilarmo faced the group of leading citizens. Behind the overdressed merchant were his three colleagues—those who had earlier met Elric and Moonglum in the tavern.

One of the accusing citizens pointed a chubby finger towards the north and Nikorn's palace.

"So—Nikorn was an enemy of all other traders in Bakshaan. That I accept. But now a horde of bloody-handed reavers attacks his castle with the aid of demons—and Elric of Melniboné leads them! You know that you are responsible—the gossip's all over the city. You employed Elric—and this is what's happened!"

"But we didn't know he would go to such lengths to kill Nikorn!" Fat Tormiel wrung his hands, his face aggrieved and afraid. "You are wronging us. We only . . ."

"We're wronging *you*!" Faratt, spokesman for his fellow citizens, was thick-lipped and florid. He waved his hands in angry exasperation. "When Elric and his jackals have done with Nikorn—they'll come to the city. Fool! That is what the albino sorcerer planned to begin with. He was only mocking you—for you provided him with an excuse. Armed men we can fight—but not foul sorcery!"

"What shall we do? What shall we do? Bakshaan will be razed within the day!" Tormiel turned on Pilarmo. "This was your idea—you think of a plan!"

Pilarmo stuttered: "We could pay a ransom—bribe them—give them enough money to satisfy them."

"And who shall give this money?" asked Faratt.

Again the argument began.

Elric looked with distaste at Theleb K'aarna's broken corpse. He turned away and faced a blanch-featured Moonglum who said hoarsely: "Let's away, now, Elric. Yishana awaits you in Bakshaan as she promised. You must keep your end of the bargain I made for you."

Elric nodded wearily. "Aye—the Imrryrians seem to have taken the castle by the sound of it. We'll leave them to their spoiling and get out while we may. Will you allow me a few moments here, alone? The sword rejects the soul."

Moonglum sighed thankfully. "I'll join you in the courtyard within the quarter hour. I wish to claim some measure of the spoils." He left clattering down the stairs while Elric remained standing over his enemy's body. He spread out his arms, the sword, dripping blood, still in his hand.

"Dyvim Tvar," he cried, "you and our countrymen have been avenged. Let any evil one who holds the soul of Dyvim Tvar release it now and take instead the soul of Theleb K'aarna."

Within the room something invisible and intangible—but sensed all the same—flowed and hovered over the sprawled body of Theleb K'aarna. Elric looked out of the window and thought he heard the beating of dragon wings—smelled the acrid breath of dragons—saw a shape winging across the dawn sky bearing Dyvim Tvar the Dragon Master away.

Elric half-smiled. "The gods of Melniboné protect thee wherever thou art," he said quietly and turned away from the carnage, leaving the room.

On the stairway, he met Nikorn of Ilmar.

The merchant's rugged face was full of anger. He trembled with rage. There was a big sword in his hand.

"So I've found you, wolf," he said. "I gave you your life—and you have done this to me!"

Elric said tiredly: "It was to be. But I gave my word that I would not take your life and, believe me, I would not, Nikorn, even had I not pledged my word."

Nikorn stood two steps from the door blocking the exit. "Then I'll take yours. Come—engage!" He moved out into the courtyard, half-stumbled over an Imrryrian corpse, righted himself and waited, glowering, for Elric to emerge. Elric did so, his runesword sheathed.

"No."

"Defend yourself, wolf!"

Automatically, the albino's right hand crossed to his sword-hilt, but he still did not unsheathe it. Nikorn cursed and aimed a well-timed blow which barely missed the white-faced sorcerer. He skipped back and now he tugged out Stormbringer, still reluctant, and stood poised and wary, waiting for the Bakshaanite's next move.

Elric intended simply to disarm Nikorn. He did not want to kill or maim this brave man who had spared him when he had been entirely at the other's mercy.

Nikorn swung another powerful stroke at Elric and the albino parried. Stormbringer was moaning softly, shuddering and pulsating. Metal clanged and then the fight was on in full earnest as Nikorn's rage turned to calm, possessed fury. Elric was forced to defend himself with all his skill and power. Though older than the albino, and a city merchant, Nikorn was a superb swordsman. His speed was fantastic and, at times, Elric was not on the defensive only because he desired it.

But something was happening to the runeblade. It was twisting in Elric's hand and forcing him to make a counter-attack. Nikorn backed away—a light akin to fear in his eyes as he realized the potency of Elric's hell-forged steel. The merchant fought grimly—and Elric did not fight at all. He felt entirely in the power of the whining sword which hacked and cut at Nikorn's guard.

Stormbringer suddenly shifted in Elric's hand. Nikorn screamed. The runesword left Elric's grasp and plunged on its own accord towards the heart of his opponent.

"No!" Elric tried to catch hold of his blade but could not. Stormbringer plunged into Nikorn's great heart and wailed in demoniac triumph. "No!" Elric got hold of the hilt and tried to pull it from Nikorn. The merchant shrieked in hell-brought agony. He should have been dead.

He still half-lived.

"It's taking me—the thrice-damned thing is taking me!" Nikorn gurgled horribly, clutching at the black steel with hands turned to claws. "Stop it, Elric—I beg you, stop it! *Please*!"

Elric tried again to tug the blade from Nikorn's heart. He could not. It was rooted in flesh, sinew and vitals. It moaned greedily, drinking into it all that was the being of Nikorn of Ilmar. It sucked the life-force from the dying man and all the while its voice was soft and disgustingly sensuous. Still Elric struggled to pull the sword free. It was impossible. "Damn you!" he moaned. "This man was almost my friend—I gave him my word not to kill him." But Stormbringer, though sentient, could not hear its master.

Nikorn shrieked once more, the shriek dying to a low, lost whimper. And then his body died.

It died—and the soul-stuff of Nikorn joined the souls of the countless others, friends, kin and enemies who had gone to feed that which fed Elric of Melniboné.

Elric sobbed.

"Why is this curse upon me? Why?"

He collapsed to the ground in the dirt and the blood.

Minutes later, Moonglum came upon his friend lying face downward. He grasped Elric by his shoulder and turned him. He shuddered when he saw the albino's agony-racked face.

"What happened?"

Elric raised himself on one elbow and pointed to where Nikorn's body lay a few feet away. "Another, Moonglum. Oh, curse this blade!"

Moonglum said uncomfortably: "He would have killed you no doubt. Do not think about it. Many a word's been broken through no fault of he who gave it. Come, my friend, Yishana awaits us in the Tavern of the Purple Dove."

Elric struggled upright and began to walk slowly towards the battered gates of the castle where horses awaited them.

As they rode for Bakshaan, not knowing what was troubling the people of that city, Elric tapped Stormbringer which hung, once more, at his side. His eyes were hard and moody, turned inwards on his own feelings.

"Be wary of this devil-blade, Moonglum. It kills the foe—but savours the blood of friends and kinfolk most."

Moonglum shook his head quickly, as if to clear it, and looked away. He said nothing.

Elric made as if to speak again but then changed his mind. He needed to talk, then. He needed to—but there was nothing to say at all.

Pilarmo scowled. He stared, hurt-faced, as his slaves struggled with his chests of treasure, lugging them out to pile them in the street beside his great house. In other parts of the city, Pilarmo's three colleagues were also in various stages of heartbreak. Their treasure, too, was being dealt with in a like manner. The burghers of Bakshaan had decided who was to pay any possible ransom.

And then a ragged citizen was shambling down the street, pointing behind him and shouting.

"The albino and his companion—at the north gate!"

The burghers who stood near to Pilarmo exchanged glances. Faratt swallowed.

He said: "Elric comes to bargain. Quick. Open the treasure chests and tell the city guard to admit him." One of the citizens scurried off.

Within a few minutes, while Faratt and the rest worked frantically to expose Pilarmo's treasure to the gaze of the approaching albino, Elric was galloping up the street, Moonglum beside him. Both men were expressionless. They knew enough not to show their puzzlement.

"What's this?" Elric said, casting a look at Pilarmo.

Faratt cringed. "Treasure," he whined. "Yours, Lord Elric—for you and your men. There's much more. There is no need to use sorcery.

No need for your men to attack us. The treasure here is fabulous—its value is enormous. Will you take it and leave the city in peace?"

Moonglum almost smiled, but he controlled his features.

Elric said coolly: "It will do. I accept it. Make sure this and the rest is delivered to my men at Nikorn's castle or we'll be roasting you and your friends over open fires by the morrow."

Faratt coughed suddenly, trembling. "As you say, Lord Elric. It shall be delivered."

The two men wheeled their horses in the direction of the Tavern of the Purple Dove. When they were out of earshot Moonglum said: "From what I gathered, back there, it's Master Pilarmo and his friends who are paying that unasked-for toll."

Elric was incapable of any real humour, but he half-chuckled. "Aye. I'd planned to rob them from the start—and now their own fellows have done it for us. On our way back, we shall take our pick of the spoils."

He rode on and reached the tavern. Yishana was waiting there, nervously, dressed for traveling.

When she saw Elric's face she sighed with satisfaction and smiled silkily. "So Theleb K'aarna is dead," she said. "Now we can resume our interrupted relationship, Elric."

The albino nodded. "That was my part of the bargain—you kept yours when you helped Moonglum to get my sword back for me." He showed no emotion.

She embraced him, but he drew back. "Later," he murmured. "But this is one promise I shall not break, Yishana."

He helped the puzzled woman mount her waiting horse. They rode back towards Pilarmo's house.

She asked: "And what of Nikorn—is he safe? I liked that man."

"He died." Elric's voice was strained.

"How?" she asked.

"Because, like all merchants," Elric answered, "he bargained too hard."

There was an unnatural silence among the three as they made their horses speed faster towards the gates of Bakshaan, and Elric did not stop when the others did, to take their pick of Pilarmo's riches. He rode on, unseeing, and the others had to spur their steeds in order to catch up with him, two miles beyond the city.

Over Bakshaan, no breeze stirred in the gardens of the rich. No winds came to blow cool on the sweating faces of the poor. Only the sun blazed in the heavens, round and red, and a shadow, shaped like a dragon, moved across it once, and then was gone.

*Here is a further adventure of Elric of Melniboné in which he and Moonglum enter the dreaded forest of Troos— and Elric wins a wife.*

*—John Carnell, SCIENCE FANTASY No. 54, August 1962*

# KINGS IN DARKNESS

(with James Cawthorn)

Three Kings in Darkness lie,
Gutheran of Org, and I,
Under a bleak and sunless sky—
The third Beneath the Hill.

—*Song of Veerkad*

## CHAPTER ONE

ELRIC, LORD OF the lost and sundered Empire of Melniboné, rode like a fanged wolf from a trap—all slavering madness and mirth. He rode from Nadsokor, City of Beggars, and there was hate in his wake for he had been recognized as their old enemy before he could obtain the secret he had sought there. Now they hounded him and the grotesque little man who rode laughing at Elric's side; Moonglum the Outlander, from Elwher and the Unmapped East.

The flames of brands devoured the velvet of the night as the yelling, ragged throng pushed their bony nags in pursuit of the pair.

Starvelings and tattered jackals that they were, there was strength in their gaudy numbers, and long knives and bone bows glinted in the brandlight. They were too strong for a couple of men to fight, too few to represent serious danger in a hunt, so Elric and Moonglum had chosen to leave the city without dispute and now sped towards the full and rising moon which stabbed its sickly beams through the darkness to show them the disturbing waters of the Varkalk River and a chance of escape from the incensed mob.

They had half a mind to stand and face the mob, since the Varkalk was their only alternative. But they knew well what the beggars would do to them, whereas they were uncertain what would become of them once they had entered the river. The horses reached the sloping banks of the Varkalk and reared, with hoofs lashing.

Cursing, the two men spurred the steeds and forced them down towards the water. Into the river the horses plunged, snorting and spluttering. Into the river which led a roaring course towards the hell-spawned Forest of Troos which lay within the borders of Org, country of necromancy and rotting, ancient evil.

Elric blew water away from his mouth and coughed. "They'll not follow us to Troos, I think," he shouted at his companion.

Moonglum said nothing. He only grinned, showing his white teeth and the unhidden fear in his eyes. The horses swam strongly with the current and behind them the ragged mob shrieked in frustrated bloodlust while some of their number laughed and jeered.

"Let the forest do our work for us!"

Elric laughed back at them, wildly, as the horses swam on down the dark, straight river, wide and deep, towards a sun-starved morning, cold and spiky with ice. Scattered, slim-peaked crags loomed on either side of the flat plain, through which the river ran swiftly. Green-tinted masses of jutting blacks and browns spread colour through the rocks and the grass was waving on the plain as if for some purpose. Through the dawnlight, the beggar crew chased along the banks, but eventually gave up their quarry to return, shuddering, to Nadsokor.

When they had gone, Elric and Moonglum made their mounts swim towards the banks and climb them, stumbling, to the top where rocks and grass had already given way to sparse forest land which rose starkly on all sides, staining the earth with sombre shades. The foliage waved jerkily, as if alive—sentient.

It was a forest of malignantly erupting blooms, blood-coloured and sickly-mottled. A forest of bending, sinuously smooth trunks, black and shiny; a forest of spiked leaves of murky purples and gleaming greens—certainly an unhealthy place if judged only by the odour of rotting vegetation which was almost unbearable, impinging as it did upon the fastidious nostrils of Elric and Moonglum.

Moonglum wrinkled his nose and jerked his head in the direction they had come. "Back now?" he enquired. "We can avoid Troos and cut swiftly across a corner of Org to be in Bakshaan in just over a day. What say you, Elric?"

Elric frowned. "I don't doubt they'd welcome us in Bakshaan with the same warmth we received in Nadsokor. They'll not have forgotten the destruction we wrought there—and the wealth we acquired from their merchants. No, I have a fancy to explore the forest a little. I have heard tales of Org and its unnatural forest and should like to investigate the truth of them. My blade and sorcery will protect us, if necessary."

Moonglum sighed. "Elric—this once, let us not court the danger."

Elric smiled icily. His scarlet eyes blazed out of his dead white skin with peculiar intensity. "Danger? It can bring only death."

"Death is not to my liking, just yet," Moonglum said. "The fleshpots of Bakshaan, or if you prefer—Jadmar—on the other hand . . ."

But Elric was already urging his horse onward, heading for the forest. Moonglum sighed and followed.

Soon dark blossoms hid most of the sky, which was dark enough, and they could see only a little way in all directions. The rest of the forest seemed vast and sprawling; they could sense this, though sight of most of it was lost in the depressing gloom.

Moonglum recognized the forest from descriptions he had heard from mad-eyed travelers who drank purposefully in the shadows of Nadsokor's taverns.

"This is the Forest of Troos, sure enough," he said to Elric. "It's told of how the Doomed Folk released tremendous forces upon the Earth and caused terrible changes among men, beasts and vegetation. This forest is the last they created, and the last to perish."

"A child will always hate its parents at certain times," Elric said mysteriously.

"Children of whom to be extremely wary, I should think," Moonglum retorted. "Some say that when they were at the peak of their power, they had no gods to frighten them."

"A daring people, indeed," Elric replied, with a faint smile. "They have my respect. Now fear and the gods are back and that, at least, is comforting."

Moonglum puzzled over this for a short time, and then, eventually, said nothing.

He was beginning to feel uneasy.

The place was full of malicious rustlings and whispers, though no living animal inhabited it, as far as they could tell. There was a discomforting absence of birds, rodents or insects and, though they normally had no love for such creatures, they would have appreciated their company in the disconcerting forest.

In a quavering voice, Moonglum began to sing a song in the hope that it would keep his spirits up and his thoughts off the lurking forest.

"A grin and a word is my trade;
From these, my profit is made.
Though my body's not tall and my courage is small,
My fame will take longer to fade."

So singing, with his natural amiability returning, Moonglum rode after the man he regarded as a friend—a friend who possessed something akin to mastery over him, though neither admitted it.

Elric smiled at Moonglum's song. "To sing of one's own lack of size and absence of courage is not an action designed to ward off one's enemies, Moonglum."

"But this way I offer no provocation," Moonglum replied glibly. "If I sing of my shortcomings, I am safe. If I were to boast of my talents, then someone might consider this to be a challenge and decide to teach me a lesson."

"True," Elric assented gravely, "and well-spoken."

He began pointing at certain blossoms and leaves, remarking upon their alien tint and texture, referring to them in words which Moonglum could not understand, though he knew the words to be part of a sorcerer's vocabulary. The albino seemed to be untroubled by the fears which beset the Eastlander, but often, Moonglum knew, appearances with Elric could hide the opposite of what they indicated.

They stopped for a short break while Elric sifted through some of the samples he had torn from trees and plants. He carefully placed his prizes in his belt pouch but would say nothing of why he did so to Moonglum.

"Come," he said, "Troos's mysteries await us."

But then a new voice, a woman's, said softly from the gloom: "Save the excursion for another day, strangers."

Elric reined his horse, one hand at Stormbringer's hilt. The voice had had an unusual effect upon him. It had been low, deep and had, for a moment, sent the pulse in his throat throbbing. Incredibly, he sensed that he was suddenly standing on one of Fate's roads, but where the road would take him, he did not know. Quickly, he controlled his mind and then his body and looked towards the shadows from where the voice had come.

"You are very kind to offer us advice, madam," he said sternly. "Come, show yourself and give explanation . . ."

She rode then, very slowly, on a black-coated gelding that pranced with a power she could barely restrain. Moonglum drew an appreciative breath for although heavy-featured, she was incredibly beautiful. Her face and bearing was patrician, her eyes were grey-green, combining enigma and innocence. She was very young. For all her obvious womanhood and beauty, Moonglum aged her at seventeen or little more.

Elric frowned: "Do you ride alone?"

"I do now," she replied, trying to hide her obvious astonishment at the albino's colouring. "I need aid—protection. Men who will escort me safely to Karlaak. There, they will be paid."

"Karlaak, by the Weeping Waste? It lies the other side of Ilmiora, a hundred leagues away and a week's traveling at speed." Elric did not wait for her to reply to this statement. "We are not hirelings, madam."

"Then you are bound by the vows of chivalry, sir, and cannot refuse my request."

Elric laughed shortly. "Chivalry, madam? We come not from the upstart nations of the South with their strange codes and rules of behaviour. We are nobles of older stock whose actions are governed by our own desires. You would not ask what you do, if you knew our names."

She wetted her full lips with her tongue and said almost timidly: "You are . . . ?"

"Elric of Melniboné, madam, called Elric Womanslayer in the West, and this is Moonglum of Elwher; he has no conscience."

She said: "There are legends—the white-faced reaver, the hell-driven sorcerer with a blade that drinks the souls of men . . ."

"Aye, that's true. And however magnified they are with the retelling, they cannot hint, those tales, at the darker truths which lie in their origin. Now, madam, do you still seek our aid?" Elric's voice was gentle, without menace, as he saw that she was very much afraid, although she had managed to control the signs of fear and her lips were tight with determination.

"I have no choice. I am at your mercy. My father, the Senior Senator of Karlaak, is very rich. Karlaak is called the City of the Jade Towers, as you will know, and such rare jades and ambers we have. Many could be yours."

"Be careful, madam, lest you anger me," warned Elric, although Moonglum's bright eyes lighted with avarice. "We are not nags to be hired or goods to be bought. Besides which," he smiled disdainfully, "I am from crumbling Imrryr, the Dreaming City, from the Isle of the Dragon, hub of Ancient Melniboné, and I know what beauty really is. Your baubles cannot tempt one who has looked upon the milky Heart of Arioch, upon the blinding iridescence that throbs from the Ruby Throne, of the languorous and unnamable colours in the Actorios stone of the Ring of Kings. These are more than jewels, madam—they contain the lifestuff of the universe."

"I apologize, Lord Elric, and to you Sir Moonglum."

Elric laughed, almost with affection. "We are grim clowns, lady, but the Gods of Luck aided our escape from Nadsokor and we owe them a debt. We'll escort you to Karlaak, City of the Jade Towers, and explore the Forest of Troos another time."

Her thanks were tempered by the wary look in her eyes.

"And now we have made introductions," said Elric, "perhaps you would be good enough to give your name and tell us your story."

"I am Zarozinia from Karlaak, a daughter of the Voashoon, the most powerful clan in south-eastern Ilmiora. We have kinsmen in the trading cities on the coasts of Pikarayd and I went with two cousins and my uncle to visit them."

"A perilous journey, Lady Zarozinia."

"Aye and there are not only natural dangers, sir. Two weeks ago we made our goodbyes and began the journey home. Safely we crossed the Straits of Vilmir and there employed men-at-arms, forming a strong caravan to journey through Vilmir and so to Ilmiora. We skirted Nadsokor since we had heard that the City of Beggars is inhospitable to honest travelers . . ."

Here, Elric smiled: "And sometimes to dishonest travelers, as we can appreciate."

Again the expression on her face showed that she had some difficulty in equating his obvious good humour with his evil reputation. "Having skirted Nadsokor," she continued, "we came this way and reached the borders of Org wherein, of course, Troos lies. Very warily we traveled, knowing dark Org's reputation, along the fringes of the forest. And then we were ambushed and our hired men-at-arms deserted us."

"Ambushed, eh?" broke in Moonglum. "By whom, madam, did you know?"

"By their unsavoury looks and squat shapes they seemed natives. They fell upon the caravan and my uncle and cousins fought bravely but were slain. One of my cousins slapped the rump of my gelding and sent it galloping so that I could not control it. I heard—terrible screams—mad, giggling shouts—and when I at last brought my horse to a halt, I was lost. Later I heard you approach and waited in fear for you to pass, thinking you also were of Org, but when I heard your accents and some of your speech, I thought that you might help me."

"And help you we shall, madam," said Moonglum bowing gallantly from the saddle. "And I am indebted to you for convincing Lord Elric here of your need. But for you, we should be deep in this awful forest by now and experiencing strange terrors no doubt. I offer my sorrow for your dead kinfolk and assure you that you will be protected from now onwards by more than swords and brave hearts, for sorcery can be called up if needs be."

"Let's hope there'll be no need," frowned Elric. "You talk blithely of sorcery, friend Moonglum—you who hate the art."

Moonglum grinned.

"I was consoling the young lady, Elric. And I've had occasion to be grateful for your horrid powers, I'll admit. Now I suggest that we make camp for the night and so refreshed be on our way at dawn."

"I'll agree to that," said Elric, glancing almost with embarrassment at the girl. Again he felt the pulse in his throat and this time he had more difficulty in controlling it.

The girl also seemed fascinated by the albino. There was an attraction between them which might be strong enough to throw both their destinies along wildly different paths than any they had guessed.

Night came again quickly, for the days were short in those parts. While Moonglum tended the fire, nervously peering around him, Zarozinia, her richly embroidered cloth-of-gold gown shimmering in the firelight, walked gracefully to where Elric sat sorting the herbs he had collected. She glanced at him cautiously and then seeing that he was absorbed, stared at him with open curiosity.

He looked up and smiled faintly, his eyes for once unprotected, his strange face frank and pleasant. "Some of these are healing herbs," he said, "and others are used in summoning spirits. Yet others give unnatural strength to the imbiber and some turn men mad. They will be useful to me."

She sat down beside him, her thick-fingered hands pushing her black hair back. Her small breasts lifted and fell rapidly.

"Are you really the terrible evil-bringer of the legends, Lord Elric? I find it hard to credit."

"I have brought evil to many places," he said, "but usually there has already been evil to match mine. I seek no excuses, for I know what I am and I know what I have done. I have slain malignant sorcerers and destroyed oppressors, but I have also been responsible for slaying fine men, and a woman, my cousin, whom I loved, I killed—or my sword did."

"And you are master of your sword?"

"I often wonder. Without it, I am helpless." He put his hand around Stormbringer's hilt. "I should be grateful to it." Once again his red eyes seemed to become deeper, protecting some bitter emotion rooted at the core of his soul.

"I'm sorry if I revived unpleasant recollection . . ."

"Do not feel sorry, Lady Zarozinia. The pain is within me—you did not put it there. In fact I'd say you relieve it greatly by your presence."

Half-startled, she glanced at him and smiled. "I am no wanton, sir," she said, "but . . ."

He got up quickly.

"Moonglum, is the fire going well?"

"Aye, Elric. She'll stay in for the night." Moonglum cocked his head on one side. It was unlike Elric to make such empty queries, but Elric said nothing further so the Eastlander shrugged, turned away to check his gear.

Since he could think of little else to say, Elric turned and said quietly, urgently: "I'm a killer and a thief, not fit to . . ."

"Lord Elric, I am . . ."

"You are infatuated by a legend, that is all."

"No! If you feel what I feel, then you'll know it's more."

"You are young."

"Old enough."

"Beware. I must fulfill my destiny."

"Your destiny?"

"It is no destiny at all, but an awful thing called doom. And I have no pity except when I see something in my own soul. Then I have pity—and I pity. But I hate to look and this is part of the doom which drives me. Not Fate, nor the Stars, nor Men, nor Demons, nor Gods. Look at me, Zarozinia—it is Elric, poor white chosen plaything of the Gods of Time—Elric of Melniboné who causes his own gradual and terrible destruction."

"It is suicide!"

"Aye. I drive myself to slow death. And those who go with me suffer also."

"You speak falsely, Lord Elric—from guilt-madness."

"Because I am guilty, lady."

"And does Sir Moonglum go to doom with you?"

"He is unlike others—he is indestructible in his own self-assurance."

"I am confident, also, Lord Elric."

"But your confidence is that of youth, it is different."

"Need I lose it with my youth?"

"You have strength. You are as strong as we are. I'll grant you that."

She opened her arms, rising. "Then be reconciled, Elric of Melniboné."

And he was. He seized her, kissing her with a deeper need than that of passion. For the first time Cymoril of Imrryr was forgotten as they lay down, together on the soft turf, oblivious of Moonglum who polished away at his curved sword with wry jealousy.

They all slept and the fire waned.

Elric, in his joy, had forgotten, or not heeded, that he had a watch to take and Moonglum, who had no source of strength by himself, stayed awake for as long as he could but sleep overcame him.

In the shadows of the awful trees, figures moved with shambling caution.

The misshapen men of Org began to creep inwards towards the sleepers.

Then Elric opened his eyes, aroused by instinct, stared at Zarozinia's peaceful face beside him, moved his eyes without turning his head and saw the danger. He rolled over, grasped Stormbringer and tugged the runeblade from its sheath. The sword hummed, as if in anger at being awakened.

"Moonglum! Danger!" Elric bellowed in fear, for he had more to protect than his own life. The little man's head jerked up. His curved sabre was already across his knees and he jumped to his feet, ran towards Elric as the men of Org closed in.

"I apologize," he said.

"My fault, I . . ."

And then the men of Org were at them. Elric and Moonglum

stood over the girl as she came awake, saw the situation and did not scream. Instead she looked around for a weapon but found none. She remained still, where she was, the only thing to do.

Smelling like offal, the gibbering creatures, some dozen of them, slashed at Elric and Moonglum with heavy blades like cleavers, long and dangerous.

Stormbringer whined and smote through a cleaver, cut into a neck and beheaded the owner. Blood gurgled from the corpse as it slumped back across the fire. Moonglum ducked beneath a howling cleaver, lost his balance, fell, slashed at his opponent's legs and hamstrung him so that he collapsed shrieking. Moonglum stayed on the ground and lunged upwards, taking another in the heart. Then he sprang to his feet and stood shoulder to shoulder with Elric while Zarozinia got up behind them.

"The horses," grunted Elric. "If it's safe, try to get them."

There were still seven natives standing and Moonglum groaned as a cleaver sliced flesh from his left arm, retaliated, pierced the man's throat, turned slightly and sheared off another's face. They pressed forward, taking the attack to the incensed foe. His left hand covered with his own blood, Moonglum painfully pulled his long poignard from its sheath and held it with his thumb along the handle, blocked an opponent's swing, closed in and killed him with a ripping upward thrust of the dagger, the action of which caused his wound to pound with agony.

Elric held his great runesword in both hands and swung it in a semi-circle, hacking down the howling misshapen things. Zarozinia darted towards the horses, leapt onto her own and led the other two towards the fighting men. Elric smote at another and got into his saddle, thanking his own forethought to leave the equipment on the horses in case of danger. Moonglum quickly joined him and they thundered out of the clearing.

"The saddle-bags," Moonglum called in greater agony than that created by his wound. "We've left the saddle-bags!"

"What of it? Don't press your luck, my friend."

"But all our treasure's in them!"

Elric laughed, partly in relief, partly from real humour. "We'll retrieve them, friend, never fear."

"I know you, Elric. You've no value for the realities."

But even Moonglum was laughing as they left the enraged men of Org behind them and slowed to a canter.

Elric reached and hugged Zarozinia. "You have the courage of your noble clan in your veins," he said.

"Thank you," she replied, pleased with the compliment, "but we cannot match such swordmanship as that displayed by you and Moonglum. It was fantastic."

"Thank the blade," he said shortly.

"No. I will thank you. I think you place too much reliance upon that hell weapon, however powerful it is."

"I need it."

"For what?"

"For my own strength and, now, to give strength to you."

"I'm no vampire," she smiled, "and need no such fearful strength as that supplies."

"Then be assured that I do," he told her gravely. "You would not love me if the blade did not give me what I need. I am like a spineless sea-thing without it."

"I do not believe that, but will not dispute with you now."

They rode for a while without speaking.

Later, they stopped, dismounted, and Zarozinia put herbs that Elric had given her upon Moonglum's wounded arm and began to bind it.

Elric was thinking deeply. The forest rustled with macabre, sensuous sounds. "We're in the heart of Troos," he said, "and our intention to skirt the forest has been forestalled. I have it in mind to call on the King of Org and so round off our visit."

Moonglum laughed. "Shall we send our swords along first? And bind our own hands?" His pain was already eased by the herbs which were having quick effect.

"I mean it. We owe, all of us, much to the men of Org. They slew Zarozinia's uncle and cousins, they wounded you and they now have our treasure. We have many reasons for asking the king for recompense. Also, they seem stupid and should be easy to trick."

"Aye. The king will pay us back for our lack of common sense by tearing our limbs off."

"I'm in earnest. I think we should go."

"I'll agree that I'd like our wealth returned to us. But we cannot risk the lady's safety, Elric."

"I am to be Elric's wife, Moonglum. Therefore if he visits the King of Org, I shall come too."

Moonglum lifted an eyebrow. "A quick courtship."

"She speaks the truth, however. We shall all go to Org—and sorcery will protect us from the king's uncalled-for wrath."

"And still you wish for death and vengeance, Elric," shrugged Moonglum, mounting. "Well, it's all the same to me since your roads, whatever else, are profitable ones. You may be the Lord of Bad Luck by your own reckoning, but you bring good luck to me, I'll say that."

"No more courting death," smiled Elric, "but we'll have some revenge, I hope."

"Dawn will be with us soon," Moonglum said. "The Orgian citadel lies six hours' ride from here by my working, south-south-east by the Ancient Star, if the map I memorized in Nadsokor was correct."

"You have an instinct for direction that never fails, Moonglum. Every caravan should have such a man as you."

"We base an entire philosophy on the stars in Elwher," Moonglum replied. "We regard them as the master plan for everything that happens on Earth. As they revolve around the planet they see all things, past, present and future. They are our gods."

"Predictable gods, at least," said Elric and they rode off towards Org with light hearts considering the enormity of their risk.

## Chapter Two

Little was known of the tiny kingdom of Org save that the Forest of Troos lay within its boundaries and to that, other nations felt, it was welcome. The people were unpleasant to look upon, for the most part, and their bodies were stunted and strangely altered. Legend had it that they were the descendants of the Doomed Folk. Their rulers, it was said, were shaped like normal men in so far as their outward bodily appearance went, but their minds were warped more horribly than the limbs of their subjects.

The inhabitants were few and were generally scattered, ruled by their king from his citadel which was also called Org.

It was for this citadel that Elric and his companions rode and, as they did so, Elric explained how he planned to protect them all from the natives of Org.

In the forest he had found a particular leaf which, when used with certain invocations (which were harmless in that the invoker was in little danger of being harmed by the spirits he marshaled) would invest that person, and anyone else to whom he gave the drug distilled from the leaf, with temporary invulnerability.

The spell somehow reknitted the skin and flesh structure so that it could withstand any edge and almost any blow. Elric explained, in a rare garrulous mood, how the drug and spell combined to achieve the effect, but his archaicisms and esoteric words meant little to the other two.

They stopped an hour's ride from where Moonglum expected to find the citadel so that Elric could prepare the drug and invoke the spell.

He worked swiftly over a small fire, using an alchemist's pestle and mortar, mixing the shredded leaf with a little water. As the brew bubbled on the fire, he drew peculiar runes on the ground, some of which were twisted into such alien forms that they seemed to disappear into a different dimension and reappear beyond it.

"Bone and blood and flesh and sinew,
Spell and spirit bind anew;
Potent potion work the life charm,
Keep its takers safe from harm."

So Elric chanted as a small pink cloud formed in the air over the fire, wavered, re-formed into a spiral shape which curled downwards into the bowl. The brew spluttered and then was still. The albino sorcerer said: "An old boyhood spell, so simple that I'd near forgotten it. The leaf for the potion grows only in Troos and therefore it is rarely possible to perform."

The brew, which had been liquid, had now solidified and Elric broke it into small pellets. "Too much," he warned, "taken at one time is poison, and yet the effect can last for several hours. Not always, though, but we must accept that small risk." He handed both of them a pellet which they received dubiously. "Swallow them just before we reach the citadel," he told them, "or in the event of the men of Org finding us first."

Then they mounted and rode on again.

*Some miles to the south-east of Troos, a blind man sang a grim song in his sleep and so woke himself . . .*

They reached the brooding citadel of Org at dusk. Guttural voices shouted at them from the battlements of the square-cut ancient dwelling place of the Kings of Org. The thick rock oozed moisture and was corroded by lichen and sickly, mottled moss. The only entrance large enough for a mounted man to pass through was reached by a path almost a foot deep in evil-smelling black mud.

"What's your business at the Royal Court of Gutheran the Mighty?"

They could not see who asked the question.

"We seek hospitality and an audience with your liege," called Moonglum cheerfully, successfully hiding his nervousness. "We bring important news to Org."

A twisted face peered down from the battlements. "Enter strangers and be welcome," it said unwelcomingly.

The heavy wooden drawgate shifted upwards to allow them entrance and the horses pushed their way slowly through the mud and so into the courtyard of the citadel.

Overhead, the grey sky was a racing field of black tattered clouds which streamed towards the horizon as if to escape the horrid boundaries of Org and the disgusting Forest of Troos.

The courtyard was covered, though not so deeply, with the same foul mud as had impaired their progress to the citadel. It was full of heavy, unmoving shadow. On Elric's right, a flight of steps went up to an arched entrance which was hung, partially, with the same unhealthy lichen he had seen on the outer walls and, also, in the Forest of Troos.

Through this archway, brushing at the lichen with a pale, beringed hand, a tall man came and stood on the top step, regarding the visitors through heavy-lidded eyes. He was, in contrast to the others, handsome, with a massive, leonine head and long hair as white as Elric's; although the hair on the head of this great, solid man was somewhat dirty, tangled, unbrushed. He was dressed in a heavy jerkin of quilted, embossed leather, a yellow kilt which reached to his ankles and he carried a wide-bladed dagger, naked in his belt. He was older than Elric, aged between forty and fifty and his powerful if somewhat decadent face was seamed and pock-marked.

He stared at them in silence and did not welcome them; instead he signed to one of the battlement guards who caused the drawgate to be lowered. It came down with a crash, blocking off their way of escape.

"Kill the men and keep the woman," said the massive man in a low monotone. Elric had heard dead men speak in that manner.

As planned, Elric and Moonglum stood either side of Zarozinia and remained where they were, arms folded.

Puzzled, shambling creatures came warily at them, their loose trousers dragging in the mud, their hands hidden by the long shapeless sleeves of their filthy garments. They swung their cleavers. Elric felt a faint shock as the blade thudded onto his arm, but that was all. Moonglum's experience was similar.

The men fell back, amazement and confusion on their bestial faces.

The tall man's eyes widened. He put one ring-covered hand to his thick lips, chewing at a nail.

"Our swords have no effect upon them, king! They do not cut and they do not bleed. What are these folk?"

Elric laughed theatrically. "We are not common folk, little human, be assured. We are the messengers of the gods and come to your king with a message from our great masters. Do not worry, we shall not harm you since we are in no danger of being harmed. Stand aside and make us welcome."

Elric could see that King Gutheran was puzzled and not absolutely taken in by his words. Elric cursed to himself. He had measured their intelligence by those he had seen. This king, mad or not, was much more intelligent, was going to be harder to deceive. He led the way up the steps towards glowering Gutheran.

"Greetings, King Gutheran. The gods have, at last, returned to Org and wish you to know this."

"Org has had no gods to worship for an eternity," said Gutheran hollowly, turning back into the citadel. "Why should we accept them now?"

"You are impertinent, king."

"And you are audacious. How do I know you come from the gods?" He walked ahead of them, leading them through the low-roofed halls.

"You saw that the swords of your subjects had no effect upon us."

"True. I'll take that incident as proof for the moment. I suppose there must be a banquet in your—honour—I shall order it. Be welcome, messengers." His words were ungracious but it was virtually impossible to detect anything from Gutheran's tone, since the man's voice stayed at the same pitch.

Elric pushed his heavy riding cloak back from his shoulders and said lightly: "We shall mention your kindness to our masters."

The Court was a place of gloomy halls and false laughter and although Elric put many questions to Gutheran, the king would not answer them, or did so by means of ambiguous phrases which meant nothing. They were not given chambers wherein they could refresh themselves but instead stood about for several hours in the main hall of the citadel and Gutheran, while he was with them and not giving orders for the banquet, sat slumped on his throne and chewed at his nails, ignoring them.

"Pleasant hospitality," whispered Moonglum.

"Elric—how long will the effects of the drug last?" Zarozinia had remained close to him. He put his arm around her shoulders. "I do not know. Not much longer. But it has served its purpose. I doubt if they will try to attack us a second time. However, beware of other attempts, subtler ones, upon our lives."

The main hall, which had a higher roof than the others and was completely surrounded by a gallery which ran around it well above the floor, fairly close to the roof, was chilly and unwarmed. No fires burned in the several hearths, which were open and let into the floor, and the walls dripped moisture and were undecorated; damp, solid stone, time-worn and gaunt. There were not even rushes upon the floor which was strewn with old bones and pieces of decaying food.

"Hardly house-proud, are they?" commented Moonglum looking around him with distaste and glancing at brooding Gutheran who was seemingly oblivious of their presence.

A servitor shambled into the hall and whispered a few words to the king. He nodded and arose, leaving the Great Hall.

Soon men came in, carrying benches and tables and began to place them about the hall.

The banquet was, at last, due to commence. And the air had menace in it.

The three visitors sat together on the right of the king who had donned a richly jeweled chain of kingship, whilst his son and several pale-faced female members of the royal line sat on the left, unspeaking even among themselves.

Prince Hurd, a sullen-faced youth who seemed to bear a resentment against his father, picked at the unappetizing food which was served them all.

He drank heavily of the wine which had little flavour but was strong, fiery stuff and this seemed to warm the company a little.

"And what do the gods want of us poor folk of Org?" Hurd said, staring hard at Zarozinia with more than friendly interest.

Elric answered: "They ask nothing of you but your recognition. In return they will, on occasions, help you."

"That is all?" Hurd laughed. "That is more than those from the Hill can offer, eh, father?"

Gutheran turned his great head slowly to regard his son.

"Yes," he murmured, and the word seemed to carry warning.

Moonglum said: "The Hill—what is that?"

He got no reply. Instead a high-pitched laugh came from the entrance to the Great Hall. A thin, gaunt man stood there staring ahead with a fixed gaze. His features, though emaciated, strongly resembled Gutheran's. He carried a stringed instrument and plucked at the gut so that it wailed and moaned with melancholy insistence.

Hurd said savagely: "Look, father, 'tis blind Veerkad, the minstrel, your brother. Shall he sing for us?"

"Sing?"

"Shall he sing his songs, father?"

Gutheran's mouth trembled and twisted and he said after a moment: "He may entertain our guests with an heroic ballad if he wishes, but . . ."

"But certain other songs he shall not sing . . ." Hurd grinned maliciously. He seemed to be tormenting his father deliberately in some way which Elric could not guess. Hurd shouted at the blind man: "Come Uncle Veerkad—sing!"

"There are strangers present," said Veerkad hollowly above the wail of his own music. "Strangers in Org."

Hurd giggled and drank more wine. Gutheran scowled and continued to tremble, gnawing at his nails.

Elric called: "We'd appreciate a song, minstrel."

"Then you'll have the song of the Three Kings in Darkness, strangers, and hear the ghastly story of the Kings of Org."

"No!" shouted Gutheran, leaping from his place, but Veerkad was already singing:

"Three Kings in Darkness lie,
Gutheran of Org, and I,

Under a bleak and sunless sky—
The third Beneath the Hill.
When shall the third arise?
Only when another dies . . ."

"Stop!" Gutheran got up in an obviously insane rage and stumbled across the table, trembling in terror, his face blanched, striking at the blind man, his brother. Two blows and the minstrel fell, slumping to the floor and not moving. "Take him out! Do not let him enter again." The king shrieked and foam flecked his lips.

Hurd, sober for a moment, jumped across the table, scattering dishes and cups and took his father's arm.

"Be calm, father. I have a new plan for our entertainment."

"You! You seek my throne. 'Twas you who goaded Veerkad to sing his dreadful song. You know I cannot listen without . . ." He stared at the door. "One day the legend shall be realized and the Hill-King shall come. Then shall I, you and Org perish."

"Father," Húrd was smiling horribly, "let the female visitor dance for us a dance of the gods."

"What?"

"Let the woman dance for us, father."

Elric heard him. By now the drug must have worn off. He could not afford to show his hand by offering his companions further doses. He got to his feet.

"What sacrilege do you speak, prince?"

"We have given you entertainment. It is the custom in Org for our visitors to give us entertainment also."

The hall was filled with menace. Elric regretted his plan to trick the men of Org. But there was nothing he could do. He had intended to exact tribute from them in the name of the gods, but obviously these mad men feared more immediate and tangible dangers than any the gods might represent.

He had made a mistake, put the lives of his friends in danger as well as his own. What should he do? Zarozinia murmured: "I have learned dances in Ilmiora where all ladies are taught the art. Let me dance for them. It might placate them and bedazzle them to make our work easier."

"Arioch knows our work is hard enough now. I was a fool to have conceived this plan. Very well, Zarozinia, dance for them, but with caution." He shouted at Hurd: "Our companion will dance for you, to show you the beauty that the gods create. Then you must pay the tribute, for our masters grow impatient."

"The tribute?" Gutheran looked up. "You mentioned nothing of tribute."

"Your recognition of the gods must take the form of precious stones and metals, King Gutheran. I thought you to understand that."

"You seem more like common thieves than uncommon messengers, my friends. We are poor in Org and have nothing to give away to charlatans."

"Beware of your words, king!" Elric's clear voice echoed warningly through the hall.

"We'll see the dance and then judge the truth of what you've told us."

Elric seated himself, grasped Zarozinia's hand beneath the table as she arose, giving her comfort.

She walked gracefully and confidently into the centre of the hall and there began to dance. Elric, who loved her, was amazed at her splendid grace and artistry. She danced the old, beautiful dances of Ilmiora, entrancing even the thick-skulled men of Org and, as she danced, a great golden Guest Cup was brought in.

Hurd leaned across his father and said to Elric: "The Guest Cup, lord. It is our custom that our guests drink from it in friendship."

Elric nodded, annoyed at being disturbed in his watching of the wonderful dance, his eyes fixed on Zarozinia as she postured and glided. There was silence in the hall.

Hurd handed him the cup and absently he put it to his lips; seeing this Zarozinia danced onto the table and began to weave along it to where Elric sat. As he took the first sip, Zarozinia cried out and, with her foot, knocked the cup from his hand. The wine splashed onto Gutheran and Hurd who half rose, startled. "It was drugged, Elric. They drugged it!"

Hurd lashed at her with his hand, striking her across the face. She fell from the table and lay moaning slightly on the filthy floor. "Bitch! Would the messengers of the gods be harmed by a little drugged wine?"

Enraged, Elric pushed aside Gutheran and struck savagely at Hurd so that the young man's mouth gushed blood. But the drug was already having effect. Gutheran shouted something and Moonglum drew his sabre, glancing upwards. Elric was swaying, his senses were jumbled and the scene had an unreal quality. He saw servants grasp Zarozinia but could not see how Moonglum was faring. He felt sick and dizzy, could hardly control his limbs.

Summoning up his last remaining strength, Elric clubbed Hurd down with one tremendous blow. Then he collapsed into unconsciousness.

## Chapter Three

There was the cold clutch of chains about his wrists and a thin drizzle was falling directly onto his face which stung where Hurd's nails had ripped it.

He looked about him. He was chained between two stone menhirs upon an obvious burial barrow of gigantic size. It was night and a pale moon hovered in the heavens above him. He looked down at the group of men below. Hurd and Gutheran were among them. They grinned at him mockingly.

"Farewell, messenger. You will serve us a good purpose and placate the Ones from the Hill!" Hurd called as he and the others scurried back towards the citadel which lay, silhouetted, a short distance away.

Where was he? What had happened to Zarozinia—and Moonglum? Why had he been chained thus upon—realization and remembrance came—*the Hill*!

He shuddered, helpless in the strong chains which held him. Desperately he began to tug at them, but they would not yield. He searched his brain for a plan, but he was confused by torment and worry for his friends' safety. He heard a dreadful scuttling sound from below and saw a ghastly white shape dart into the gloom. Wildly he struggled in the rattling iron which held him.

In the Great Hall of the citadel, a riotous celebration was now reaching the state of an ecstatic orgy. Gutheran and Hurd were totally drunk, laughing insanely at their victory.

Outside the hall, Veerkad listened and hated. Particularly he hated his brother, the man who had deposed and blinded him to prevent his study of sorcery by means of which he had planned to raise the King from Beneath the Hill.

"The time has come, at last," he whispered to himself and stopped a passing servant.

"Tell me—where is the girl kept?"

"In Gutheran's chamber, master."

Veerkad released the man and began to grope his way through the gloomy corridors up twisting steps, until he reached the room he sought. Here he produced a key, one of many he'd had made without Gutheran's knowing, and unlocked the door.

Zarozinia saw the blind man enter and could do nothing. She was gagged and bound with her own dress and still dazed from the blow Hurd had given her. They had told her of Elric's fate, but Moonglum had so far escaped them, guards hunted him now in the stinking corridors of Org.

"I've come to take you to your companion, lady," smiled blind Veerkad, grasping her roughly with strength that his insanity had given him. Picking her up, he fumbled his way towards the door. He knew the passages of Org perfectly, for he had been born and had grown up among them.

But two men were in the corridor outside Gutheran's chambers. One of them was Hurd, Prince of Org, who resented his father's appropriation of the girl and desired her for himself. He saw Veerkad bearing the girl away and stood silent while his uncle passed.

The other man was Moonglum, who observed what was happening from the shadows where he had hidden from the searching guards. As Hurd followed Veerkad, on cautious feet, Moonglum followed him.

Veerkad went out of the citadel by a small side door and carried his living burden towards the looming Burial Hill.

All about the foot of the monstrous barrow swarmed the leprous-white ghouls who sensed the presence of Elric, the folk of Org's sacrifice to them.

Now Elric understood.

These were the things that Org feared more than the gods. These were the living-dead ancestors of those who now reveled in the Great Hall. Perhaps these were actually the Doomed Folk. Was that their doom? Never to rest? Never to die? Just to degenerate into mindless ghouls? Elric shuddered.

Now desperation brought back his memory. His voice was an agonized wail to the brooding sky and the pulsing earth.

"Arioch! Destroy the stones. Save your servant! Arioch—master—aid me!"

It was not enough. The ghouls gathered together and began to scuttle, gibbering up the barrow towards the helpless albino.

"*Arioch! These are the things that would forsake your memory! Aid me to destroy them!*"

The earth trembled and the sky became overcast, hiding the moon but not the white-faced, bloodless ghouls who were now almost upon him.

And then a ball of fire formed in the sky above him and the very sky seemed to shake and sway around it. Then, with a roaring crash two bolts of lightning slashed down, pulverizing the stones and releasing Elric.

He got to his feet, knowing that Arioch would demand his price, as the first ghouls reached him.

He did not retreat, but in his rage and desperation leapt among them, smashing and flailing with the lengths of chain. The ghouls fell back and fled, gibbering in fear and anger, down the Hill and into the barrow.

Elric could now see that there was a gaping entrance to the barrow below him, black against the blackness. Breathing heavily, he found that his belt pouch had been left him. From it he took a length of slim, gold wire and began frantically to pick at the locks of the manacles.

Veerkad chuckled to himself and Zarozinia hearing him was almost mad with terror. He kept drooling the words into her ear: "When shall the third arise? Only when another dies. When that other's blood flows red—we'll hear the footfalls of the dead. You and I, we shall resurrect him and such vengeance will he wreak upon my cursed brother. Your blood, my dear, it will be that released him." He felt that the ghouls were gone and judged them placated by their feast. "Your lover has been useful to me," he laughed as he began to enter the barrow. The smell of death almost overpowered the girl as the blind madman bore her downwards into the heart of the Hill.

Hurd, sobered after his walk in the colder air, was horrified when he saw where Veerkad was going; the barrow, the Hill of the King, was the most feared spot in the land of Org. Hurd paused before the black entrance and turned to run. Then, suddenly, he saw the form of Elric, looming huge and bloody, descending the barrow slope, cutting off his escape.

With a wild yell he fled into the Hill passage.

Elric had not previously noticed the prince, but the yell startled him and he tried to see who had given it but was too late. He began to run down the steep incline towards the entrance of the barrow. Another figure came scampering out of the darkness.

"Elric! Thank the stars and all the gods of Earth! You live!"

"Thank Arioch, Moonglum. Where's Zarozinia?"

"In there—the mad minstrel took her with him and Hurd followed. They are all insane, these kings and princes, I see no sense to their actions."

"I have an idea that the minstrel means Zarozinia no good. Quickly, we must follow."

"By the stars, the stench of death! I have breathed nothing like it—not even at the great battle of the Eshmir Valley where the armies of Elwher met those of Kaleg Vogun, usurper prince of the Tanghensi, and half a million corpses strewed the valley from end to end."

"If you've no stomach . . ."

"I wish I had none. It would not be so bad. Come . . ."

They rushed into the passage, led by the far-away sounds of Veerkad's maniacal laughter and the somewhat nearer movements of a fear-maddened Hurd who was now trapped between two enemies and yet more afraid of a third.

Hurd blundered along in the blackness, sobbing to himself in his terror.

In the phosphorescent Central Tomb, surrounded by the mummified corpses of his ancestors, Veerkad chanted the resurrection ritual before the great coffin of the Hill-King—a giant thing, half as tall again as Veerkad who was tall enough. Veerkad was forgetful for his own safety and thinking only of vengeance upon his brother Gutheran. He held a long dagger over Zarozinia who lay huddled and terrified upon the ground near the coffin.

The spilling of Zarozinia's blood would be the culmination of the ritual and then—

Then Hell would, quite literally, be let loose. Or so Veerkad planned. He finished his chanting and raised the knife just as Hurd came screeching into the Central Tomb with his own sword drawn. Veerkad swung round, his blind face working in thwarted rage.

Savagely, without stopping for a moment, Hurd ran his sword into Veerkad's body, plunging the blade in up to the hilt so that its bloody point appeared sticking from his back. But the other, in his groaning death spasms, locked his hands about the prince's throat. Locked them immovably.

Somehow, the two men retained a semblance of life and, struggling with each other in a macabre death-dance, swayed about the glowing chamber. The coffin of the Hill-King began to tremble and shake slightly, the movement hardly perceptible.

So Elric and Moonglum found Veerkad and Hurd. Seeing that both were near dead, Elric raced across the Central Tomb to where Zarozinia lay, unconscious, mercifully, from her ordeal. Elric picked her up and made to return.

He glanced at the throbbing coffin.

"Quickly, Moonglum. That blind fool has invoked the dead, I can tell. Hurry, my friend, before the hosts of hell are upon us."

Moonglum gasped and followed Elric as he ran back towards the cleaner air of night.

"Where to now, Elric?"

"We'll have to risk going back to the citadel. Our horses are there and our goods. We need the horses to take us quickly away, for I fear there's going to be a terrible blood-letting soon if my instinct is right."

"There should not be too much opposition, Elric. They were all drunk when I left. That was how I managed to evade them so easily. By now, if they continued drinking as heavily as when last I saw them, they'll be unable to move at all."

"Then let's make haste."

They left the Hill behind them and began to run towards the citadel.

## Chapter Four

Moonglum had spoken truth. Everyone was lying about the Great Hall in drunken sleep. Open fires had been lit in the hearths and they blazed, sending shadows skipping around the hall. Elric said softly: "Moonglum, go with Zarozinia to the stables and prepare our horses. I will settle our debt with Gutheran first." He pointed. "See, they have heaped their booty upon the table, gloating in their apparent victory."

Stormbringer lay upon a pile of burst sacks and saddle-bags which contained the loot stolen from Zarozinia's uncle and cousins and from Elric and Moonglum.

Zarozinia, now conscious but confused, left with Moonglum to locate the stables and Elric picked his way towards the table, across the sprawled shapes of drunken men of Org, around the blazing fires and caught up, thankfully, his hell-forged runeblade.

Then he leapt over the table and was about to grasp Gutheran, who still had his fabulously gemmed chain of kingship around his neck, when the great doors of the hall crashed open and a howling blast of icy air sent the torches dancing and leaping. Elric turned, Gutheran forgotten, and his eyes widened.

Framed in the doorway stood the King from Beneath the Hill.

The long-dead monarch had been raised by Veerkad whose own blood had completed the work of resurrection. He stood in rotting robes, his fleshless bones covered by tight, tattered skin. His heart did not beat, for he had none; he drew no breath, for his lungs had been eaten by the creatures which feasted on such things. But, horribly, he lived . . .

The King from the Hill. He had been the last great ruler of the Doomed Folk who had, in their fury, destroyed half the Earth and created the Forest of Troos. Behind the dead king crowded the ghastly hosts who had been buried with him in a legendary past.

The massacre began!

What secret vengeance was being reaped, Elric could only guess at—but whatever the reason, the danger was still very real.

Elric pulled out Stormbringer as the awakened horde vented their anger upon the living. The hall became filled with the shrieking, horrified screams of the unfortunate Orgians. Elric remained, half-paralyzed in his horror, beside the throne. Aroused, Gutheran woke up and saw the King from the Hill and his host. He screamed, almost thankfully:

"At last I can rest!"

And fell dying in a seizure, robbing Elric of his vengeance.

Veerkad's grim song echoed in Elric's memory. The Three Kings in Darkness—Gutheran, Veerkad and the King from Beneath the Hill. Now only the last lived—and he had been dead for millennia.

The King's cold, dead eyes roved the hall and saw Gutheran sprawled upon his throne, the ancient chain of office still about his throat. Elric wrenched it off the body and backed away as the King from Beneath the Hill advanced. And then his back was against a pillar and there were feasting ghouls everywhere else.

The dead King came nearer and then, with a whistling moan which came from the depths of his decaying body, launched himself at Elric who found himself fighting desperately against the Hill-King's clawing, abnormal strength, cutting at flesh that neither bled nor suffered pain. Even the sorcerous runeblade could do nothing against this horror that had no soul to take and no blood to let.

Frantically, Elric slashed and hacked at the Hill-King but ragged nails raked his flesh and teeth snapped at his throat. And above everything came the almost overpowering stench of death as the ghouls, packing the Great Hall with their horrible shapes, feasted on the living and the dead.

Then Elric heard Moonglum's voice calling and saw him upon the gallery which ran around the hall. He held a great oil jar.

"Lure him close to the central fire, Elric. There may be a way to vanquish him. Quickly man, or you're finished!"

In a frantic burst of energy, the Melnibonéan forced the giant king towards the flames. Around them, the ghouls fed off the remains of their victims, some of whom still lived, their screams calling hopelessly over the sound of carnage.

The Hill-King now stood, unfeeling, with his back to the leaping central fire. He still slashed at Elric. Moonglum hurled the jar.

It shattered upon the stone hearth, spraying the King with blazing oil. He staggered, and Elric struck with his full power, the man and the blade combining to push the Hill-King backwards. Down went the King into the flames and the flames began to devour him.

A dreadful, lost howling came from the burning giant as he perished.

Flames licked everywhere throughout the Great Hall and soon the place was like Hell itself, an inferno of licking fire through which the ghouls ran about, still feasting, unaware of their destruction. The way to the door was blocked.

Elric stared around him and saw no way of escape—save one.

Sheathing Stormbringer, he ran a few paces and leapt upwards, just grasping the rail of the gallery as flames engulfed the spot where he had been standing.

Moonglum reached down and helped him to clamber across the rail.

"I'm disappointed, Elric," he grinned, "you forgot to bring the treasure."

Elric showed him what he grasped in his left hand—the jewel-encrusted chain of kingship.

"This bauble is some reward for our hardships," he smiled, holding up the glittering chain. "I stole nothing, by Arioch! There are no kings left in Org to wear it! Come let's join Zarozinia and get our horses."

They ran from the gallery as masonry began to crash downwards into the Great Hall.

They rode fast away from the halls of Org and looking back saw great fissures appear in the walls and heard the roar of destruction as the flames consumed everything that had been Org. They destroyed the seat of the monarchy, the remains of the Three Kings in Darkness, the present and the past. Nothing would be left of Org save an empty burial mound and two corpses, locked together, lying where their ancestors had lain for centuries in the Central Tomb. They destroyed the last link with the previous age and cleansed the Earth of an ancient evil. Only the dreadful Forest of Troos remained to mark the coming and the passing of the Doomed Folk.

And the Forest of Troos was a warning.

Weary and yet relieved, the three saw the outlines of Troos in the distance, behind the blazing funeral pyre.

And yet, in his happiness, Elric had a fresh problem on his mind now that danger was past.

"Why do you frown now, love?" asked Zarozinia.

"Because I think you spoke the truth. Remember you said I placed too much reliance on my runeblade here?"

"Yes—and I said I would not dispute with you."

"Agreed. But I have a feeling that you were partially right. On the burial mound and in it I did not have Stormbringer with me—and yet I fought and won, because I feared for your safety." His voice was quiet. "Perhaps, in time, I can keep my strength by means of certain herbs I found in Troos and dispense with the blade for ever?"

Moonglum shouted with laughter hearing these words.

"Elric—I never thought I'd witness this. You daring to think of dispensing with that foul weapon of yours. I don't know if you ever shall, but the thought is comforting."

"It is, my friend, it is." He leaned in his saddle and grasped Zarozinia's shoulders, pulling her dangerously towards him as they galloped without slackening speed. And as they rode he kissed her, heedless of their pace.

"A new beginning!" he shouted above the wind. "A new beginning, my love!"

And then they all rode laughing towards Karlaak by the Weeping Waste, to present themselves, to enrich themselves, and to attend the strangest wedding the Northern lands had ever witnessed.

*The tide of evil surrounding Elric is beginning to change since his marriage to Zarozinia ("Kings in Darkness," No. 54) but he is still called upon to exert his necromantic powers in order to save a fellow sorcerer as well as his own city.*

*—John Carnell,* SCIENCE FANTASY *No. 55, October 1962*

# THE CARAVAN OF FORGOTTEN DREAMS

(originally titled The Flame Bringers)

## Chapter One

BLOODY-BEAKED HAWKS soared on the frigid wind. They soared high above a mounted horde inexorably moving across the Weeping Waste.

The horde had crossed two deserts and three mountain ranges to be there and hunger drove them onwards. They were spurred on by remembrances of stories heard from travelers who had come to their Eastern homeland, by the encouragements of their thin-lipped leader who swaggered in his saddle ahead of them, one arm wrapped around a ten-foot lance decorated with the gory trophies of his pillaging campaigns.

The riders moved slowly and wearily, unaware that they were nearing their goal.

Far behind the horde, a stocky rider left Elwher, the singing, boisterous capital of the Eastern World, and came soon to a valley.

The hard skeletons of trees had a blighted look and the horse kicked earth the colour of ashes as its rider drove it fiercely through the sick wasteland that had once been gentle Eshmir, the golden garden of the East.

A plague had smitten Eshmir and the locust had stripped her of her beauty. Both plague and locust went by the same name—Terarn Gashtek, Lord of the Mounted Hordes, sunken-faced carrier of destruction; Terarn Gashtek, insane blood-drawer, the shrieking flame bringer. And that was his other name—Flame Bringer.

The rider who witnessed the evil that Terarn Gashtek had brought to gentle Eshmir was named Moonglum. Moonglum was riding, now, for Karlaak by the Weeping Waste, the last outpost of the Western civilization of which those in the Eastlands knew little. In Karlaak, Moonglum knew he would find Elric of Melniboné who now dwelt permanently in his wife's graceful city. Moonglum was desperate to reach Karlaak quickly, to warn Elric and to solicit his help.

He was small and cocky, with a broad mouth and a shock of red hair, but now his mouth did not grin and his body was bent over the horse as he pushed it on towards Karlaak. For Eshmir, gentle Eshmir, had been Moonglum's home province, and with his ancestors had formed him into what he was.

So, cursing, Moonglum rode for Karlaak.

But so did Terarn Gashtek. And already the Flame Bringer had reached the Weeping Waste. The horde moved slowly, for they had wagons with them which had at one time dropped far behind but now the supplies they carried were needed. As well as provisions, one of the wagons carried a bound prisoner who lay on his back cursing Terarn Gashtek and his slant-eyed battle-mongers.

Drinij Bara was bound by more than strips of leather, that was why he cursed, for Drinij Bara was a sorcerer who could not normally be held in such a manner. If he had not succumbed to his weakness for wine and women just before the Flame Bringer had come down on the town in which he was staying, he would not have been trussed so, and Terarn Gashtek would not now have Drinij Bara's soul.

Drinij Bara's soul reposed in the body of a small, black-and-white cat—the cat which Terarn Gashtek had caught and carried with him always, for, as was the habit of Eastern sorcerers, Drinij Bara had hidden his soul in the body of the cat for protection. Because of this he was now slave to the Lord of the Mounted Hordes, and had to obey him lest the man slay the cat and so send his soul to hell.

It was not a pleasant situation for the proud sorcerer, but he did not deserve less.

There was on the pale face of Elric of Melniboné some slight trace of an earlier haunting, but his mouth smiled and his crimson eyes were at peace as he looked down at the young, black-haired woman with whom he walked in the terraced gardens of Karlaak.

"Elric," said Zarozinia, "have you found your happiness?"

He nodded. "I think so. Stormbringer now hangs amid cobwebs in your father's armoury. The drugs I discovered in Troos keep me strong, my eyesight clear, and need to be taken only occasionally. I need never think of traveling or fighting again. I am content, here, to spend my time with you and study the books in Karlaak's library. What more would I require?"

"You compliment me overmuch, my lord. I would become complacent."

He laughed. "Rather that than you were doubting. Do not fear, Zarozinia, I possess no reason, now, to journey on. Moonglum, I miss, but it was natural that he should become restless of residence in a city and wish to revisit his homeland."

"I am glad you are at peace, Elric. My father was at first reluctant to let you live here, fearing the black evil that once accompanied you, but three months have proved to him that the evil has gone and left no fuming berserker behind it."

Suddenly there came a shouting from below them, in the street a man's voice was raised and he banged at the gates of the house.

"Let me in, damn you, I must speak with your master."

A servant came running: "Lord Elric—there is a man at the gates with a message. He pretends friendship with you."

"His name?"

"An alien one—Moonglum, he says."

"Moonglum! His stay in Elwher has been short. Let him in!"

Zarozinia's eyes held a trace of fear and she held Elric's arm fiercely. "Elric—pray he does not bring news to take you hence."

"No news could do that. Fear not, Zarozinia." He hurried out of the garden and into the courtyard of the house. Moonglum rode hurriedly through the gates, dismounting as he did so.

"Moonglum, my friend! Why the haste? Naturally, I am pleased to see you after such a short time, but you have been riding hastily—why?"

The little Eastlander's face was grim beneath its coating of dust and his clothes were filthy from hard riding.

"The Flame Bringer comes with sorcery to aid him," he panted. "You must warn the city."

"The Flame Bringer? The name means nothing—you sound delirious, my friend."

"Aye, that's true, I am. Delirious with hate. He destroyed my homeland, killed my family, my friends and now plans conquests in the West. Two years ago he was little more than an ordinary desert raider but then he began to gather a great horde of barbarians around him and has been looting and slaying his way across the Eastern lands. Only Elwher has not suffered from his attacks, for the city was too great for even him to take. But he has turned two thousand miles of pleasant country into a burning waste. He plans world conquest, rides westwards with five hundred thousand warriors!"

"You mentioned sorcery—what does this barbarian know of such sophisticated arts?"

"Little himself, but he has one of our greatest wizards in his power—Drinij Bara. The man was captured as he lay drunk between two wenches in a tavern in Phum. He had put his soul into the body of a cat so that no rival sorcerer might steal it while he slept. But Terarn Gashtek, the Flame Bringer, knew of this trick, seized the cat and bound its legs, eyes and mouth, so imprisoning Drinij Bara's soul. Now the sorcerer is his slave—if he does not obey the barbarian, the cat will be killed by an iron blade and Drinij Bara's soul will go to hell."

"These are unfamiliar sorceries to me," said Elric. "They seem little more than superstitions."

"Who knows that they may be—but so long as Drinij Bara believes what he believes, he will do as Terarn Gashtek dictates. Several proud cities have been destroyed with the aid of his magic."

"How far away is this Flame Bringer?"

"Three days' ride at most. I was forced to come hence by a longer route, to avoid his outriders."

"Then we must prepare for a siege."

"No, Elric—you must prepare to flee!"

"To flee—should I request the citizens of Karlaak to leave their beautiful city unprotected, to leave their homes?"

"If they will not—you must, and take your bride with you. None can stand against such a foe."

"My own sorcery is no mean thing."

"But one man's sorcery is not enough to hold back half a million men also aided by sorcery."

"And Karlaak is a trading city—not a warrior's fortress. Very well, I will speak to the Council of Elders and try to convince them."

"You must convince them quickly, Elric, for if you do not Karlaak will not stand half a day before Terarn Gashtek's howling bloodletters."

"They are stubborn," said Elric as the two sat in his private study later that night. "They refuse to realize the magnitude of the danger. They refuse to leave and I cannot leave them for they have welcomed me and made me a citizen of Karlaak."

"Then we must stay here and die?"

"Perhaps. There seems to be no choice. But I have another plan. You say that this sorcerer is a prisoner of Terarn Gashtek. What would he do if he regained his soul?"

"Why he would take vengeance upon his captor. But Terarn Gashtek would not be so foolish as to give him the chance. There is no help for us there."

"What if we managed to aid Drinij Bara?"

"How? It would be impossible."

"It seems our only chance. Does this barbarian know of me or my history?"

"Not as far as I know."

"Would he recognize you?"

"Why should he?"

"Then I suggest we join him."

"Join him—Elric, you are no more sane than when we rode as free travelers together!"

"I know what I am doing. It would be the only way to get close to him and discover a subtle way to defeat him. We will set off at dawn, there is no time to waste."

"Very well. Let's hope your old luck is good, but I doubt it now, for you've forsaken your old ways and the luck went with them."

"Let us find out."

"Will you take Stormbringer?"

"I had hoped never to have to make use of that hell-forged blade again. She's a treacherous sword at best."

"Aye—but I think you'll need her in this business."

"Yes, you're right. I'll take her."

Elric frowned, his hands clenched. "It will mean breaking my word to Zarozinia."

"Better break it—than give her up to the Mounted Hordes."

Elric unlocked the door to the armoury, a pitch torch flaring in one hand. He felt sick as he strode down the narrow passage lined with dulled weapons which had not been used for a century.

His heart pounded heavily as he came to another door and flung off the bar to enter the little room in which lay the disused regalia of Karlaak's long-dead War Chieftains—and Stormbringer. The black blade began to moan as if welcoming him as he took a deep breath of the musty air and reached for the sword. He clutched the hilt and his body was racked by an unholy sensation of awful ecstasy. His face twisted as he sheathed the blade and he almost ran from the armoury towards cleaner air.

Elric and Moonglum mounted their plainly equipped horses and, garbed like common mercenaries, bade urgent farewell to the Councilors of Karlaak.

Zarozinia kissed Elric's pale hand.

"I realize the need for this," she said, her eyes full of tears, "but take care, my love."

"I shall. And pray that we are successful in whatever we decide to do."

"The White Gods be with you."

"No—pray to the Lords of the Darks, for it is their evil help I'll need in this work. And forget not my words to the messenger who is to ride to the south-west and find Dyvim Slorm."

"I'll not forget," she said, "though I worry lest you succumb again to your old black ways."

"Fear for the moment—I'll worry about my own fate later."

"Then farewell, my lord, and be lucky."

"Farewell, Zarozinia. My love for you will give me more power even than this foul blade here." He spurred his horse through the gates and then they were riding for the Weeping Waste and a troubled future.

## Chapter Two

Dwarfed by the vastness of the softly turfed plateau which was the Weeping Waste, the place of eternal rains, the two horsemen drove their hard-pressed steeds through the drizzle.

A shivering desert warrior, huddled against the weather, saw them come towards him. He stared through the rain trying to make out details of the riders, then wheeled his stocky pony and rode swiftly back in the direction he had come. Within minutes he had reached a large group of warriors attired like himself in furs and tasseled iron helmets. They carried short bone bows and quivers of long arrows fletched with hawk feathers. There were curved scimitars at their sides.

He exchanged a few words with his fellows and soon they were all lashing their horses towards the two riders.

"How much further lies the camp of Terarn Gashtek, Moonglum?" Elric's words were breathless, for both men had ridden for a day without halt.

"Not much further, Elric. We should be—look!"

Moonglum pointed ahead. About ten riders came swiftly towards them. "Desert barbarians—the Flame Bringer's men. Prepare for a fight—they won't waste time parleying."

Stormbringer scraped from the scabbard and the heavy blade seemed to aid Elric's wrist as he raised it, so that it felt almost weightless.

Moonglum drew both his swords, holding the short one with the same hand with which he grasped his horse's reins.

The Eastern warriors spread out in a half circle as they rode down on the companions, yelling wild war-shouts. Elric reared his mount to a savage standstill and met the first rider with Stormbringer's point full in the man's throat. There was a stink like brimstone as it pierced flesh and the warrior drew a ghastly choking breath as he died, his eyes staring out in full realization of his terrible fate—that Stormbringer drank souls as well as blood.

Elric cut savagely at another desert man, lopping off his sword arm and splitting his crested helmet and the skull beneath. Rain and sweat ran down his white, taut features and into his glowing crimson eyes, but he blinked it aside, half-fell in his saddle as he turned to defend himself against another howling scimitar, parried the sweep, slid his own runeblade down its length, turned the blade with a movement of his wrist and disarmed the warrior. Then he plunged his sword into the man's heart and the desert warrior yelled like a wolf at the moon, a long baying shout before Stormbringer took his soul.

Elric's face was twisted in self-loathing as he fought intently with superhuman strength. Moonglum stayed clear of the albino's sword for he knew its liking for the lives of Elric's friends.

Soon only one opponent was left. Elric disarmed him and had to hold his own greedy sword back from the man's throat.

Reconciled to the horror of his death, the man said something in a guttural tongue which Elric half-recognized. He searched his memory and realized that it was a language close to one of the many ancient tongues which, as a sorcerer, he had been required to learn years before.

He said in the same language: "Thou art one of the warriors of Terarn Gashtek the Flame Bringer."

"That is true. And you must be the White-faced Evil One of legends. I beg you to slay me with a cleaner weapon than that which you hold."

"I do not wish to kill thee at all. We were coming hence to join Terarn Gashtek. Take us to him."

The man nodded hastily and clambered back on his horse.

"Who are you who speaks the High Tongue of our people?"

"I am called Elric of Melniboné—dost thou know the name?"

The warrior shook his head. "No, but the High Tongue has not been spoken for generations, save by shamans—yet you're no shaman but, by your dress, seem a warrior."

"We are both mercenaries. But speak no more. I will explain the rest to thy leader."

They left a jackal's feast behind them and followed the quaking Easterner in the direction he led them.

Fairly soon, the low-lying smoke of many campfires could be observed and at length they saw the sprawling camp of the barbarian warlord's mighty army.

The camp encompassed over a mile of the great plateau. The barbarians had erected skin tents on rounded frames and the camp had the aspect of a large primitive town. Roughly in the centre was a much larger construction, decorated with a motley assortment of gaudy silks and brocades.

Moonglum said in the Western tongue: "That must be Terarn

Gashtek's dwelling. See, he has covered its half-cured hides with a score of Eastern battle-flags." His face grew grimmer as he noted the torn standard of Eshmir, the lion-flag of Okara and the blood-soaked pennants of sorrowing Chang Shai.

The captured warrior led them through the squatting ranks of barbarians who stared at them impassively and muttered to one another. Outside Terarn Gashtek's tasteless dwelling was his great war-lance decorated with more trophies of his conquests—the skulls and bones of Eastern princes and kings.

Elric said: "Such a one as this must not be allowed to destroy the reborn civilization of the Young Kingdoms."

"Young kingdoms are resilient," remarked Moonglum, "but it is when they are old that they fall—and it is often Terarn Gashtek's kind that tear them down."

"While I live he shall not destroy Karlaak—nor reach as far as Bakshaan."

Moonglum said: "Though, in my opinion, he'd be welcome to Nadsokor. The City of Beggars deserves such visitors as the Flame Bringer. If we fail, Elric, only the sea will stop him—and perhaps not that."

"With Dyvim Slorm's aid—we shall stop him. Let us hope Karlaak's messenger finds my kinsman soon."

"If he does not we shall be hard put to fight off half a million warriors, my friend."

The barbarian shouted: "Oh, Conqueror—mighty Flame Bringer—there are men here who wish to speak with you."

A slurred voice snarled: "Bring them in."

They entered the badly smelling tent which was lighted by a fire flickering in a circle of stones. A gaunt man, carelessly dressed in bright captured clothing, lounged on a wooden bench. There were several women in the tent, one of whom poured wine into a heavy golden goblet which he held out.

Terarn Gashtek pushed the woman aside, knocking her sprawling and regarded the newcomers. His face was almost as fleshless as the skulls hanging outside his tent. His cheeks were sunken and his slanting eyes narrow beneath thick brows.

"Who are these?"

"Lord, I know not—but between them they slew ten of our men and would have slain me."

"You deserved no more than death if you let yourself be disarmed. Get out—and find a new sword quickly or I'll let the shamans have your vitals for divination." The man slunk away.

Terarn Gashtek seated himself upon the bench once more.

"So, you slew ten of my blood-letters, did you, and came here to boast to me about it? What's the explanation?"

"We but defended ourselves against your warriors—we sought no quarrel with them." Elric now spoke the cruder tongue as best he could.

"You defended yourselves fairly well, I grant you. We reckon three soft-living house-dwellers to one of us. You are a Westerner, I can tell that, though your silent friend has the face of an Elwherite. Have you come from the East or the West?"

"The West," Elric said, "we are free traveling warriors, hiring our swords to those who'll pay or promise us good booty."

"Are all Western warriors as skillful as you?" Terarn Gashtek could not hide his sudden realization that he might have underestimated the men he hoped to conquer.

"We are a little better than most," lied Moonglum, "but not much."

"What of sorcery—is there much strong magic here?"

"No," said Elric, "the art has been lost to most."

The barbarian's thin mouth twisted into a grin, half of relief, half of triumph. He nodded his head, reached into his gaudy silks and produced a small black-and-white bound cat. He began to stroke its back. It wriggled but could do no more than hiss at its captor. "Then we need not worry," he said.

"Now, why did you come here? I could have you tortured for days for what you did, slaying ten of my best outriders."

"We recognized the chance of enriching ourselves by aiding you, Lord Flame Bringer," said Elric. "We could show you the richest towns, lead you to ill-defended cities that would take little time to fall. Will you enlist us?"

"I've need of such men as you, true enough. I'll enlist you readily—but mark this, I'll not trust you until you've proved loyal to me. Find yourselves quarters now—and come to the feast, tonight. There I'll be able to show you something of the power I hold. The power which will smash the strength of the West and lay it waste for ten thousand miles."

"Thanks," said Elric. "I'll look forward to tonight."

They left the tent and wandered through the haphazard collection of tents and cooking fires, wagons and animals. There seemed little food, but wine was in abundance and the taut, hungry stomachs of the barbarians were placated with that.

They stopped a warrior and told him of Terarn Gashtek's orders to them. The warrior sullenly led them to a tent.

"Here—it was shared by three of the men you slew. It is yours by right of battle, as are the weapons and booty inside."

"We're richer already," grinned Elric with feigned delight.

In the privacy of the tent, which was less clean than Terarn Gashtek's, they debated.

"I feel uncommonly uncomfortable," said Moonglum, "surrounded by this treacherous horde. And every time I think of what they made of Eshmir, I itch to slay more of them. What now?"

"We can do nothing now—let us wait until tonight and see what develops." Elric sighed. "Our task seems impossible—I have never seen so great a horde as this."

"They are invincible as they are," said Moonglum. "Even without Drinij Bara's sorcery to tumble down the walls of cities, no single nation could withstand them and, with the Western nations squabbling among themselves, they could never unite in time. Civilization itself is threatened. Let us pray for inspiration—your dark gods are at least sophisticated, Elric, and we must hope that they'll resent the barbarian's intrusion as much as we do."

"They play strange games with their human pawns," Elric replied, "and who knows what they plan?"

Terarn Gashtek's smoke-wreathed tent had been further lighted by rush torches when Elric and Moonglum swaggered in, and the feast, consisting primarily of wine, was already in progress.

"Welcome, my friends," shouted the Flame Bringer, waving his goblet. "These are my captains—come, join them!"

Elric had never seen such an evil-looking group of barbarians. They were all half-drunk and, like their leader, had draped a variety of looted articles of clothing about themselves. But their swords were their own.

Room was made on one of the benches and they accepted wine which they drank sparingly.

"Bring in our slave!" yelled Terarn Gashtek. "Bring in Drinij Bara our pet sorcerer." Before him on the table lay the bound and struggling cat and beside it an iron blade.

Grinning warriors dragged a morose-faced man close to the fire and forced him to kneel before the barbarian chief. He was a lean man and he glowered at Terarn Gashtek and the little cat. Then his eyes saw the iron blade and his gaze faltered.

"What do you want with me now?" he said sullenly.

"Is that the way to address your master, spell-maker? Still, no matter. We have guests to entertain—men who have promised to lead us to fat merchant cities. We require you to do a few minor tricks for them."

"I'm no petty conjuror. You cannot ask this of one of the greatest sorcerers in the world!"

"We do not ask—we order. Come, make the evening lively. What do you need for your magic-making? A few slaves—the blood of virgins? We shall arrange it."

"I'm no mumbling shaman—I need no such trappings."

Suddenly the sorcerer saw Elric. The albino felt the man's powerful mind tentatively probing his own. He had been recognized as a fellow sorcerer. Would Drinij Bara betray him?

Elric was tense, waiting to be denounced. He leaned back in his chair and, as he did so, made a sign with his hand which would be recognized by Western sorcerers—would the Easterner know it?

He did. For a moment he faltered, glancing at the barbarian leader. Then he turned away and began to make new passes in the air, muttering to himself.

The beholders gasped as a cloud of golden smoke formed near the roof and began to metamorphose into the shape of a great horse bearing a rider which all recognized as Terarn Gashtek. The barbarian leader leaned forward, glaring at the image.

"What's this?"

A map showing great land areas and seas seemed to unroll beneath the horse's hoofs. "The Western lands," cried Drinij Bara. "I make a prophecy."

"What is it?"

The ghostly horse began to trample the map. It split and flew into a thousand smoky pieces. Then the image of the horseman faded, also, into fragments.

"Thus will the mighty Flame Bringer rend the bountiful nations of the West," shouted Drinij Bara.

The barbarians cheered exultantly, but Elric smiled thinly. The Eastern wizard was mocking Terarn Gashtek and his men.

The smoke formed into a golden globe which seemed to blaze and vanish.

Terarn Gashtek laughed. "A good trick, magic-maker—and a true prophecy. You have done your work well. Take him back to his kennel!"

As Drinij Bara was dragged away, he glanced questioningly at Elric but said nothing.

Later that night, as the barbarians drank themselves into a stupor, Elric and Moonglum slipped out of the tent and made their way to the place where Drinij Bara was imprisoned.

They reached the small hut and saw that a warrior stood guard at the entrance. Moonglum produced a skin of wine and, pretending drunkenness, staggered towards the man. Elric stayed where he was.

"What do you want, Outlander?" growled the guard.

"Nothing my friend, we are trying to get back to our own tent, that's all. Do you know where it is?"

"How should I know?"

"True—how should you? Have some wine—it's good—from Terarn Gashtek's own supply."

The man extended a hand. "Let's have it."

Moonglum took a swig of the wine. "No, I've changed my mind. It's too good to waste on common warriors."

"Is that so?" The warrior took several paces towards Moonglum. "We'll find out won't we? And maybe we'll mix some of your blood with it to give it flavour, my little friend."

Moonglum backed away. The warrior followed.

Elric ran softly towards the tent and ducked into it to find Drinij Bara, wrists bound, lying on a pile of uncured hides. The sorcerer looked up.

"You—what do you want?"

"We've come to aid you, Drinij Bara."

"Aid me? But why? You're no friend of mine. What would you gain? You risk too much."

"As a fellow sorcerer, I thought I'd help you," Elric said.

"I thought you were that. But, in my land, sorcerers are not so friendly to one another—the opposite, in fact."

"I'll tell you the truth—we need your aid to halt the barbarian's bloody progress. We have a common enemy. If we can help you regain your soul, will you help?"

"Help—of course. All I do is plan the way I'll avenge myself. But for my sake be careful—if he suspects that you're here to aid me, he'll slay the cat and slay us, too."

"We'll try to bring the cat to you. Will that be what you need?"

"Yes. We must exchange blood, the cat and I, and my soul will then pass back into my own body."

"Very well, I'll try to—" Elric turned, hearing voices outside. "What's that?"

The sorcerer replied fearfully. "It must be Terarn Gashtek—he comes every night to taunt me."

"Where's the guard?" The barbarian's harsh voice came closer as he entered the little tent. "What's . . . ?" He saw Elric standing above the sorcerer.

His eyes were puzzled and wary. "What are you doing here, Westerner—and what have you done with the guard?"

"Guard?" said Elric, "I saw no guard. I was looking for my own tent and heard this cur cry out, so I entered. I was curious, anyway, to see such a great sorcerer clad in filthy rags and bound so."

Terarn Gashtek scowled. "Any more of such unwary curiosity my friend, and you'll be discovering what your own heart looks like. Now, get hence—we ride on in the morning."

Elric pretended to flinch and stumbled hurriedly from the tent.

A lone man in the livery of an Official Messenger of Karlaak goaded his horse southwards. The mount galloped over the crest of a hill and the messenger saw a village ahead. Hurriedly he rode into it, shouting at the first man he saw.

"Quickly, tell me—know you ought of Dyvim Slorm and his Imrryrian mercenaries? Have they passed this way?"

"Aye—a week ago. They went towards Rignariom by Vilmir's border, to offer their services to the Ilmioran Pretender."

"Were they mounted or on foot?"

"Both."

"Thanks, friend," cried the messenger behind him and galloped out of the village in the direction of Rignariom.

The messenger from Karlaak rode through the night—rode along a recently made trail. A large force had passed that way. He prayed that it had been Dyvim Slorm and his Imrryrian warriors.

In the sweet-smelling garden city of Karlaak, the atmosphere was tense as the citizens waited for news they knew they could not expect for some time. They were relying on both Elric and on the messenger. If only one were successful, there would be no hope for them. Both had to be successful. Both.

## Chapter Three

The tumbling sound of moving men cut through the weeping morning and the hungry voice of Terarn Gashtek lashed at them to hurry.

Slaves packed up his tent and threw it into a wagon. He rode forward and wrenched his tall war-lance from the soft earth, wheeled his horse and rode westwards, his captains, Elric and Moonglum among them, behind him.

Speaking the Western tongue, Elric and Moonglum debated their problem. The barbarian was expecting them to lead him to his prey, his outriders were covering wide distances so that it would be impossible to lead him past a settlement. They were in a quandary for it would be disgraceful to sacrifice another township to give Karlaak a few days' grace, yet . . .

A little later two whooping outriders came galloping up to Terarn Gashtek.

"A town, lord! A small one and easy to take!"

"At last—this will do to test our blades and see how easy Western flesh is to pierce. Then we'll aim at a bigger target." He turned to Elric: "Do you know this town?"

"Where does it lie?" asked Elric thickly.

"A dozen miles to the south-west," replied the outrider.

In spite of the fact that the town was doomed, Elric felt almost relieved. They spoke of the town of Gorjhan.

"I know it," he said.

Cavim the Saddler, riding to deliver a new set of horse furniture to an outlying farm, saw the distant riders, their bright helmets caught by a sudden beam of sunlight. That the riders came from off the Weeping Waste was undoubtable—and he recognized menace in their massed progress.

He turned his mount about and rode with the speed of fear, back the way he had come to the town of Gorjhan.

The flat, hard mud of the street trembled beneath the thudding hoofs of Cavim's horse and his high, excited shout knifed through shuttered windows.

"*Raiders come! 'Ware the raiders!*"

Within a quarter of an hour, the head-men of the town had met in hasty conference and debated whether to run or to fight. The older men advised their neighbours to flee the raiders, other younger men preferred to stay ready, armed to meet a possible attack. Some argued that their town was too poor to attract any raider.

The townspeople of Gorjhan debated and quarreled and the first wave of raiders came screaming to their walls.

With the realization that there was no time for further argument came the realization of their doom, and they ran to the ramparts with their pitiful weapons.

Terarn Gashtek roared through the milling barbarians who churned the mud around Gorjhan: "Let's waste no time in siege. Fetch the sorcerer!"

They dragged Drinij Bara forward. From his garments, Terarn Gashtek produced the small black-and-white cat and held an iron blade at its throat.

"Work your spell, sorcerer, and tumble the walls quickly."

The sorcerer scowled, his eyes seeking Elric, but the albino averted his own eyes and turned his horse away.

The sorcerer produced a handful of powder from his belt pouch and hurled it into the air where it became first a gas, then a flickering ball of flame and finally a face, a dreadful unhuman face, formed in the flame.

"Dag-Gadden the Destroyer," intoned Drinij Bara, "you are sworn to our ancient pact—will you obey me?"

"I must, therefore I will. What do you command?"

"That you obliterate the walls of this town and so leave the men inside naked, like crabs without their shells."

"My pleasure is to destroy and destroy I shall." The flaming face faded, altered, shrieked a searing course upward and became a blossoming scarlet canopy which hid the sky.

Then it swept down over the town and, in the instant of its passing, the walls of Gorjhan groaned, crumbled and vanished.

Elric shuddered—if Dag-Gadden came to Karlaak, such would be their fate.

Triumphant, the barbarian battlemongers swept into the defenseless town.

Careful to take no part in the massacre, Elric and Moonglum were also helpless to aid the slaughtered townspeople. The sight of the senseless, savage bloodshed around them enervated them. They ducked into a small house which seemed so far untouched by the pillaging barbarians. Inside they found three cowering children huddled around an older girl who clutched an old scythe in her soft hands. Shaking with fear, she prepared to stand them off.

"Do not waste our time, girl," Elric said, "or you'll be wasting your lives. Does this house have a loft?"

She nodded.

"Then get to it quickly. We'll make sure you're unharmed."

They stayed in the house, hating to observe the slaughter-madness which had come upon the howling barbarians. They heard the dreadful sounds of carnage and smelled the stench of dead flesh and running blood.

A barbarian, covered in blood which was not his own, dragged a woman into the house by her hair. She made no attempt to resist, her face stunned by the horror she had witnessed.

Elric growled: "Find another nest, hawk—we've made this our own."

The man said: "There's room enough here for what I want."

Then, at last, Elric's clenched muscles reacted almost in spite of him. His right hand swung over to his left hip and the long fingers locked around Stormbringer's black hilt. The blade leapt from the scabbard as Elric stepped forward and, his crimson eyes blazing his sickened hatred, he smashed his sword down through the man's body. Unnecessarily, he clove again, hacking the barbarian in two. The woman remained where she lay, conscious but unmoving.

Elric picked up her inert body and passed it gently to Moonglum. "Take her upstairs with the others," he said brusquely.

The barbarians had begun to fire part of the town, their slaying all but done. Now they looted. Elric stepped out of the doorway.

There was precious little for them to loot but, still hungry for violence, they spent their energy on smashing inanimate things and setting fire to the broken, pillaged dwellings.

Stormbringer dangled loosely in Elric's hand as he looked at the blazing town. His face was a mask of shadow and frisking light as the fire threw up still longer tongues of flames to the misty sky.

Around him, barbarians squabbled over the pitiful booty; and occasionally a woman's scream cut above the other sounds, intermingled with rough shouts and the clash of metal.

Then he heard voices which were pitched differently to those in the immediate vicinity. The accents of the reavers mingled with a new tone—a whining, pleading tone. A group led by Terarn Gashtek came into view through the smoke.

Terarn Gashtek held something bloody in his hand—a human hand, severed at the wrist—and behind him swaggered several of his captains holding a naked old man between them. Blood ran over his body and gushed from his ruined arm, spurting sluggishly.

Terarn Gashtek frowned when he saw Elric. Then he shouted: "Now Westerner, you shall see how we placate our gods with better gifts than meal and sour milk as this swine once did. He'll soon be dancing a pretty measure, I'll warrant—won't you, Lord Priest?"

The whining note went out of the old man's voice then and he stared with fever-bright eyes at Elric. His voice rose to a frenzied and high-pitched shriek which was curiously repellent.

"You dogs can howl over me!" he spat, "but Mirath and T'aargano will be revenged for the ruin of their priest and their temple—you have brought flame here and you shall die by flame." He pointed the bleeding stump of his arm at Elric—"And you—you are a traitor and have been one in many causes, I can see it written in you. Though now . . . You are—" the priest drew breath . . .

Elric licked his lips.

"I am what I am," he said, "and you are nothing but an old man soon to die. Your gods cannot harm us, for we do not pay them any respect. I'll listen no more to your senile meanderings!"

There was in the old priest's face all the knowledge of his past torment and the torment which was to come. He seemed to consider this and then was silent.

"Save your breath for screaming," said Terarn Gashtek to the uncomprehending priest.

And then Elric said: "It's bad luck to kill a priest, Flame Bringer!"

"You seem weak of stomach, my friend. His sacrifice to our own gods will bring us good luck, fear not."

Elric turned away. As he entered the house again, a wild shriek of agony seared out of the night and the laughter which followed was not pleasant.

Later, as the still-burning houses lit the night, Elric and Moonglum, carrying heavy sacks on their shoulders, clasping a woman each, moved with a simulation of drunkenness to the edge of the camp. Moonglum left the sacks and the women with Elric and went back, returning soon with three horses.

They opened the sacks to allow the children to climb out and watched the silent women mount the horses, aiding the children to clamber up.

Then they galloped away.

"Now," said Elric savagely, "we must work our plan tonight, whether the messenger reached Dyvim Slorm or not. I could not bear to witness another such sword-quenching."

Terarn Gashtek had drunk himself insensible. He lay sprawled in an upper room of one of the unburned houses.

Elric and Moonglum crept towards him. While Elric watched to see that he was undisturbed, Moonglum knelt beside the barbarian leader and, lightfingered, cautiously reached inside the man's garments. He smiled in self-approval as he lifted out the squirming cat and replaced it with a stuffed rabbit-skin he had earlier prepared for the purpose. Holding the animal tight, he arose and nodded to Elric. Together, warily, they left the house and made their way through the chaos of the camp.

"I ascertained that Drinij Bara lies in the large wagon," Elric told his friend. "Quickly, now, the main danger's over."

Moonglum said: "When the cat and Drinij Bara have exchanged blood and the sorcerer's soul is back in his body—what then, Elric?"

"Together, our powers may serve at least to hold the barbarians back, but—" he broke off as a large group of warriors came weaving towards them.

"It's the Westerner and his little friend," laughed one. "Where are you off to, comrades?"

Elric sensed their mood. The slaughter of the day had not completely satiated their blood-lust. They were looking for trouble.

"Nowhere in particular," he replied. The barbarians lurched around them, encircling them.

"We've heard much of your straight blade, stranger," grinned their spokesman, "and I'd a mind to test it against a real weapon." He grabbed his own scimitar out of his belt. "What do you say?"

"I'd spare you that," said Elric coolly.

"You are generous—but I'd rather you accepted my invitation."

"Let us pass," said Moonglum.

The barbarians' faces hardened. "Speak you so to the conquerors of the world?" said the leader.

Moonglum took a step back and drew his sword, the cat squirming in his left hand.

"We'd best get this done," said Elric to his friend. He tugged his runeblade from its scabbard. The sword sang a soft and mocking tune and the barbarians heard it. They were disconcerted.

"Well?" said Elric, holding the half-sentient blade out.

The barbarian who had challenged him looked uncertain of what to do. Then he forced himself to shout: "Clean iron can withstand any sorcery," and launched himself forward.

Elric, grateful for the chance to take further vengeance, blocked his swing, forced the scimitar back and aimed a blow which sliced the man's torso just above the hip. The barbarian screamed and died. Moonglum, dealing with a couple more, killed one but another came in swiftly and his sweeping sword sliced the little Eastlander's left shoulder. He howled—and dropped the cat. Elric stepped in, slew Moonglum's opponent, Stormbringer wailing a triumphant dirge. The rest of the barbarians turned and ran off.

"How bad is your wound?" gasped Elric, but Moonglum was on his knees staring through the gloom.

"Quick, Elric—can you see the cat? I dropped it in the struggle. If we lose it—we too are lost."

Frantically, they began to hunt through the camp.

But they were unsuccessful, for the cat, with the dexterity of its kind, had wriggled free of its bindings and hidden itself.

A few moments later they heard the sounds of uproar coming from the house which Terarn Gashtek had commandeered.

"He's discovered that the cat's been stolen!" exclaimed Moonglum. "What do we do now?"

"I don't know—keep searching and hope he does not suspect us."

They continued to hunt, but with no result. While they searched, several barbarians came up to them. One of them said:

"Our leader wishes to speak with you."

"Why?"

"He'll inform you of that. Come on."

Reluctantly, they went with the barbarians to be confronted by a raging Terarn Gashtek. He clutched the stuffed rabbit skin in one clawlike hand and his face was warped with fury.

"My hold over the sorcerer has been stolen from me," he roared. "What do you know of it?"

"I don't understand," said Elric.

"The cat is missing—I found this rag in its place. You were caught talking to Drinij Bara recently, I think you were responsible."

"We know nothing of this," said Moonglum.

Terarn Gashtek growled: "The camp's in disorder, it will take a day to reorganize my men—once loosed like this they will obey no-one. But when I've restored order, I shall question the whole camp. If you tell the truth, then you will be released, but meanwhile you will be given all the time you need to speak with the sorcerer." He jerked his head. "Take them away, disarm them, bind them and throw them in Drinij Bara's kennel."

As they were led away, Elric muttered: "We must escape and find that cat, but meanwhile we need not waste this opportunity to confer with Drinij Bara."

Drinij Bara said in the darkness: "No, Brother Sorcerer, I will not aid you. I will risk nothing until the cat and I are united."

"But Terarn Gashtek cannot threaten you any more."

"What if he recaptures the cat—what then?"

Elric was silent. He shifted his bound body uncomfortably on the hard boards of the wagon. He was about to continue his attempts at persuasion when the awning was thrown aside and he saw another trussed figure thrown towards them. Through the blackness he said in the Eastern tongue: "Who are you?"

The man replied in the language of the West: "I do not understand you."

"Are you, then, a Westerner?" asked Elric in the common speech.

"Yes—I am an Official Messenger from Karlaak. I was captured by these odorous jackals as I returned to the city."

"What? Are you the man we sent to Dyvim Slorm, my kinsman? I am Elric of Melniboné."

"My lord, are we all, then, prisoners? Oh, gods—Karlaak is truly lost."

"Did you get to Dyvim Slorm?"

"Aye—I caught up with him and his band. Luckily they were nearer to Karlaak than we suspected."

"And what was his answer to my request?"

"He said that a few young ones might be ready, but even with sorcery to aid him it would take some time to get to the Dragon Isle. There is a chance."

"A chance is all we need—but it will be no good unless we accomplish the rest of our plan. Somehow Drinij Bara's soul must be regained so that Terarn Gashtek cannot force him to defend the barbarians. There is one idea I have—a memory of an ancient kinship that we of Melniboné had for a being called Meerclar. Thank the gods that I discovered those drugs in Troos and I still have my strength. Now, I must call my sword to me."

He closed his eyes and allowed his mind and body first to relax completely and then concentrate on one single thing—the sword Stormbringer.

For years the evil symbiosis had existed between man and sword and the old attachments lingered.

He cried: "Stormbringer! Stormbringer, unite with your brother! Come, sweet runeblade, come hell-forged kinslayer, your master needs thee . . ."

Outside, it seemed that a wailing wind had suddenly sprung up. Elric heard shouts of fear and a whistling sound. Then the covering of the wagon was sliced apart to let in the starlight and the moaning blade quivered in the air over his head. He struggled upwards, already feeling nauseated at what he was about to do, but he was reconciled that he was not, this time, guided by self-interest but by the necessity to save the world from the barbarian menace.

"Give me thy strength, my sword," he groaned as his bound hands grasped the hilt. "Give my thy strength and let us hope it is for the last time."

The blade writhed in his hands and he felt an awful sensation as its power, the power stolen vampirelike, from a hundred brave men, flowed into his shuddering body.

He became possessed of a peculiar strength which was not by any means wholly physical. His white face twisted as he concentrated on controlling the new power and the blade, both of which threatened to possess him entirely. He snapped his bonds and stood up.

Barbarians were even now running towards the wagon. Swiftly he cut the leather ropes binding the others and, unconscious of the nearing warriors, called a different name.

He spoke a new tongue, an alien tongue which normally he could not remember. It was a language taught to the Sorcerer Kings of Melniboné, Elric's ancestors, even before the building of Imrryr, the Dreaming City, over ten thousand years previously.

"Meerclar of the Cats, it is I, your kinsman, Elric of Melniboné, last of the line that made vows of friendship with you and your people. Do you hear me, Lord of the Cats?"

*Far beyond the Earth, dwelling within a world set apart from the physical laws of space and time which governed the planet, glowing in a deep warmth of blue and amber, a manlike creature stretched itself and yawned, displaying tiny, pointed teeth. It pressed its head languidly against its furry shoulder—and listened.*

*The voice it heard was not that of one of its people, the kind he loved and protected. But he recognized the language. He smiled to himself as remembrance came and he felt the pleasant sensation of fellowship. He remembered a race which, unlike other humans (whom he disdained) had shared his qualities—a race which, like him, loved pleasure, cruelty and sophistication for its own sake. The race of Melnibonéans.*

*Meerclar, Lord of the Cats, Protector of the Feline Kind, projected himself gracefully towards the source of the voice.*

"*How may I aid thee?" he purred.*

"We seek one of your folk, Meerclar, who is somewhere close to here."

"*Yes, I sense him. What do you want of him?*"

"Nothing which is his—but he has two souls, one of them not his own."

"*That is so—his name is Fiarshern of the great family of Trrrechoww. I will call him. He will come to me.*"

Outside, the barbarians were striving to conquer their fear of the supernatural events taking place in the wagon. Terarn Gashtek cursed them: "There are five hundred thousand of us and a few of them. Take them now!"

His warriors began to move cautiously forward.

Fiarshern, the cat, heard a voice which it knew instinctively to be that of one which it would be foolish to disobey. It ran swiftly towards the source of that voice.

"Look—the cat—there it is. Seize it quickly."

Two of Terarn Gashtek's men jumped forward to do his bidding, but the little cat eluded them and leapt lightly into the wagon.

"*Give the human back its soul, Fiarshern*," said Meerclar softly. The cat moved towards its human master and dug its delicate teeth into the sorcerer's veins.

A moment later Drinij Bara laughed wildly. "My soul is mine again. Thank you, great Cat Lord. Let me repay you!"

"*There is no need*," smiled Meerclar mockingly, "*and, anyway, I perceive that your soul is already bartered. Goodbye, Elric of Melniboné. I was pleased to answer your call, though I see that you no longer follow the ancient pursuits of your fathers. Still, for the sake of old loyalties I do not begrudge you this service. Farewell, I go back to a warmer place than this inhospitable one."*

The Lord of the Cats faded and returned to the world of blue and amber warmth where he once more resumed his interrupted sleep.

"Come, Brother Sorcerer," cried Drinij Bara exultantly. "Let us take the vengeance which is ours."

He and Elric sprang from the wagon, but the two others were not quite so quick to respond.

Terarn Gashtek and his men confronted them. Many had bows with long arrows fitted to them.

"Shoot them down swiftly," yelled the Flame Bringer. "Shoot them now before they have time to summon further demons!"

A shower of arrows whistled towards them. Drinij Bara smiled, spoke a few words as he moved his hands almost carelessly. The arrows stopped in midflight, turned back and each uncannily found the throat of the man who had shot it. Terarn Gashtek gasped and wheeled back, pushing past his men and, as he retreated, shouted for them to attack the four.

Driven by the knowledge that if they fled they would be doomed, the great mass of barbarians closed in.

Dawn was bringing light to the cloud-ripped sky as Moonglum looked upwards. "Look, Elric," he shouted, pointing.

"Only five," said the albino. "Only five—but perhaps enough."

He parried several lashing blades on his own sword and, although he was possessed of superhuman strength, all the power seemed to have left the sword so that it was only as useful as an ordinary blade. Still fighting, he relaxed his body and felt the power leave him, flowing back into Stormbringer.

Again the runeblade began to whine and thirstily sought the throats and hearts of the savage barbarians.

Drinij Bara had no sword, but he did not need one, he was using subtler means to defend himself. All around him were the gruesome results, boneless masses of flesh and sinew.

The two sorcerers and Moonglum and the messenger forced their way through the half-insane barbarians who were desperately attempting to overcome them. In the confusion it was impossible to work out a coherent plan of action. Moonglum and the messenger grabbed scimitars from the corpses of the barbarians and joined in the battle.

Eventually, they had reached the outer limits of the camp. A whole mass of barbarians had fled, spurring their mounts westwards. Then Elric saw Terarn Gashtek, holding a bow. He saw the Flame Bringer's intention and shouted a warning to his fellow sorcerer who had his back to the barbarian. Drinij Bara, yelling some disturbing incantation, half-turned, broke off, attempted to begin another spell, but the arrow pierced his eye.

He screamed: "*No!*"

Then he died.

Seeing his ally slain, Elric paused and stared at the sky and the great wheeling beasts which he recognized.

Dyvim Slorm, son of Elric's cousin Dyvim Tvar the Dragon Master, had brought the legendary dragons of Imrryr to aid his kinsman. But most of the huge beasts slept, and would sleep for another century—only five dragons had been aroused. As yet, Dyvim Slorm could do nothing for fear of harming Elric and his comrades.

Terarn Gashtek, too, had seen the magnificent beasts. His grandiose plans of conquest were already fading and, thwarted, he ran towards Elric.

"You white-faced filth," he howled, "you have been responsible for all this—and you will pay the Flame Bringer's price!"

Elric laughed as he brought up Stormbringer to protect himself from the incensed barbarian. He pointed to the sky: "These, too, can be called Flame Bringers, Terarn Gashtek—and are better named than thou!"

Then he plunged the evil blade full into Terarn Gashtek's body and the barbarian gave a choking moan as his soul was drawn from him.

"Destroyer, I may be, Elric of Melniboné," he gasped, "but my way was cleaner than yours. May you and all you hold dear be cursed for eternity!"

Elric laughed, but his voice shook slightly as he stared at the barbarian's corpse. "I've rid myself of such curses once before, my friend. Yours will have little effect, I think." He paused. "By Arioch, I hope I'm right. I'd thought my fate cleansed of doom and curses, but perhaps I was wrong . . ."

The huge horde of barbarians was nearly all mounted now and fleeing westwards. They had to be stopped for, at the pace they were traveling, they would soon reach Karlaak and only the gods knew what they would do when they got to the unprotected city.

Above him, he heard the flapping of thirty-foot wings and scented the familiar smell of the great flying reptiles which had pursued him years before when he had led a reaver fleet on the attack of his home-city. Then he heard the curious notes of the Dragon Horn and saw that Dyvim Slorm was seated on the back of the leading beast, a long spearlike goad in his gauntleted right hand.

The dragon spiraled downward and its great bulk came to rest on the ground thirty feet away, its leathery wings folding back along its length. The Dragon Master waved to Elric.

"Greetings, King Elric, we barely managed to arrive in time I see."

"Time enough, kinsman," smiled Elric. "It is good to see the son of Dyvim Tvar again. I was afraid you might not answer my plea."

"Old scores were forgotten at the Battle of Bakshaan when my father Dyvim Tvar died aiding you in the siege of Nikorn's fortress. I regret only the younger beasts were ready to be awakened. You'll remember the others were used but a few years past."

"I remember," said Elric. "May I beg another favour Dyvim Slorm?"

"What is that?"

"Let me ride the chief dragon. I am trained in the arts of the

Dragon Master and have good reason for riding against the barbarians—we were forced to witness insensate carnage a while ago and may, perhaps, pay them back in their own coin."

Dyvim Slorm nodded and swung off his mount. The beast stirred restlessly and drew back the lips of its tapering snout to reveal teeth as thick as a man's arm, as long as a sword. Its forked tongue flickered and it turned its huge, cold eyes to regard Elric.

Elric sang to it in the old Melnibonéan speech, took the goad and the Dragon Horn from Dyvim Slorm and carefully climbed into the high saddle at the base of the dragon's neck. He placed his booted feet into the great silver stirrups.

"Now, fly, dragon brother," he sang, "up, up and have your venom ready."

He heard the snap of displaced air as the wings began to beat and then the great beast was clear of the ground and soaring upwards into the grey and brooding sky.

The other four dragons followed the first and, as he gained height, sounding specific notes on the horn to give them directions, he drew his sword from its scabbard.

Centuries before, Elric's ancestors had ridden their dragon steeds to conquer the whole of the Western World. There had been many more dragons in the Dragon Caves in those days. Now only a handful remained, and of those only the youngest had slept sufficiently long to be awakened.

High in the wintry sky climbed the huge reptiles and Elric's long white hair and stained black cloak flew behind him as he sang the exultant Song of the Dragon Masters and urged his charges westwards.

> Wild wind-horses soar the cloud-trails,
> Unholy horn doth sound its blast,
> You and we were first to conquer,
> You and we shall be the last!

Thoughts of love, of peace, of vengeance even were lost in that reckless sweeping across the glowering skies which hung over that ancient Age of the Young Kingdoms. Elric, archetypal, proud and disdainful in his knowledge that even his deficient blood was the blood of the Sorcerer Kings of Melniboné, became detached.

He had no loyalties then, no friends and, if evil possessed him, then it was a pure, brilliant evil, untainted by human drivings.

High soared the dragons until below them was the heaving black mass, marring the landscape, the fear-driven horde of barbarians who, in their ignorance, had sought to conquer the lands beloved of Elric of Melniboné.

"Ho, dragon brothers—loose your venom—burn—burn! And in your burning cleanse the world!"

Stormbringer joined in the wild shout and, diving, the dragons swept across the sky, down upon the crazed barbarians, shooting streams of combustible venom which water could not extinguish, and the stink of charred flesh drifted upwards through the smoke and flame so that the scene became a scene of hell—and proud Elric was a Lord of Demons reaping awful vengeance.

He did not gloat, for he had done only what was needed, that was all. He shouted no more but turned his dragon mount back and upward, sounding his horn and summoning the other reptiles to him. And as he climbed, the exultation left him and was replaced by cold horror.

I am still a Melnibonéan, he thought, and cannot rid myself of that whatever else I do. And, in my strength I am still weak, ready to use this cursed blade in any small emergency. With a shout of loathing, he flung the sword away, flung it into space. It screamed like a woman and went plummeting downwards towards the distant earth.

"There," he said, "it is done at last." Then, in calmer mood, he returned to where he had left his friends and guided his reptilian mount to the ground.

Dyvim Slorm said: "Where is the sword of your forefathers, King Elric?" But the albino did not answer, just thanked his kinsman for the loan of the dragon leader. Then they all remounted the dragons and flew back towards Karlaak to tell them the news.

Zarozinia saw her lord riding the first dragon and knew that Karlaak and the Western World were saved, the Eastern World avenged. His stance was proud but his face was grave as he went to meet her outside the city. She saw in him a return of an earlier sorrow which he had thought forgotten. She ran to him and he caught her in his arms, holding her close but saying nothing.

He bade farewell to Dyvim Slorm and his fellow Imrryrians and, with Moonglum and the messenger following at a distance, went into the city and thence to his house, impatient of the congratulations which the citizens showered upon him.

"What is it, my lord?" Zarozinia said as, with a sigh, he sprawled wearily upon the great bed. "Can speaking help?"

"I'm tired of swords and sorcery, Zarozinia, that is all. But at last I have rid myself once and for all of that hellblade which I had thought my destiny to carry always."

"Stormbringer you mean?"

"What else?"

She said nothing. She did not tell him of the sword which, apparently of its own volition, had come screaming into Karlaak and passed into the armoury to hang, in its old place, in darkness there.

He closed his eyes and drew a long, sighing breath.

"Sleep well, my lord," she said softly. With tearful eyes and a sad mouth she lay herself down beside him.

She did not welcome the morning.

# MISSION TO ASNO!

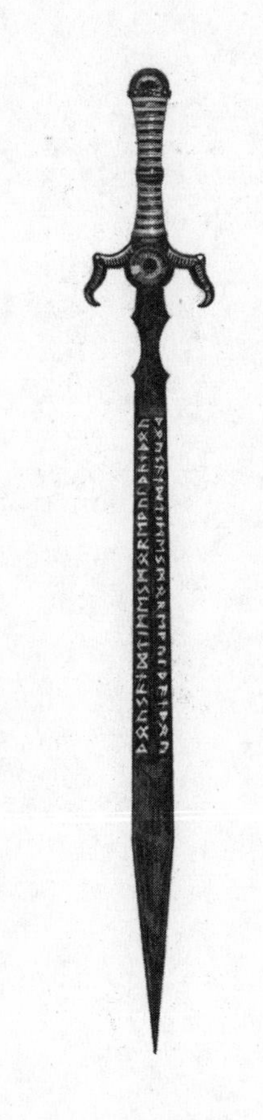

*But before Elric there was Sojan, first in the fanzines and then professionals. Here is the second appearance of Sojan, my first serial fantasy hero, in* Tarzan Weekly. *I make no apologies for its shortcomings or failures of prescience, etc. I was young, largely oblivious to my good fortune and thoroughly enjoying myself. But not quite as sophisticated as I liked to think . . .*

## MISSION TO ASNO!

(1957)

MOTORS PURRING, CAPTAINS shouting orders, the rustle of the canvas gun-covers being drawn back, gay flags, flashing steel, flying cloaks of many hues; a Hatnorian war-fleet rose rapidly into the sky.

On the deck of the flagship stood a tall, strong figure—that of Sojan, nicknamed "Shieldbearer," second in command to the great War Lord of Hatnor himself—Nornos Kad.

At his side was a long broadsword, upon his back his round shield; his right hand rested on the butt of his heavy air-pistol—an incredibly powerful weapon. Clad in a jerkin of sky-blue, a divided kilt of deep crimson and boots of dark leather, over his shoulder his leathern war-harness, he was the typical example of a Zylorian mercenary, whose love of bright garb was legendary.

The great war-fleet was destined for Asno—a country far to the north of Hatnor where the king, so the spies told, was raising an army of mercenaries to attack Yundrot—a colony of the Hatnorian Empire.

To stop a major war, Nornos Kad decided to send a mighty fleet to crush the attack before it started. Having other business, he assigned Sojan to take his place and instructed him to completely wipe out any signs of an attack.

Only too pleased at the chance of battle, Sojan had readily assented and was now on his way—the entire fleet under his command.

Soon the fleet was winging its way over Asno—a land of snow and ice, fierce beasts, great tracts of uninhabited ice-fields—uninhabited, that is, by *civilized* beings.

In another hour it would be over Boitil, the capital city.

"Gunners, take your positions!" Sojan roared through cupped hands and picking up a megaphone—for there was no radio on Zylor—shouted the same orders, which went from ship to ship until every gunner was seated in his seat, guns loaded and ready for firing.

"Drop two hundred feet!" Sojan roared again to the steersman, and repeated these orders to the other captains, who in turn shouted them to their own steersmen.

"Prepare hand weapons and fasten down loose fixtures, check gas-bag coverings, every man to position!" Sojan shouted when the ships had all dropped two hundred feet.

"Slow speed!" The ships slowed into "second-speed."

In Zylorian naval terms there are five speeds: "Speed No. 1" is fastest possible, "Speed No. 2" is a fifth of this slower, and so on. When a commander gives the order to slow when traveling at Speed No. 1, the ship automatically adjusts to Speed No. 2; if going at No. 2 and told to slow, it changes to No. 3.

Now they were over the outskirts of the city, dropping lower and lower until Sojan thought that they would touch the very towers of Boitil, scanning the squares and flying-fields for signs of the army. Halfway over the city a message was passed to Sojan that a great army camp had been spotted—just on the outskirts of the city. At the same time someone yelled for him to look, and doing so he saw that a fleet almost as large as his own was rising from flying-fields all over the vast city.

"Prepare for battle!" he shouted.

As one, the safety catches of the guns were pushed off.

"Shoot as you will!" Sojan ordered.

There was a muffled "pop" and the hiss of escaping air as the explosive shells of the Hatnorian craft were sent on their mission of destruction. Almost at once the enemy retaliated.

Two Hatnorian ships, one only slightly damaged, the other a mass of roaring yellow and blue flame, dropped earthwards.

For twelve hours the great air-battle was fought, developing into ship-to-ship duels as the opposing sides became mixed. Bit by bit the battle moved southwards until it was over the great ice wastes.

But expert handling of their craft, superior marksmanship and a slightly superior weight of numbers on the part of the Hatnorian fleet was slowly but surely weakening the Asnogian fleet. Sojan, now with a gun mounted on the officer's platform, was taking an active part in the battle. His uncanny ability to hit almost whatever he aimed at was taking great toll. Everywhere ships were hurtling earthwards, crashing in an inferno of flame, or merely bouncing gently when a gas-bag was only slightly punctured.

At last, one by one, the enemy began to flee. The other ships, seeing their companions escape, disengaged and followed them. The hired ships, manned mainly by mercenaries, flew in every direction but that of Asno, while the Asnogian craft turned and headed for their home base. In this direction went the Hatnorian fleet, re-forming to a close formation and turning to No. 1 speed. If they overtook a ship it was ruthlessly shot down; but half a dozen or so were lucky and escaped them. In three hours they were back over Asno and bombing the troop encampment with incendiaries until nothing remained of the great camp but smouldering fabric and twisted steel. Through the south gate of the city streamed forth ragged bands of hired soldiers, bent on escaping while they could. The planned attack on a Hatnorian colony had not even begun. A just reprisal on Nornos Kad's part. A reprisal carried out in full by Sojan. But his business was not finished and, landing on part of an undamaged airfield, Sojan ordered the frightened commanding officer to take him to King Tremorn of Asno.

"I bring a message from my Emperor!" he cried when he was in the vast chamber which housed the king's court. All around him stood courtiers and servants, worried and anxious to hear his terms. Great pillars supported the roof and brilliant tapestries hung from the ceiling. Murals on the walls depicted scenes of battles, on land, water and in the air.

"Speak your message," ordered the king. "What are your terms? I admit that I am beaten! For the present!" he added.

"For all time, sir, while a member of the Nornos family sits on the throne of Hatnor!" Sojan replied. "Now, do you wish to hear my terms?"

"Speak!"

"The first is that you acknowledge allegiance to Hatnor and pay a tribute of five hundred young men to train in our armies every tenth year. The second is that you disband any army you still have, save for policing your city. On signs of attack, you will notify the Empire, who will come to your aid. As a member of the Empire you will be subject to all laws and trading terms of the Empire and in times of major war shall enlist two-thirds of your fighting strength in the armies of Hatnor and the remaining third if called upon. You will not make warships or weapons of war, save hand weapons, for your own use, but all warships and arms shall be sent direct to the capital. Do you recognize these terms?"

The king paused and, turning to his *major domo*, whispered a few words to him. The man nodded.

"Yes, I recognize your terms," he sighed.

"Then sign your name and oath to this document and seal it with your royal seal. Upon the breaking of your word, the lapse shall be punished according to the magnitude."

Sojan handed the paper to a courtier who carried it to the king. The act of bowing to a king is unknown upon the planet Zylor, instead the subject places his right hand upon his heart to signify complete allegiance.

So it was that Sojan achieved his purpose. But more adventures were yet to come before he could return to his palace at Hatnor.

# ORIGINS

*Early artwork associated with Elric's first appearances in magazines and books*

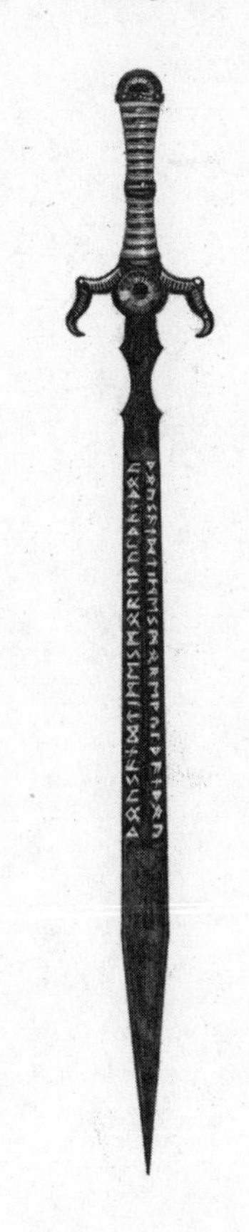

Title page illustration by James Cawthorn, for "Mission to Asno!" *Tarzan Adventures*, vol. 7, no. 25, September 1957.

Cover artwork by Eric Parker, for "The Affair of the Bronze Basilisk," *Sexton Blake Library*, 3rd series, no. 49, June 1943; this was Monsieur Zenith the Albino's very last story.

Cover artwork by Brian Lewis, for "The Dreaming City," *Science Fantasy*, vol. 16, no. 47, June 1961; this was Elric of Melniboné's very first story.

Cover artwork by James Cawthorn, for "The Flame Bringers," *Science Fantasy*, vol. 19, no. 55, October 1962.

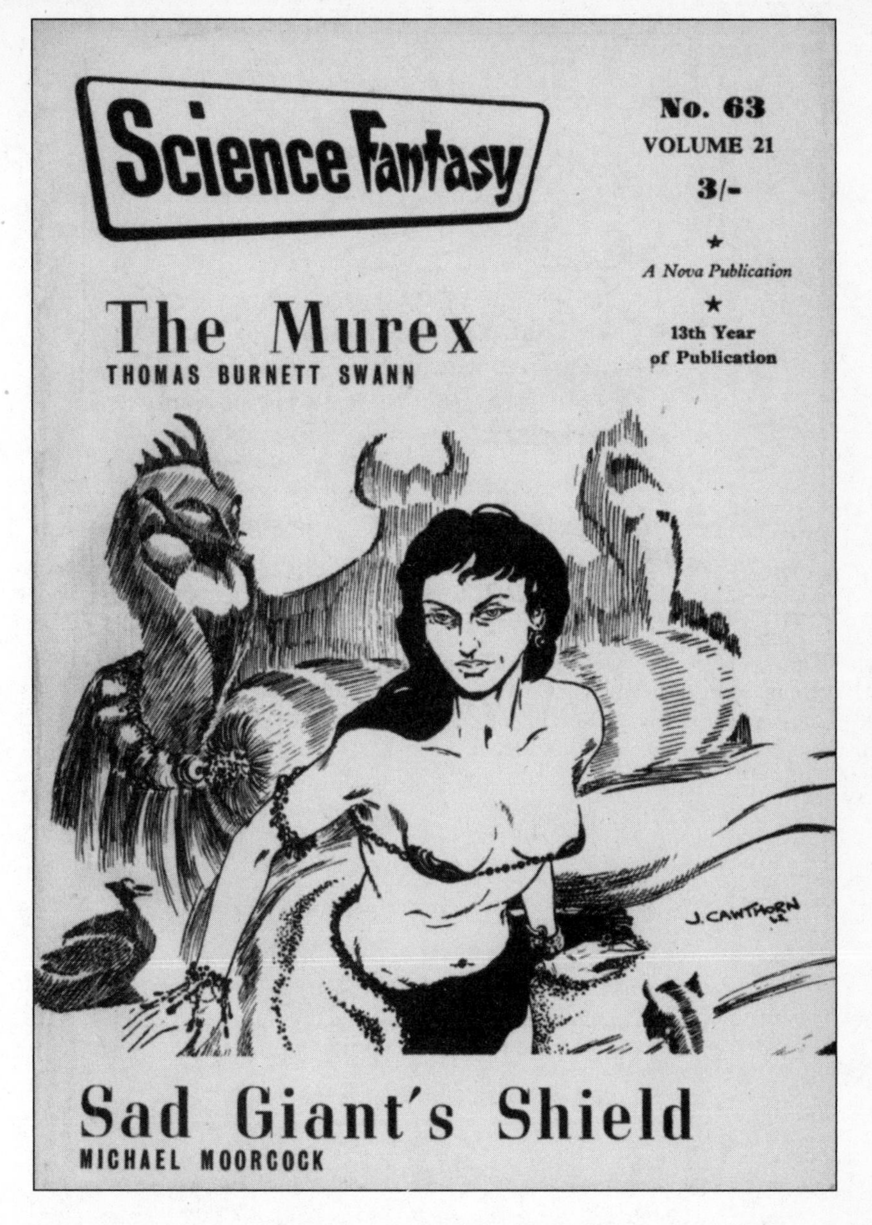


Cover artwork by James Cawthorn, for "Sad Giant's Shield," *Science Fantasy*, vol. 21, no. 63, February 1964.

"The Age of the Young Kingdoms" map by James Cawthorn, 1962; first published accompanying "The Singing Citadel," in *The Fantastic Swordsmen*, edited by L. Sprague de Camp, Pyramid Books, 1967.

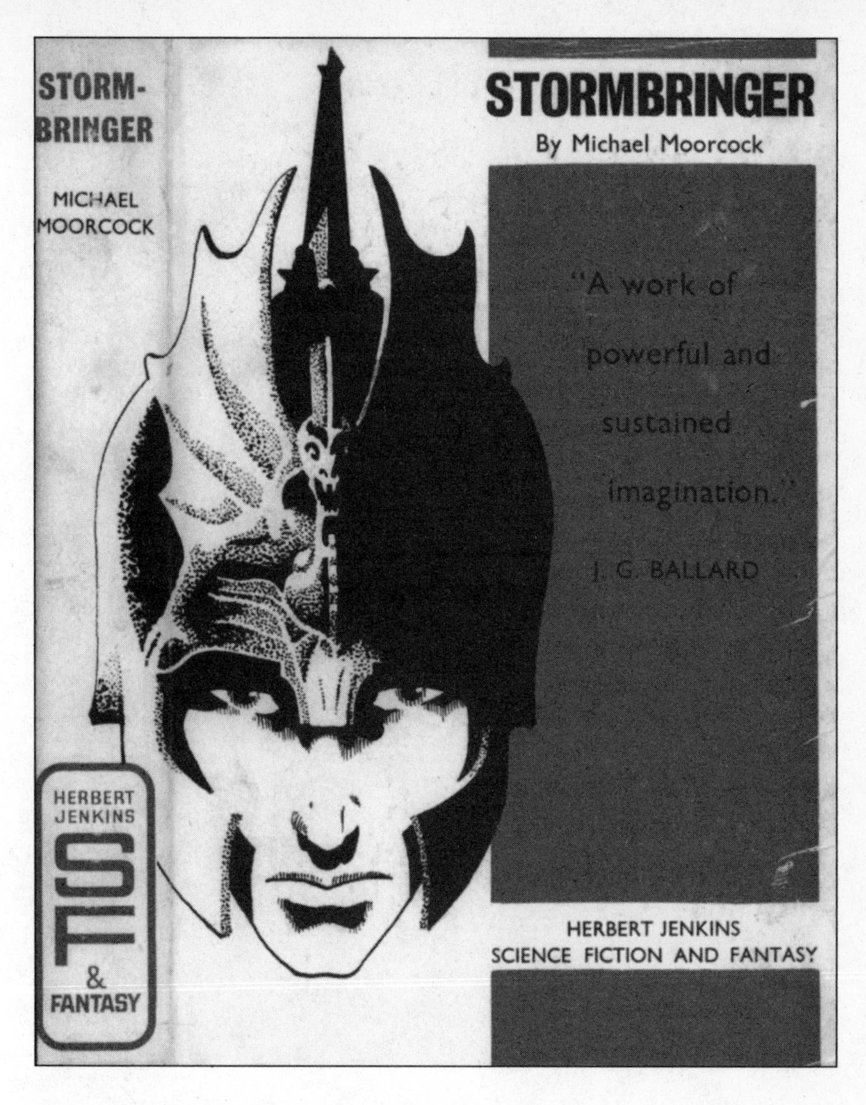


Cover artwork by James Cawthorn, for *Stormbringer*, first edition, Herbert Jenkins, 1965.

# STORMBRINGER

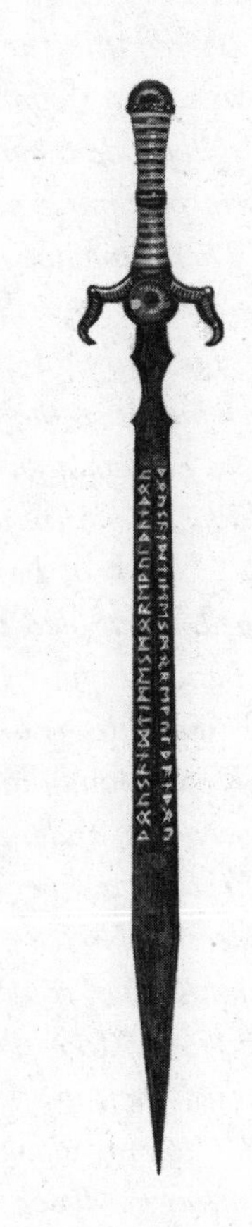

*To our great surprise, the series was hugely popular with readers. Ted Carnell, still at a point where I think he was trying anything to get the magazine's circulation back up, commissioned an Elric serial. We planned four quasi-independent episodes, separately titled, which would fit together and become a novel, though any story could be read individually. Then came the news from Ted that the magazines were going under unless buyers could be found. He, at any rate, had found a new job editing a quarterly SF anthology* New Writings in SF. *We would run the final Elric story in the final issue of* Science Fantasy, *even though it meant also featuring my more New Wave story "The Deep Fix" under the James Colvin name and cutting short my "Aspects of Fantasy" series. No more Elric stories in future, I sighed. I was glad I'd had a chance to finish the series with a bit of a bang. Happily Compact Books bought the titles, and* New Worlds *went to me and* Science Fantasy *to the heroic-fantasy-hating Kyril Bonfiglioli, a friend of mine. Friendship didn't come between Bon and his ferocious dislike of the burgeoning genre. Asked if he'd like a supernatural adventure story in his new start-up, he shuddered. "No way, Mike. I would wather take cyanide," he lisped with his usual courtesy. He saw Lovecraft and Peake as the same: "All wight, Mike, if you like your dahkness* uttah!*" he would add in his over-the-top affected voice, fixing himself another whisky and milk ("foh my ulcah . . ." he explained). So Elric appeared in book form, in hardback in the UK and paperback in the United States. Eventually new stories were commissioned. But not for a while. For quite some time, these were all there were, with* Stormbringer *trimmed to fit the page requirements of the book publisher who still had circulating libraries as a main customer. That was another reason for returning to the orig-*

*inal magazine narrative which appears here pretty much as it did in the early 1960s. At the time the first stories were being published comment about them was appearing almost as swiftly as it might these days on the web, via the great network of fanzines which, while mainly produced in the United States and UK also appeared in Italy, Switzerland, France, Germany, Scandinavia, Japan and elsewhere.*

*For J. G. Ballard, whose enthusiasm for Elric gave me encouragement to begin this particular book, my first attempt at a full-length novel, and for Jim Cawthorn, whose illustrations based on my ideas in turn gave me inspiration for certain scenes in this book, and for Dave Britton, who kept the magazines in which the serial first appeared and who kindly loaned them to me so that I could restore this novel to its original shape and length.*

*So far, the earlier Elric stories have dealt with his random and rather aimless wanderings in the ancient world, but, in fact, they were all part of a larger pattern which begins to become apparent in the following novelette. It is the beginning of the big battle between Order and Chaos.*

*—John Carnell, SCIENCE FANTASY No. 59, June 1963*

## Prologue

THERE CAME A time when there was great movement upon the Earth and above it, when the destiny of Men and Gods was hammered out upon the forge of Fate, when monstrous wars were brewed and mighty deeds were designed. And there rose up in this time, which was called the Age of the Young Kingdoms, heroes. Greatest of these heroes was a doom-driven adventurer who bore a crooning runeblade that he loathed.

His name was Elric of Melniboné, king of ruins, lord of a scattered race that had once ruled the ancient world. Elric, sorcerer and swordsman, slayer of kin, despoiler of his homeland, white-faced albino, last of his line.

Elric, who had come to Karlaak by the Weeping Waste and had married a wife in whom he found some peace, some surcease from the torment in him.

And Elric, who had within him a greater destiny than he knew, now dwelt in Karlaak with Zarozinia, his wife, and his sleep was troubled, his dream dark, one brooding night in the Month of Anemone . . .

## BOOK ONE

# DEAD GOD'S HOMECOMING

In which, at long last, Elric's fate begins to be revealed to him as the forces of Law and Chaos gather strength for the final battle which will decide the future of Elric's world . . .

## Chapter One

ABOVE THE ROLLING Earth great clouds tumbled down and bolts of lightning charged groundwards to slash the midnight black, split trees in twain and sear through roofs that cracked and broke.

The dark mass of forest trembled with the shock and out of it crept six hunched, unhuman figures who paused to stare beyond the low hills towards the outline of a city. It was a city of squat walls and slender spires, of graceful towers and domes; and it had a name which the leader of the creatures knew. Karlaak by the Weeping Waste it was called.

Not of natural origin, the storm was ominous. It groaned around the city of Karlaak as the creatures skulked past the open gates and made their way through shadows towards the elegant palace where Elric slept. The leader raised an axe of black iron in its clawed hand. The group came to a stealthy halt and regarded the sprawling palace which lay on a hill surrounded by languorously scented gardens. The earth shook as lightning lashed it and thunder prowled across the turbulent sky.

"Chaos has aided us in this matter," the leader grunted. "See—already the guards fall in magic slumber and our entrance is thus made simple. The Lords of Chaos are good to their servants."

He spoke the truth. Some supernatural force had been at work and the warriors guarding Elric's palace had dropped to the ground, their snores echoing the thunder. The servants of Chaos crept past the prone guards, into the main courtyard and from there into the darkened palace. Unerringly they climbed twisting staircases, moved softly along gloomy corridors, to arrive at length outside the room where Elric and his wife lay in uneasy sleep.

As the leader laid a hand upon the door, a voice cried out from within the room: "*What's this? What things of hell disrupt my rest?*"

"He sees us!" sharply whispered one of the creatures.

"No," the leader said, "he sleeps—but such a sorcerer as this Elric is not so easily lulled into a stupor. We had best make speed and do our work, for if he wakes it will be the harder!"

He twisted the handle and eased the door open, his axe half raised. Beyond the bed, heaped with tumbled furs and silks, lightning gashed the night again, showing the white face of the albino close to that of his dark-haired wife.

Even as they entered, he rose stiffly in the bed and his crimson eyes opened, staring out at them. For a moment the eyes were glazed and then the albino forced himself awake, shouting: "Begone, you creatures of my dreams!"

The leader cursed and leapt forward, but he had been instructed not to slay this man. He raised the axe threateningly.

"Silence—your guards cannot aid you!"

Elric jumped from the bed and grasped the thing's wrist, his face close to the fanged muzzle. Because of his albinism he was physically weak and required magic to give him strength. But so quickly did he move, that he had wrested the axe from the creature's hand and smashed the shaft between its eyes. Snarling, it fell back, but its comrades jumped forward. There were five of them, huge muscles moving beneath their furred skins.

Elric clove the skull of the first as others grappled with him. His body was spattered with the thing's blood and brains and he gasped in disgust at the foetid stuff. He managed to wrench his arm away and bring the axe up and down into the collarbone of another. But then he felt his legs gripped and he fell, confused but still battling. Then there came a great blow on his head and pain blazed through him. He made an effort to rise, failed and fell back insensible.

Thunder and lightning still disturbed the night when, with throbbing head, he awoke and got slowly to his feet using a bedpost as support. He stared dazedly around him.

Zarozinia was gone. The only other figure in the room was the stiff corpse of the beast he had killed. His black-haired girl-wife had been abducted.

Shaking, he went to the door and flung it open, calling for his guards, but none answered him.

His runesword Stormbringer hung in the city's armoury and would take time to get. His throat tight with pain and anger, he ran down the corridors and stairways, dazed with anxiety, trying to grasp the implications of his wife's disappearance.

Above the palace, thunder still crashed, eddying about in the noisy night. The palace seemed deserted and he had the sudden feeling that he was completely alone, that he had been abandoned. But as he ran out into the main courtyard and saw the insensible guards he realized at once that their slumber could not be natural. Realization was coming even as he ran through the gardens, through the gates and down to the city, but there was no sign of his wife's abductors.

Where had they gone?

He raised his eyes to the shouting sky, his white face stark and twisted with frustrated anger. There was no sense to it. Why had they taken her? He had enemies, he knew, but none who could summon such supernatural help. Who, apart from himself, could work this mighty sorcery that made the skies themselves shake and a city sleep?

To the house of Lord Voashoon, Chief Senator of Karlaak and father of Zarozinia, Elric ran panting like a wolf. He banged with his fists upon the door, yelling at the astonished servants within.

"Open! It is Elric. Hurry!"

The doors gaped back and he was through them. Lord Voashoon

came stumbling down the stairs into the chamber, his face heavy with sleep.

"What is it, Elric?"

"Summon your warriors. Zarozinia has been abducted. Those who took her were demons and may be far from here by now—but we must search in case they escaped by land."

Lord Voashoon's face became instantly alert and he shouted terse orders to his servants between listening to Elric's explanation of what had happened.

"And I must have entrance into the armoury," Elric concluded. "I must have Stormbringer!"

"But you renounced the blade for fear of its evil power over you!" Lord Voashoon reminded him quietly.

Elric replied impatiently. "Aye—but I renounced the blade for Zarozinia's sake, too. I must have Stormbringer if I am to bring her back. The logic is simple. Quickly, give me the key."

In silence Lord Voashoon fetched the key and led Elric to the armoury where the weapons and armour of his ancestors were held, unused for centuries. Through the dusty place strode Elric to a dark alcove that seemed to contain something which lived.

He heard a soft moaning from the great black battle-blade as he reached out a slim-fingered white hand to take it. It was heavy, yet perfectly balanced, a two-handed broadsword of prodigious size, with its wide crosspiece and its blade smooth and broad, stretching for over five feet from the hilt. Near the hilt, mystic runes were engraved and even Elric did not know what they fully signified.

"Again I must make use of you, Stormbringer," he said as he buckled the sheath about his waist, "and I must conclude that we are too closely linked now for less than death to separate us."

With that he was striding from the armoury and back to the courtyard where mounted guards were already sitting nervous steeds, awaiting his instructions.

Standing before them, he drew Stormbringer so that the sword's strange, black radiance flickered around him, his white face, as pallid as bleached bone, staring out of it at the horsemen.

"You go to chase demons this night. Search the countryside, scour forest and plain for those who have done this thing to our princess! Though it's likely that her abductors used supernatural means to make their escape, we cannot be sure. So search—and search well!"

All through the raging night they searched but could find no trace of either the creatures or Elric's wife. And when dawn came, a smear of blood in the morning sky, his men returned to Karlaak where Elric awaited them, now filled with the nigromantic vitality which his sword supplied.

"Lord Elric—shall we retrace our trail and see if daylight yields a clue?" cried one.

"He does not hear you," another murmured as Elric gave no sign.

But then Elric turned his pain-racked head and he said bleakly, "Search no more. I have had time to meditate and must seek my wife with the aid of sorcery. Disperse. You can do nothing further."

Then he left them and went back towards his palace, knowing that there was still one way of learning where Zarozinia had been taken. It was a method which he ill-liked, yet it would have to be employed.

Curtly, upon returning, Elric ordered everyone from his chamber, barred the door and stared down at the dead thing. Its congealed blood was still on him, but the axe with which he had slain it had been taken away by its comrades.

Elric prepared the body, stretching out its limbs on the floor. He drew the shutters of the windows so that no light filtered into the room, and lit a brazier in one corner. It swayed on its chains as the oil-soaked rushes flared. He went to a small chest by the window and took out a pouch. From this he removed a bunch of dried herbs and with a hasty gesture flung them on the brazier so that it gave off a sickly odour and the room began to fill with smoke. Then he stood over the corpse, his body rigid, and began to sing an incantation in the old language of his forefathers, the Sorcerer Emperors of Melniboné. The song seemed scarcely akin to human speech, rising and falling from a deep groan to a high-pitched shriek.

The brazier speared flaring red light over Elric's face and grotesque shadows skipped about the room. On the floor the dead corpse began to stir, its ruined head moving from side to side. Elric drew his runesword and placed it before him, his two hands on the hilt. "Arise, soulless one!" he commanded.

Slowly, with jerky movements, the creature raised itself stiffly upright and pointed a clawed finger at Elric, its glazed eyes staring as if beyond him.

"All this," it whispered, "was pre-ordained. Think not that you can escape your fate, Elric of Melniboné. You have tampered with my corpse and I am a creature of Chaos. My masters will avenge me."

"How?"

"Your destiny is already laid down. You will know soon enough."

"Tell me, dead one, why did you come to abduct my wife? Who sent you hither? Where has my wife been taken?"

"Three questions, Lord Elric. Requiring three answers. You know that the dead who have been raised by sorcery can answer nothing directly."

"Aye—that I know. So answer as you can."

"Then listen well for I may recite only once my rede and then must return to the nether regions where my being may peacefully rot to nothing. Listen:

"Beyond the ocean brews a battle;
Beyond the battle blood shall fall.
If Elric's kinsman ventures with him
(Bearing a twin of that he bears)
To a place where, man-forsaken,
Dwells the one who should not live,
Then a bargain shall be entered.
Elric's wife shall be restored."

With this the thing fell to the floor and did not stir thereafter.

Elric went to the window and opened the shutters. Used as he was to enigmatic verse-omens, this one was difficult to unravel. As daylight entered the room, the rushes sputtered and the smoke faded. *Beyond the ocean* . . . There were many oceans.

He resheathed his runesword and climbed onto the disordered bed to lie down and contemplate the rede. At last, after long minutes of this contemplation, he remembered something he had heard from a traveler who had come to Karlaak, from Tarkesh, a nation of the Western Continent, beyond the Pale Sea.

The traveler had told him how there was trouble brewing between the land of Dharijor and the other nations of the West. Dharijor had contravened treaties she had signed with her neighbouring kingdoms and had signed a new one with the Theocrat of Pan Tang. Pan Tang was an unholy island dominated by its dark aristocracy of warrior-wizards. It was from here that Elric's old enemy, Theleb K'aarna, had come. Its capital of Hwamgaarl was called the City of Screaming Statues and until recently its residents had had little contact with the folk of the outside world. Jagreen Lern was the new Theocrat and an ambitious man. His alliance with Dharijor could only mean that he sought more power over the nations of the Young Kingdoms. The traveler had said that strife was sure to break out at any moment since there was ample evidence that Dharijor and Pan Tang had entered a war alliance.

Now, as his memory improved, Elric related this information with the news he had had recently that Queen Yishana of Jharkor, a neighbouring kingdom to Dharijor, had recruited the aid of Dyvim Slorm and his Imrryrian mercenaries. And Dyvim Slorm was Elric's only kinsman. This meant that Jharkor must be preparing for battle against Dharijor. The two facts were too closely linked with the prophecy to be ignored.

Even as he thought upon it, he was gathering his clothes together and preparing for a journey. There was nothing for it but to go to Jharkor and speedily, for there he was sure to meet his kinsman. And there, also, there would soon be a battle if all the evidence were true.

Yet the prospect of the journey, which would take many days, caused a cold ache to grow in his heart as he thought of the weeks to come in which he would not know how his wife fared.

"No time for that," he told himself as he laced up his black quilted jacket. "Action is all that's required of me now—and speedy action."

He held the sheathed runeblade before him, staring beyond it into space. "I swear by Arioch that those who have done this, whether they be man or immortal, shall suffer from their deed. Hear me, Arioch! That is my oath!"

But his words found no answer and he sensed that Arioch, his patron demon, had either not heard him or else heard his oath and was unmoved.

Then he was striding from the death-heavy chamber, yelling for his horse.

## Chapter Two

Where the Sighing Desert gave way to the borders of Ilmiora, between the coasts of the Eastern Continent and the lands of Tarkesh, Dharijor, Jharkor and Shazaar, there lay the Pale Sea.

It was a cold sea, a morose and chilling sea, but ships preferred to cross from Ilmiora to Dharijor by means of it, rather than chance the weirder dangers of the Straits of Chaos which were lashed by eternal storms and inhabited by malevolent sea-creatures.

On the deck of an Ilmioran schooner, Elric of Melniboné stood wrapped in his cloak, shivering and staring gloomily at the cloud-covered sky.

The captain, a stocky man with blue, humorous eyes, came struggling along the deck towards him. He had a cup of hot wine in his hands. He steadied himself by clinging to a piece of rigging and gave the cup to Elric.

"Thanks," said the albino gratefully. He sipped the wine. "How soon before we make the port of Banarva, captain?"

The captain pulled the collar of his leather jerkin about his unshaven face. "We're sailing slow, but we should sight the Tarkesh peninsula well before sunset." Banarva was in Tarkesh, one of its chief trading posts. The captain leaned on the rail. "I wonder how long these waters will be free for ships now that war's broken out between the kingdoms of the West. Both Dharijor and Pan Tang have been notorious in the past for their piratical activities. They'll soon extend them under the guise of war, I'll warrant."

Elric nodded vaguely, his mind on other things than the prospect of piracy.

Disembarking in the chilly evening at the port of Banarva, Elric soon saw ample evidence that war darkened the lands of the Young Kingdoms. There were rumours rife, talk of nothing but battles gained and warriors lost. From the confused gossip, he could get no clear impression of how the war went, save that the decisive battle was yet to be fought.

Loquacious Banarvans told him that all over the Western Continent men were marching. From Myyrrhn, he heard, the winged men were flying. From Jharkor, the White Leopards, Queen Yishana's personal guard, ran towards Dharijor, while Dyvim Slorm and his mercenaries pressed northwards to meet them.

Dharijor was the strongest nation of the West and Pan Tang was a formidable ally, more for her people's occult knowledge than for her numbers. Next in power to Dharijor came Jharkor, who, with her allies Tarkesh, Myyrrhn and Shazaar, was still not as strong as those who threatened the security of the Young Kingdoms.

For some years Dharijor had sought an opportunity for conquest and the hasty alliance against her had been made in an effort to stop her before she had fully prepared for conquest. Whether this effort would succeed, Elric did not know, and those who spoke to him were equally uncertain.

The streets of Banarva were packed with soldiers and supply trains of horses and oxen. The harbour was filled with warships and it was difficult to find lodgings since most inns and many private houses had been requisitioned by the army. And it was the same all over the Western Continent. Everywhere, men strapped metal about them, bestrode heavy chargers, sharpened their arms, and rode beneath bright silken banners to slay and to despoil.

Here, without doubt, Elric reflected, he would find the battle of the prophecy. He tried to forget his tormented longing for news of Zarozinia and turned his moody eyes towards the west. Stormbringer hung like an anchor at his side and he fingered it constantly, hating it even as it fed him his vitality.

He spent the night in Banarva and by morning had hired a good horse and was riding through the sparse grassland towards Jharkor.

Across a war-torn world rode Elric, his crimson eyes burning with a fierce anger at the sights of wanton destruction he witnessed. Although he had himself lived by his sword for many years and had committed acts of murder, robbery and urbicide, he disliked the senselessness of wars such as this, of men who killed one another for only the vaguest of reasons. It was not that he pitied the slain or hated the slayers; he was too remote from ordinary men to care greatly about what they did. Yet, in his own tortured way, he was an idealist who, because he lacked peace and security himself, resented the sights of strife which the war brought to him. His ancestors, he knew, had also been remote, yet they had delighted in the conflicts of the men of the Young Kingdoms, observing them from a distance and judging themselves above such activities; above the morass of sentiment and emotion in which these new men struggled. For ten thousand years the Sorcerer Emperors of Melniboné had ruled this world, a race without conscience or moral creed, unneedful of reasons for their acts of conquest, seeking no excuses for their natural malicious tendencies. But Elric, the last in the direct line of emperors, was not like them. He was capable of cruelty and malevolent sorcery, had little pity, yet could love and hate more violently than ever his ancestors. And these strong passions, perhaps, had been the cause of his breaking with his homeland and traveling the world to compare himself against these new men since he could find none in Melniboné who shared his feelings. And it was because of these twin forces of love and hate that he had returned to have vengeance on his cousin Yyrkoon who had put Cymoril, Elric's betrothed, into a magic slumber and usurped the kingship of Melniboné, the Dragon Isle, the last territory of the fallen Bright Empire. With the aid of a fleet of reavers, Elric had razed Imrryr in his vengeance-taking, destroyed the Dreaming City and scattered for ever the race who had founded it so that the last survivors were now mercenaries roaming the world to sell their arms to whoever bid highest. Love and hate; they had led him to kill Yyrkoon who deserved death and, inadvertently, Cymoril, who did not. Love and hate. They welled in him now as bitter smoke stung his throat and he passed a straggling group of townspeople who were fleeing, without knowledge of their direction, from the latest depredation of the roving Dharijorian troops who had struck far into this part of Tarkesh and had met little hindrance from the armies of King Hilran of Tarkesh whose main force was concentrated further north, readying itself for the major battle.

Now Elric rode close to the Western Marches, near the Jharkorian border. Here lived sturdy foresters and harvesters in better times. But now the forests were blackened and burned and the crops of the fields were ruined.

His journey, which was speedy for he wasted no time, took him through one of the stark forests where remnants of trees cast cold silhouettes against the grey, seething sky. He raised the hood of his cloak over his head so that the heavy black fabric completely hid his face, and rode on as rain rushed suddenly down and beat through the skeleton trees, sweeping across the distant plains beyond so that all the world seemed grey and black with the hiss of the rain a constant and depressing sound.

Then, as he passed a ruined hovel which was half cottage and half hole in the earth, a cawing voice called out:

"*Lord Elric!*"

Astonished that he should be recognized, he turned his bleak face in the direction of the voice, pushing his hood back as he did so. A ragged figure appeared in the hole's opening. It beckoned him closer. Puzzled, he walked his horse towards the figure and saw that it was an old man, or perhaps a woman, he couldn't tell.

"You know my name. How?"

"Thou art a legend throughout the Young Kingdoms. Who could not recognize that white face and heavy blade thou art carrying?"

"True, perhaps, but I have a notion there is more to this than chance recognition. Who are you and how do you know the High Speech of Melniboné?" Elric deliberately used the coarse common speech.

"Thou shouldst know that all who practise dark sorcery use the High Tongue of those who are past masters in its arts. Wouldst thou guest with me a while?"

Elric looked at the hovel and shook his head. He was fastidious at the best of times. The wretch smiled and made a mock bow, resorting to the common speech and saying: "So the mighty lord disd fle and will, we can see none of the bigger conflict save for a few arce related details.”

“hat may be so,” said Elric impatiently, “but I'm greatly angered t being involved and require my wife's release. I have no notion why we, together, must make the bargain for her return, neither can I guess what it is we have that those who captured her want. But, if the omens are sent by the same agents, then we had best do as we are told, for the meantime, until we can see matters more clearly. Then, perhaps, we can act upon our *own* volition.”

“That's wise,” Dyvim Slorm nodded, “and I'm with you in it.” He smiled slightly and added: “Whether I like it or not, I fancy.”

Elric said: “Where lies the main army of Dharijor and Pan Tang? I heard it was gathering.”

“It has gathered—and marches closer. The impending battle will decide who rules the Western lands. I'm committed to Yishana's side, not only because she has employed us to aid her, but because I felt that if the warped lords of Pan Tang dominate these nations, then tyranny will come upon them and they will threaten the security of the whole world. It is a sad thing when a Melnibonéan has to consider such problems.” He smiled ironically. “Aside from that, I like them not, these sorcerous upstarts—they seek to emulate the Bright Empire.”

“Aye,” Elric said. “They are an island culture, as ours was. They are sorcerers and warriors as our ancestors were. But their sorcery is less healthy than ever ours was. Our ancestors committed frightful deeds, yet it was *natural* to them. These newcomers, more human than we, have perverted their humanity whereas we never possessed it in the same degree. There will never be another Bright Empire, nor can their power last more than ten thousand years. This is a fresh age, Dyvim Slorm, in more than one way. The time of subtle sorcery is on the wane. Men are finding new means of harnessing natural power.”

“Our knowledge is ancient,” Dyvim Slorm agreed, “yet, so old is it that it has little relation to present events, I think. Our logic and learning are suited to the past . . .”



dains to grace my poor home. But does he not perhaps wonder why the fire which raged through this forest a while ago did not, in fact, harm me?”

“Aye,” said Elric thoughtfully, “that is an interesting riddle.”

The hag took a step towards him. “Soldiers came not a month gone—from Pan Tang they were. Devil Riders with their hunting tigers running with them. They despoiled the harvest and burned even the forests that those who fled them might not eat game or berries here. I lived in this forest all my life, doing a little simple magic and prophecy for my needs. But when I saw the walls of flame soon to engulf me, I cried the name of a demon I knew—a thing from Chaos which, latterly, I had dared not summon. It came.

“ ‘Save me,’ I cried, ‘And what would ye do in return?’ said the demon. ‘Anything,’ I quoth. ‘Then bear this message for my masters,’ it said. ‘When the kinslayer known as Elric of Melniboné shall pass this way, tell him that there is one kinsman he shall not slay and he will be found in Sequaloris. If Elric loves his wife, he will play his role. If he plays it well, his wife shall be returned.’ So I fixed the message in my mind and now give it thee as I swore.”

“Thanks,” said Elric, “and what did you give in the first place for the power to summon such a demon?”

“Why, my soul, of course. But it was an old one and not of much worth. Hell could be no worse than this existence.”

“Then why did you not let yourself burn, your soul unbartered?”

“I wish to live,” said the wretch, smiling again. “Oh, life is good. My own life, perhaps, is squalid, yet the life around me, that is what I love. But let me not keep you, my lord, for you have weightier matters on your mind.” Once more the wretch gave a mock bow as Elric rode off, puzzled, but encouraged. His wife still lived and was safe. But what bargain must he strike before he could get her back?

Savagely he goaded his horse into a gallop, heading for Sequaloris in Jharkor. Behind him, faintly through the beating rain, he heard a cackling at once mocking and miserable.

Now his direction was not so vague, and he rode at great speed, but cautiously, avoiding the roving bands of invaders, until at length the arid plains gave way to the lusher wheatlands of the Sequa province of Jharkor. Another day's ride and Elric entered the small walled city of Sequaloris which had so far not suffered attack. Here, he discovered preparations for war and learned news that was of greater interest to him.

The Imrryrian mercenaries, led by Dyvim Slorm, Elric's cousin and son of Dyvim Tvar, Elric's old friend, were due to arrive next day in Sequaloris.

There had been a certain enmity between Elric and the Imrryrians since the albino had been the direct cause of their need to leave the ruins of the Dreaming City and live as mercenaries. But those times were past, long since, and on two previous occasions he and the Imrryrians had fought on the same side. He was their leader by right and the ties of tradition were strong in the elder race. Elric prayed to Arioch that Dyvim Slorm would have some clue to his wife's whereabouts.

At noon of the next day the mercenary army rode swaggering into the city. Elric met them close to the city gate. The Imrryrian warriors were obviously weary from the long ride and were loaded with booty since, before Yishana sent for them, they had been raiding in Shazaar close to the Marshes of the Mist. They were different from any other race, these Imrryrians, with their tapering faces, slanting eyes and high cheekbones. They were pale and slim with long, soft hair drifting to their shoulders. The finery they wore was not stolen, but definitely Melnibonéan in design; shimmering cloths of gold, blue and green, metals of delicate workmanship and intricately patterned. They carried lances with long, sweeping heads and there were slender swords at their sides. They sat arrogantly in their saddles, convinced of their superiority over other mortals, and were, as Elric, not quite human in their unearthly beauty.

He rode up to meet Dyvim Slorm, his own sombre clothes contrasting with theirs. He wore a tall-collared jacket of quilted leather, black and buckled in by a broad, plain belt at which hung a poignard and Stormbringer. His milk-white hair was held from his eyes by a fillet of black bronze and his breeks and boots were also black. All this black set off sharply his white sk
glowing eyes.

Dyvim Slorm bowed in his saddle, showing only slig

"Cousin Elric. So the omen was true."

"What omen, Dyvim Slorm?"

"A falcon's—your name bird if I remember."

It had been customary for Melnibonéans to identify newbo
dren with birds of their choice; thus Elric's was a falcon, hunting
of prey.

"What did it tell you, cousin?" Elric asked eagerly.

"It gave a puzzling message. While we had barely gone from the Marshes of the Mist, it came and perched on my shoulder and spoke in human tongue. It told me to come to Sequaloris and there I would meet my king. From Sequaloris we were to journey together to join Yishana's army and the battle, whether won or lost, would resolve the direction of our linked destinies thereafter. Do you make sense of that, cousin?"

"Some," Elric frowned. "But come—I have a place reserved for you at the inn. I will tell you all I know over wine—if we can find decent wine in this forsaken hamlet. I need help, cousin; as much help as I can obtain, for Zarozinia has been abducted by supernatural agents and I have a feeling that this and the wars are but two elements in a greater play."

"Then quickly, to the inn. My curiosity is further piqued. This matter increases in interest for me. First falcons and omens, now abductions and strife! What else, I wonder, are we to meet!"

With the Imrryrians straggling after them through the cobbled streets, scarcely a hundred warriors but hardened by their outlawed life, Elric and Dyvim Slorm made their way to the inn and there, in haste, Elric outlined all he had learned.

Before replying, his cousin sipped his wine and carefully placed the cup upon the board, pursing his lips. "I have a feeling in my bones that we are puppets in some struggle between the gods. For all our blood

"I think you are right," said Elric, whose mingled emotions were suited neither to past, present nor future. "Aye, it is fitting that we should be wanderers, for we have no place in this world."

They drank in silence, moodily, their minds on matters of philosophy. Yet, for all this, Elric's thoughts were forever turning to Zarozinia and the fear of what might have befallen her. The very innocence of this girl, her vulnerability and her youth had been, to some degree at least, his salvation. His protective love for her had helped to keep him from brooding too deeply on his own doom-filled life and her company had eased his melancholy. The strange rede of the dead creature lingered in his memory. Undoubtedly the rede had referred to a battle, and the falcon which Dyvim Slorm had seen had spoken of one also. The battle was sure to be the forthcoming one between Yishana's forces and those of Sarosto of Dharijor and Jagreen Lern of Pan Tang. If he was to find Zarozinia then he must go with Dyvim Slorm and there take part in the conflict. Though he might perish, he reasoned that he had best do as the omens ordered—otherwise he could lose even the slight chance of ever seeing Zarozinia again. He turned to his cousin.

"I'll make my way with you tomorrow, and use my blade in the battle. Whatever else, I have the feeling that Yishana will need every warrior against the Theocrat and his allies."

Dyvim Slorm agreed. "Not only *our* doom but the doom of nations will be at stake in this . . ."

## Chapter Three

Ten terrible men drove their yellow chariots down a black mountain which vomited blue and scarlet fire and shook in a spasm of destruction.

In such a manner, all over the globe, the forces of nature were disrupted and rebellious. Though few realized it, the Earth was changing.

The Ten knew why, and they knew of Elric and how their knowledge linked with him.

The night was pale purple and the sun hung a bloody globe over the mountains, for it was late summer. In the valleys, cottages were burning as smoking lava smacked against the straw roofs.

Sepiriz, in the leading chariot, saw the villagers running, a confused rabble—like ants whose hills had been scattered. He turned to the blue-armoured man behind him and he smiled almost gaily.

"See them run," he said. "See them run, brother. Oh, the joy of it—such forces there are at work!"

" 'Tis good to have woken at this time," his brother agreed, shouting over the rumbling noise of the volcano.

Then the smile left Sepiriz and his eyes narrowed. He lashed at his twin horses with a bull-hide whip, so that blood laced the flanks of the great black steeds as they galloped even faster down the steep mountain.

In the village, one man saw the Ten in the distance. He shrieked, voicing his fear in a warning:

"The fire has driven them out of the mountain. Hide—escape! The men from the volcano have awakened—they are coming. The Ten have awakened according to the prophecy—it is the end of the world!" Then the mountain gushed a fresh spewing of hot rock and flaming lava and the man was struck down, screamed as he burned, and died. He died needlessly, for the Ten had no interest in him or his fellows.

Sepiriz and his brothers rode straight through the village, their chariot wheels rattling on the coarse street, the hoofs of their horses pounding.

Behind them, the mountain bellowed.

"To Nihrain!" cried Sepiriz. "Speedily, brethren, for there is much work to do. A blade must be brought from limbo and a pair of men must be found to carry it to Xanyaw!"

Joy filled him as he saw the earth shuddering about him and heard the gushing of fire and rock behind him. His black body glistened, reflecting the flames of the burning houses. The horses leaned in their harness, dragging the bucking chariot at wild speed, their hoofs blurred movement over the ground so that it often seemed they flew.

Perhaps they did, for the steeds of Nihrain were known to be different from ordinary beasts.

Now they flung themselves along a gorge, now up a mountain path, making their speedy way towards the Chasm of Nihrain, the ancient home of the Ten who had not returned there for two thousand years.

Again, Sepiriz laughed. He and his brothers bore a terrible responsibility, for though they had no loyalty to men or gods, they were Fate's spokesmen and thus bore an awful knowledge within their immortal skulls.

For centuries they had slept in their mountain chamber, dwelling close to the dormant heart of the volcano since extremes of heat and cold bothered them little. Now the spewing rock had awakened them and they knew that their time had come—the time for which they had been waiting for millennia.

This was why Sepiriz sang in joy. At last he and his brothers were to be allowed to perform their ultimate function. And this involved two Melnibonéans, the two surviving members of the royal line of the Bright Empire.

Sepiriz knew they lived—they had to be alive, for without them Fate's scheme was impossible. But there were those upon the Earth, Sepiriz knew, who were capable of cheating Fate, so powerful were they. Their minions lay everywhere, particularly among the new race of men, but ghouls and demons were also their tools.

This made his chosen task the harder.

But now—to Nihrain! To the hewn city and there to draw the threads of destiny into a finer net. There was still a little time, but it was running short; and Time the Unknown, was master of all . . .

The pavilions of Queen Yishana and her allies were grouped thickly about a series of small, wooded hills. The trees afforded cover from a distance and no campfires burned to give away their position. Also the sounds of the great army were as muted as possible. Outriders went to and fro, reporting the enemy's positions and keeping wary eyes open for spies.

But Elric and his Imrryrians were unchallenged as they rode in, for the albino and his men were easily recognizable and it was well-known that the feared Melnibonéan mercenaries had elected to aid Yishana.

Elric said to Dyvim Slorm: "I had best pay my respects to Queen Yishana, on account of our old bond, but I do not want her to know of my wife's disappearance—otherwise she may try to hinder me. We shall just say that I have come to aid her, out of friendship."

Dyvim Slorm nodded, and Elric left his cousin to tend to making camp, while he went at once to Yishana's tent where the tall queen awaited him impatiently.

The look in her eyes was shielded as he entered. She had a heavy, sensuous face that was beginning to show signs of aging. Her long hair was black and shone around her head. Her breasts were large and her hips broader than Elric remembered. She was sitting in a padded chair and the table before her was scattered with battle-maps and writing materials, parchment, ink and quills.

"Good morning, wolf," said she with a half-smile that was at once sardonic and provocative. "My scouts reported that you were riding with your countrymen. This is pleasant. Have you forsaken your new wife to return to subtler pleasures?"

"No," he said.

He stripped off his heavy riding cloak and flung it on a bench. "Good morning, Yishana. You do not change. I've half a suspicion that Theleb K'aarna gave you a draught of the waters of Eternal Life before I killed him."

"Perhaps he did. How goes your marriage?"

"Well," he said as she moved closer and he felt the warmth of her body.

"And now I'm disappointed," she smiled ironically and shrugged. They had been lovers on different occasions, in spite of the fact that Elric had been partially responsible for her brother's death during the raid on Imrryr. Dharmit of Jharkor's death had put her on the throne and, being an ambitious woman, she had not taken the news with too much sadness. Elric had no wish to resume the relationship, however.

He turned immediately to the matter of the forthcoming battle.

"I see you're preparing for more than a skirmish," he said. "What forces have you and what are your chances of winning?"

"There are my own White Leopards," she told him, "five hundred picked warriors who run as swiftly as horses, are as strong as mountain cats and as ferocious as blood-mad sharks—they are trained to kill and killing is all they know. Then there are my other troops—infantry and cavalry, some eighty lords in command. The best cavalry are from Shazaar, wild riders but clever fighters and well-disciplined. Tarkesh has sent fewer men since I understand King Hilran needed to defend his southern borders against a heavy attack. However, there are almost a thousand and fifty foot-soldiers and some two hundred mounted men from Tarkesh. In all we can put perhaps six thousand trained warriors on the field. Serfs, slaves and the like are also fighting, but they will of course serve only to meet the initial onslaught and will die in the early part of the battle."

Elric nodded. These were standard military tactics. "And what of the enemy?"

"We have more numbers—but they have Devil Riders and hunting tigers. There are also some beasts they keep in cages—but we cannot guess what they are since the cages are covered."

"I heard that the men of Myyrrhn are flying hither. The import must be great for them to leave their eyries."

"If we lose this battle," she said gravely, "Chaos could easily engulf the Earth and rule over it. Every oracle from here to Shazaar says the same thing, that Jagreen Lern is but the tool of less natural masters, that he is aided by the Lords of Chaos. We are not only fighting for our lands, Elric, we are fighting for the human race!"

"Then let us hope we win," he said.

Elric stood among the captains as they surveyed the mobilizing army. Tall Dyvim Slorm was by his side, his golden shirt loose on his slim body and his manner confident, arrogant. Also here were hardened soldiers of many smaller campaigns; short, dark-faced men from Tarkesh with thick armour and black, oiled hair and beards. The half-naked winged men from Myyrrhn had arrived, with their brooding eyes, hawklike faces, their great wings folded on their backs, quiet, dignified, seldom speaking. The Shazaarian commanders were there also, in jackets of grey, brown and black, in rust-coloured bronze armour. With them stood the captain of Yishana's White Leopards, a long-legged, thick-bodied man with blond hair tied in a knot at the back of his bull-necked head, silver armour bearing the emblazon of a leopard, albino like Elric, rampant and snarling.

The time of the battle was drawing close . . .

Now, in the grey dawn, the two armies advanced upon each other, coming from opposite ends of a wide valley, flanked by low, wooded, hills.

The army of Pan Tang and Dharijor moved, a tide of dark metal, up the shallow valley to meet them. Elric, still unarmoured, watched as they approached, his horse stamping the turf. Dyvim Slorm, beside him, pointed and said: "Look—there are the plotters—Sarosto on the left and Jagreen Lern on the right!"

The leaders headed their army, banners of dark silk rustling above their helms. King Sarosto and his thin ally, aquiline Jagreen Lern in glowing scarlet armour that seemed to be red hot and may have been. On his helm was the Merman crest of Pan Tang, for he claimed kinship with the sea-people. Sarosto's armour was dull, murky yellow, emblazoned with the Star of Dharijor upon which was the Cleft Sword which history said was borne by Sarosto's ancestor Atarn the City-Builder.

Behind them, instantly observable, came the Devil Riders of Pan Tang on their six-legged reptilian mounts, bred by sorcery it was said. Swarthy and with introspective expressions on their sharp faces, they carried long, curved sabres, naked at their belts. Prowling among them came over a hundred hunting tigers, trained like dogs, with tusklike teeth and claws that could rend a man to the bone with a single sweep. Beyond the rolling army as it moved towards them, Elric could just see the tops of the mysterious cage-wagons. What weird beasts did *they* contain? he wondered.

Then Yishana shouted a command.

The archers' arrows spread a rattling black cloud above them as Elric led the first wave of infantry down the hill to meet the van of the enemy army. That he should be forced to risk his life embittered him, but if he was ever to discover Zarozinia's whereabouts he had to play out his ordered part and pray that he lived.

The main force of cavalry followed the infantry, flanking it with orders to encircle the enemy if possible. Brightly clad Imrryrians and bronze-armoured Shazaarians were to one side. Blue-armoured Tarkeshites with brilliant plumes of red, purple and white, long lances leveled, and gold-armoured Jharkorians, longswords already unscabbarded, galloped on the other side. In the centre of Elric's advance phalanx loped Yishana's White Leopards and the queen herself rode beneath her banner, behind the first phalanx, leading a battalion of knights.

Down they rushed towards the enemy whose own arrows rose upwards and then swept down to clash against helmets or thud into flesh.

Now the sound of war-shouts smashed through the still dawn as they streaked down the slopes and clashed.

Elric found himself confronting lean Jagreen Lern, and the snarling Theocrat met Stormbringer's swing with a flame-red buckler which successfully protected him—proving the shield to be treated against sorcerous weapons.

Jagreen Lern's features wrinkled into a malicious smile as he recognized Elric. "I was told you'd be here, Whiteface. I know you Elric and I know your doom!"

"Too many men appear to know my destiny better than I," said the albino. "But perhaps if I slay you, Theocrat, I may force the secret from you before you die?"

"Oh, no! That is not my masters' plan at all."

"Well, mayhap 'tis mine!"

He struck again at Jagreen Lern, but again the blade was turned, screaming its anger. He felt it move in his hand, felt it throb with chagrin, for normally the hell-forged blade could slice through metal however finely tempered.

In Jagreen Lern's gauntleted right hand was a huge war-axe which he now swung at the unprotected head of Elric's horse. This was odd since he was in a position to strike at Elric himself. The albino jerked his steed's head to one side, avoided the blow and drove again point first at Jagreen Lern's midriff. The runeblade shrieked as it failed to pierce the armour. The war-axe swung again and Elric brought up his sword as protection but, in astonishment, was driven back in his saddle by the force of the blow, barely able to control his horse, one foot slipping from the stirrup.

Jagreen Lern struck again and successfully split the skull of Elric's horse which crumpled to its knees, blood and brains gushing, great eyes rolling as it died.

Flung from the beast, Elric rose painfully and readied himself for Jagreen Lern's next blow. But to his surprise, the sorcerer-king turned away and moved into the thick of the battle.

"Sadly your life is not mine to take, Whiteface! That is the prerogative of other powers. If you live and we are the victors—I will seek you out, perhaps."

Unable, in his dazed condition, to make sense of this, Elric looked desperately around for another horse and saw a Dharijorian mount, its head and foreparts well protected by dented black armour, running loose and away from the fight.

Swiftly, he leapt for its harness and caught a dangling rein, steadied the beast, got a foot into a stirrup and swung himself up in the saddle which was uncomfortable for an unarmoured man. Standing in the stirrups, Elric rode it back into the battle.

He hewed his way through the enemy knights, slaying now a Devil Rider, now a hunting tiger that lashed at him with bared fangs, now a gorgeously armoured Dharijorian commander, now two foot-soldiers who struck at him with halberds. His horse reared like a monster and, desperately, he forced it closer to the standard of Yishana until he could see one of the heralds.

Yishana's army was fighting bravely, but its discipline was lost. It must regroup if it was to be most effective.

"*Recall the cavalry!*" Elric yelled. "*Recall the cavalry!*"

The young herald looked up. He was badly pressed by two Devil Riders. His attention diverted, he was skewered on a Devil Rider's blade and shrieked as the two men butchered him.

Cursing, Elric rode closer and struck one of the attackers in the side of the head. The man toppled and fell into the churned mud of the field. The other Rider turned, only to meet howling Stormbringer's point, and he died yelling, as the runeblade drank his soul.

The herald, still mounted, was dead in the saddle, his body a mass of cuts. Elric leaned forward, tearing the bloody horn from around the corpse's neck. Placing it to his lips, he sounded the Cavalry Recall and caught a glimpse of horsemen turning. Now he saw the standard itself begin to fall and realized that the standard-bearer was slain. He rose in the saddle and grasped the pole which bore the bright flag of Jharkor and, with this in one hand, the horn at his lips, attempted to rally his forces.

Slowly, the remnants of the battered army gathered around him. Then Elric, taking control of the battle, did the only thing he could—took the sole course of action which might save the day.

He sounded a long, wailing note on the horn. In response to this he heard the beating of heavy wings as the men of Myyrrhn rose into the air.

Observing this, the enemy released the traps of the mysterious cages.

Elric groaned with despair.

A weird hooting preceded the sight of giant owls, thought extinct even in Myyrrhn the land of their origin, circling skyward.

The enemy had prepared against a threat from the air and, by some means, had produced the age-old enemies of the men of Myyrrhn.

Only slightly daunted by this unexpected sight, the men of Myyrrhn, armed with long spears, attacked the great birds. The embattled warriors on the ground were showered with blood and feathers. Corpses of men and birds began to flop downwards, crushing infantry and cavalry beneath them.

Through this confusion, Elric and the White Leopards of Yishana cut their way into the enemy to join up with Dyvim Slorm and his Imrryrians, the remnants of the Tarkeshite cavalry, and about a hundred Shazaarians, who had survived. Looking upwards, Elric saw that most of the great owls were destroyed, but only a handful of the men of Myyrrhn had survived the fight in the air. These, having done what they could against the owls, were themselves circling about preparing to leave the battle. Obviously they realized the hopelessness of it all.

Elric called to Dyvim Slorm as their forces joined: "The battle's lost—Sarosto and Jagreen Lern rule here now!"

Dyvim Slorm hefted his longsword in his hand and gave Elric a look of assent. "If we're to live to keep our destiny, we'd best make speed away from here!" he cried.

There was little more they could do.

"Zarozinia's life is more important to me than anything else!" Elric yelled. "Let's look to our own predicament!"

But the weight of the enemy forces was like a vice, crushing Elric and his men. Blood covered Elric's face from a blow he had received on the forehead. It clogged his eyes so that he had to keep raising his left hand to his face to get rid of the stuff.

His right arm ached as he lifted Stormbringer again and again, hacking and stabbing about him, desperate now, for although the dreadful blade had a life, almost an intelligence, of its own, even it could not supply the vitality which Elric needed to remain entirely fresh. In a way he was glad, for he hated the runesword, though he had to depend on the force which flowed from it to him.

Stormbringer more than slew Elric's attackers—it drank their souls, and some of that life-force was passed on to the Melnibonéan monarch . . .

Now the ranks of the enemy fell back and seemed to open. Through this self-made breach, animals came running. Animals with gleaming eyes and red, fang-filled jaws. Animals with claws.

The hunting tigers of Pan Tang.

Horses screamed as the tigers leapt and rent them, tearing down mount and man and slashing at the throats of their victims. The tigers raised bloody snouts and stared around for a new prey. Terrified, many of Elric's small force fell back shouting. Most of the Tarkeshite knights broke and fled the field, precipitating the flight of the Jharkorians whose maddened horses bore them away and were soon followed by the few remaining Shazaarians still mounted. Soon only Elric, his Imrryrians and about forty White Leopards stood against the might of Dharijor and Pan Tang.

Elric raised his horn and sounded the Retreat, wheeled his black steed about and raced up the valley, Imrryrians behind him. But the White Leopards fought on to the last. Yishana had said that they knew nothing but how to kill. Evidently they also knew how to die.

Elric and Dyvim Slorm led the Imrryrians up the valley, half-thankful that the White Leopards covered their retreat. The Melnibonéan had seen nothing of Yishana since he had clashed with Jagreen Lern. He wondered what had become of her.

As they turned a bend in the valley, Elric understood the full battle-plan of Jagreen Lern and his ally—for a strong, fresh force of foot-soldiers and cavalry had assembled at the other end of the valley, for the purpose of cutting off any retreat made by his army.

Scarcely thinking, Elric urged his horse up the slopes of the hills, his men following, ducking beneath the low branches of the birch trees as the Dharijorians rushed towards them, spreading out to cut off their escape.

* * *

Elric turned his horse about and saw that the White Leopards were still fighting around the standard of Jharkor and he headed back in that direction, keeping to the hills. Over the crest of the hills he rode, Dyvim Slorm and a handful of Imrryrians with him, and then they were galloping for open countryside while the knights of Dharijor and Pan Tang gave chase. They had obviously recognized Elric and wished either to kill or to capture him.

Ahead Elric could see that the Tarkeshites, Shazaarians and Jharkorians who had earlier fled had taken the same route out as he had. But they no longer rode together, were scattering away.

Elric and Dyvim Slorm fled westwards across unknown country while the other Imrryrians, to take attention off their leaders, rode to the north-east towards Tarkesh and perhaps a few days of safety.

The battle was won. The minions of evil were the victors and an age of terror had settled on the lands of the Young Kingdoms in the West.

Some days later, Elric, Dyvim Slorm, two Imrryrians, a Tarkeshite commander called Yedn-pad-Juizev, badly wounded in the side, and a Shazaarian foot-soldier, Orozn, who had taken a horse away from the battle, were temporarily safe from pursuit and were trudging their horses wearily towards a range of slim-peaked mountains which loomed black against the red evening sky.

They had not spoken for some hours. Yedn-pad-Juizev was obviously dying and they could do nothing for him. He knew this also and expected nothing, merely rode with them for company. He was very tall for a Tarkeshite, his scarlet plume still bobbing on his dented blue-metal helmet, his breastplate scarred and smeared with his own blood and others'. His beard was black and shiny with oil, his nose a jutting crag on the rock of his soldier's face, his eyes half-glazed. He was bearing the pain well. Though they were impatient to reach the comparative safety of the mountain range, the others matched their pace to his, half in respect and half in fascination that a man could cling to life for so long.

Night came and a great yellow moon hung in the sky over the mountains. The sky was completely clear of cloud and stars shone brightly. The warriors wished that the night had been dark, storm-covered, for they could have then sought more security in the shadows. As it was the night was lighted and they could only hope that they reached the mountains soon—before the hunting tigers of Pan Tang discovered their tracks and they died under the rending claws of those dreadful beasts.

Elric was in a grim and thoughtful mood. For a while the Dharijorian and Pan Tang conquerors would be busy consolidating their new-won empire. Perhaps there would be quarrels between them when this was done, perhaps not. But soon, anyway, they would be very powerful and threatening the security of other nations on the Southern and Eastern Continents.

But all this, however much it overshadowed the fate of the whole world, meant little to Elric for he still could not clearly see his way to Zarozinia. He remembered the dead creature's prophecy, part of which had now come about. But still it meant little. He felt as if he were being driven constantly westwards, as if he must go further and further into the sparsely settled lands beyond Jharkor. Was it here his destiny lay? Was it here that Zarozinia's captors were? *Beyond the ocean brews a battle; Beyond the battle blood shall fall . . .*

Well, had the blood fallen, or was it yet to fall? What was the "twin" that Elric's kinsman, Dyvim Slorm, bore? Who was the one who should not live?

Perhaps the secret lay in the mountains ahead of them?

Beneath the moon they rode, and at last came to a gorge. Halfway along it they located a cave and lay down inside to rest.

* * *

In the morning, Elric was awakened by a sound outside the cave. Instantly he drew Stormbringer and crept to the mouth of the cave. What he saw caused him to sheathe the blade and call in a soft voice to the battered man who was riding up the gorge towards the cave. "Here, herald! We are friends!"

The man was one of Yishana's heralds. His surcoat was in ribbons, his armour crumpled on his body. He was swordless and without a helmet, a young man with his face made gaunt by weariness and despair. He looked up and relief came when he recognized Elric.

"My lord Elric—they said you were slain on the field."

"I'm glad they did, since that makes pursuit less likely. Come inside."

The others were awake now—all but one. Yedn-pad-Juizev had died, sleeping, in the night. Orozn yawned and jerked a thumb at the corpse. "If we do not find food soon, I'll be tempted to eat our dead friend."

The man looked at Elric for response to this jest, but seeing the albino's expression he was abashed and retreated to the depths of the cave grumbling and kicking at loose stones.

Elric leaned against the wall of the cave near the opening. "What news have you?" he asked.

"Dark news, my lord. From Shazaar to Tarkesh black misery prevails and iron and fire beat across nations like an unholy storm. We are fully conquered. Only small bands of men carry on a hopeless struggle against the enemy. Some of our folk are already talking of turning bandit and preying on each other, so desperate have times become."

Elric nodded. "Such is what happens when foreign allies are beaten on friendly soil. What of Queen Yishana?"

"She fared ill, my lord. Clad in metal, she battled against a score of men before expiring—her body torn asunder by the force of their attack. Sarosto took her head for a keepsake and added it to other trophies including the hands of Karnarl, his half-brother who opposed him over the Pan Tang alliance, the eyes of Penik of Nargesser, who raised an army against him in that province. Theocrat Jagreen Lern ordered that all other prisoners be tortured to death and hanged in chains through the lands as warning against insurrection. They are an unholy pair, my lord!"

Elric's mouth grew tight when he heard this. Already it was becoming clear to him that his only route was westwards, for the conquerors would soon search him out if he went back. He turned to Dyvim Slorm. The Imrryrian's shirt was in rags and his left arm covered in dried blood.

"Our destiny appears to lie in the west," he said quietly.

"Then let us make speed," said his cousin, "for I am impatient to get it over and at least learn whether we live or perish in this enterprise. We gained nothing by our encounter with the enemy, but wasted time."

"I gained something," Elric said, remembering his fight with Jagreen Lern. "I gained the knowledge that Jagreen Lern *is* connected in some way with the kidnapping of my wife—and if he had aught to do with it, I'll claim my vengeance no matter what."

"Now," said Dyvim Slorm. "Let us make haste to the west."

## Chapter Four

They drove deeper into the mountains that day, avoiding the few hunting parties sent out by the conquerors, but the two Imrryrians, recognizing that their leaders were on a special journey, left to go in another direction. The herald was gone southward to spread his gloomy news so that only Elric, Dyvim Slorm and Orozn were left. They did not welcome Orozn's company, but bore with it for the meanwhile.

Then, after a day, Orozn disappeared and Elric and Dyvim Slorm ranged deeper into the black crags, riding through towering, oppressive canyons or along narrow paths.

Snow lay on the mountains, bright white against sharp black, filling gorges, making paths slippery and dangerous. Then one evening they came to a place where the mountains opened out into a wide valley and they rode with difficulty down the foothills of the mountains, their tracks making great black scars in the snow and their horses steaming, their breath billowing white in the cold air.

They observed a rider coming across the valley floor towards them. One rider they did not fear, so they waited for him to approach. To their surprise it was Orozn, clad in fresh garments of wolfskin and deer hide. He greeted them in a friendly manner.

"I have come seeking you both. You must have taken a more difficult route than mine."

"From where have you come?" Elric asked; his face was drawn, his cheekbones emphasized by the sunken skin. He looked more like a wolf than ever with his red eyes gleaming. Zarozinia's fate weighed heavily on his mind.

"There is a settlement nearby. Come, I will take you to it."

They followed Orozn for some way and it was getting near nightfall, the setting sun staining the mountains scarlet, when they reached the opposite side of the valley, dotted with a few birch trees and, further up, a cluster of firs.

Orozn led them into this grove.

They came screaming out of the dark, a dozen swarthy men, possessed by hatred—and something else. Weapons were raised in mailed hands. By their armour, these men were from Pan Tang. Orozn must have been captured and persuaded to lead Elric and his cousin into ambush.

Elric turned his horse, rearing.

"Orozn! You betrayed us!"

But Orozn was riding. He looked back once, his pale face tortured with guilt. Then his eyes darted away from Elric and Dyvim Slorm and he frowned, rode down the moss-wet hill back into the howling darkness of the night.

Elric lifted Stormbringer from his belt, gripped the hilt, blocked a blow from a brass-studded mace, slid his sword down the handle and sheared off his attacker's fingers. He and Dyvim Slorm were soon surrounded, yet he fought on, Stormbringer shrilling a wild, lawless song of death.

But Elric and Dyvim Slorm were still weak from the rigours of their past adventures. Not even Stormbringer's evil strength was sufficient fully to revitalize Elric's deficient veins and he was filled with fear—not of the attackers, but of the fact that he was doomed to die or be captured. And he had the feeling that these warriors had no knowledge of their master's part in the matter of the prophecy, did not realize that, perhaps, he was not meant to die at that moment.

In fact, he decided, as he battled, a great mistake was about to be perpetrated . . .

"Arioch!" he cried in his fear to the demon-god of Melniboné. "Arioch! Aid me! Blood and souls for thine aid!"

But that intractable entity sent no aid.

Dyvim Slorm's long blade caught a man just below his gorget and pierced him through the throat. The other Pan Tang horsemen threw themselves at him but were driven back by his sweeping sword. Dyvim Slorm shouted: "Why do we worship such a god when whim decides him so often?"

"Perhaps he thinks our time has come!" Elric yelled back as his runeblade drank another foe's life-force.

Tiring fast, they fought on until a new sound broke above the clash of arms—the sound of chariots and low, moaning cries.

Then they were sweeping into the mêlée, black men with handsome features and thin, proud mouths, their magnificent bodies half-naked as their cloaks of white fox fur streamed behind them and their javelins were flung with terrible accuracy at the bewildered men of Pan Tang.

Elric sheathed his sword and remained ready to fight or flee. "This is the one—the white-faced one!" cried a black charioteer as he saw Elric. The chariots rolled to a halt, tall horses stamping and snorting. Elric rode up to the leader.

"I am grateful," he said, half falling from his saddle in weariness. He turned the droop of his shoulders into a bow. "You appear to know me—you are the third I've met while on this quest who recognizes me without my being able to return the compliment."

The leader tugged the fox cape about his naked chest and smiled with his thin lips. "I'm named Sepiriz and you will know me soon enough. As for you, we have known of you for thousands of years. Elric are you not—last king of Melniboné?"

"That is true."

"And you," Sepiriz addressed Dyvim Slorm, "are Elric's cousin. Together you represent the last of the pure line of Melniboné."

"Aye," Dyvim Slorm agreed, curiosity in his eyes.

"Then we have been waiting for you to pass this way. There was a prophecy . . ."

"*You* are the captors of Zarozinia?" Elric reached for his sword.

Sepiriz shook his head. "No, but we can tell you where she is. Calm yourself. Though I realize the agony of mind you must be suffering, I will be better able to explain all I know back in our own domain."

"First tell us who you are," Elric demanded.

Sepiriz smiled slightly. "You know us, I think—or at least you know of us. There was a certain friendship between your ancestors and our folk in the early years of the Bright Empire." He paused a moment before continuing: "Have you ever heard legends, in Imrryr perhaps, of the Ten from the mountain? The Ten who sleep in the mountain of fire?"

"Many times." Elric drew in his breath. "Now I recognize you by description. But it is said that you sleep for centuries in the mountain of fire. Why are you roaming abroad in this manner?"

"We were driven by an eruption from our volcano home which had been dormant for two thousand years. Such movements of nature have been taking place all over the Earth of late. Our time, we knew, had come to awaken again. We were servants of Fate—and our mission is strongly bound up with your destiny. We bear a message for you from Zarozinia's captor—and another from a different source. Would you return now, with us, to the Chasm of Nihrain and learn all we can tell you?"

Elric pondered for a moment, then he lifted his white face and said: "I am in haste to claim vengeance, Sepiriz. But if what you can tell me will lead me closer to claiming it, I'll come."

"Then come!" The black giant jerked the reins of his horse and turned the chariot about.

It was a journey of a day and a night to the Chasm of Nihrain, a huge gaping fissure high in the mountains, a place avoided by all; it had supernatural significance for those who dwelt near the mountains.

The lordly Nihrain conversed little on the journey and at last they were above the chasm, driving their chariots down the steep path which wound into its dark depths.

About half a mile down no light penetrated, but they saw ahead of them flickering torches that illuminated part of the carved outline of an unearthly mural or betrayed a gaping opening in the solid rock. Then, as they guided their horses down further, they saw, in detail, the awe-inspiring city of Nihrain which outsiders had not glimpsed for many centuries. The last of the Nihrain now lived here; ten immortal men of a race older even than that of Melniboné which had a history of twenty thousand years.

Huge columns rose above them, hewn ages before from the living rock, giant statues and wide balconies, many-tiered. Windows a hundred feet high and sweeping steps cut into the face of the chasm. The Ten drove their yellow chariots through a mighty gate and into the caverns of Nihrain, carved to their entire extent with strange symbols and stranger murals. Here slaves, wakened from a sleep of centuries to tend their masters, ran forward. Even these did not fully bear resemblance to the men that Elric knew.

Sepiriz gave the reins to a slave as Elric and Dyvim Slorm dismounted, staring about them in awe.

He said: "Now—to my own chambers and there I'll inform you of what you wish to know—and what you must do."

Led by Sepiriz, the kinsmen stalked impatiently through galleries and into a large chamber full of dark sculpture. A number of fires burned behind this hall, in big grates. Sepiriz folded his great body in a chair and bade them sit in two similar chairs, carved from solid blocks of ebony. When they were all seated before one of the fires, Sepiriz took a long breath, staring around the hall, perhaps remembering its earlier history.

Somewhat angered by this show of casualness, Elric said impatiently: "Forgive me, Sepiriz—but you promised to pass on your message to us."

"Yes," Sepiriz said, "but so much do I have to tell you that I must pause one moment to collect my thoughts." He settled himself in the chair before continuing.

"We know where your wife is," he said at last, "and know also that she is safe. She will not be harmed since she is to be bargained for something which you possess."

"Then tell me the *whole* story," Elric demanded bleakly.

"We were friendly with your ancestors, Elric. And we were friendly with those they superseded, the ones who forged that blade you bear."

Elric was interested in spite of his anxiety. For years he had attempted to rid himself of the runesword, but had never succeeded. All his efforts had failed and he still needed to carry it, although drugs now gave him most of his strength.

"Would you be rid of your sword, Elric?" Sepiriz said.

"Aye—it's well known."

"Then listen to this tale.

"We know for whom and for what the blade—and its twin—were forged. They were made for a special purpose and for special men. Only Melnibonéans may carry them, and of those only the blood of the royal line."

"There is no hint of any special purpose for the swords in Melnibonéan history or legend," Elric said leaning forward.

"Some secrets are best kept fully guarded," Sepiriz said calmly. "Those blades were forged to destroy a group of very powerful beings. Among them are the Dead Gods."

"The Dead Gods—but, by their very name, *you* must know that they perished long ages ago."

"They 'perished' as you say. In human terms they are dead. But they *chose* to die, chose to rid themselves of material shape and hurled their lifestuff into the blackness of eternity, for in those days they were full of fear."

Elric had no real conception of what Sepiriz described but he accepted what the Nihrainian said and listened on.

"One of them has returned," Sepiriz said.

"Why?"

"To get, at any cost, two things which endanger him and his fellow gods—wherever they may be they can still be harmed by these things."

"They are . . . ?"

"They have the earthly appearance of two swords, runecarved and sorcerous—Mournblade and Stormbringer."

"This!" Elric touched his blade. "Why should the gods fear this? And the other went to limbo with my cousin Yyrkoon whom I killed many years ago. It is lost."

"That is not true. We recovered it—that was part of Fate's purpose for us. We have it here in Nihrain. The blades were forged for your ancestors who drove the Dead Gods away by means of them. They were made by other unhuman smiths who were also enemies of the Dead Gods. These smiths were compelled to combat evil *with* evil, although they, themselves, were not pledged to Chaos, but to Law. They forged the swords for several reasons—ridding the world of the Dead Gods was but one!"

"The other reasons?"

"Those you shall learn in times to come—for our relationship will not be ended until the whole destiny has been worked out. We are obliged not to reveal the other reasons until the proper time. You have a dangerous destiny, Elric, and I do not envy it."

"But what is the message you have?" Elric said impatiently.

"Due to the disturbance created by Jagreen Lern, one of the Dead Gods has been enabled to return to Earth, as I told you. He has gathered acolytes about him. They kidnapped your wife."

Elric felt a mood of deep despair creep over him. Must he defy such power as this?

"Why . . . ?" he whispered.

"Darnizhaan is aware that Zarozinia is important to you. He wishes to barter her for the two swords. We, in this matter, are merely messengers. We must give up the sword we keep, at the request of you or Dyvim Slorm, for they rightfully belong to any of the royal line. Darnizhaan's terms are simple. He will dispatch Zarozinia to limbo unless you give him the blades which threaten his existence. Her death, it would not be death as we know it, would be unpleasant and eternal."

"And if I agreed to do that, what would happen?"

"All the Dead Gods would return. Only the power of the swords keeps them from doing so now!"

"And what would happen if the Dead Gods came back?"

"Even without the Dead Gods, Chaos threatens to conquer the planet, but with them it would be utterly invincible, its effect immediate. Evil would sweep the world. Chaos would plunge this Earth into a stinking inferno of terror and destruction. You have already had a taste of what is happening, and Darnizhaan has only been back for a short time."

"You mean the defeat of Yishana's armies and the conquest by Sarosto and Jagreen Lern?"

"Exactly. Jagreen Lern has a pact with Chaos—all the Lords of Chaos, not merely the Dead Gods—for Chaos fears Fate's plan for Earth's future and would attempt to tamper with it by gaining domination of our planet. The Lords of Chaos are strong enough without the help of the Dead Gods. Darnizhaan must be destroyed."

"I have an impossible choice, Sepiriz. If I give up Stormbringer I can probably survive on herbs and the like. But if I do give it up for Zarozinia, then Chaos will be unleashed to its full extent and I will have a monstrous crime upon my conscience."

"The choice is yours alone to make."

Elric deliberated but could think of no way of solving the problem.

"Bring the other blade," he said at last.

Sepiriz rejoined them a while later, with a scabbarded sword that seemed little different from Stormbringer.

"So, Elric—is the prophecy explained?" he asked, still keeping hold of Mournblade.

"Aye—here is the twin of that I bear. But the last part—where are we to go?"

"I will tell you in a moment. Though the Dead Gods, and the powers of Chaos, are aware that we possess the sister blade, they do not know whom we really serve. Fate, as I told you, is our master, and Fate has wrought a fabric for this Earth which would be hard to alter. But it *could* be altered and we are entrusted to see that Fate is not cheated. You are about to undergo a test. How you fare in it, what your decision is, will decide what we must tell you upon your return to Nihrain."

"You wish me to return here?"

"Yes."

"Give me Mournblade," Elric said quickly.

Sepiriz handed him the sword and Elric stood there with one twin blade in each hand, as if weighing something between them.

Both blades seemed to moan in recognition and the powers swam through his body so that he seemed to be built of steel-hard fire.

"I remember now that I hold them both that their powers are greater than I realize. There is one quality they possess when paired, a quality we may be able to use against this Dead God." He frowned. "But more of that in a moment." He stared sharply at Sepiriz. "Now tell me, where is Darnizhaan?"

"The Vale of Xanyaw in Myyrrhn!"

Elric handed Mournblade to Dyvim Slorm who accepted it gingerly.

"What will your choice be?" Sepiriz asked.

"Who knows?" Elric said with bitter gaiety. "Perhaps there is a way to beat this Dead God . . .

"But I tell you this, Sepiriz—given the opportunity I shall make that god rue his homecoming, for he has done the one thing that can move me to real anger. And the anger of Elric of Melniboné and his sword Stormbringer can destroy the world!"

Sepiriz rose from his chair, his eyebrows lifting.

"And gods, Elric, can it destroy gods?"

## Chapter Five

Elric rode like a giant scarecrow, gaunt and rigid on the massive back of the Nihrainian steed. His grim face was set fast in a mask that hid emotion and his crimson eyes burned like coals in their sunken sockets. The wind whipped his hair this way and that, but he sat straight, staring ahead, one long-fingered hand gripping Stormbringer's hilt.

Occasionally Dyvim Slorm, who bore Mournblade both proudly and warily, heard the blade moan to its sister and felt it shudder at his side. Only later did he begin to ask himself what the blade might make him, what it would give him and demand of him. After that, he kept his hand away from it as much as possible.

Close to the borders of Myyrrhn, a pack of Dharijorian hirelings—native Jharkorians in the livery of the conquerors—came upon them. Unsavoury louts they were, who should have known better than to ride across Elric's path. They steered their horses towards the pair, grinning. The black plumes of their helmets nodded, armour straps creaked and metal clanked. The leader, a squint-eyed bully with an axe at his belt, pulled his mount short in front of Elric.

At a direction from its master, the albino's horse came to a stop. His expression unchanged, Elric drew Stormbringer in an economic, catlike gesture. Dyvim Slorm copied him, eyeing the silently laughing men. He was surprised at how easily the blade sprang from its scabbard.

Then, with no challenges, Elric began to fight.

He fought like an automaton, quickly, efficiently, expressionlessly, cleaving the leader's shoulder plate in a stroke that cut through the man from shoulder to stomach in one raking movement which peeled back armour and flesh, rupturing the body so that a great scarlet gash appeared in the black metal and the leader wept as he slowly died, sprawling for a moment over his horse before slumping from the mount, one leg high, caught in a stirrup strap.

Stormbringer let out a great metallic purr of pleasure and Elric directed arm and blade about him, emotionlessly slaying the horsemen as if they were unarmed and chained, so little chance did they have.

Dyvim Slorm, unused to the semi-sentient Mournblade, tried to wield her like an ordinary sword but she moved in his hand, making cleverer strokes than he. A peculiar sense of power, at once sensual and cool, poured into him and he heard his voice yelling exultantly, realized what his ancestors must have been like in war.

The fight was quickly done with and leaving the soul-drained corpses on the ground behind them, they were soon in the land of Myyrrhn. Both blades had now been commonly blooded.

Elric was now better able to think and act coherently, but he could spare nothing for Dyvim Slorm while intratemporally asking nothing of his cousin who rode at his side, frustrated in that he was not called upon for his help.

Elric let his mind drift about in time, encompassing past, present and future and forming it into a whole—a pattern. He was suspicious of pattern, disliking shape, for he did not trust it. To him, life was chaotic, chance-dominated, unpredictable. It was a trick, an illusion of the mind, to be able to see a pattern to it.

He knew a few things, judged nothing.

He knew he bore a sword which physically and psychologically he needed to bear. It was an unalterable admission of a weakness in him, a lack of confidence in either himself or the philosophy of cause and effect. He believed himself a realist.

He knew that he loved, obscurely at times, his wife Zarozinia and would die if it meant she would not be harmed.

He knew that, if he were to survive and keep the freedom he had won and fought to hold, he must journey to the Dead God's lair and do what he saw fit to do when he had managed to assess the situation. He knew that for all his admission of Chaos he would be better able to do what he wished in a world ordered by some degree of Law.

The wind had been warm but now, nearing dusk, it grew colder. A low, cloudy sky with the heavy banks of grey picked out against the lighter shades of grey like islands in a cold sea. And there was a smell of smoke in Elric's nostrils, the frantic chirruping of birds in his ears and the sound of a whistling boy heard over the droning wind.

Dyvim Slorm turned his horse in the direction of the whistling, rode into scrub, leaned down in the saddle and hauled himself up with a wriggling youngster gripped by the slack of his shirt.

"Where are you from, lad?" Dyvim Slorm asked.

"From a village a mile or two away, sir," the boy replied, out of breath and scared.

He looked with wide eyes at Elric, fascinated by the tall albino's stern and pitiless mien.

He turned his head sharply to stare up at Dyvim Slorm. "Is that not Elric Friendslayer?" he said.

Dyvim Storm released the boy and said, "Where lies the Vale of Xanyaw?"

"North-west of here—it is no place for mortals. Is that not Elric Friendslayer, sir, tell me?"

Dyvim Slorm glanced miserably at his cousin and did not reply to the boy. Together they urged their horses north-west and Elric's pace was even more urgent.

Through the bleak night they rode, buffeted by a vicious wind.

And as they came closer to the Vale of Xanyaw, the whole sky, the earth, the air became filled with heavy, throbbing music. Melodious, sensual, great chords of sound, on and on it rose and fell, and following it came the white-faced ones.

Each had a black cowl and a sword which split at the end into three curved barbs. Each grinned a fixed grin. The music followed them as they came running like mad things at the two men who reined in their horses, restraining the urge to turn and flee. Elric had seen horrors in his life, had seen much that would make others insane, but for some reason these shocked him more deeply than any. They were men, ordinary men by the look of them—but men possessed by an unholy spirit.

Prepared to defend themselves, Elric and Dyvim Slorm drew their blades and waited for the encounter, but none came. The music and the men rushed past them and away beyond them in the direction from which they had come.

Overhead, suddenly, they heard the beat of wings, a shriek from out of the sky and a ghastly wail. Fleeing, two women rushed by and Elric was disturbed to see that the women were from the winged race of Myyrrhn, but were wingless. These, unlike a woman Elric remembered, had had their wings deliberately hacked off. They paid no attention to the two riders, but disappeared, running into the night, their eyes blank and their faces insane.

"What is happening, Elric?" cried Dyvim Slorm, resheathing his runeblade, his other hand striving to control the prancing horse.

"I know not. What *does* happen in a place where the Dead Gods' rule has come back?"

All was rushing noise and confusion; the night was full of movement and terror.

"Come!" Elric slapped his sword against his mount's rump and sent the beast into a jerking gallop, forcing himself and the steed forward into the terrible night.

Then mighty laughter greeted them as they rode between hills into the Vale of Xanyaw. The valley was pitch-black and alive with menace, the very hills seeming sentient. They slowed their pace as they lost their sense of direction, and Elric had to call to his unseen cousin, to make sure he was still close. The echoing laughter sounded again, roaring from out of the dark, so that the earth shook. It was as if the whole planet laughed in ironic mirth at their efforts to control their fears and push on through the valley.

Elric wondered if he had been betrayed and this was a trap set by the Dead Gods. What proof had he that Zarozinia was here? Why had he trusted Sepiriz? Something slithered against his leg as it passed him and he put his hand on the hilt of his sword, ready to draw it.

But then, shooting upwards into the dark sky, there arose, seemingly from the very earth, a huge figure which barred their way. Hands on hips, wreathed in golden light, a face of an ape, somehow blended with another shape to give it dignity and wild grandeur, its body alive and dancing with colour and light, its lips grinning with delight and knowledge—Darnizhaan, the Dead God!

"*Elric!*"

"Darnizhaan!" cried Elric fiercely, craning his head to stare up at the Dead God's face. He felt no fear now. "I have come for my wife!"

Around the Dead God's heels appeared acolytes with wide lips and pale, triangular faces, conical caps on their heads and madness in their eyes. They giggled and shrilled and shivered in the light of Darnizhaan's grotesque and beautiful body. They gibbered at the two riders and mocked them, but they did not move away from the Dead God's heels.

Elric sneered. "Degenerate and pitiful minions," he said.

"Not so pitiful as you, Elric of Melniboné," laughed the Dead God. "Have you come to bargain, or to give your wife's soul into my custody, so that she may spend eternity dying?"

Elric did not let his hate show on his face.

"I would destroy you; it is instinctive for me to do so. But—"

The Dead God smiled, almost with pity. "*You* must be destroyed, Elric. You are an anachronism. Your time is gone."

"Speak for yourself, Darnizhaan!"

"I *could* destroy you."

"But you will not." Though passionately hating the being, Elric also felt a disturbing sense of comradeship for the Dead God. Both of them represented an age that was gone; neither was really part of the new Earth.

"Then I will destroy her," the Dead God said. "That I could do with impunity."

"Zarozinia! Where is she?"

Once again Darnizhaan's mighty laughter shook the Vale of Xanyaw. "Oh, what have the old folk come to? There was a time when no man of Melniboné, particularly of the royal line, would admit to

caring for another mortal soul, especially if they belonged to the beast-race, the new race of the age you call that of the Young Kingdoms. What? Are you mating with animals, King of Melniboné? Where is your blood, your cruel and brilliant blood? Where the glorious malice? Where the evil, Elric?"

Peculiar emotions stirred in Elric as he remembered his ancestors, the Sorcerer Emperors of the Dragon Isle. He realized that the Dead God was deliberately awakening these emotions and, with an effort, he refused to let them dominate him.

"That is past," he shouted, "a new time has come upon the Earth. Our time will soon be gone—and yours is *over*!"

"No, Elric. Mark my words, whatever happens. The dawn is over and will soon be swept away like dead leaves before the wind of morning. The Earth's history has not even begun. You, your ancestors, these men of the new races even, you are nothing but a *prelude to history*. You will all be forgotten if the real history of the world begins. But we can avert that—we can survive, conquer the Earth and hold it against the Lords of Law, against Fate herself, against the Cosmic Balance—we *can* continue to live, but you *must* give me the swords!"

"I fail to understand you," Elric said, his lips thin and his teeth tight in his skull. "I am here to bargain or do battle for my wife."

"You do not understand," the Dead God guffawed, "because we are all of us, gods and men, but shadows playing puppet parts before the true play begins. You would best not fight me—rather side with me, for I know the truth. We share a common destiny. We do not, any of us, exist. The old folk are doomed, you, myself and my brothers, unless you give me the swords. We must not fight one another. Share our frightful knowledge—the knowledge that turned us insane. There is nothing, Elric—no past, present, or future. *We do not exist, any of us!*"

Elric shook his head quickly. "I do not understand you, still. I would not understand you if I could. I desire only the return of my wife—not baffling conundra!"

Darnizhaan laughed again. "No! You shall not have the woman unless we are given control of the swords. You do not realize their properties. They were not only designed to destroy us or exile us—their destiny is to destroy the world as we know it. If you retain them, Elric, you will be responsible for wiping out your own memory for those who come after you."

"I'd welcome that," Elric said.

Dyvim Slorm remained silent, not altogether in sympathy with Elric. The Dead God's argument seemed to contain truth.

Darnizhaan shook his body so that the golden light danced and its area widened momentarily. "Keep the swords and all of us will be as if we had *never* existed," he said impatiently.

"So be it," Elric's tone was stubborn, "do you think I wish the memory to live on—the memory of evil, ruin and destruction? The memory of a man with deficient blood in his veins—a man called Friendslayer, Womanslayer and many other such names?"

Darnizhaan spoke urgently, almost in terror. "Elric, you have been duped! Somewhere you have been given a conscience. You must join with us. Only if the Lords of Chaos can establish their reign will we survive. If they fail, we shall be obliterated!"

"*Good!*"

"Limbo, Elric. *Limbo!* Do you understand what that means?"

"I do not care. Where is my wife?"

Elric blocked the truth from his mind, blocked out the terror in the meaning of the Dead God's words. He could not afford to listen or fully to comprehend. He must save Zarozinia.

"I have brought the swords," said he, "and wish my wife to be returned to me."

"Very well," the Dead God smiled hugely in his relief. "At least if we keep the blades, in their true shape, beyond the Earth, we may be able to retain control of the world. In your hands they could destroy not only us but you, your world, all that you represent. Beasts would rule the Earth for millions of years before the age of intelligence began again. And it would be a duller age than this. We do not wish it to occur. But if you had *kept* the swords, it would have come about almost inevitably!"

"Oh, be silent!" Elric cried. "For a god, you talk too much. Take the swords—and give me back my wife!"

At the Dead God's command, some of the acolytes scampered away. Elric saw their gleaming bodies disappear into the darkness. He waited nervously until they returned, carrying the struggling body of Zarozinia. They set her on the ground and Elric saw that her face bore the blank look of shock.

"Zarozinia!"

The girl's eyes roamed about before they saw Elric. She began to move towards him, but the acolytes held her back, giggling.

Darnizhaan stretched forward two gigantic, glowing hands.

"The swords first."

Elric and Dyvim Slorm put them into his hands. The Dead God straightened up, clutching his prizes and roaring his mirth. Zarozinia was now released and she ran forward to grasp her husband's hand, weeping and trembling. Elric leaned down and stroked her hair, too disturbed to say anything.

Then he turned to Dyvim Slorm, shouting: "Let us see if our plan will work, cousin!"

Elric stared up at Stormbringer writhing in Darnizhaan's grasp. "Stormbringer! *Kerana soliem, o'glara . . .*"

Dyvim Slorm also called to Mournblade in the High Tongue of Melniboné, the mystic, sorcerous tongue which had been used for rune-casting and demon-raising all through Melniboné's twenty thousand years of history.

Together, they commanded the blades, as if they were actually wielding them in their hands, so that merely by shouting orders, Elric and Dyvim Slorm began their work. This was the remembered quality of both blades when paired in a common fight. The blades twisted in Darnizhaan's glowing hands. He started backwards, his shape faltering, sometimes manlike, sometimes beastlike, sometimes totally alien. But he was evidently horrified, this god.

Now the swords wrenched themselves from the clutching hands and turned on him. He fought against them, fending them off as they wove about in the air, whining malevolently, triumphantly, attacking him with vicious power. At Elric's command, Stormbringer slashed at the supernatural being and Dyvim Slorm's Mournblade followed its example. Because the runeblades were also supernatural, Darnizhaan was harmed dreadfully whenever they struck his form.

"Elric!" he raved, "Elric—you do not know what you are doing! Stop them! Stop them! You should have listened more carefully to what I told you. Stop them!"

But Elric in his hate and malice urged on the blades, made them plunge into the Dead God's being time after time so that his shape sometimes faltered, faded, the colours of its bright beauty dulling. The acolytes fled upwards into the vale, convinced that their lord was doomed. Their lord, also, was so convinced. He made one lunge towards the mounted men and then the fabric of his being began to shred before the blades' attack; wisps of his bodystuff seemed to break away and drift into the air to be swallowed by the black night.

Viciously and ferociously, Elric goaded the blades while Dyvim Slorm's voice blended with his in a cruel joy to see the bright being destroyed.

"*Fools!*" he screamed, "*in destroying me, you destroy yourselves!*"

But Elric did not listen and at last there was nothing left of the Dead God and the swords crept back to lie contentedly in their masters' hands.

Quickly, with a sudden shudder, Elric scabbarded Stormbringer.

He dismounted and helped his girl-wife onto the back of his great stallion and then swung up into the saddle again. It was very quiet in the Vale of Xanyaw.

## Chapter Six

Three people, bent in their saddles with weariness, reached the Chasm of Nihrain days later. They rode down the twisting paths into the black depths of the mountain city and were there welcomed by Sepiriz whose face was grave, though his words were encouraging.

"So you were successful, Elric," he said with a small smile.

Elric paused while he dismounted and aided Zarozinia down. He turned to Sepiriz. "I am not altogether satisfied with this adventure," he said grimly, "though I did what I had to in order to save my wife. I would speak with you privately, Sepiriz."

The black Nihrainian nodded gravely. "When we have eaten," he said, "we will talk alone."

They walked wearily through the galleries, noting that there was considerably more activity in the city now, but there was no sign of Sepiriz's nine brothers. He explained their absence as he led Elric and his companions towards his own chamber. "As servants of Fate they have been called to another plane where they can observe something of the several different possible futures of the Earth and thus keep me informed of what I must do here."

They entered the chamber and found food ready and, when they had satisfied their hunger, Dyvim Slorm and Zarozinia left the other two.

The fire from the great hearth blazed. Elric and Sepiriz sat together, unspeaking, hunched in their chairs.

At last, without preamble, Elric told Sepiriz the story of what had happened, what he remembered of the Dead God's words, how they had disturbed him—even struck him as being true.

When he had finished, Sepiriz nodded. "It is so," he said. "Darnizhaan spoke the truth. Or, at least, he spoke most of the truth, as he understood it."

"You mean we will all soon cease to exist? That it will be as if we had never breathed, or thought, or fought?"

"That is likely."

"But why? It seems unjust."

"Who told you that the world was just?"

Elric smiled, his own suspicions confirmed. "Aye, as I expected, there is no justice."

"But there *is*," Sepiriz said, "justice of a kind—justice which must be carved from the chaos of existence. Man was not born to a world of justice. But he can *create* such a world!"

"I'd agree to that," Elric said, "but what are all our strivings for if we are doomed to die and the results of our actions with us?"

"That is not absolutely the case. Something will continue. Those who come after us will inherit something from us."

"What is that?"

"An Earth free of the major forces of Chaos."

"You mean a world free of sorcery, I presume . . . ?"

"Not entirely free of sorcery, but Chaos and sorcery will not dominate the world of the future as it does this world."

"Then that *is* worth striving for, Sepiriz," Elric said almost with relief. "But what part do the runeblades play in the scheme of things?"

"They have two functions. One, to rid this world of the great dominating sources of evil—"

"But they *are* evil, themselves!"

"Just so. It takes a strong evil to battle a strong evil. The days that will come will be when the forces of good can overcome those of evil. They are not yet strong enough. That, as I told you, is what we must strive for."

"And what is the other purpose of the blades?"

"That is their final purpose—your destiny. I can tell you now. I *must* tell you now, or let you live out your destiny unknowing."

"Then tell me," Elric said impatiently.

"Their ultimate purpose is to destroy this world!"

Elric stood up. "Ah, no, Sepiriz. That I cannot believe. Shall I have such a crime on my conscience?"

"It is not a crime, it is in the nature of things. The era of the Bright Empire, even that of the Young Kingdoms, is drawing to a close. Chaos formed this Earth and, for aeons, Chaos ruled. Men were created to put an end to that rule."

"But my ancestors worshipped the powers of Chaos. My patron demon, Arioch, is a Duke of Hell, one of the prime Lords of Chaos!"

"Just so. You, and your ancestors, were not true men at all, but an intermediary type created for a purpose. You understand Chaos as no true men ever could understand it. You can control the forces of Chaos as no true men ever could. And, as a manifestation of the Champion Eternal, you can weaken the forces of Chaos—for you know the qualities of Chaos. Weaken them is what you *have* done. Though worshipping the Lords of Chance, your race was the first to bring some kind of order to the Earth. The people of the Young Kingdoms have inherited this from you—and have consolidated it. But, as yet, Chaos is still that much stronger. The runeblades, Stormbringer and Mournblade, this more orderly age, the wisdom your race and mine have gained, all will go towards creating the basis for the true beginnings of Mankind's history. That history will not begin for many thousands of years, the type may take on a lowlier form, become more beastlike before it re-evolves, but when it does, it will re-evolve into a world bereft of the stronger forces of Chaos. It will have a fighting chance. We are all doomed, but *they* need not be."

"So that is what Darnizhaan meant when he said we were just puppets, acting out our parts before the true play began . . ." Elric sighed deeply, the weight of his mighty responsibility was heavy on his soul. He did not welcome it; but he accepted it.

Sepiriz said gently: "It is your purpose, Elric of Melniboné. Hitherto, your life has appeared comparatively meaningless. All through it you have been searching for some purpose for living, is that not true?"

"Aye," Elric agreed with a slight smile, "I've been restless for many a year since my birth; restless the more between the time when Zarozinia was abducted and now."

"It is fitting that you should have been," Sepiriz said, "for there *is* a purpose for you—Fate's purpose. It is this destiny that you have sensed all your mortal days. You, the last of the royal line of Melniboné, must complete your destiny in the times which are to follow closely upon these. The world is darkening—nature revolts and rebels against the abuses to which the Lords of Chaos put it. Oceans seethe and forests sway, hot lava spills from a thousand mountains, winds shriek their angry torment and the skies are full of awful movement. Upon the face of the Earth, warriors are embattled in a struggle which will decide the fate of the world, linked as the struggle is, with greater conflicts among gods. Women and little children die on a million funeral pyres upon this continent alone. And soon the conflict will spread to the next continent and the next. Soon all the men of the Earth will have chosen sides and Chaos might easily win. It would win but for one thing: you and your sword Stormbringer."

"Stormbringer. It has brought enough storms for me. Perhaps this time it can calm one. And what if Law should win?"

"And if Law should win—then that, too, will mean the decline and death of this world—we shall all be forgotten. But if Chaos should

win—then doom will cloud the very air, agony will sound in the wind and foul misery will dominate a plunging, unsettled world of sorcery and evil hatred. But you, Elric, with your sword and our aid, could stop this. It must be done."

"Then let it be done," Elric said quietly, "and if it must be done—then let it be done well."

Sepiriz said: "Armies will soon be marshaled to drive against Pan Tang's might. These must be our first defense. Thereafter, we shall call upon you to fulfill the rest of your destiny."

"I'll play my part, willingly," Elric replied, "for, whatever else, I have a mind to pay the Theocrat back for his insults and the inconvenience he has caused me. Though perhaps he didn't instigate Zarozinia's abduction, he aided those who did, and he shall die slowly for that."

"Go then, speedily, for each moment wasted allows the Theocrat to consolidate further his new-won empire."

"Farewell," said Elric, now more than ever anxious to leave Nihrain and return to familiar lands. "I know we'll meet again, Sepiriz, but I pray it be in calmer times than these."

Now the three of them rode eastwards, towards the coast of Tarkesh where they hoped to find a secret ship to take them across the Pale Sea to Ilmiora and thence to Karlaak by the Weeping Waste. They rode their magical Nihrain horses, careless of danger, through a war-wasted world, strife-ruined and miserable under the heel of the Theocrat.

Elric and Zarozinia exchanged many glances, but they did not speak much, for they were both moved by a knowledge of something which they could not speak of, which they dared not admit. She knew they would not have much time together even when they returned to Karlaak, she saw that he grieved and she grieved also, unable to understand the change that had come upon her husband, only aware that the black sword at his side would never, now, hang in the armoury again. She felt she had failed him, though this was not the case.

As they topped a hill and saw smoke drifting, black and thick across the plains of Toraunz, once beautiful, now ruined, Dyvim Slorm shouted from behind Elric and his bride: "One thing, cousin—whatever happens, we must have vengeance on the Theocrat and his ally."

Elric pursed his lips.

"Aye," he said, and glanced again at Zarozinia whose eyes were downcast.

Now the Western lands from Tarkesh to Myyrrhn were sundered by the servitors of Chaos. Was this truly to be the final conflict that would decide whether Law or Chaos would dominate the future? The forces of Law were weak and scattered. Could this possibly be the final paroxysm on Earth of the great Lords of Evil? Now, between armies, one part of the world's fate was being decided. The lands groaned in the torment of bloody conflict.

What other forces must Elric fight before he accomplished his final destiny and destroyed the world he knew? What else before the Horn of Fate was blown—to herald in the night?

Sepiriz, no doubt, would tell him when the time came.

But meanwhile more material scores had to be settled. The lands to the east must be made ready for war. The sea-lords of the Purple Towns must be approached for aid, the kings of the South marshaled for attack on the Western Continent. It would take time to do all this.

Part of Elric's mind welcomed the time it would take.

Part of him was reluctant to continue his heavy destiny, for it would mean the end of the Age of the Young Kingdoms, the death of the memory of the Age of the Bright Empire which his ancestors had dominated for ten thousand years.

The sea was at last in sight, rolling its troubled way towards the horizon to meet a seething sky. He heard the cry of gulls and smelled the tang of the salt air in his nostrils.

With a wild shout he clapped his steed's flanks and raced down towards the sea . . .

*In this second long novelette concerning Elric's place in the random scheme of events wherein Order and Chaos are fighting for supremacy of the Earth, the part being played by the mystic runeswords is of paramount importance.*

*—John Carnell, SCIENCE FANTASY No. 61, October 1963*

## BOOK TWO

# BLACK SWORD'S BROTHERS

In which a million blades decide an issue
between Elric and the Lords of Chaos . . .

## Chapter One

ONE DAY THERE came a gathering of kings, captains, and warlords to the peaceful city of Karlaak in Ilmiora by the Weeping Waste.

They did not come in great pomp or with grandiose gestures. They came grim-faced and hurriedly to answer the summons of Elric, who dwelt again in Karlaak with his lately-rescued wife Zarozinia. And they gathered in a great chamber which had once been used by the old rulers of Karlaak for the planning of wars. To this same purpose Elric now put it.

Illuminated by flaring torches, a great coloured map of the world was spread behind the dais on which Elric stood. It showed the three major continents of the East, West and South. That of the West, comprising Jharkor, Dharijor, Shazaar, Tarkesh, Myyrrhn and the Isle of Pan Tang, was shaded black, for all these lands were now the conquered Empire of the Pan Tang-Dharijor alliance which threatened the security of the assembled nobles.

Some of the men who stood armoured before Elric were exiles from the conquered lands—but there were few. Few also were Elric's Imrryrian kinsmen who had fought at the Battle of Sequa and had been defeated with the massed army that had sought to resist the combined might of the evil alliance. At the head of the eldritch Imrryrians stood Dyvim Slorm, Elric's cousin. At his belt, encased in a sturdy scabbard, was the runesword Mournblade, twin to the one Elric wore.

Here also was Montan, Lord of Lormyr, standing with fellow rulers from the Southlands—Jerned of Filkhar, Hozel of Argimiliar, and Kolthak of Pikarayd, adorned in painted iron, velvet, silk and wool.

The sea-lords from the Isle of the Purple Towns were less gaudily clad with helms and breastplates of plain bronze, jerkins, breeks and boots of unstained leather and great broadswords at their hips. Their faces were all but hidden by their long shaggy hair and thick, curling beards.

All these, kings and sea-lords alike, were inclined to stare at Elric suspiciously, since years before he had led their royal predecessors on the raid of Imrryr—though it had left many thrones clear for those who now sat on them.

In another group stood the nobles of that part of the Eastern Continent lying to the east of the Sighing Desert and the Weeping Waste. Beyond these two barren stretches of land were the kingdoms of Eshmir, Chang Shai and Okara, but there was no contact between Elric's part of the world and theirs—save for the small, red-headed man beside him—his friend Moonglum of Elwher, an Eastern adventurer.

The Regent of Vilmir, uncle of the ten-month-old king, headed this last group made up of senators from the city-states comprising Ilmiora; the red-clothed archer Rackhir representing the city of Tanelorn; and various merchant princes from towns coming under the indirect rule of Vilmir as protectorates.

A mighty gathering, representing the massed power of the world.

But would even this be sufficient, Elric wondered, to wipe out the growing menace from the Westlands?

His white albino's face was stern, his red eyes troubled as he addressed the men he had caused to come here.

"As you know, my lords, the threat of Pan Tang and Dharijor is not likely to remain confined to the Western Continent for much longer. Though barely two months have passed since their victory was achieved, they are already marshaling a great fleet aimed at crushing the power of those kings dependent, largely, on their ships for livelihood and defense."

He glanced at the sea-lords of the Purple Towns and the kings of the Southern Continent.

"We of the East, it seems, are not regarded as so much of a danger to their immediate plans and, if we did not unite now, they would have a greater chance of success by conquering first the Southern seapower and then the scattered cities of the East. We must form an alliance which can match their strength."

"How do you know this is their plan, Elric?"

The voice was that of Hozel of Argimiliar, a proud-faced man inclined it was said to fits of insanity, the inbred offspring of a dozen incestuous unions.

"Spies, refugees—and supernatural sources. They have all reported it."

"Even without these reports, we could be sure that this is, indeed, their plan," growled Kargan Sharpeyes, spokesman for the sea-lords. He looked directly at Hozel with something akin to contempt. "And Jagreen Lern of Pan Tang might also seek allies amongst the Southerners. There are some who would rather capitulate to a foreign conqueror than lose their soft lives and easily earned treasure."

Hozel smiled coldly at Kargan. "There are some, too, whose animal suspicions might cause them to make no move against the Theocrat until it was too late."

Elric said hastily, aware of age-old bitternesses between the hardy sea-lords and their softer neighbours: "But worst of all they would be best aided by internal feuds in our ranks, brothers. Hozel—take it for granted that I speak truly and that my information is exact."

Montan, Lord of Lormyr, his face, beard and hair all shaded grey, said haughtily: "You of the North and East are weak. We of the South are strong. Why should we lend you our ships to defend your coasts? I do not agree with your logic, Elric. It will not be the first time it has led good men astray—to their deaths!"

"I thought we had agreed to bury old disputes!" Elric said, close to anger, for the guilt of what he had done was still in him.

"Aye," nodded Kargan. "A man who can't forget the past is a man who cannot plan for the future. I say Elric's logic is good!"

"You traders were always too reckless with your ships and too gullible when you heard a smooth tongue. That's why you now envy our riches." Young Jerned of Filkhar smiled in his thin beard, his eyes on the floor.

Kargan fumed. "Too honest, perhaps, is the word you should have used, Southerner! Belatedly our forefathers learned how the fat Southlands were cheating them. Their forefathers raided your coasts, remember? Maybe we should have continued their practice! Instead, we settled, traded—and your bellies swelled from the profits of our sweat! Gods! I'd not trust the word of a Southern—"

Elric leaned forward to interrupt, but was interrupted himself by Hozel who said impatiently: "The fact is this. The Theocrat is more likely to concentrate his first attacks on the East. For these reasons: The Eastlands are weak. The Eastlands are poorly defended. The Eastlands are closer to his shores and therefore more accessible. Why should he risk his recently united strength on the stronger Southlands, or risk a more hazardous sea-crossing?"

"Because," Elric said levelly, "his ships will be magic-aided and distance will not count. Because the South is richer and will supply him with metals, food—"

"Ships and men!" spat Kargan.

"So! You think we already plan treachery!" Hozel glanced first at Elric and then at Kargan. "Then why summon us here in the first place?"

"I did not say that," Elric said hastily. "Kargan spoke his own thoughts, not mine. Calm yourselves—we *must* be united—or perish before superior armies and supernatural might!"

"Oh, no!" Hozel turned to the other Southern monarchs. "What say you, my peers? Shall we lend them our ships and warriors to protect their shores as well as ours?"

"Not when they are so ungratefully spurned," Jerned murmured.

"Let Jagreen Lern expend his energies upon them. When he looks towards the South he will be weakened, and we shall be ready for him!"

"You are fools!" Elric cried urgently. "Stand with us or we'll all perish! The Lords of Chaos are behind the Theocrat. If he succeeds in his ambitions it will mean more than conquest by a human schemer—it will mean that we shall all be subjected to the horror of total anarchy, on the Earth and above it. The human race is threatened!"

Hozel stared hard at Elric and smiled. "Then let the human race protect itself and not fight under an unhuman leader. 'Tis well-known that the men of Melniboné are not true men at all."

"Be that as it may." Elric lowered his head and lifted a thin, white hand to point at Hozel. The king shivered and held his ground with obvious effort. "But I know more than that, Hozel of Argimiliar. I know that the men of the Young Kingdoms are only the gods' first mouldings—shadow-things who precede the race of real men, even as we preceded you. And I know more! I know that if we do not vanquish both Jagreen Lern and his supernatural allies, then men will be swept from the boiling face of a maddened planet, their destiny unfulfilled!"

Hozel swallowed and spoke, his voice trembling.

"I've seen your muttering kind in the market places, Elric. Men who prophesy all kinds of dooms that never take place—mad-eyed men such as you. But we do not let them live in Argimiliar. We fry them slowly, finger by finger, inch by inch until they admit their omens are fallacious! Perhaps we'll have that opportunity, yet!"

He swung about and half-ran from the hall. For a moment the other Southern monarchs stood staring irresolutely after him.

Elric said urgently: "Heed him not, my lords. I swear on my life that my words are true!"

Jerned said softly, half to himself: "That could mean little. There are rumours you're immortal."

Moonglum came close to his friend and whispered: "They are unconvinced, Elric. 'Tis plain they're not our men."

Elric nodded. To the Southern nobles he said: "Know this: Though you foolishly reject my offer of an alliance, the day will come when you will regret your decision. I have been insulted in my own palace, my friends have been insulted and I curse you for the upstart fools you are. But when the time comes for you to learn the error of this decision I swear that we shall aid you, if it is in our power. Now go!"

Disconcerted, the Southerners straggled from the hall in silence.

Elric turned to Kargan Sharpeyes. "What have you decided, sea-lord?"

"We stand with you," Kargan said simply. "My brother Smiorgan Baldhead always spoke well of you and I remember his words rather than the rumours which followed his death under your leadership. Moreover," he smiled broadly, "it is in our nature to believe that whatever a Southern weakling decides must therefore be wrong. You have the Purple Towns as allies—and our ships, though fewer than the combined fleets of the South, are smooth-sailing fighting ships and well-equipped for war."

"I must warn you that we stand little chance without Southern aid," Elric said gravely.

"I'm doubtful if they'd have been more than an encumbrance with their guile and squabblings," Kargan replied. "Besides—have you no sorcery to help us in this?"

"I plan to seek some tomorrow," Elric told him. "Moonglum and myself will be leaving my cousin Dyvim Slorm in charge here while we go to Sorcerers' Isle, beyond Melniboné. There, among the hermit practitioners of the White Arts, I might find means of contacting the Lords of Law. I, as you know, am half-sworn to Chaos, though I fight it, and am finding increasingly that my own demon-god is somewhat loath to aid me these days. At present, the White Lords are weak, beaten back, just as we are on Earth, by the increasing power of the Dark Ones. It is hard to contact them. The hermits can likely help me."

Kargan nodded. " 'Twould be a relief to us of the Purple Towns to know that we were not too strongly leagued with dark spirits, I must admit."

Elric frowned. "I agree, of course. But our position is so weak that we must accept *any* help—be it black or white. I presume that there is dispute among the Masters of Chaos as to how far they should go—that is why some of my own help still comes from Chaos. This blade that hangs at my side, and the twin which Dyvim Slorm bears, are both evil. Yet they were forged by creatures of Chaos to bring an end, on Earth at least, to the Masters' rule here. Just as my blood-loyalties are divided, so are the swords' loyalties. We have no supernatural allies we can wholly rely upon."

"I feel for you," Kargan said gruffly, and it was obvious that he did. No man could envy Elric's position or Elric's destiny.

Orgon, Kargan's cousin-in-law, said bluntly: "We'll to bed now. Has your kinsman your full confidence?"

Elric glanced at Dyvim Slorm and smiled. "My full confidence—he knows as much as I about this business. He shall speak for me since he knows my basic plans."

"Very well. We'll confer with him tomorrow and, if we do not see you before we leave, do well for us on Sorcerers' Isle."

The sea-lords left.

Now, for the first time, the Regent of Vilmir spoke. His voice was clear and cool. "We, too, have confidence in you and your kinsman, Elric. Already we know you both for clever warriors and cunning planners. Vilmir has good cause to know it from your exploits in Bakshaan and elsewhere throughout our territories. We, I feel, have the good sense to bury old scores." He turned to the merchant princes for confirmation and they nodded their agreement.

"Good," Elric said. He addressed the gaunt-faced archer, Rackhir, his friend, whose legend almost equaled his own.

"You come as a spokesman of Tanelorn, Rackhir. This will not be the first time we have fought the Lords of Chaos."

"True," Rackhir nodded. "Most recently we averted a threat with certain aid from the Grey Lords—but Chaos had caused the gateways to the Grey Lords to be closed to mortals. We can offer you only our warriors' loyalty."

"We shall be grateful for that." Elric paced the dais. There was no need to ask the senators of Karlaak and the other cities of Ilmiora, for they had agreed to support him, come what may, long before the other rulers were called.

The same was true of the bleak-faced band who made up the refugees from the West, headed by Viri-Sek, the winged youth from Myyrrhn, last of his line since all the other members of the ruling family had been slain by Jagreen Lern's minions.

Just beyond the walls of Karlaak was a sea of tents and pavilions over which the banners of many nations waved sluggishly in the hot, moist wind. At this moment, Elric knew, the proud lords of the South were uprooting their standards and packing their tents, not looking at the war-battered warriors of Shazaar, Jharkor and Tarkesh who stared at them in puzzlement. Sight of those dull-eyed veterans should have decided the Southern nobles to ally themselves with the East, but evidently it had not.

Elric sighed and turned his back on the others to contemplate the great map of the world with its shaded dark areas.

"Now only a quarter is black," he said softly to Moonglum. "But the dark tide spreads farther and faster and soon we may all be engulfed."

"We'll dam the flow—or try to—when it comes," Moonglum said with attempted jauntiness. "But meanwhile your wife would spend some time with you before we leave. Let's both to bed and trust our dreams are light!"

## Chapter Two

Two nights later they stood on the quayside in the city of Jadmar while a cold wind sliced its way inland.

"There she is," Elric said, pointing down at the small boat rocking and bumping in the water below.

"A small craft," Moonglum said dubiously. "She scarcely looks seaworthy."

"She'll stay afloat longer than a larger vessel in a heavy storm." Elric clambered down the iron steps. "Also," he added, as Moonglum put a cautious foot on the rung above him, "she'll be less noticeable and won't draw the attention of any enemy vessels which might be scouting in these waters."

He jumped and the boat rocked crazily. He leaned over, grasped a rung and steadied the boat so that Moonglum could climb aboard.

The cocky little Eastlander pushed a hand through his shock of red hair and stared up at the troubled sky.

"Bad weather for this time of year," he noted. "It's hard to understand. All the way from Karlaak we've had every sort of weather, freak snow-storms, thunder-storms, hail and winds as hot as a furnace blast. Those rumours were disturbing, too—a rain of blood in Bakshaan, balls of fiery metal falling in the west of Vilmir, unprecedented earthquakes in Jadmar a few hours before we arrived. It seems nature has gone insane."

"Not far from the truth," Elric said grimly, untying the mooring line. "Lift the sail will you, and tack into the wind?"

"What do you mean?" Moonglum began to loosen the sail. It billowed into his face and his voice was muffled. "Jagreen Lern's hordes haven't reached this part of the world yet."

"They haven't needed to. I told you the forces of nature were being disrupted by Chaos. We have only experienced the backwash of what is going on in the West. If you think these weather conditions are peculiar, you would be horrified by the effect which Chaos has on those parts of the world where its rule is almost total!"

"I wonder if you haven't taken on too much in this fight." Moonglum adjusted the sail and it filled to send the little boat scudding between the two long harbour walls towards the open sea.

As they passed the beacons, guttering in the cold wind, Elric gripped the tiller tighter, taking a south-westerly course past the Vilmirian peninsula. Overhead the stars were sometimes obscured by the tattered shreds of clouds streaming before the cold, unnatural blast of the wind. Spray splashed in his face, stinging it in a thousand places, but he ignored it. He had not answered Moonglum, for he also had doubts about his ability to save the world from Chaos.

Moonglum had learned to judge his friend's moods. For some years before they had traveled the world together and had learned to respect one another. Lately, since Elric had near-permanent residence in his wife's city of Karlaak, Moonglum had continued to travel and had been in command of a small mercenary army patrolling the Southern Marches of Pikarayd, driving back the barbarians inhabiting the hinterland of that country. He had immediately relinquished this command when Elric's news reached him and now, as the tiny ship bore them towards a hazy and peril-fraught destiny, savoured the familiar mixture of excitement and perturbation which he had felt a dozen times before when their escapades had led them into conflict with the unknown supernatural forces so closely linked with Elric's destiny. He had come to accept as a fact that his destiny was bound to Elric's and felt, in the deepest places of his being, that when the time came they would both die together in some mighty adventure.

*Is this death imminent?* he wondered, as he concentrated on the sail and shivered in the blasting wind. Not yet, perhaps, but he felt, fatalistically, that it was not far away, for the time was looming when the only deeds of men would be dark, desperate and great and even these might not serve to form a bastion against the inrush of the creatures of Chaos.

Elric, himself, contemplated nothing, kept his mind clear and relaxed as much as he could. His quest for the aid of the White Lords was one which could well prove fruitless, but he chose not to dwell on this until he knew for certain whether their help could be invoked or not.

Dawn came swimming over the horizon, showing a heaving waste of grey water with no land in sight. The wind had dropped and the air was warmer. Banks of purple clouds bearing veins of saffron and scarlet, poured into the sky, like the smoke of some monstrous pyre. Soon they were sweating beneath a moody sun and the wind had dropped so that the sail hardly moved and yet, at the same time, the sea began to heave as if lashed by a storm.

The sea was moving like a living entity thrashing in nightmare-filled sleep. Moonglum glanced at Elric from where he lay sprawled in the prow of the boat. Elric returned the gaze, shaking his head and releasing his half-conscious grip of the tiller. It was useless to attempt steering the boat in conditions like these. The boat was being swept about by the wild waves, yet no water seemed to enter it, no spray wet them. Everything had become unreal, dreamlike and for a while Elric felt that even if he had wished to speak, he would not have been able to.

Then, in the distance at first, they heard a low droning which grew to a whining shriek and suddenly the boat was sent half-flying over the rolling waves and driven down into a trench. Above them, the blue and silver water seemed for a moment to be a wall of metal—and then it came crashing down towards them.

His mood broken, Elric clung to the tiller, yelling: "Hang on to the boat, Moonglum! Hang on, or you're lost!"

Tepid water groaned down and they were flattened beneath it as if swatted by a gigantic palm. The boat dropped deeper and deeper until it seemed they would be crushed on the bottom by the surging blow. Then, they were flung upwards again, and down, and as he glimpsed the boiling surface, Elric saw three mountains pushing themselves upwards, gouting flame and lava. The boat wallowed, half-full of water, and they set to frantically baling it out as the boat was swirled back and forth, being driven nearer and nearer to the new-formed volcanoes.

Elric dropped his baling pan and flung his weight against the tiller, forcing the boat away from the mountains of fire. It responded sluggishly, but began to drift in the opposite direction.

Elric saw Moonglum, pale-faced, attempting to shake out the sodden sail. The heat from the volcanoes was hardly bearable. He glanced upwards to try and get some kind of bearing, but the sun seemed to have swollen and broken so that he saw a million fragments of flame.

"This is the work of Chaos, Moonglum!" he shouted. "And only a taste, I fancy, of what it can become!"

"They must know we are here and seek to destroy us!" Moonglum swept sweat from his eyes with the back of his hand.

"Perhaps, but I think not." Now he looked up again and the sun seemed almost normal. He took a bearing and began to steer the boat away from the mountains of fire, but they were many miles off their original course.

He had planned to sail to the south of Melniboné, Isle of the

Dragon, and avoid the Dragon Sea lying to the north, for it was well-known that the last great sea-monsters still roamed this stretch. But now it was obvious that they were, in fact, north of Melniboné and being driven further north all the time—towards Pan Tang!

There was a no chance of heading for Melniboné itself—he wondered if the Isle of the Dragon had even survived the monstrous upheavals. He would have to make straight for Sorcerers' Isle if he could.

The ocean was calmer now, but the water had almost reached boiling point so that every drop that fell on his skin seemed to scald him. Bubbles formed on the surface and it was as if they sailed in a gigantic witch's cauldron. Dead fish and half-reptilian forms drifted about, as thick as seaweed, threatening to clog the boat's passage. But the wind, though strong, had begun to blow in one direction and Moonglum grinned in relief as it filled the sail.

Slowly, through the death-thick waters, they managed to steer a south-westerly course towards Sorcerers' Isle as clouds of steam formed on the ocean and obscured their view.

Hours later, they had left the heated waters behind and were sailing beneath clear skies on a calm sea. They allowed themselves to doze. In less than a day they would reach Sorcerers' Isle, but now they were overcome by the reaction to their experience and wondered, dazedly, how they had lived through the awful storm.

Elric jerked his eyes open with a shock. He was certain he had not slept long, yet the sky was dark and a cold drizzle was falling. As the drops touched his head and face, they oozed down it like viscous jelly. Some of it entered his mouth and he hastily spat out the bitter-tasting stuff.

"Moonglum," he called through the gloom, "what's the hour, do you know?"

The Eastlander's sleep-heavy voice answered dazedly. "I know not. I'd swear it is not night already."

Elric gave the tiller a tentative push. The boat did not respond. He looked over the side.

It seemed they were sailing through the sky itself. A dully luminous gas seemed to swirl about the hull, but he could see no water. He shuddered. Had they left the plane of Earth? Were they sailing through some frightful, supernatural sea? He cursed himself for sleeping, feeling helpless; more helpless than when he had fought the storm. The heavy, gelatinous rain beat down strongly and he pulled the hood of his cloak over his white hair. From his belt pouch he took flint and tinder and the tiny light was just sufficient to show him Moonglum's half-mad eyes. The little Eastlander's face was taut with fear. Elric had never seen such fear on his friend's face, and knew that with a little less self-control, his own face would assume a similar expression.

"Our time has ended." Moonglum trembled. "I fear that we're dead, at last, Elric."

"Don't prattle such emptiness, Moonglum. I have heard of no afterlife such as this." But secretly, Elric wondered if Moonglum's words were true. The ship seemed to be moving rapidly through the gaseous sea, being driven or drawn to some unknown destination. Yet Elric could swear that the Lords of Chaos had no knowledge of his boat.

Faster and faster the little craft moved and then, with relief, they heard the familiar splash of water about its keel and it was surging through the salt-sea again. For a short while longer the viscous rain continued to fall and then even that was gone.

Moonglum sighed as the blackness slowly gave way to light and they saw again a normal ocean about them.

"What was it, then?" he ventured, finally.

"Another manifestation of ruptured nature." Elric attempted to keep his voice calm. "Some warp in the barrier between the realm of men and the realm of Chaos, perhaps? Don't question our luck in surviving it. We are again off-course, and," he pointed to the horizon, "a natural storm seems to be brewing yonder."

"A natural storm I can accept, no matter how dangerous," Moonglum murmured, and made swift preparations, furling the sail as the wind increased and the sea churned.

In a way, Elric welcomed the storm when it finally struck them. At least it obeyed natural laws and could be fought by natural means. The rain refreshed their faces, the wind swept through their hair and they battled the storm with fierce enjoyment, the plucky boat riding the waves.

But, in spite of this, they were being driven further and further north-east, towards the conquered coasts of Shazaar, in the opposite direction to their goal.

The healthy storm raged on until all thoughts of destiny and supernatural danger were driven from their minds and their muscles ached and they gasped with the shock of cold waves on their drenched bodies.

The boat reeled and rocked, their hands were sore from the tightness of their grip on wood and rope, but it was as if Fate had singled them out to live, or perhaps for a death that would be less clean, for they continued to ride the heaving waters.

Then, with a shock, Elric saw rocks rearing and Moonglum shouted in recognition: "*The Serpent's Teeth!*"

The Serpent's Teeth lay close to Shazaar and were one of the most feared hazards of the shore-hugging traders of the West. Elric and Moonglum had seen them before, from a distance, but now the storm was driving them nearer and nearer, and though they struggled to keep the boat away, they seemed bound to be smashed to their deaths on the jagged rocks.

A wave surged under the boat, lifted them and bore them down. Elric clung to the side of the boat and thought he heard Moonglum's wild shout above the noise of the storm before they were flung towards the Serpent's Teeth.

"*Farewell!*"

And then there was a terrifying sound of smashing timbers, the feel of sharp rock lacerating his rolling body, and he was beneath the waves, fighting his way to the surface to gasp in air before another wave tossed him and grazed his arm against the rocks.

Desperately, encumbered by the life-giving runesword at his belt, he attempted to swim for the looming cliffs of Shazaar, conscious that even if he lived, he had returned to enemy soil and his chances of reaching the White Lords were now almost non-existent.

## Chapter Three

Elric lay exhausted on the cold shingle, listening to the musical sound that the tide made as it drew back over the stones. Another sound joined that of the surf, and he recognized it as the crunch of boots. Someone was coming towards him. In Shazaar it was most likely to be an enemy. He rolled over and began scrambling to his feet, drawing the last reserves from his worn-out body. His right hand had half-drawn Stormbringer from its scabbard before he realized that it was Moonglum, bent with weariness, standing grinning before him.

"Thank the gods, you live!" Moonglum lowered himself to the shingle and leaned back with his arms supporting his weight, regarding the now calm sea and the towering Serpent's Teeth in the distance.

"Aye, we live," Elric squatted down, moodily, "but for how long in this ruined land, I cannot guess. Somewhere, perhaps, we can find a ship—but it will mean seeking a town or city and we're a marked pair, easily recognized by our physical appearance."

Moonglum shook his head and laughed lightly. "You're still the gloomy one, friend. Be thankful for your life, say I."

"Small mercies are all but useless in this conflict," Elric said. "Rest, now, Moonglum, while I watch, then you can take my place. There was no time to lose when we began this adventure, and now we've lost days."

Moonglum gave no argument, but allowed himself immediately to sleep and when he awoke, much refreshed though aching still, Elric slept until the moon was high and shining brightly in the clear sky.

They trudged through the night, the sparse grass of the coast region giving way to wet, blackened ground. It was as if a holocaust had raged over the countryside, followed by a rainstorm which had left behind it a marsh of ashes. Remembering the grassy plains of this part of Shazaar, Elric was horrified, unable to tell whether men or the creatures of Chaos had caused such wanton ruin.

Noon was approaching, with a hint of weird disturbances in the bright-clouded sky, when they saw a long line of people coming towards them. They flattened themselves behind a small rise and peered cautiously over it as the party drew nearer. These were no enemy soldiers, but gaunt women and starving children, men who staggered in rags, and a few battered riders, obviously the remnants of some defeated band of partisans who had held out against Jagreen Lern.

"I think we'll find friends, of sorts, here," Elric muttered thankfully, "and perhaps some information which will help us."

They arose and walked towards the wretched herd. The riders quickly grouped around the civilians and drew their weapons, but before any challenges could be given, someone cried from the enclosed ranks:

"Elric of Melniboné! Elric—have you returned with news of rescue?"

Elric didn't recognize the voice, but he knew his face was a legend, with its dead white skin and glowing crimson eyes.

"I'm seeking rescue myself, friend," he said with poorly assumed cheerfulness. "We were shipwrecked on your coasts while on a journey which we hoped would help us lift the yoke of Jagreen Lern from off the Westlands, but unless we find another ship, our chances are poor."

"Which way did you sail, Elric?" said the unseen spokesman.

"We sailed to Sorcerers' Isle in the south-west, there to invoke the aid, if we could, of the White Lords," Moonglum replied.

"Then you were going in the wrong direction!"

Elric straightened his back and tried to peer into the throng. "Who are you to tell us that?"

There was a disturbance in the crowd and a bent, middle-aged man with long, curling moustachios adorning his fair-skinned face broke from the ranks and stood leaning on a staff. The riders drew back their horses so that Elric could see him properly.

"I am named Ohada the Seer, once famous in Aflitain as an oracle. But Aflitain was razed in the sack of Shazaar and I was lucky enough to escape with these few people who are all from Aflitain, one of the last cities to fall before Pan Tang's sorcerous might. I have a message of great import for you, Elric. It is for your ears only and I received it from one you know—one who may help you and, indirectly, us."

"You have piqued my curiosity and raised my hopes," Elric beckoned with his hand. "Come, seer, tell me your news and let's all trust it is as good as you hint."

Moonglum took a step back as the seer approached. Both he and the Aflitainians watched with curiosity as Ohada whispered to Elric. Elric himself had to strain to catch the words. "I bear a message from a strange man called Sepiriz. He says that what you have failed to do, he has done, but there is something which you must do that he cannot. He says to go to the carved city and there he will enlighten you further."

"Sepiriz! How did he contact you?"

"I am clairvoyant. He came to me in a dream."

"Your words could be treacherous, designed to lead me into Jagreen Lern's hands."

"Sepiriz added one thing to me—he told me that we should meet on this very spot. Could Jagreen Lern know that?"

"Unlikely—but, by the same reckoning, could *anyone* know that?" He nodded. "Thanks, seer." Then he shouted to the riders. "We need a pair of horses—your best!"

"Our horses are valuable to us," grumbled a knight in torn armour, "they are all we have."

"My companion and I need to move swiftly if we are to save the world from Chaos. Come, risk a pair of horses against the chance of vengeance on your conquerors."

"Aye, very well." The knight dismounted and so did the man beside him. They led their steeds up to Elric and Moonglum.

"Use them with care, Elric."

Elric took the reins and swung himself into the saddle, the huge runesword slapping at his side. "I will," said he. "What are your plans now?"

"We'll fight on, as best we can."

"Would it not be wiser to hide in the mountains or the Marshes of the Mist?"

"If you had witnessed the depravity and terror of Jagreen Lern's rule, you would not make such an enquiry," the knight said bleakly. "Though we cannot hope to win against a warlock whose servants can command the very earth to heave like the ocean, pull down floods of salt water from the sky, and send green clouds scudding down to destroy helpless children in nameless ways, we shall take what vengeance we can. This part of the continent is calm beside what is going on elsewhere. Dreadful geological changes are taking place. You would not recognize a hill or forest ten miles north. And those that you passed one day might well have changed or disappeared the next."

"We have witnessed something of the like on our sea journey," Elric nodded. "I wish you a long life of revenge, friend. I myself have scores to settle with Jagreen Lern and his accomplice."

"His accomplice? You mean King Sarosto of Dharijor?" A thin smile crossed the knight's haggard face. "You'll take no vengeance on Sarosto. He was assassinated soon after our forces were vanquished at the battle of Sequa. Though nothing was proved, it is common knowledge that he was killed at the orders of the Theocrat who now rules unchallenged." The knight shrugged. "And who can stand for long against Jagreen Lern, let alone his captains?"

"Who are these captains?"

"Why, he has summoned all the Dukes of Hell to him. Whether they will accept his mastery much longer, I do not know. It is our belief that Jagreen Lern will be the next to die—and Hell unchecked will rule in his place!"

"I hope not," Elric said softly, "for I won't be cheated of my vengeance."

The knight sighed. "With the Dukes of Hell as his allies, Jagreen Lern will soon rule the world."

"Let us hope I can find a means of disposing of that dark aristocracy, and keeping my vow to slay Jagreen Lern," Elric said and, with a wave of thanks to the seer and the two knights, turned his horse towards the mountains of Jharkor, Moonglum in his wake.

They got little rest on their perilous ride to the mountain home of Sepiriz, for, as the knight had told them, the ground itself seemed alive and anarchy ruled everywhere. Afterwards, Elric remembered little, save a feeling of utter horror and the noise of unholy screechings in his ear, dark colours, gold, reds, blue, black, and the flaring orange that was everywhere the sign of Chaos on Earth.

In the mountain regions close to Nihrain, they found that the rule of Chaos was not so complete as in other parts. This proved that Sepiriz and his nine black brothers were exerting at least some control against the forces threatening to engulf them.

Through steep gorges of towering black rock, along treacherous mountain paths, down slopes that rattled with loose stones and seemed likely to start an avalanche, they pressed deeper and deeper into the heart of the ancient mountains. These were the oldest mountains in the world, and they held one of the Earth's most ancient secrets—the domain of the immortal Nihrain who had ruled for centuries even before the coming of the Melnibonéans. At last, they came to the Hewn City of Nihrain, its towering palaces, temples and fortresses carved into the living black granite, hidden in the depths of the chasm that might have been bottomless. Virtually cut off from all but the faintest filterings of sunlight, it had brooded here since earliest times.

Down the narrow paths they guided their reluctant steeds until they had reached a huge gateway, its pillars carved with the figures of titans and half-men looming above them, so that Moonglum gasped and immediately fell silent, overawed by the genius which could accomplish the twin feats of gigantic engineering and powerful art.

In the caverns, also carved to represent scenes from the legends of the Nihrain, Sepiriz awaited them, a welcoming smile on his thin-lipped ebony face.

"Greetings, Sepiriz," Elric dismounted and allowed slaves to lead his horse away. Moonglum did likewise, a trifle warily.

"I was informed correctly," Sepiriz clasped Elric's shoulders in his hands. "I am glad for I learned you were bound to Sorcerers' Isle to seek the White Lords' help."

"True. Is their help, then, unobtainable?"

"Not yet. We ourselves are trying to contact them, with the aid of the hermit magicians of the island, but so far Chaos has blocked our attempts. But there is work for you and your sword closer to home. Come to my chamber and refresh yourselves. We have some wine which will revitalize you and when you have drunk your fill I'll tell you what task Fate has decided for you now."

Sitting in his chair, sipping his wine and glancing around Sepiriz's dark chamber, lighted only by the fires which burned in its several grates, Elric searched his mind for some clue to the unidentifiable impressions which seemed to drift just below the surface of his conscious brain. There was something mysterious about the chamber, a mystery that was not solely created by its vastness and the shadows that filled it. Without knowing why, Elric thought that though it was bounded by miles of solid rock in all directions, it had no proper dimensions that could be measured by the means normally employed; it was as if it extended into planes that did not conform to the Earth's space and time—planes that were, in fact, timeless and spaceless. He felt that he might attempt to cross the chamber from one wall to the other—but could walk for ever without ever reaching the far wall. He made an attempt to dismiss these thoughts and put down his cup, breathing in deeply. There was no doubt that the wine relaxed and invigorated him. He pointed to the wine-jar on the stone table and said to Sepiriz: "A man might easily become addicted to such a brew!"

"I'm addicted already," Moonglum grinned, pouring himself another cup.

Sepiriz shook his head. "It has a strange quality, our Nihrain wine. It tastes pleasant and refreshes the weary, yet once his strength is regained, the man who drinks it then is nauseated. That is why we still have some of it left. But our stocks are low—the vines from which it was made have long since passed from the Earth."

"A magic potion," Moonglum said, replacing his cup on the table.

"If you like so to designate it. Elric and I are of an earlier age when what you call magic was part of normal life and Chaos ruled entirely, if more quietly than now. You men of the Young Kingdoms are perhaps right to be suspicious of sorcery, for we hope to ready the world for Law soon and then, perhaps, you'll find similar brews by more painstaking methods, methods you can understand better."

"I doubt it," Moonglum laughed.

Elric sighed. "If we are not luckier than we have been, we'll see Chaos unleashed on the globe and Law forever vanquished," he said gloomily.

"And no luck for us if Law is triumphant, eh?" Sepiriz poured himself a cup of the wine.

Moonglum looked sharply at Elric, understanding that much more of his friend's unenviable predicament.

"You said there was work for me and my sword, Sepiriz," Elric said. "What's its nature?"

"You have already learned that Jagreen Lern has summoned some of the Dukes of Hell to captain his men and keep his conquered lands under control?"

"Yes."

"You understand the import of this? Jagreen Lern has succeeded in making a sizable breach in the Law-constructed barrier which once kept the creatures of Chaos from wholly ruling the planet. He is forever widening this breach as his power increases. This explains how he could summon such a mighty assembly of hell's nobility where, in the past, it was hard to bring one to our plane. Arioch is among them . . ."

"Arioch!" Arioch had always been Elric's patron demon, the principal god worshipped by his ancestors. That matters had reached such a stage conveyed to him, deeper than anything else, that he was now a total outcast, unprotected either by Law or Chaos.

"Your only close supernatural ally is your sword," Sepiriz said grimly. "And, perhaps, its brothers."

"What brothers? There is only the sister sword Mournblade, which Dyvim Slorm has!"

"Do you remember that I told you how the twin swords were actually only an earthly manifestation of their supernatural selves?" Sepiriz said calmly.

"I do."

"Well, I can tell you now that Stormbringer's 'real' being is related to other supernatural forces on another plane. I know how to summon them, but these entities are also creatures of Chaos and therefore, as far as you're concerned, somewhat hard to control. They could well get out of hand—perhaps even turn against you. Stormbringer, as you have discovered in the past, is bound to you by ties even stronger than those which bind it to its brothers who are lesser beings altogether, but its brothers outnumber it, and Stormbringer might not be able to protect you against them."

"Why have I never known this?"

"You *have* known it, in a way. Do you remember times when you have called to the Dark Ones for help and help has come?"

"Yes. You mean that this help has been supplied by Stormbringer's brethren?"

"Much of the time, yes. Already they are used to coming to your help. They are not what you and I would call intelligent, though sentient, and are therefore not so strongly bound to Chaos as its reasoning servants. They can be controlled, to a degree, by anyone who has power such as you have over one of their brothers. If you need their help, you will need to remember a rune which I shall tell you later."

"And what is my task?"

"To destroy the Dukes of Hell."

"Destroy the—Sepiriz, that's *impossible*. They are Lords of Chaos, one of the most powerful groups in the whole Realm of Chance. Sepiriz, I could not do it!"

"True. But you control one of the mightiest weapons. Of course, no mortal can destroy the dukes entirely—all he can hope to do is banish them to their own plane by wrecking the substance which they use for bodies on Earth. That is your task. Already there are hints that the Dukes of Hell—namely Arioch, and Balan, and Maluk—have taken some of Jagreen Lern's power from him. The fool still thinks he can rule over such supernatural might as they represent. It suits them, perhaps, to let him think so, but it is certain that with these friends Jagreen Lern can defeat the Southlands with a minimum of expenditure in arms, ships or men. Without them, he could do it—but it would take more time and effort and therefore give us a slight advantage to prepare against him while he subdues the Southlands."

Elric did not bother to ask Sepiriz how he knew of the Southerners' decision to fight Jagreen Lern alone. Sepiriz obviously had many powers as was proved by his ability to contact Elric through the seer. "I have sworn to help the Southlands in spite of their refusal to side with us against the Theocrat," he said calmly.

"And you'll keep your oath—by destroying the dukes if you can."

"Destroying Arioch, and Balan, and Maluk . . ." Elric whispered the names, fearful that even here he might invoke them.

"Arioch has always been an unhelpful demon," Moonglum pointed out. "Many's the time in the past he has refused to aid you, Elric."

"Because," Sepiriz said, "he already had some knowledge that you and he were to fight in the future."

Though the wine had refreshed his body, Elric's mind was close to snapping. The strain on his soul was almost at breaking point. To fight the demon-god of his ancestors . . . The old blood was still strong in him, the old loyalties still present.

Sepiriz rose and gripped Elric's shoulder, staring with black eyes into the dazed and smouldering crimson ones.

"You have pledged yourself to this mission, remember?"

"Aye, pledged—but Sepiriz—the Dukes of Hell—Arioch—I—oh, I wish that I were dead now . . ."

"You have much to do before you'll be allowed to die, Elric," Sepiriz said quietly. "You must realize how important you and your great sword are to Fate's cause. Remember your pledge!"

Elric drew himself upright, nodded vaguely. "Even had I been given this knowledge before I made that pledge, I would still have made it. But . . ."

"What?"

"Do not place too much faith on my ability to fulfill this part, Sepiriz."

The black Nihrain said nothing. Moonglum's normally animated face was grave and miserable as he looked at Elric standing in the mighty hall, the firelight writhing around him, his arms folded on his chest, the huge broadsword hanging straight at his side, and a look of stunned shock on his white face. Sepiriz walked away into the darkness and returned later with a white tablet on which old runes were engraved. He handed it to the albino.

"Memorize the spell," Sepiriz said softly, "and then destroy the tablet. But remember, only use it in extreme adversity for, as I warned you, Stormbringer's brethren may refuse to aid you."

Elric made an effort and controlled his emotions. Long after Moonglum had gone to rest, he studied the rune under the guidance of the Nihrainian, learning not only how to vocalize it, but also the twists of logic which he would have to understand, and the state of mind into which he must put himself if it were to be effective.

When both he and Sepiriz were satisfied, Elric allowed a slave to take him to his sleeping chamber, but slumber came hard to him and he spent the night in restless torment until the slave came to wake him the next morning and found him fully dressed and ready to ride for Pan Tang where the Dukes of Hell were assembled.

## Chapter Four

Through the stricken lands of the West rode Elric and Moonglum, astride sturdy Nihrain steeds that seemed to need no rest and contained no fear. The Nihrain horses were a special gift, for they had certain additional powers to their unnatural strength and endurance. Sepiriz had told them how, in fact, the steeds did not have full existence on the earthly plane and that their hoofs did not touch the ground in the strict sense, but touched the stuff of their other plane. This gave them the ability to appear to gallop on air—or water.

Scenes of terror were everywhere to be found. At one time they saw a frightful sight; a wild and hellish mob destroying a village built around a castle. The castle itself was in flames and on the horizon a mountain gouted smoke and fire—yet another volcano in lands previously free of them. Though the looters had human shape, they were degenerate creatures, spilling blood and drinking it with equal abandon. And directing them without joining their orgy, Elric and Moonglum saw what seemed to be a corpse astride the living skeleton of a horse, bedecked in bright trappings, a flaming sword in its hand and a golden helm on its head.

They skirted the scene and rode fast away from it, through mists that looked and smelled like blood, over steaming rivers dammed with death, past rustling forests that seemed to follow them, beneath skies often filled with ghastly, winged shapes bearing even ghastlier burdens.

At other times, they met groups of warriors, many of them in the armour and trappings of the conquered nations, but depraved and obviously sold to Chaos. These they fought or avoided, depending on circumstance and, when at last they reached the cliffs of Jharkor and saw the sea which would take them to the Isle of Pan Tang, they knew they had ridden through a land to which Hell had come.

Along the cliffs they galloped, high above the churning, grey sea, the lowering sky dark and cold; down to the beaches to pause for a second time on the water's edge.

"Come!" Elric cried, urging his horse forward. "To Pan Tang!"

Scarcely stopping, they rode their magical steeds over the water towards the evil-heavy island of Pan Tang, where Jagreen Lern and his terrible allies prepared to sail with their giant fleet and smash the seapower of the South before conquering the Southlands themselves.

"Elric!" Moonglum called above the whining wind. "Should we not proceed with more caution?"

"Caution? What need of that when the Dukes of Hell must surely know their turncoat servant comes to fight them!"

Moonglum pursed his long lips, disturbed, for Elric was in a wild, maddened mood. He got little comfort, also, from the knowledge that Sepiriz had charmed his shortsword and his sabre both, with one of the few white spells he had at his command.

Now the bleak cliffs of Pan Tang rose into sight, spray-lashed and ominous, the sea moaning about them as if in some special torture which Chaos could inflict on nature itself.

And also around the island a peculiar darkness hovered, shifting and changing.

They entered the darkness as the Nihrain steeds pounded up the steep, rocky beach of Pan Tang, a place that had always been ruled by its black priesthood, a grim theocracy that had sought to emulate the legendary Sorcerer Emperors of the Bright Empire of Melniboné. But Elric, last of those emperors, and landless now, with few subjects, knew that the dark arts had been natural and lawful to his ancestors, whereas these human beings had perverted themselves to worship an unholy hierarchy they barely understood.

Sepiriz had given them their route and they galloped across the turbulent land towards the capital—Hwamgaarl, City of Screaming Statues.

Pan Tang was an island of green, obsidian rock that gave off bizarre reflections; rock that seemed alive.

Soon they could see the looming walls of Hwamgaarl in the distance. As they drew nearer, an army of black-cowled swordsmen, chanting a particularly horrible litany, seemed to rise from the ground ahead and block their way.

Elric had no time to spare for these, recognizable as a detachment of Jagreen Lern's warrior-priests.

"Up, steed!" he cried, and the Nihrain horse leapt skywards, passing over the disconcerted priests with a fantastic bound. Moonglum did likewise, his laughter mocking the swordsmen as he and his friend thundered on towards Hwamgaarl. Their way was clear for some distance, since Jagreen Lern had evidently expected the detachment to hold the pair for a long time. But, when the City of Screaming Statues was barely a mile away, the ground began to grumble and gaping cracks split its surface. This did not overly disturb them, for the Nihrain horses had no use for earthly terrain in any case.

The sky above heaved and shook itself, the darkness became flushed with streaks of luminous ebony, and from the fissures in the ground, monstrous shapes sprang up!

Vulture-headed lions, fifteen feet high, prowled in hungry anticipation towards them, their feathered manes rustling as they approached.

To Moonglum's frightened astonishment, Elric laughed and the Eastlander knew his friend had gone mad. But Elric was familiar with this ghoulish pack, since his ancestors had formed it for their own purposes a dozen centuries before. Evidently, Jagreen Lern had discovered the pack lurking on the borders between Chaos and Earth and had utilized it without being aware of how it had been created.

Old words formed on Elric's pale lips, and he spoke affectionately to the towering bird-beasts. They ceased their progress towards him, and glanced uncertainly around them, their loyalties evidently divided. Feathered tails lashed, claws worked in and out of pads, scraping great gashes in the obsidian rock. And, taking advantage of this, Elric and Moonglum walked their horses through them, and emerged just as a droning but angry voice rapped from the heavens, ordering, in the High Tongue of Melniboné: "*Destroy them!*"

One lion-vulture bounded uncertainly towards the pair. Another followed it, and another, till the whole pack raced to catch them.

"Faster!" Elric whispered to the Nihrain horse, but the steed could hardly keep the distance separating them. There was nothing for it but to turn. Deep in the recesses of his memory, he recalled a certain spell he had learned as a child. All the old spells of Melniboné had been passed on to him by his father, with the warning that, in these times, many of them were virtually useless. But there had been one—the spell for calling the vulture-headed lions, and another spell . . . Now he remembered it! The spell for sending them back to the domain of Chaos. Would it work?

He adjusted his mind, sought the words he needed as the beasts plunged on towards him.

> "Creatures! Matik of Melniboné made thee
> From stuff of unformed madness!
> If thou wouldst live as thou art now,
> Get hence, or Matik's brew again shall be!"

The creatures paused and, desperately, Elric repeated the spell, afraid that he had made a small mistake, either within his mind, or in the words.

Moonglum, who had drawn his horse up beside Elric, did not dare speak his fears, for he knew the albino sorcerer must not be hindered whilst spell-making. He watched in trepidation as the leading beast gave voice to a cawing roar.

But Elric heard the sound with relief, for it meant the beasts had understood his threat and were still bound to obey the spell. Slowly, half-reluctantly, they crawled down into the fissures, and vanished.

Sweating, Elric said triumphantly: "Luck is with us so far! Jagreen Lern either underestimated my powers, or else this is all he could summon with his own! More proof, perhaps, that Chaos uses him, and not the other way about!"

"Tempt not such luck by speaking of it," Moonglum warned. "From what you'd told me, these are puny things compared with what we must soon face."

Elric shot an angry look at his friend. He did not like to think of his coming task.

Now they neared the huge walls of Hwamgaarl. At intervals along these walls, which slanted outwards at an angle to encumber potential besiegers, they saw the screaming statues—once men and women whom Jagreen Lern and his forefathers had turned to rock but allowed them to retain their life and ability to speak. They spoke little, but screamed much, their ghastly shouts rolling over the disgusting city like the tormented voices of the damned—and damned they were. These sobbing waves of sound were horrifying, even to Elric's ears, familiar with such sounds. Then another noise blended with this as the mighty portcullis of Hwamgaarl's main gate squealed upwards and from it poured a host of well-armed men.

"Evidently, Jagreen Lern's powers of sorcery have been exhausted for the meantime and the Dukes of Hell disdain to join him in a fight against a pair of mere mortals!" Elric said, reaching for the hilt of the black runesword.

Moonglum was beyond speech. Wordlessly, he drew both his own charmed blades, knowing he must fight and vanquish his own fears before he could encounter the men who ran at him.

With a wild howl that drowned out the screams from the statues, Stormbringer climbed from the scabbard and stood in Elric's hand, waiting in anticipation for the new souls it might drink, for the lifestuff which it could pass on to Elric and fill him with dark and stolen vitality.

Elric half-cringed at the feel of his blade in his damp hand. But he shouted to the advancing soldiers: "See, jackals! See the sword! Forged by Chaos to vanquish Chaos! Come, let it drink your souls and spill your blood! We are ready for you!"

He did not wait but, with Moonglum behind him, spurred the Nihrain horse into their ranks, hewing about him with something of the old delight.

Now, so symbiotically linked with the hellblade was he, that a hungry joy of killing swept through him, the joy of soul-stealing which drew a surging, unholy vitality into his deficient veins.

Though there were over a hundred warriors blocking his path, he smashed a bloody trail through them and Moonglum, seized by something akin to his friend's mood, was equally successful in dispatching all who came against him. Familiar with horror as they were, the soldiers soon became loath to approach the screaming runesword as it shone with a peculiarly brilliant light—a black light that pierced the blackness itself.

Laughing in his half-insane triumph, Elric felt the callous joy that his ancestors must have felt long ago, when they conquered the world and made it kneel to the Bright Empire. Chaos was, indeed, fighting Chaos—but Chaos of an older, cleaner sort, come to destroy the perverted upstarts who thought themselves as mighty as the wild Dragon Lords of Melniboné! Through the red ruin they had made of the enemy's ranks the pair plunged until the gateway gaped like a monster's maw before them. Without pausing, Elric rode laughing through it and people scuttled to hiding as he entered, in bizarre triumph, the City of Screaming Statues.

"Where now?" gasped Moonglum, all fear driven from him.

"To the Theocrat's Temple-Palace, of course. There Arioch and his fellow dukes no doubt await us!"

Through the echoing streets of the city they rode, proud and terrible, as if with an army at their backs. Dark buildings towered above them, but not a face dared peep from a window. Pan Tang had planned to rule the world—and it might yet—but, for the moment, its denizens were fully demoralized by the sight of two men taking their huge city by storm.

As they reached the wide plaza, Elric and Moonglum pulled their horses to a halt and observed the huge bronze shrine swinging on its chains in the centre. Beyond it rose Jagreen Lern's palace, all columns and towers, ominously quiet. Even the statues had ceased to scream, and the horses' hoofs made no sound as Elric and Moonglum approached the shrine. The blood-reddened runesword was still in Elric's two hands and he raised it upwards and to one side as he reached the brazen shrine. Then he took a mighty sweep at the chains supporting it. The supernatural blade bit into the metal and severed the links. The crash as the shrine dropped and smashed, scattering the bones of Jagreen Lern's ancestors, was magnified a thousand times by the silence. The noise echoed throughout Hwamgaarl and every inhabitant left alive knew what it signified.

"Thus I challenge thee, Jagreen Lern!" Elric shouted, aware that these words would also be heard by everyone. "I have come to pay the debt I promised! Come, puppet!" He paused, even his triumph not sufficient fully to quench his hesitation at what he must do now. "Come! Bring Hell's Dukes with you—"

Moonglum swallowed, his eyes rolling as he studied Elric's twisted face, but the albino continued:

"Bring Arioch. Bring Balan. Bring Maluk! Bring the proud princes of Chaos with you, for I have come to send them back to their own realm for ever!"

The silence again enfolded his high challenge, and he heard its echoes die away in the far places of the city.

Then, from somewhere inside the palace, he heard a movement. His heart pounded against his rib-cage, threatening to break through the bones and hang throbbing on his chest as proof of his mortality. He heard a sound like the clopping of monstrous hoofs and, ahead of this noise, the measured steps that must be those of a man.

His eyes fixed themselves on the great, golden doors of the palace, half-hidden in the shadows that the columns threw. The doors silently began to open. Then a high-shouldered figure, dwarfed by the size of the doors, stepped forth and stood there, regarding Elric with a horrible anger smouldering in its face.

On his body, scarlet armour glowed as if red-hot. On his left arm was a shield of the same stuff and in his hand a steel sword. He had a narrow, aquiline head with a closely trimmed black beard and moustache. On his elaborate helm was the Merman Crest of Pan Tang. Jagreen Lern said, in a voice that trembled with rage: "So, Elric, you have kept part of your word, after all. How I wish I'd been able to kill you at Sequa when I had the chance, but then I had a bargain with Darnizhaan . . ."

"Step forward, Theocrat," Elric said with sudden calm. "I'll give you the chance again and meet you fairly in single combat."

Jagreen Lern sneered. "Fairly? With that blade in your hands?

Once I met it and did not perish, but now it burns with the souls of my best warrior-priests. I know its power. I would not be so foolish as to stand against it. No—let those you have challenged meet you."

He stepped to one side. The doors gaped wider and, if Elric expected to see giant figures to emerge, he was disappointed. The dukes had assumed human proportions and the forms of men. But there was a power about them that filled the air as they moved to stand, disdainful of Jagreen Lern, upon the topmost step of the palace.

Elric looked upon their beautiful, smiling faces and shuddered again, for there was a kind of love on their faces, love mingled with pride and confidence, so that, for a moment, he was filled with the wish to jump from his horse and fling himself at their feet to plead forgiveness for what he had become. All the longing and the loneliness within him seemed to well up and he knew that these lovely beings would claim him, protect him, care for him . . .

"Well, Elric," said Arioch, the leader, softly. "Would you repent and return to us?"

The voice was silvery in its beauty, and Elric half-made to dismount, but then he clapped his hands to his ears, the runesword hanging by its wrist-throng, and cried: "*No! No! I must do what I must! Your time, like mine, is over!*"

"Do not speak thus, Elric," Balan said persuasively, "our rule has hardly begun. Soon the Earth and all its creatures will be part of the Realm of Chaos and a wild and splendid era will begin!" His words passed Elric's hands and whispered in his skull. "Chaos has never been so powerful on Earth—not even in earliest days. We shall make you great. We shall make you a Lord of Chaos, equal to ourselves! We give you immortality, Elric. If you behave so foolishly, you will bring yourself only death, and none shall remember you."

"I know that! I would not wish to be remembered in a world ruled by Law!"

Maluk laughed softly. "That will never come to pass. We block every move that Law makes to try to bring help to Earth."

"And this is why you must be destroyed!" Elric cried.

"We are immortal—we can never be slain!" Arioch said, and there was a tinge of impatience in his voice.

"Then I shall send you back to Chaos in such a way that you shall never have power on the Earth again!"

Elric swung his runeblade into his hand and it trembled there, moaning quietly, as if unsure of itself, just as he was.

"See!" Balan walked partway down the steps. "See—even your trusted sword knows that we speak truth!"

"You speak a sort of truth," Moonglum said in a quavering tone, astonished at his own bravery. "But I remember something of a greater truth—a law that should bind both Chaos and Law—the Law of the Balance. That balance is held over the Earth and it has been ordained that Chaos and Law must keep it straight. Sometimes the Balance tips one way, sometimes another—and thus are the ages of the Earth created. But an unequal balance of this magnitude is *wrong*. In your struggling, you of Chaos may have forgotten this!"

"We have forgotten it for good reason, mortal. The Balance has tipped to such an extent in our favour that it is no longer adjustable. We triumph!"

Elric used this pause to collect himself. Sensing his renewed strength, Stormbringer responded with a confident purr.

The dukes also sensed it and glanced at one another.

Arioch's beautiful face seemed to flare with anger and his pseudobody glided down the steps towards Elric, his fellow dukes following.

Elric's steed backed away a few paces.

A blot of living fire appeared in Arioch's hand and it shot towards the albino. He felt cold pain in his chest and he staggered in the saddle.

"Your body is unimportant, Elric. But think of a similar blow to your soul!" The façade of patience was dropping from Arioch.

Elric flung back his head and laughed. Arioch had betrayed himself. If he had remained calm, he would have had a greater advantage, but now he showed himself perturbed, whatever he had said to the contrary.

"Arioch, you aided me in the past, aided me to live. You will regret that!"

"There's still time to undo my folly, upstart man!" Another bolt came streaking towards him, but he passed Stormbringer before it and, in relief, saw that it deflected the unholy weapon.

But against such might they were surely doomed, unless they could invoke some supernatural aid. But Elric dared not risk summoning his runesword's brothers. Not yet. He must think of some other means. As he retreated before the searing bolts, Moonglum behind him whispering almost impotent charms, he thought of the vulture-lions he had sent back to Chaos. Perhaps he could recall them—for a different purpose.

The spell was fresh in his mind, requiring a slightly changed mental state and scarcely changed wording. Calmly, mechanically deflecting the bolts of the dukes, whose features had changed hideously to retain their previous beauty but take on an increasingly malevolent look, he uttered the spell.

> "Creatures! Matik of Melniboné made thee,
> From stuff of unformed madness!
> If thou wouldst live, then aid me now.
> Come hither, or Matik's brew again shall be!"

From out of the rolling darks of the plaza, the beaked beasts prowled. Elric yelled at the dukes. "Mortal weapons cannot harm you! But these are beasts of your own plane! Sample their ferocity!" In the bizarre tongue of Melniboné, he ordered the vulture-lions upon the dukes.

Apprehensively, Arioch and his fellows backed towards the steps again, calling their own commands to the giant animals, but the things advanced, gathering speed.

Elric saw Arioch shout, rave, and then his body seemed to split asunder and rise in a new, less recognizable shape as the beasts attacked. All was suddenly ragged colour, shrill sound and disordered matter. Behind the embattled demons, Elric saw Jagreen Lern running back into his palace. Hoping that the creatures he had summoned would hold the dukes, Elric rode his horse around the boiling mass and galloped up the steps.

Through the doors, the two men rode, catching a glimpse of the terrified Theocrat running before them.

"Your allies were not so strong as you believed, Jagreen Lern!" Elric yelled as he bore down upon his enemy. "Why, you foolish latecomer, did you think your knowledge matched that of a Melnibonéan!"

Jagreen Lern began to climb a winding staircase, labouring up the steps, too afraid to look back. Elric laughed again and pulled his horse to a stop, watching the running man.

"Dukes! Dukes!" sobbed Jagreen Lern as he climbed. "Do not desert me now!"

Moonglum whispered. "Surely those creatures will not defeat the aristocracy of hell?"

Elric shook his head. "I do not expect them to, but if I finish Jagreen Lern, at least it could put an end to his conquests and demon-summoning." He spurred the Nihrain steed up the steps after the Theocrat who heard him coming and flung himself into a room. Elric heard a bar fall and bolts squeal.

When he reached the door, it fell in at a blow of his sword and he was in a small chamber. Jagreen Lern had disappeared.

Dismounting, Elric went to a small door in the farthest corner of the room and again demolished it. A narrow stair led upwards, obviously into a tower. Now he could take his vengeance, he thought, as he reached yet another door at the top of the stair and drew back his sword to smite it. The blow fell, but the door held.

"Curse the thing, it is protected by charms!"

He was about to aim another blow, when he heard Moonglum's urgent calling from below.

"Elric! Elric—they've defeated the creatures. They are returning to the palace!"

He would have to leave Jagreen Lern for the meantime. He sprang down the steps, into the chamber and out onto the stair. In the hall he saw the flowing shapes of the unholy trinity. Halfway up the stair, Moonglum was quaking.

"Stormbringer," said Elric, "it is time to summon your brothers."

The sword moved in his hand, as if in assent. He began to chant the difficult rune that Sepiriz had taught him. Stormbringer moaned a counterpoint to the dirge as the battle-worn dukes assumed different shapes and began to rise menacingly towards Elric.

Then, in the air all about him, he saw shapes appear, shadowy shapes half on his own plane, half on the plane of Chaos. He saw them stir and suddenly it seemed as if the air was filled with a million swords, each a twin to Stormbringer!

Acting on instinct, Elric released his grip on his blade and flung it towards the rest. It hung in the air before them and they seemed to acknowledge it. "Lead them, Stormbringer! Lead them against the dukes—or your master perishes and you'll not drink another human soul again!"

The sea of swords rustled and a dreadful moaning emanated from them. The dukes flung themselves upwards towards the albino and he recoiled before the evil hatred that poured from the twisting shapes.

Glancing down, he saw Moonglum slumped in his saddle and did not know if he had perished or fainted.

Then the swords rushed upon the reaching dukes and Elric's head swam with the sight of a million blades plunging into the stuff of their beings.

The ululating noise of the battle filled his ears, the dreadful sight of the toiling conflict clouded his vision. Without Stormbringer's vitality, he felt weak and limp. He felt his knees shake and crumple and he could do nothing to aid the Black Sword's brothers as they clashed with the Dukes of Hell.

He collapsed, aware that if he witnessed further horror he would become totally insane. Thankfully, he felt his mind go blank and then, at last, he was unconscious, unable to know which would win.

## Chapter Five

His body itched. His arms and back ached. His wrists pounded with agony. Elric opened his eyes.

Immediately opposite him, spreadeagled in chains against the wall he saw Moonglum. Dull flame flickered in the centre of the place and he felt pain on his naked knee, looked down and saw Jagreen Lern.

The Theocrat spat at him.

"So," Elric said thickly, "I failed. You triumph after all."

Jagreen Lern did not look triumphant. Rage still burned in his eyes.

"Oh, how shall I punish you?" he whispered.

"Punish me? Then—?" Elric's heartbeat increased.

"Your final spell succeeded," the Theocrat said flatly, turning away to contemplate the brazier. "Both your allies and mine vanished and all my attempts to contact the dukes have proved fruitless. You achieved your threat—or your minions did—you sent them back to Chaos for ever!"

"My sword—what of that?"

The Theocrat smiled bitterly. "That's my only pleasure. Your sword vanished with the others. You are weak and helpless now, Elric. You are mine to maim and torture until the end of my life."

Elric was dumbfounded. Part of him rejoiced that the dukes had been beaten. Part of him lamented the loss of his sword. As Jagreen Lern had emphasized, without the blade, he was less than half a man, for his albinism weakened him. Already, his eyesight was dimmer and he felt no response in his limbs.

Jagreen Lern looked up at him.

"Enjoy the comparatively painless days left you, Elric. I leave you to anticipate what I have in store for you. I must away and instruct my men in the final preparations for the war-fleet soon to sail against the South. I won't waste time with crude torture now, for all the while I shall be scheming the most exquisite tortures conceivable. You shall take long years to die, I swear."

He left the cell and, as the door slammed, Elric heard Jagreen Lern instructing the guard.

"Keep the brazier at full blast. Let them sweat like damned souls. Feed them enough to keep them alive, once every three days. They will soon be crying for water. Give them only sufficient to sustain their lives. They deserve far worse than this and they'll get their deserts when my mind has had time to work on the problem."

A day later, the real agony began. Their bodies gave out the last of their sweat. Their tongues were swollen in their heads and all the time as they groaned in their torment they were aware that this terrible torture would be nothing to what they might expect. Elric's weakened body would not respond to his desperate struggling and at length his mind dulled, the agony became constant and familiar, and time was non-existent.

Finally, through a pain-thick daze, he recognized a voice. It was the hate-filled voice of Jagreen Lern.

Others were in the chamber. He felt their hands seize him and his body was suddenly light as he was borne, moaning, from the cell.

Though he heard disjointed phrases, he could make no sense of Jagreen Lern's words. He was taken to a dark place that rolled about, hurting his scorched chest.

Later, he heard Moonglum's voice and strained to hear the words.

"Elric! What's happening? We're aboard a ship at sea, I'd swear!"

But Elric mumbled without interest. His deficient body was weakening faster than would a normal man's. He thought of Zarozinia, whom he would never see again. He knew he would not live to know whether Law or Chaos finally won, or even if the Southlands would stand against the Theocrat.

And these problems were fading in his mind again.

Then the food started to come and the water and it revived him somewhat. At one stage, he opened his eyes and stared upwards into the thinly smiling face of Jagreen Lern.

"Thank the gods," said the Theocrat. "I feared we'd lost you. You're a delicate case to be sure, my friend. You must stay alive longer than this. To begin my entertainment, I have arranged for you to sail on my own flagship. We are now crossing the Dragon Sea, our fleet well-protected by charms against the monsters roaming these parts." He frowned. "Thanks to you, we haven't the same call for the charms which would have borne us safely through the Chaos-torn waters. The seas are almost normal for the moment. But that will soon be changed."

Elric's old spirit returned for a moment and he glared at his enemy, too weak to voice the loathing he felt.

Jagreen Lern laughed softly and stirred Elric's gaunt white head with the toe of his boot. "I think I can brew a drug which will give you a little more vitality."

The food, when it came, was foul-tasting, and had to be forced between Elric's mumbling lips, but after a while he was able to sit up and observe the huddled body of Moonglum. Evidently, the little man had totally succumbed to his torture. To his surprise, Elric discovered he was unfettered and he crawled the agonizing distance between himself and the Eastlander, shaking Moonglum's shoulder. He groaned, but did not otherwise respond.

A shaft of light suddenly struck through the darkness of the hold and Elric blinked, looking up to see that the hatch-cover had been prised aside and Jagreen Lern's bearded face stared down at him.

"Good, good. I see the brew had its effect. Come, Elric, smell the invigorating sea and feel the warm sun on your body. We are not many miles from the coasts of Argimiliar and our scout ships report quite a sizable fleet sailing hence."

Elric cursed. "By Arioch, I hope they send you all to the bottom!"

Jagreen Lern pursed his lips, mockingly. "By whom? Arioch? Do you not remember what ensued in my own palace? Arioch cannot be invoked. Not by you—not by me. Your stinking spells saw to that."

He turned to an unseen lieutenant. "Bind him and bring him on deck. You know what to do with him."

Two warriors dropped into the hold and grasped the still-weak Elric, tying his arms and legs and manhandling him onto the deck. He gasped as the sun's glare struck his eyes.

"Prop him up so he may see all," Jagreen Lern ordered.

The warriors obeyed, and Elric was lifted to a standing position, seeing Jagreen Lern's huge, black flagship with its silken deck canopies flapping in a steady westerly breeze, its three banks of straining oarsmen and its tall ebony mast, bearing a sail of dark red.

Beyond the ship's rails, Elric saw a massive fleet surging in the flagship's wake. As well as the vessels of Pan Tang and Dharijor, there were many from Jharkor, Shazaar and Tarkesh, but on every scarlet sail the Merman blazon of Pan Tang was painted.

Despair filled Elric, for he knew that the Southlands, however strong, could not match a fleet like this.

"We have been at sea for only three days," said Jagreen Lern, "but thanks to a witch-wind, we're almost at our destination. A scout ship has recently reported that the Lormyrian navy, hearing rumours of our superior seapower, is sailing to join with us. A wise move of King Montan—for the moment, at any rate. I'll make use of him for the time being and, when his usefulness is over, I'll kill him for a treacherous turncoat."

"Why do you tell me all this?" Elric whispered, his teeth gritted against the pain that came with any slight movement of his face or body.

"Because I want you to witness for yourself the defeat of the South. The merchant princes sail against us—and we shall easily crush them. I want you to know that what you sought to avert will come to pass. After we have subdued the South and sucked her of her treasures, we'll vanquish the Isle of the Purple Towns and press forward to sack Vilmir and Ilmiora. That will be an easy matter, don't you agree? We have allies other than those you defeated."

When Elric did not reply, Jagreen Lern gestured impatiently to his men.

"Tie him to the mast so that he may get a good view of the battle. I'll put a protective charm around his body, for I do not want him to be killed by a stray arrow and cheat me of my full vengeance."

Elric was borne up and roped to the mast, but he was scarcely aware of it, for his head lolled on his right shoulder, only semiconscious.

The massive fleet plunged onwards, certain of victory.

By mid-afternoon, Elric was aroused from his stupor by the shout of the helmsman.

"Sail to the south-east! Lormyrian fleet approaches!"

With impotent anger, Elric saw the fifty two-masted ships, their bright sails contrasting with the sombre scarlet of Jagreen Lern's vessels, come into line with the others.

Lormyr, though a smaller power than Argimiliar, had a larger navy. Elric judged that King Montan's treachery had cost the South more than a quarter of its strength.

Now he knew there was absolutely no hope for the South and that Jagreen Lern's certainty of victory was well-founded.

Night fell and the huge fleet lay at anchor. A guard came to feed Elric a mushy porridge containing another dose of the drug. As he revived, his anger increased, and Jagreen Lern paused by the mast on two occasions, taunting him savagely.

"Soon after dawn we shall meet the Southern fleet," Jagreen Lern smiled, "and by noon what is left of it will float as bloody driftwood behind us as we press on to establish our reign over those nations who so foolishly relied on their seapower as defense."

Elric remembered how he had warned the kings of the Southlands that this was likely to happen if they stood alone against the Theocrat. But he wished that he had been wrong. With the defeat of the South, the conquest of the East seemed bound to follow and, when Jagreen Lern ruled the world, Chaos would dominate and the Earth revert to the stuff from which it had been formed millions of years before.

All through that moonless night, he brooded. He pulled his thoughts together, summoning all his strength for a plan that was, as yet, only a shadow in the back of his mind.

## Chapter Six

The rattle of anchors woke him.

Blinking in the light of the watery sun, he saw the Southern fleet on the horizon, riding gracefully in hollow pomp towards the ships of Jagreen Lern. Either, he thought, the Southern kings were very brave, or else they did not understand the strength of their enemies.

Beneath him, on Jagreen Lern's foredeck, a great catapult rested, and slaves had already filled its cup with a large ball of flaming pitch. Normally, Elric knew, such catapults were an encumbrance, since when they reached that size they were difficult to rewind and gave lighter war-engines the advantage. Yet obviously Jagreen Lern's engineers were not fools. Elric noted extra mechanisms on the big catapult and realized they were equipped to rewind rapidly.

The wind had dropped and five hundred pairs of muscles strove to row Jagreen Lern's galley along. On the deck, in disciplined order, his warriors took their posts beside the great boarding platforms that would drop down on the opponent's ships and grapple them at the same time as they formed a bridge between the vessels.

Elric was forced to admit that Jagreen Lern had used foresight. He had not relied wholly on supernatural aid. His ships were the best equipped he had ever seen. The Southern fleet, he decided, was doomed. To fight Jagreen Lern was insanity.

But the Theocrat had made one mistake. He had, in his gnawing desire for vengeance, ensured that Elric's vitality was restored for a few hours and this vitality extended to his mind as well as his body.

Stormbringer had vanished. With the sword he was, among men, all but invincible. Without it, he was helpless. These were facts. Therefore he must somehow regain the blade. But how? It had returned to the plane of Chaos with its brothers, presumably drawn back there by the overwhelming power of the rest.

He must contact it.

He dare not summon the entire horde of blades with the spell, that would be tempting providence too far.

He heard the sudden *thwack* and roar as the giant catapult discharged its first shot. The flame-shrouded pitch went arching over the ocean and landed short, boiling the sea around it as it guttered and sank. Swiftly the war-engine was rewound, and Elric marveled at the speed as another ball of flaring pitch was forked into its cup. Jagreen Lern looked up at him and laughed.

"My pleasure will be short. There are not enough of them to put up a long fight. Watch them perish, Elric!"

Elric said nothing, pretended to be dazed and frightened.

The next fireball struck one of the leading ships directly and Elric saw tiny figures scampering about, striving desperately to quench the spreading pitch, but within a minute the whole ship was ablaze, a gouting mass of flame as the figures now jumped overboard, unable to save their vessel.

The air around him sounded to the rushing heat of the fireballs and, within range now, the Southerners retaliated with their lighter machines until it seemed the sky was filled with a thousand comets and the heat almost equaled that which Elric had experienced in the torture chamber. Black smoke began to drift as the brass beaks of the ships' rams ground through timbers, impaling ships like skewered fish. The hoarse yells of fighting men began to be heard, and the clash of iron as the first few opposing warriors met.

But now he only vaguely heard the sounds, for he was thinking deeply.

Then, when at last his mind was ready, he called in a desperate and agonized voice that human ears could not hear above the noise of war: "Stormbringer!"

His straining mind echoed the shout and he seemed to look beyond the turbulent battle, beyond the ocean, beyond the very Earth to a place of shadows and terror. Something moved there. Many things moved there.

"Stormbringer!"

He heard a curse from beneath him and saw Jagreen Lern pointing up at him. "Gag the white-faced sorcerer." Jagreen Lern's eyes met Elric's and the Theocrat sucked in his lips, deliberating a bare moment before adding: "And if that doesn't put an end to his babbling—best slay him!"

The lieutenant began to climb the mast towards Elric.

"Stormbringer! Your master perishes!"

He struggled in the biting ropes, but could hardly move.

"Stormbringer!"

All his life he had hated the sword he relied on so much; which he was relying on more and more, but now he called for it as a lover calls for his betrothed.

The warrior grasped his foot and shook it. "Silence! You heard my master!"

With insane eyes, Elric looked down at the warrior who shuddered and drew his sword, hanging to the mast with one hand and readying himself to make a stab at Elric's vitals.

"Stormbringer!" Elric sobbed the name. He *must* live. Without him, Chaos would surely rule the world.

The man lunged at Elric's body—yet the blade did not reach the albino. Then Elric remembered, with sudden humour, that Jagreen Lern had placed a protective spell about him! The Theocrat's own magic had saved his enemy!

"Stormbringer!"

Now the warrior gasped and the sword dropped from his fingers. He seemed to grapple with something invisible at his throat and Elric saw the man's fingers sliced off and blood spurt from the stumps. Then, slowly, a shape materialized and, with bounding relief, the albino saw that it was a sword—his own runesword impaling the warrior and sucking out his soul!

The warrior dropped, but Stormbringer hung in the air and then turned to slash the ropes restraining Elric's hands and then nestled firmly, with horrid affection, in its master's right fist.

At once the stolen lifestuff of the warrior began to pour through Elric's being and the pain of his body vanished. Quickly he grasped a piece of the sail's rigging and cut away the rest of his bonds until he was swinging by one hand on the rope.

"Now, Jagreen Lern, we'll see who takes vengeance, finally," he grimaced as he swung towards the deck and dropped lightly upon it, the unholy vitality from the sword surging through him to fill him with a godlike ecstasy. He had never known it so strong before.

But then he noted that the boarding platforms had been lowered and only a skeleton crew remained on the flagship. Jagreen Lern must have led his main strength onto the ship which was now held fast by grapples.

Close by was a great barrel of pitch, used to form the fireballs.

Close to that was a flaring torch used to ignite them. Elric seized the brand and flung it into the pitch.

"Though Jagreen Lern may win this battle, his flagship shall go to the bottom with the Southern fleet," he said grimly, and dashed for the hold where he had been imprisoned, aware that Moonglum lay helpless there.

He wrenched up the hatch-cover and stared down at the pitiful figure of his friend. Evidently, he had been left to starve to death. A rat chittered away as the light shone down.

Elric jumped into the hold and saw, with horror, that part of Moonglum's right arm had been gnawed already. He heaved the body onto his shoulder, aware that the heart still beat, though faintly, and clambered back up to the deck. How to ensure his friend's safety and still take vengeance on Jagreen Lern was a problem. But Elric moved towards the boarding platform which he guessed the Theocrat to have crossed. As he did so, three warriors leapt towards him. One of them cried: "The albino! The reaver escapes!"

Elric struck him down with a blow that required only a slight movement of his wrist. The Black Sword did the rest. The others retreated, remembering how Elric had entered Hwamgaarl.

New energy flowed through him. For every corpse he created, his strength increased—a stolen strength, but necessary if he was to survive and win the day for Law.

He ran, untroubled by his burden, over the boarding platform and onto the deck of the Southern ship. Up ahead he saw the standard of Argimiliar and a little group of men around it, headed by King Hozel himself, his face gaunt as he stared at the knowledge of his own death. A deserved death, thought Elric grimly, but nonetheless when Hozel died it would mean another victory for Chaos.

Then he heard a shout of a different quality, thought for a moment that he had been observed, but one of Hozel's men was pointing to the north and mouthing something.

Elric looked in that direction and saw the brave sails of the Purple Towns. They were fighting ships, better equipped for battle than those of the merchant princes. Their brightly painted sails caught the

light. The only rich decoration the austere sea-lords allowed themselves was upon their sails. Elric's old friend Kargan must command them.

But they had arrived belatedly. Even if they had sailed with the other Southern vessels it would have been unlikely that they could have turned the day against Pan Tang.

At that moment, staring around him, Jagreen Lern saw Elric and bellowed at his men who moved forward warily and reluctantly, approaching the albino in a wide semi-circle.

Elric cursed the brave sea-lords who had added a further factor to his indecision.

Menacingly he swung the moaning runeblade about him as he advanced to meet the half-terrified Pan Tang warriors. They dropped back, some of them groaning as the blade touched them. The way was now clear to Jagreen Lern.

But the ships of the Purple Towns were drawing closer, almost within catapult range.

Elric looked directly into Jagreen Lern's frightened face and snarled: "I doubt if my blade has the strength to pierce your burning armour with one blow, and one blow is all I have time for. I leave you now, Theocrat, but remember that even if you conquer all the world including the unknown lands of the East, I'll have my sword drink your black soul at length."

With that he dropped Moonglum's unconscious body overboard and dived after it into the choppy sea.

The blade gave him superhuman strength and he swam towards the leading ship of the sea-lords, which he recognized as Kargan's, dragging Moonglum's body after him.

Now, behind him, Jagreen Lern and his men saw their own flagship blazing. Elric had done his work well.

That, too, would serve to divert attention from Kargan's fleet.

Trusting to the sea-lords' famed seamanship, he swam directly in the path of the leading galleon, shouting Kargan's name.

The ship veered slightly and he saw bearded faces at the rail, saw ropes flicker towards him and grasped one, letting them haul him upwards with his burden.

As the seamen pulled them both over the rail, Elric saw Kargan staring at him with shocked eyes. The sea-lord was dressed in the tough brown leather armour of his folk. He had an iron cap on his massive head and his black beard bristled. "Elric! We thought you dead—lost on your voyage south!"

Elric spat salt water from his mouth and said urgently: "Turn your fleet, Kargan! Turn it back the way it has come, there is no hope of saving the Southlanders—they are doomed. We must preserve our forces for a later struggle."

Hesitating momentarily, Kargan gave the order which was swiftly relayed to the rest of his sixty-strong fleet.

As the ships turned away, Elric noted that hardly a Southern ship remained afloat. For more than a mile the water burned and the sputtering of the flaming, sinking ships was blended with the screams of the maimed and drowning.

"With the Southern seapower crushed so decisively," Kargan said, watching the physician who was tending to Moonglum, "the lands will not last long before Pan Tang's marching hordes. Like us, the South relied too much on its ships. It has taught me that we must strengthen our land defenses if we are to have any chance at all."

"From now on we'll use your island as our main headquarters," Elric said. "We'll fortify the whole place and from there keep in close touch with what is happening in the South. How is my friend, physician?"

The physician looked up. "These are no battle-made wounds. He's been hurt sorely, but he'll live. He should recover to perfect fitness given a month or so of rest."

"He'll have it," Elric promised. He gripped the runesword at his belt and wondered what other tasks lay in store for them before the last great battle between Law and Chaos was joined.

Chaos would soon rule more than half the world, in spite of the powerful blow he had dealt it in forever sentencing the Dukes of Hell to their own plane; the more power that Jagreen Lern gathered, the more the threat from Chaos would increase.

He sighed and looked northwards.

Two days later they returned to the Isle of the Purple Towns, the fleet remaining in the largest harbour of Utkel since it was thought wise to have it at hand and not disperse it.

All that following night, Elric talked with the sea-lords, ordered messengers to Vilmir and Ilmiora and, towards morning, there came a polite knock on the door of the room.

Kargan got up to open it and stared in astonishment at the tall, black-faced man who stood there.

"Sepiriz!" Elric cried. "How did you come here?"

"On horseback," smiled the giant, "and you know the power of the Nihrain steeds. I had come to warn you. We have, at last, managed to contact the White Lords but they can do little as yet. Somehow a path to their plane must be made through the barricades which Chaos has constructed against them. Jagreen Lern's ships have vomited their contents on the Southern shores and his warriors swarm inland. There is nothing we can do now to stop his conquests there. Once consolidated, his earthly power increased, he will be able to summon more and more allies from Chaos."

"Then where does my next task lie?" Elric asked softly.

"I am not sure yet. But that is not what I came for. Your blade's sojourn with its brothers has strengthened it. You notice how swiftly it pours power into your body now?"

"True. Yet I seem ever more reliant upon that power." He spoke flatly. "The power is stronger, but I am weaker, it seems."

Sepiriz said gravely: "That power is evilly gained and evil in itself. The blade's strength will continue to increase but as Chaos-begotten power fills your being, you will have to fight yet more strongly to control the force within you. That also will take strength. So, you see, you must use part of the strength to fight the strength itself."

Elric sighed and grasped Sepiriz's arm.

"Thanks for the warning, friend, but when I beat the Dukes of Hell, to whom I formerly pledged allegiance, I did not expect to escape with a mere scratch or a flesh-wound. Know this, Sepiriz," he turned to the watching sea-lords, "and know this all of you."

He drew the groaning runeblade from its scabbard and held it aloft so that it shone and flared in its awful power.

"This blade was forged by Chaos to conquer Chaos and that is my destiny, too. Though the world crumbles and turns to boiling gas, I shall live now. I swear by the Cosmic Balance that Law shall triumph and the New Age come to this Earth."

Taken aback by this grim vow, the sea-lords glanced at one another and Sepiriz smiled.

"Let us hope so, Elric," he said. "Let us hope so."

*This is the third novelette in the quartette dealing with Elric's final influence in the great battle between Order and Chaos. Here, the forces of Order are almost beaten, but Elric, himself a part of Chaos, still hopefully fights on against impossible odds.*

*—John Carnell, SCIENCE FANTASY No. 63, February 1964*

## BOOK THREE

# SAD GIANT'S SHIELD

Thirteen times thirteen, the steps to the sad giant's lair;
And the Chaos Shield lies there.
Seven times seven are the elder trees
Twelve times twelve warriors he sees
But the Chaos Shield lies there.
And the hero fair will the sad giant dare
And a red sword wield for the sad giant's shield
On a mournful victory day.

—*The Chronicle of the Black Sword*

## Chapter One

ACROSS THE WHOLE world the shadow of anarchy had fallen. Neither god, nor man, nor that which ruled both could clearly read the future and see the fate of Earth as the forces of Chaos increased their strength both personally and through their human minions.

From Westland mountain, over the agitated ocean to Southland plain, Chaos now held its monstrous sway. Tormented, miserable, unable to hope any longer for liberation from the corroding, warping influence of Chaos, the remnants of races fled over the two continents already fallen to the human minions of Disorder, led by their warped Theocrat Jagreen Lern of Pan Tang, aquiline, high-shouldered and greedy for power, in his glowing scarlet armour, controlling human vultures and supernatural creatures alike as he widened his black boundaries.

Upon the face of the Earth all was disruption and roaring anguish, save for the thinly populated, already threatened Eastern Continent and the Isle of the Purple Towns, which now readied itself to withstand Jagreen Lern's initial onslaught. The onrushing tide of Chaos must soon sweep the world unless some great force could be summoned to halt it.

Bleakly, bitterly, the few who still resisted Jagreen Lern, under the command of Elric of Melniboné, talked of strategy and tactics in the full knowledge that more than these were needed to beat back Jagreen Lern's unholy horde.

Desperately, Elric attempted to utilize the ancient sorcery of his emperor forefathers to contact the White Lords of Law; but he was unused to seeking such aid and, as well, the forces of Chaos were now so strong, that those of Law could no longer gain easy access to the Earth as they had contrived to do in earlier times.

As they prepared for the coming fight, Elric and his allies went about the preparation with heavy souls and a sense of the futility of such action. And, in the back of Elric's mind, was the constant knowledge that even if he won against Chaos, the very act of winning would destroy the world he knew and leave it ripe for the forces of Law to rule—and there would be no place in such a world for the wild albino sorcerer.

Beyond the earthly plane, in their bordering realms, the Lords of the Higher Worlds watched the struggle, and even they did not realize Elric's entire destiny.

Chaos triumphed. Chaos blocked the efforts of Law on each occasion they tried to pass through the domain of Chaos, now the only road to Earth. And the Lords of Law shared Elric's frustration.

And, if Chaos and Law were observing the Earth and her struggle, who watched these? For Chaos and Law were but the twin weights in a balance and the hand that held the Balance, though it rarely deigned to interfere in their struggle, still less in the affairs of men, had reached the rare state of a decision to alter the status quo. Which weight would drop? Which rise? Could men decide? Could the lords decide? Or could only the Cosmic Hand remould the pattern of the Earth, reforming her stuff, changing her spiritual constituents and placing her on a different path, a fresh course of destiny?

Perhaps all would play some part before the outcome was decided.

The great zodiac influencing the universe and its Ages, had completed its twelve cycles and the cycles would soon begin again. The wheel would spin and, when it stopped its spinning, which symbol would dominate, how changed would it be?

Great movements on the Earth and beyond it; great destinies being shaped, great deeds being planned and, marvelously, could it just be possible that in spite of the Lords of the Higher Worlds, in spite of the Cosmic Hand, in spite of the myriad supernatural denizens that swarmed the multiverse, that Man might decide the issue?

Even one man?

One man, one sword, one destiny?

Elric of Melniboné sat hunched in his saddle, watching the warriors bustle to and fro around him in the city square of Bakshaan. Here, years before, he had conducted a siege against the city's leading merchant, tricked others and left rich, but such scores that they held against him were now forgotten, pushed from their minds by the threat of war and the knowledge that if Elric's command could not save them, nothing could. The walls of the city were being widened and heightened, warriors being trained in the use of unfamiliar war-engines. From being a lazy merchant city, Bakshaan had become a functional place, ready for battle when it came.

For a month, Elric had been riding the length and breadth of the Eastern kingdoms of Ilmiora and Vilmir, overseeing preparations, building the strength of the two nations into an efficient war machine.

Now he studied parchments handed him by his lieutenants and, recalling all the old tactical skill of his ancestors, gave them his decisions.

The sun was setting and heavy black clouds hung against a sharp, metallic blue sky, stretching over the horizon. Elric loosened his cloak strings and allowed the folds of the garment to enclose him, for a chill had come.

Then, as he silently regarded the sky to the west, he frowned as he noticed something like a flashing golden star appear, moving swiftly towards him.

Ever wary for signs of the coming of Chaos, he turned in his saddle shouting:

"Every man to his position! 'Ware the golden globe!"

The thing approached rapidly until soon it was hanging over the city, all men looking up at it in astonishment, their hands on their weapons. As black night fell, the clouds admitting no moonlight, the globe began to fall towards the spires of Bakshaan, a strange luminescence pulsing from it. Elric tugged Stormbringer from its scabbard and black fire flickered along the blade as it gave out a low moaning sound. The globe touched the cobbles of the city square—broke into a million fragments that glowed for a moment before vanishing.

Elric laughed in relief, resheathing Stormbringer as he saw who now stood in the place of the golden globe.

"Sepiriz, my friend. You choose strange means of transport to carry you from the Chasm of Nihrain."

The tall, black-faced seer smiled, his white pointed teeth gleaming. "I have so few carriages of that type that I must only use them when pressed. I come with news for you—much news."

"I hope it is good, for we have enough bad to last us for ever."

"It is mixed. Where can we converse in private?"

"My headquarters are in yonder mansion," Elric pointed at a richly decorated house on the far side of the square.

Inside, Elric poured yellow wine for his guest. Kelos the merchant, whose house this was, had not accepted the requisitioning altogether willingly and, partly because of this, Elric maliciously made free with all Kelos's best.

Sepiriz took the goblet and sipped the strong wine.

"Have you succeeded in contacting the White Lords again, Sepiriz?" Elric asked.

"We have."

"Thank the gods. Are they willing to give their aid to us?"

"They have always been so willing—but they have not yet made a sufficient breach in the defenses that Chaos has set up around this planet. However, the fact that I have at last managed to contact them is a better sign than we've had these past months."

"So—the news *is* good," Elric said cheerfully.

"Not altogether. Jagreen Lern's fleet has set sail again—and they head towards the Eastern Continent, with thousands of ships—and supernatural allies, too."

"It was only what I expected, Sepiriz. My work's done here, anyway. I'll ride for the Isle of the Purple Towns at once, for I must lead the fleet against Jagreen Lern."

"Your chances of winning will be all but non-existent, Elric," Sepiriz warned him gravely. "Have you heard of the Ships of Hell?"

"I've heard of them—do they not sail the depths of the sea, taking on board dead mariners as crews?"

"They do—they're things of Chaos and far larger than even the largest mortal warship. You'd never withstand them, even if you did not have the Theocrat's fleet to fight as well."

"I'm aware the fight will be hard, Sepiriz—but what else can we do? I have a weapon against Chaos in my blade here—or so you tell me."

"Not enough, that bodkin—you still have no *protection* against the Dark Lords. That is what I have to tell you of—a personal armament for yourself to help you in your struggle, though you'll have to win it from its present possessor."

"Who owns it?"

"A giant who broods in eternal misery in a great castle on the edge of the world, beyond the Sighing Desert. Mordaga is his name and he was once a god, but is now made mortal for sins he committed against his fellow gods long ages ago."

"Mortal? Yet he has lived so long?"

"Aye. Mordaga is mortal—though his life-span's considerably greater than an ordinary man's. He is obsessed with the knowledge that he must one day die. That is what saddens him."

"And the weapon?"

"Not a weapon exactly—a shield. A shield with a purpose—one that Mordaga had made for himself when he raised a rebellion in the domain of the gods and sought to make himself greatest of them, and even wrest the Eternal Balance from He who holds it. For this he was banished to Earth and informed that he would one day die—slain by a mortal's blade. The shield, as you might guess, is proof against the workings of Chaos."

"How so?"

"The chaotic forces, if powerful enough, can disrupt any defense made of lawful matter; no construction based on the principles of order can withstand for long the ravages of sheer chaos, as we know." Sepiriz leaned forward a little. "Stormbringer has shown you that the only weapon effective against Chaos is something of Chaos-manufacture. The same can be said for the Chaos Shield. This itself is Chaotic in nature and therefore there is nothing organized in it on which the random forces can act and destroy. It meets Chaos with Chaos, and so the hostile powers are subverted."

"If I had only had such a shield of late—things might have gone better for us all!"

"I could not tell you of it. I am merely the servant of Fate and cannot act unless it is sanctioned by that which I serve. Perhaps, as I have guessed, it is willing to see Chaos sweep the world before it is defeated—if indeed it *is* defeated—so that it can completely change the nature of our planet before the new cycle begins. Change it will—but whether it will be ruled in the future primarily by Law or Chaos, that is in your hands, Elric!"

"How would I recognize this shield?"

"By the eight-arrowed Sign of Chaos which radiates from its boss. It is a heavy, round shield, made as a buckler for a giant. But, with the vitality you receive from your runesword, you will have the strength to carry it, have no fear. But first you must have the courage to win it from

its present possessor. Mordaga is aware of the prophecy, told him by his fellow gods before they cast him forth."

"Are you, too, aware of it?"

"I am. In our language it forms a simple rhyme:

> "Mordaga's pride; Mordaga's doom,
> Mordaga's fate shall be
> To die as men when slain by men,
> Four men of destiny."

"Four men? Who are the other three?"

"Those you will know of when the time comes for you to seek the

Chaos Shield. Which will you do? Go to the Purple Towns—or will you go to find the shield?"

"I wish that I had the time to embark on a quest of that kind, but I have not. I must go to rally my men, shield or no."

"You will be defeated."

"We shall see, Sepiriz."

"Very well, Elric. Since so little of your destiny is in your own hands, we should allow you to take just one decision at times," Sepiriz said sympathetically.

"Fate is kind," Elric commented ironically. He rose from his seat. "I'll begin the journey straightway, for there's no time to lose."

## Chapter Two

With his milk-white hair streaming behind him and his red eyes blazing with purpose, Elric lashed his stallion through the cold darkness of the night, through a disturbed land which awaited Jagreen Lern's attack in trepidation, for it could mean not only their deaths, but the drawing of their souls into the servitude of Chaos.

Already the standards of a dozen Western and Southern monarchs fluttered with Jagreen Lern's as the kings of the conquered lands chose his command rather than death—and placed their peoples under his dominance so that they became marching, blank-faced creatures with enslaved souls, their wives and children dead, tormented or feeding the blood-washed altars of Pan Tang where the priests send up invocations to the Chaos Lords, and, ever-willing to further their power on Earth, the lords answered with support.

And not only the entities themselves, but the stuff of their own weird cosmos was entering the Earth, so that where their power was the land heaved like the sea, or the sea flowed like lava, mountains changed shape and trees sprouted ghastly blossoms never seen on Earth before—all nature was unstable and it could not be long until Earth was wholly one with the Realm of Chaos.

Wherever Jagreen Lern conquered, the warping influence of Chaos was manifest. The very spirits of nature were tortured into becoming what they should not be—air, fire, water and earth, all became unstable, for Jagreen Lern and his allies were tampering not only with the lives and souls of men, but the very constituents of the planet itself. And there was none of sufficient power to punish them for these crimes. None.

With this knowledge within him, Elric's progress was swift and wild, as he strove to reach the Isle of the Purple Towns before his pitifully inadequate fleet sailed to do battle with Chaos.

Two days later he arrived in the port of Uhaio, at the tip of the smallest of the three Vilmirian peninsulas, and took ship at once to the Isle of the Purple Towns, where he disembarked and rode into the interior towards the ancient fortress *Ma-ha-kil-agra*, which had withstood every siege ever made against it, and was regarded as the most impregnable construction in the whole of the lands still free from Chaos. Its name was in an older language than any known to those who lived in the current Age of the Young Kingdoms. Only Elric knew what the name signified. The fortress had been there long before the present races came to dominance, even before Elric's ancestors had begun their conquerings. *Ma-ha-kil-agra*—the Fortress of Evening, where long ago, a lonely race had come to die.

As he arrived in the courtyard, Moonglum, the Eastlander, came rushing from the entrance of a tower.

"Elric! We have been awaiting your arrival, for time grows scarce before we must embark against the enemy. We have sent out shipborne spies to estimate the size and power of Jagreen Lern's fleet. Only four returned and all were uselessly insane. The fifth has just come back, but—"

"But what?"

"See for yourself. He has been—altered, Elric."

"Altered! Altered! Let me see him. Take me to him." Elric nodded curtly to the other captains who had come out to greet him. He passed them and followed behind Moonglum through the stone corridors of the fortress, lit badly by sputtering rushes.

Leading Elric to an antechamber, Moonglum stopped outside, running his fingers through his thick, red hair. "He is therein. Would you care to interview him alone? I'd rather not set eyes on him again!"

"Very well." Elric opened the door, wondering how this spy would be changed. Sitting at the plain wooden table, was the remains of a man. It looked up. As Moonglum had warned him—it had been altered.

Elric felt pity for the man, but he was not nauseated or horrified like Moonglum, for in his sorcery-working he had seen far worse creatures. It was as if the whole of one side of the spy's body had become at one stage viscous, had flowed, and then coiled in a random shape. Side of head, shoulder, arm, torso, leg, all were replaced by streamers of flesh like rat's tails, lumps of matter like swollen boils, weirdly mottled. The spy spread his good hand and some of the streamers seemed to jerk and wave in unison.

Elric spoke quietly. "What magic wrought this drastic change?"

A kind of chuckle came from the lopsided face.

"I entered the Realm of Chaos, lord. And Chaos did this, it changed me as you see. The boundaries are being extended. I did not know it. I was inside before I realized what had happened. *The area of Chaos is being widened!*" He leaned forward, his shaking voice almost screaming. "With it sail the massed fleets of Jagreen Lern—great waves of warships, squadrons of invasion craft, thousands of transports, ships mounting great war engines, fire-ships—ships of all kinds, bearing a multitude of standards—the kings of the South left alive have sworn loyalty to Jagreen Lern and he has used all their resources and his own to marshal this sea-horde! As he sails, he extends the area of Chaos, so whereas his sailing is slower than normal, when he reaches us here—Chaos will be with him. I saw such ships that could be of no earthly contriving—the size of castles—each one seeming to be a dazzling combination of all colours!"

"So he *has* managed to bring more supernatural allies to his standard," Elric mused. "Those are the Ships of Hell, Sepiriz mentioned . . ."

"Aye—and even if we beat the natural craft," the messenger said, hysterically, "we could not beat both the ships of Chaos and the stuff of Chaos which boils around them and did to me what you observe! It boils, it warps, it changes constantly. That is all I know, save that Jagreen Lern and his human allies are unharmed by it as I was harmed. When this change began to take place in my body, I fled to the Dragon Isle of Melniboné, which seems to have withstood the process and is the only safe land in all the waters of the world. My body—healed—swiftly, and I chanced another sailing to bring me here."

"You were courageous," Elric said hollowly. "You will be well rewarded, I promise."

"I want only one reward, my lord."

"What is that?"

"Death. I can no longer live with the horror of my body mirroring the horror in my brains!"

"I will see to it," Elric promised. He remained brooding for a few seconds before nodding farewell to the spy and leaving the room.

Moonglum met him outside.

"It looks black for us, Elric," he said softly.

Elric sighed. "Aye—perhaps I should have gone to seek the Chaos Shield *first*."

"What's that?"

Elric explained all Sepiriz had told him.

"We could do with such a defense," Moonglum agreed. "But there it is—the priority is tomorrow's sailing. Your captains await you in the conference chamber."

"I will see them in a short while," Elric promised. "First I wish to go to my own room to collect my thoughts. Tell them I'll join them when that's done."

When he reached his room, Elric locked the door behind him, still thinking of the spy's information. He knew that without supernatural aid no ordinary fleet, no matter how large or how courageously manned, could possibly withstand Jagreen Lern. And the fact was that he had only a comparatively small fleet, no supernatural entities for allies, no means of combating the disrupting chaotic forces. If only he had the Chaos Shield beside him now . . . But it was useless to regret a decision of the kind he'd made. If he sought the shield now, he couldn't fight the battle in any case.

For weeks he had consulted the grimoires that, in the form of scrolls, tablets, books and sheets of precious metals engraved with ancient symbols, littered his room. The elementals had helped him in the past, but, so disrupted were they by Chaos, that they were weak for the most part.

He unstrapped his hellsword and flung it on the bed of tumbled silks and furs. Wryly he thought back to earlier times when he had given in to despair and how those incidents which had engendered the mood seemed merely gay escapades in comparison to the task which now weighed on his mind. Though weary, he chose not to draw Stormbringer's stolen energy into himself, for the feeling that was so close to ecstasy was leavened by the guilt—the guilt which had possessed him since a child when he had first realized that the expression on his remote father's face had not been one of love, but of disappointment that he should have spawned a deficient weakling—a pale albino, good for nothing without the aid of drugs or sorcery.

Elric sighed and went to the window to stare out over the low hills and beyond them to the sea. He spoke aloud, perhaps subconsciously, hoping that the release of the words would relieve some of the tension within him.

"I do not care for this responsibility," he said. "When I fought the Dead God he spoke of both gods and men as shadow-things, playing puppet parts before the true history of Earth began and men found their fate in their own hands. Then Sepiriz tells me I must turn against Chaos and help destroy the whole nature of the world I know or history might never begin again, and Fate's great purpose would be thwarted. Therefore *I* am the one who must be split and tempered to fulfill my destiny—*I* must know no peace of mind, must fight men and gods and the stuff of Chaos without surcease, must bring about the death of this age so that, in some far dawn-age, men who know little of sorcery or the Lords of the Higher Worlds, may move about a world where the major forces of Chaos can no longer enter, where justice may actually exist as a reality, and not as a mere concept in the minds of all philosophers."

He rubbed his red eyes with his fingers.

"So fate makes Elric a martyr that Law might rule the world. It gives him a sword of ugly evil that destroys friends and enemies alike and sucks their soul-stuff out to feed him the strength he needs. It binds me to evil and to Chaos, in order that I may *destroy* evil and Chaos—but it does not make me some senseless dolt easily convinced and a willing sacrifice. No, it makes me Elric of Melniboné and floods me with a mighty misery . . ."

"My lord speaks aloud to himself—and his thoughts are gloomy. Speak them to me, instead, so that I might help you bear them, Elric."

Recognizing the soft voice, but astonished nonetheless, Elric turned quickly towards the source and saw his wife Zarozinia standing there, her arms outstretched and a look of deep sympathy on her young face.

He took a step towards her before stopping and saying angrily: "When did you come here? Why? I told you to remain in your father's palace at Karlaak until this business is done, if ever!"

"If ever . . ." she repeated, dropping her arms to her sides with a little shrug. Though scarcely more than a girl, with her full red lips and long black hair, she bore herself as a princess must and seemed more than her age.

"Ask not *that* question," he said cynically. "It is not one we ask ourselves here. But answer mine. How did you come here and why?" He knew what her reply would be, but he spoke only to emphasize his anger which in turn was a result of his horror that she should have come so close to danger—danger which he had already rescued her from once.

"I came with my cousin Opluk's two thousand," she said, lifting her head defiantly, "when he joined the defenders of Uhaio. I came to be near my husband at a time when he may need my comforting. The gods know I've had little opportunity to discover if he does!"

Elric paced the room in agitation. "As I love you, Zarozinia, believe that I would be in Karlaak now with you had I any excuse at all. But I have not—you know my role, my destiny, my doom. You bring sorrow with your presence, not help. If this business has a satisfactory end, then we'll meet again in joy—not in misery as we now must!"

He crossed to her and took her in his arms. "Oh, Zarozinia, we should never have met, never have married. We can only hurt one another at this time. Our happiness was so brief . . ."

"If you would be hurt by me, then hurt you shall be," she said softly, "but if you would be comforted, then I am here to comfort my lord."

He relented with a sigh. "These are loving words, my dear—but they are not spoken in loving times. I have put love aside for the nonce. Try to do likewise and thus we'll both dispense with added complication."

Without anger, she drew slowly away from him and with a slight smile that had something of irony in it, pointed to the bed, where Stormbringer lay.

"I see your other mistress still shares your bed," she said. "And now you need never try to dismiss her again, for that black lord of Nihrain has given you an excuse to forever keep her by your side. Destiny—is that the word? Destiny! Ah, the deeds men have done in destiny's name. And what is destiny, Elric, can you answer?"

He shook his head. "Since you ask the question in malice, I'll not make the attempt to answer it."

She cried suddenly: "Oh, Elric! I have traveled for many days to see you, thinking you would welcome me. And now we speak in anger!"

"*Fear!*" he said urgently. "It is fear, not anger. I fear for you as I fear for the fate of the world! See me to my ship in the morning and then make speed back to Karlaak, I beg you."

"If you wish it."

She walked back into the small chamber which joined the main one.

## Chapter Three

"We talk only of defeat!" roared Kargan of the Purple Towns, beating upon the table with his fist. His beard seemed to bristle with rage.

Dawn had found all but a few of the captains retiring through weariness. Kargan, Moonglum, Elric's cousin Dyvim Slorm and moon-faced Dralab of Tarkesh, remained in the chamber, pondering tactics.

Elric answered him calmly: "We talk of defeat, Kargan, because we must be prepared for that eventuality. It seems likely, does it not? We must, if defeat seems imminent, flee our enemies, conserving our force for another attack on Jagreen Lern. We shall not have the forces to fight another major battle, so we must use our better knowledge of currents, winds and terrain to fight him from ambush on sea or land. Thus we can perhaps demoralize his warriors and take considerably more of them than they can of us."

"Aye—I see the logic," Kargan rumbled unwillingly, evidently disturbed by this talk for, if the major battle was lost, then lost also would be the Isle of the Purple Towns, bastion against Chaos for the mainland nations of Vilmir and Ilmiora.

Moonglum shifted his position, grunting slightly. "And if they drive us back, then back we must go, bending rather than breaking, and returning from other directions to attack and confuse them. It's in my mind that we'll have to move more rapidly than we'll be able to, since we'd be tired and with few provisions . . ." He grinned faintly. "Ah, forgive me for my pessimism. Ill-placed, I fear."

"No," Elric said. "We must face all this or be caught unawares. You are right. And to allow for ordered retreat, I have already sent detachments to the Sighing Desert and the Weeping Waste to bury large quantities of food and such things as extra arrows, lances and so forth. If we are forced back as far as the barrens, we'll likely fare better than Jagreen Lern, assuming that it takes him time to extend the area of Chaos and that his allies from the Higher Worlds are not overwhelmingly powerful."

"You spoke of realism . . ." said Dyvim Slorm, pursing his curving lips and raising a slanting eyebrow.

"Aye—but some things cannot be faced or considered—for if we are totally engulfed by Chaos at the outset, then we'll have no need of plans. So we plan for the other eventuality, you see."

Kargan let out his breath and rose from the table. "There's no more to discuss," he said. "I'll to bed. We must be ready to sail with the noon tide tomorrow."

They all gave signs of assent and chairs scraped as they pushed them back and left the chamber.

Bereft of human occupants, the chamber was silent save for the sputtering of the lamps and the rustle of the maps and papers as they were stirred by a warm wind.

It was late in the morning when Elric arose and found Zarozinia already up and dressed in a skirt and bodice of cloth-of-gold with a long, black-trimmed cloak of silver spreading to the floor.

He washed, shaved and ate the dish of herb-flavoured fruit she handed him.

"Why have you arrayed yourself in such finery?" he asked.

"To bid you goodbye from the harbour," she said.

"If you spoke truth last night, then you'd best be dressed in funeral red," he smiled and then, relenting, clasped her to him. He gripped her tightly, desperately, before standing back from her and taking her chin in his hand raised her face to stare down into it. "In these tragic times," he said, "there's little room for love-play and kind words. Love must be deep and strong, manifesting itself in our actions. Seek no courtly words from me, Zarozinia, but remember earlier nights when the only turbulence was our pulse-beats blending."

He was clad, himself, in Melnibonéan war regalia; with a breastplate of shiny black metal, a high-collared jerkin of black velvet, black leather breeks covered to the knee by his boots, also of black leather. Over his back was pushed a cloak of deep red, and on one thin, white finger was the Ring of Kings, the single rare Actorios stone, set in silver. His long white hair hung loose down to his shoulders, held by a bronze circlet. Stormbringer was at his hip and upon the table among the open books was a tapering black helm, engraved with old runes, its crown gradually rising into a spoke standing almost two feet from the base. At this base, dominating the eye-slits was a replica of a spread-winged dragon with gaping snout, a reminder that, as emperors of the Bright Empire, his ancestors had been Dragon Masters and that perhaps the dragons of Melniboné still slept in their underground caverns. Now he picked up this helm and fitted it over his head so that it covered the top half of his face, only his red eyes gleaming from its shadows. He refrained from pulling the side wings about his lower face but for the meantime, left them sweeping back from the bottom of the helmet.

Noting her silence, he said, with a heart already heavy, "Come, my love, let's to the harbour to astound these under-civilized allies of ours with our elegance. Have no fear that I shall not live to survive this day's battle—for Fate has not finished with me yet and protects me as a mother would her son—so that I might witness further misery until such a day when it's over for all time."

Together, they left the Fortress of Evening, riding on magical Nihrain horses, down to the harbour where the other sea-lords and captains were already assembled beneath the bright sun.

All were dressed in their finest martial glory, though none could match Elric. Old racial memories were awakened in many when they saw him and they were troubled, fearing him without knowing why, for their ancestors had had great cause to fear the Bright Emperors in the days when Melniboné ruled the world and a man accoutred as Elric commanded a million eldritch warriors. Now a bare handful of Imrryrians greeted him as he rode along the quayside, noting the ships riding at anchor with their coloured banners and heraldic devices lifting proudly in the breeze.

Dyvim Slorm was equipped in a close-fitting dragon helm, its protecting pieces fashioned to represent the entire head of a dragon, scaled in red and green and silver. His armour was lacquered yellow, though the rest of his dress was black, like Elric's. At his side was Stormbringer's sister sword Mournblade.

As Elric rode up to the group, Dyvim Slorm turned his heavily armoured head towards the open sea. There was little inkling of encroaching Chaos on the calm water or in the clear sky.

"At least we'll have good weather on our way to meet Jagreen Lern," Dyvim Slorm said.

"A small mercy," Elric smiled faintly. "Is there any more news of their numbers?"

"Before the spy who returned yesterday died he said there were at least four thousand warships, ten thousand transports—and perhaps twenty of the Chaos ships. They'll be the ones to watch since we've no idea what powers they have."

Elric nodded. Their own fleet comprised some five thousand warships, many equipped with catapults and other heavy war-engines. The transports, though they turned the odds, in numbers, to a far superior figure, would be slow, unwieldy, and of not much use in a pitched sea-battle. Also, if the battle were won, they could be dealt with later, for they would obviously follow in the rear of Jagreen Lern's war-fleet.

So, for all Jagreen Lern's numerical strength, there would be a good chance of winning a sea-fight under ordinary conditions. The disturbing factor was the presence of the supernatural ships. The spy's description had been vague. Elric needed more objective information—information he would be unlikely to receive now, until the fleets joined in battle.

In his shirt was tucked the beast-hide manuscript of an extraordinarily strong invocation used in summoning Straasha the Sea-King. He had already attempted to use it, without success, but hoped that on open sea his chances would be better, particularly since the sea-king would be angered at the disruption Jagreen Lern and his occult allies were causing in the balance of nature. Once before, long ago, the sea-king had aided him and had, Elric recalled, predicted that Elric would summon him again.

Kargan, in the thick but light sea-armour of his people which gave him the appearance of a hairy-faced armadillo, pointed as several small boats detached themselves from the fleet and sailed towards the quay.

"Here come the boats to take us to our ships, my lords!"

The gathered captains stirred, all of them with serious expressions, seeming, each and every one, to be pondering some personal problem, staring into the depths of their own hearts—perhaps trying to reach the fear which lay there; trying to reach it and tear it out and fling it from them. They all had more than the usual trepidation experienced when facing a fight—for, like Elric, they could not guess what the Chaos ships were capable of.

They were a desperate company, understanding that something less palatable than death might await them beyond the horizon.

Elric squeezed Zarozinia's arm.

"Goodbye."

"Farewell, Elric—may whatever benevolent gods there are left on the Earth protect you."

"Save your prayers for my companions," he said quietly, "for they will be less able than I to face what lies out there."

Moonglum called to him and Zarozinia: "Give her a kiss, Elric, and come to the boat. Tell her we'll be back with victory tidings!"

Elric would never have admitted such familiarity, not even with his kinsman Dyvim Slorm, from anyone but Moonglum. But he took it in good part saying softly to her: "There, you see, little Moonglum is confident—and he's usually the one with warnings of ominous portent!"

She said nothing, but kissed him lightly on the mouth, grasped his hand for a moment and then watched him as he strode down the quay and clambered into the boat which Moonglum and Kargan were steadying for him.

The oars splashed and bore the captains towards the flagship, *Timber-tearer*, Elric standing in the bow staring ahead, looking back only once when the boat drew alongside the ship and he began to climb the rope ladder up to the deck, his black helm bobbing.

* * *

Bracing himself on the deck, Elric watched the backs of the warrior-rowers as they bent to the oars, supplementing the light wind which filled the great purple sail, making it curve out in a graceful billow.

The Isle of the Purple Towns was now out of sight and green, glinting water was all that was visible around the fleet, which stretched behind the flagship, its furthest ships tiny shapes in the distance. Already the fleet was moving into battle-order, forming into five squadrons, each under the command of an experienced sea-lord from the Purple Towns, for most of the other captains were landsmen who, though quick to learn, had little experience of sea tactics.

Moonglum came stumbling along the swaying deck to stand beside his friend.

"How did you sleep last night?" he asked Elric.

"Well enough, save for a few nightmares."

"Ah, then you shared something with us all. Sleep was hard won for everyone, and when it came it was troubled. Visions of pits of monsters and demons, of horrifying shapes, of unearthly powers, they crowded our dreams."

Elric nodded, paying little attention to Moonglum. The elements of Chaos in their own beings were evidently awakening in response to the approach of the Chaos horde itself. He hoped they would be strong enough to withstand the actuality as they had survived their dreams.

"*Disturbance to forward!*"

It was the lookout's cry, baffled and perturbed. Elric cupped his hands around his mouth and tilted his head back.

"What sort of disturbance?"

"It's like nothing I've ever seen, my lord—I can't describe it."

Elric turned to Moonglum. "Relay the order through the fleet—slow the pace to one drum-beat in four, squadron commanders stand by to receive final battle orders." He strode towards the mast and began to climb up it towards the lookout's post. He climbed until he was high above the deck. The lookout swung out of his cradle, since there was only room for one.

"Is it the enemy, my lord?" he said as Elric clambered into his place. Elric stared hard towards the horizon, making out a kind of dazzling blackness that from time to time sent up sprawling gouts of stuff into the air where it hung for some moments before sinking back into the main mass. Smoky, hard to define, it crept gradually nearer, crawling over the sea towards them.

"It's the enemy," said Elric quietly.

He remained for some while in the lookout's cradle, studying the Chaos-stuff as it flung itself about in the distance, like some amorphous monster in its death-agonies. But these were not death-agonies. Chaos was far from dead.

From this vantage point, Elric also had a clear view of the fleet as it formed itself into its respective squadrons, making up a black wedge nearly a mile across at its longest point and nearly two miles deep. His own ship was a short distance in front of the rest, well in sight of the squadron commanders. Elric shouted down to Kargan whom he saw passing the mast: "Stand by to move ahead, Kargan!"

The sea-lord nodded without pausing in his stride. He was fully aware of the battle-plan, as they all were for they had discussed it long enough. The leading squadron, under the command of Elric, was comprised of their heaviest warships which would smash into the centre of the enemy fleet and seek to break its order, aiming particularly at whichever ship Jagreen Lern now used. If Jagreen Lern could be slain or captured, their victory would be more likely.

Now the dark stuff was closer and Elric could just make out the sails of the first vessels, spread out one behind the other. Then, as they came even closer, he was aware that to each side of this leading formation were great glinting shapes that dwarfed even the huge battlecraft of Jagreen Lern.

The Chaos Ships.

Elric recognized them, now, from his own knowledge of occult lore. These were the ships said normally to sail the deeps of the oceans, taking on drowned sailors as crews, captained by creatures that had never been human. It was a fleet from the deepest, gloomiest parts of the vast underwater domain which had, since the beginning of time, been disputed territory—disputed between water elementals under their king Straasha, and the Lords of Chaos, who claimed the sea-depths as their main territory on Earth, by right. Legends said that at one time Chaos had ruled the sea and Law the land. This, perhaps, explained the fear of the sea that many human beings had to this day, and the pull the sea had for others.

But the fact was that, although the elementals had succeeded in winning the shallower portions of the sea, the Chaos Lords had retained the deeper parts by means of this, their fleet of the dead. The ships themselves were not of earthly manufacture, neither were their captains originally from Earth, but their crews had once been human, and were now indestructible in any ordinary sense.

As they approached, Elric was soon in no doubt that they were, indeed, those ships. The Sign of Chaos flashed on their sails, eight amber arrows radiating from a central hub—signifying the boast of Chaos, that it contained all possibilities whereas Law was supposed, in time, to destroy possibility and result in eternal stagnation. The Sign of Law was a single arrow pointing upwards, symbolizing dynamic growth.

Elric knew that in reality Chaos was the harbinger of stagnation, for though it changed constantly, it never progressed. But, in his heart, he still felt a yearning for this state, for his past loyalties to the Lords of Chaos had suited him better to wild destruction than to stable progress.

But now Chaos must make war on Chaos; Elric must turn against those he had once been loyal to, using weapons formed by Chaotic forces to defeat those selfsame forces in these ironic times.

He clambered from the cradle and began to shin down the mast, leaping the last few feet to land on the deck as Dyvim Slorm came up. Quickly he told his cousin what he had seen.

Dyvim Slorm was astounded. "But the fleet of the dead never comes to the surface—save for . . ." his eyes widened.

Elric shrugged. "That's the legend—the fleet of the dead will rise from the depths when the final struggle comes, when Chaos shall be divided against itself, when Law shall be weak and mankind shall choose sides in the battle that will result in a new Earth dominated either by total Chaos or by almost-total Law. When Sepiriz told us this was the case, I felt a response. Since then, in studying my manuscripts, I have been fully reminded."

"Is this, then, to be the final battle?"

"It might be," Elric answered. "It is certain to be one of the last when it will be decided for all time whether Law or Chaos shall rule here."

"If we're defeated, then Chaos will undoubtedly rule."

"Perhaps, but remember that the struggle need not be decided by battles alone."

"So Sepiriz said, but if we're defeated this day, we'll have little chance to discover the truth of that." Dyvim Slorm gripped Mournblade's hilt. "Someone must wield these blades—these destiny-swords—when the time comes for the deciding duel. Our allies diminish, Elric."

"Aye. But I've a hope that we can summon a few others. Straasha, King of the Water Elementals, has ever fought against the death fleet—and he is brother to Graoll and Misha, the Wind Lords. Perhaps through Straasha, I can summon his unearthly kin. In this way we will be better matched, at least."

"I know only a fragment of the spell for summoning the water-king," Dyvim Slorm said.

"I know the whole rune. I had best make haste to meditate upon it, for our fleets will clash in two hours or less and then I'll have no time for the summoning of spirits but will have to keep tight hold on my own less some Chaos creature releases it."

Elric moved towards the prow of the ship, and, leaning over, stared into the ocean depths, turning his mind inward and contemplating the strange and ancient knowledge which lay there. He became almost hypnotized as he lost contact with his own personality and began to identify with the swirling ocean below.

Involuntarily, old words began to form in his throat and his lips began to move in the rune which his ancestors had known when they and all the elementals of the Earth had been allies and sworn to aid one another long ago in the dawn of the Bright Empire, more than ten thousand years before.

"Waters of the sea, thou gave us birth
And were our milk and mother both
In days when skies were overcast
You who were first shall be the last.

"Sea-rulers, fathers of our blood,
Thine aid is sought, thine aid is sought,
Your salt is blood, our blood your salt,
Your blood the blood of Man.

"Straasha, eternal king, eternal sea
Thine aid is sought by me;
For enemies of thine and mine
Seek to defeat our destiny, and drain away our sea."

The spoken rune was merely a vocalization of the actual invocation which was produced mentally and went plunging into the depths, through the dark green corridors of the sea until it finally found Straasha in his domain of curving, coral-coloured, womblike constructions which were only partially in the natural sea and partially in the plane where the elementals spent a large part of their immortal existence.

Straasha knew of the Ships of Hell rising to the surface and had been pleased that his domain was now cleared of them, but Elric's summons awakened his memory and he remembered the folk of Melniboné upon whom all the elementals had once looked with a sense of comradeship; he remembered the ancient invocation, and felt bound to answer it, though he knew his people were badly weakened by the effect Chaos had had in other parts of the world. Not only humans had suffered; the elemental spirits of nature had been sorely pressed as well.

But he stirred so that water and the stuff of his other plane were both disturbed. He summoned some of his followers and began to glide upwards into the domain of the Air.

* * *

Semi-conscious now, Elric knew that his invocation had met with success. Sprawled in the prow, he waited.

At last the waters heaved and broke and revealed a great green figure, with turquoise beard and hair, pale green skin that seemed made of the sea itself, and a voice that was like a rushing tide.

"*Once more Straasha answers thy summons, mortal. Our destinies are bound together. How may I aid thee, and, in aiding thee, aid myself?*"

In the throat-torturing speech of the elemental, Elric answered, telling the sea-king of the forthcoming battle and what it implied.

"*So at long last it has come to pass! I fear I cannot aid you much, for my folk are already suffering terribly from the depredations of our mutual enemy. We shall attempt to aid you if we can. That's all I promise.*"

The sea-king sank back into the waters and Elric watched him depart with a feeling of acute disappointment. It was with a brooding mind that he left the prow and went to the main cabin to tell his captains the news.

They received it with mixed feelings, for only Dyvim Slorm was used to dealing with supernaturals. Moonglum had always been dubious of Elric's powers to control his wild, elemental friends, while Kargan growled that Straasha may have been an ally of Elric's folk but had been more of an enemy to his. The four of them, however, could plan with slightly more optimism and face the coming ordeal with better confidence.

## Chapter Four

The fleet of Jagreen Lern bore towards them and, in its wake, the boiling stuff of Chaos hovered.

Elric gave the command and the rowers hauled at their oars, sending *Timber-tearer* rushing towards the enemy. So far his elemental allies had not appeared, but he could not afford to wait for them.

As *Timber-tearer* rode the foaming waves, Elric hauled his sword from its scabbard, brought the side wings of his helmet round to cover his face and cried the age-old ululating war-shout of Melniboné, a shout full of joyous evil. Stormbringer's eerie voice joined with his, giving vent to a thrumming song, anticipating the blood and the souls it would soon feast upon.

Jagreen Lern's new flagship now lay behind three rows of men-o'-war and behind the flagship were the Chaos ships.

*Timber-tearer*'s iron ram ripped into the first enemy ship and the rowers leaned on their oars, backing away and turning to pierce another ship below the water line. Showers of arrows sprayed from the holed ship and clattered on deck and armour. Several rowers went down.

Elric and his three companions directed their men from the main deck, standing so that between them they had an overall view of what was going on around them. Elric looked up suddenly, warned by some sixth sense, and saw streaking balls of green fire come curving out of the sky.

"Prepare to quench fires!" Kargan yelled and the group of men already primed for this leapt for the tubs containing a special brew which Elric had told them how to make earlier. This was spread on decks and splashed on canvas and, when the fireballs landed, they were swiftly quenched. "Don't engage unless forced to," Elric called to the seamen, "keep aiming for the flagship. If we take that, our advantage will be good!"

"Where are your allies, Elric?" Kargan asked sardonically, shuddering a little as he saw the Chaos stuff in the distance suddenly move and erupt tendrils of black matter into the sky.

"They'll come, never fear," Elric answered, but he was unsure.

Now they were in the thick of the enemy fleet, the ships of their squadron following behind, their great oars slicing through the ocean's foam. The war-engines of their own fleet sent up a constant barrage of fire and heavy stones. Only a few of Elric's craft broke through the enemy's first rank and reached the open sea, sailing towards Jagreen Lern's flagship.

As they were observed, the enemy ships sailed to protect the flagship and the scintillating ships of death, moving with fantastic speed for their size, surrounded the Theocrat's vessel.

Shouting over the waters, Kargan ordered their diminished squadron into a new formation. Moonglum shook his head in astonishment. "How can things of that size support themselves on the water?" he said to Elric.

"It's unlikely that they actually do." As their ship manoeuvred into its new position, he stared at the huge craft, twenty of them, dwarfing everything else on the sea. They seemed covered with a kind of shining fluid which flashed all the colours of the spectrum so that their outlines were hard to see and the shadowy figures moving about on their gigantic decks could not easily be observed. Wisps of dark stuff began to drift across the scene, close to the water, and Dyvim Slorm, from the lower deck, pointed and shouted: "See! Chaos comes! Where is Straasha and his folk?"

Elric shook his head, perturbed. He had expected aid by now.

"We cannot wait. We must attack!" Kargan's voice was pitched higher than usual.

A mood of bitter recklessness came upon Elric, as he gripped the rigging to steady himself on the swaying deck, then he smiled. "Come then. Let's do so!"

Speedily the squadron coursed towards the disturbing ships of death. Moonglum muttered: "We are going to our doom, Elric. No man would willingly get close to those ships. Only the dead are drawn to them, and they do not go with joy!"

But Elric ignored his friend.

A strange silence descended over the waters and the rhythmic sound of the splashing oars was sharp. The death fleet waited for them, impassively, as if they did not need to prepare for battle. He tightened his grip on Stormbringer. The blade responded to the pounding of his pulse-beat, moving in his hand with each thud of his heart, as if linked to it by veins and arteries. Now they were so close to the Chaos ships that they could make out better the figures crowding the great decks. Horribly, Elric thought he recognized some of the gaunt faces of the dead and, involuntarily, he called to the sea-folk's king.

"*Straasha!*"

The waters heaved, foamed and seemed to be attempting to rise but then subsided again. Straasha heard—but he was finding it difficult to fight against the forces of Chaos.

"*Straasha!*"

It was no good, the waters hardly moved.

In his wild despair Elric screamed to Kargan: "We cannot wait for aid. Swing the ship round the Chaos fleet and we'll attempt to reach Jagreen Lern's flagship from the rear!"

Under Kargan's expert direction, the ship swung to avoid the Ships of Hell in a wide semi-circle. Spray cascaded against Elric's face, flooding the decks with white foam. He could hardly see through it as they cleared the Chaos ships which had now engaged other craft and were altering the nature of their timbers so that they fell apart and the unfortunate crews were drowned or warped into alien shapes.

To his ears came the miserable cries of the defeated and the triumphantly surging thunder of the Chaos fleet's music as it pushed forward to destroy the Eastern ships. *Timber-tearer* was rocking badly and was hard to control, but at last they were around the hell fleet and bearing down on Jagreen Lern's vessel from behind.

Now they nearly struck the Theocrat's vessel with their ram, but were swept off-course and had to manoeuvre again. Arrows rose from the enemy's decks and thudded and rattled on their own. They retaliated as, riding a huge wave, they slid alongside the flagship and flung out grappling irons. A few held, dragging them towards the Theocrat's vessel as the men of Pan Tang strove to cut the grappling ropes. More ropes followed and then a boarding platform fell from its harness and landed squarely on Jagreen Lern's deck. Another followed it. Elric ran for the nearest platform, Kargan behind him, and they led a body of warriors over it, searching for Jagreen Lern. Stormbringer took a dozen lives and a dozen souls before Elric had gained the main deck. There a resplendent commander stood, surrounded by a group of officers. But he was not Jagreen Lern. Elric clambered up the gangway, slicing through a warrior's waist as the man sought to block his path. He yelled at the group: "Where's your cursed leader? Where's Jagreen Lern!"

The commander's face was pale for he had seen in the past what Elric and his hellblade could do.

"He's not here, Elric, I swear."

"What? Am I to be thwarted again? I know you are lying!" Elric advanced on the group who backed away, their swords ready.

"Our Theocrat does not need to protect himself by means of lies, doom-fostered one!" sneered a young officer, braver than the rest.

"Perhaps not," Elric's voice was low and menacing as he rushed towards the youth, swinging Stormbringer in a shrieking arc, "but at least I'll have your life before I put the truth of your words to the test."

The man put up his blade to block Stormbringer's swing. The runesword cut through the metal with a triumphant cry, swung back again and plunged itself into the officer's side. He gasped, but remained standing with his hands clenched.

Elric laughed. "My sword and I need revitalizing—and your soul should make an appetizer before I take Jagreen Lern's!"

"No!" the youth groaned. "Oh, no, not my soul!" His eyes widened, tears streamed from them and madness came into them for a second before Stormbringer satiated itself and Elric drew it out, replenished. He had no sympathy for the man. "Your soul would have gone to the depths of hell in any case," he said lightly. "But now I've put it to some use, at least."

Two other officers scrambled over the rail, seeking to escape their comrade's fate.

Elric hacked at the hand of one. He fell, screaming, to the deck, his hand still grasping the rail. The other he skewered in the bowels and, as Stormbringer sucked out his soul, he hung there, pleading incoherently in an effort to avert the inevitable.

So much vitality flowed into Elric that, as he rushed at the remaining group around the commander, he seemed to fly over the deck and rip into them, slicing away limbs as if they were flowers-stalks, until he encountered the commander himself. The commander said weakly: "I surrender. Do not take my soul."

"Where is Jagreen Lern?"

The commander pointed into the distance, where the Chaos fleet could be seen creating havoc amongst the Eastern ships. "There! He sails with Pyaray of Chaos whose fleet that is. You cannot reach him there for any man not protected—or not already dead—would turn to flowing flesh once he neared the fleet."

"That cursed hellspawn still cheats me," Elric grimaced. "Here's payment for your information—" Without mercy for one of the men who had wasted and enslaved two continents, Elric stuck his blade through the ornate armour and, delicately, with all the old malevolence of his sorcerer ancestors, tickled the man's heart before finishing him.

He looked around for Kargan, but couldn't see him. Then he noted that the Chaos fleet had turned back. At first he thought it was because Straasha had at last brought aid, but then he saw that the remnants of his fleet were fleeing. Jagreen Lern was victorious. Their plans, their formations, their courage—none of these had been capable of withstanding the horrible warpings of Chaos. And now the dreadful fleet was bearing down on the two flagships, locked together by their grapples. There was no chance of cutting one of them free before the fleet arrived. Elric yelled to Dyvim Slorm and Moonglum whom he saw running towards him from the other side of the deck.

"Over the side! Over, for your lives—and swim as far as you can away from here!"

They looked at him, startled, then realized the truth of his words. Others, from both sides, were already leaping into the bloody water. Elric sheathed his sword and dived. The sea was cold, for all the warm blood in it, and he gasped as he swam in the direction of Moonglum's red head, which he could see ahead and, close to it, Dyvim Slorm's honey-coloured hair. He turned once and saw the very timbers of the two ships begin to melt, to twist and curl in strange patterns as the Ships of Hell arrived. He felt very relieved he had not been aboard. He reached his companions.

"A short-term escape this," said Moonglum, spitting water from his mouth. "What now, Elric? Shall we strike for the Purple Towns?" Moonglum's capacity for facetiousness had not, it seemed, been limited by witnessing the defeat of their fleet and the advance of Chaos. The Isle was too far away.

Everywhere, the Chaos ships were disrupting nature. Soon their influence would engulf them, too.

Then, to their left they saw the water froth and form itself into what was to Elric a familiar shape.

"Straasha!"

"*I could not aid thee, I could not aid thee. Though I tried, my ancient enemy was too strong for me. Forgive me. In recompense let me take you and your friends back with me to my own land and save you, at least from Chaos.*"

"But we cannot breathe beneath the sea!"

"*You will not need to.*"

"Very well."

Trusting to the elemental's words, they allowed themselves to be dragged beneath the waters and down into the cool, green depths of the sea, deeper and deeper until no sunlight filtered there and all was wet darkness and they lived, though at normal times the pressure would have crushed them.

They seemed to travel for miles through the mysterious underwater grottoes until at last they came to a place of coral-coloured rounded constructions that seemed to drift slowly in a sluggish current. Elric knew it. The domain of Straasha the Sea-King.

The elemental bore them to the largest construction and one section of it seemed to fade away to admit them. They moved now through twisting corridors of a delicate pink texture, slightly shadowed, no longer in water. They were now on the plane of the elemental folk. In a huge circular cave, they came to rest.

With a peculiar rushing sound, the sea-king walked to a large throne of milky jade and sat upon it, his green head on his green fist.

"*Elric, once again I regret I was unable, after all, to aid you. All I can do now is have some of my folk carry you back to your own land when you have rested here for a while. We are all, it seems, helpless against this new strength which Chaos has of late.*"

Elric nodded. "Nothing can stand against its warping influence—unless it is the Chaos Shield."

Straasha straightened his back. "*The Chaos Shield. Ah, yes. It belongs to an exiled god, does it not? But his castle is virtually impregnable.*"

"Why is that?"

"*It lies upon the topmost crag of a tall and lonely mountain, reached by a hundred and sixty-nine steps. Lining these steps are forty-nine elder trees, and of these you would have to be especially wary. Also Mordaga has a guard of a hundred and forty-four warriors. I'm explicit in giving numbers, for they have a mystic value.*"

"Of the warriors I would certainly be wary. But why the elders?"

"*Each elder contains the soul of one of Mordaga's followers who was punished thus. They are vengeful trees—ever ready to take the life of anyone that comes into their domain.*"

"A hard task, to get that shield for myself," Elric mused. "But get it I must, for without it Fate's purpose would be forever thwarted—and with it I might have vengeance on the one who commands the Chaos fleet—and Jagreen Lern who sails with him."

"*Slay Pyaray, Lord of the Fleet of Hell, and, lacking his direction, the fleet itself would perish. His life-force is contained in a blue crystal set in the top of his head and striking at that with a special weapon is the only means of killing him.*"

"Thanks for that information," Elric said gratefully. "For when the time comes, I shall need it."

"What do you plan to do, Elric?" Dyvim Slorm asked.

"Put all else aside for the moment and seek the sad giant's shield. I *must*—for if I do not have it, every battle fought will be a repetition of the one we have just lost."

"I will come with you, Elric," Moonglum promised.

"I also," said Dyvim Slorm.

"We shall require a fourth if we are to carry out the prophecy," Elric said. "I wonder what became of Kargan."

Moonglum looked at the ground. "Did you not notice?"

"Notice what?"

"On board Jagreen Lern's flagship when you were hewing about you in an effort to reach the main deck. Did you not know, then, what you had done—or rather what your cursed sword did?"

Elric felt suddenly exhausted. "No. Did I—did it—*kill* him?"

"Aye."

"Gods!" He wheeled and paced the chamber, slapping his fist in his palm. "Still this hell-made blade exacts its tribute for the service it gives me. Still it drinks the souls of friends. 'Tis a wonder you two are still with me!"

"I agree it's extraordinary," Moonglum said feelingly.

"I grieve for Kargan. He was a good friend."

"Elric," Moonglum said urgently. "You know that Kargan's death was not your responsibility. It was fated."

"Aye, but why must I always be the executioner of fate? I hesitate to list the names of the good friends and useful allies whose souls my sword has stolen. I hate it enough that it must suck souls out to give me my vitality—but that it should be most partial to my friends, that is what I cannot bear. I've half a mind to venture into the heart of Chaos and there sacrifice us both! The guilt is indirectly mine, for if I was not so weak I *must* bear such a blade, many of those who have befriended me might be alive now."

"Yet the blade's major purpose seems a noble one," Moonglum said in a baffled voice. "Oh, I fail to understand all this—paradox, paradox upon paradox. Are the gods mad or are they so subtle we cannot fathom the workings of their minds?"

"It's hard enough at times like these to remember any greater purpose," Dyvim Slorm agreed. "We are pressed so sorely, that we haven't a moment for thought, but must fight the next battle and the next, forgetting often why it is we fight."

"Is the purpose, indeed, greater and not lesser," Elric smiled bitterly. "If we are the toys of the gods—are not perhaps the gods themselves mere children?"

"*These questions are of no present importance*," said Straasha from his throne.

"And at least," Moonglum told Elric, "future generations will thank Stormbringer if she fulfills her destiny."

"If Sepiriz is right," Elric said, "future generations will know nothing of any of us—blades or men!"

"Perhaps not consciously—but in the depths of their souls they will remember us. Our deeds will be spoken of as belonging to heroes with other names, that is all."

"That the world forgets me is all I ask," Elric sighed.

As if growing impatient with this fruitless discussion, the sea-king rose from his throne and said: "*Come, I will make certain that you are transported to land, if you have no objection to traveling back in the same manner as you came here?*"

"None," said Elric.

## Chapter Five

They staggered wearily onto the beach of the Isle of the Purple Towns and Elric turned back to address the sea-king, who remained in the shallows.

"Again I thank you for saving us, Lord of the Sea," he said respectfully. "And thanks also for telling me more of the sad giant's shield. By this action you have perhaps, given us the opportunity to make certain that Chaos will be swept away from the ocean—and the land, also."

"*Aahh*," the sea-king nodded, "*yet even if you are successful and the sea is unspoiled, it will mean the passing of us both, will it not?*"

"True."

"*Then let it be so, for I at least am weary of my long existence. But come—now I must return to my folk and hope to withstand Chaos for a little longer. Farewell!*"

And the sea-king sank into the waves again and vanished.

When they eventually reached the Fortress of Evening, heralds ran out to assist them.

"How went the battle? Where is the fleet?" one asked Moonglum.

"Have the survivors not yet returned?"

"Survivors? Then . . . ?"

"We were defeated," Elric said hollowly. "Is my wife still here?"

"No, she left soon after the fleet sailed, riding for Karlaak."

"Good. At least we shall have time to erect new defenses against Chaos before they reach that far. Now, we must have food and wine. We must devise a fresh plan of battle."

"Battle, my lord? With what shall we fight?"

"We shall see," Elric said, "we shall see."

Later they watched the battered survivors of the fleet sailing into the harbour. Moonglum counted despairingly. "Too few," he said. "This is a black day."

From behind them in the courtyard a trumpet sounded.

"An arrival from the mainland," Dyvim Slorm said.

They strode together down to the courtyard in time to see a scarlet-clad archer dismounting from his horse. His near-fleshless face might have been carved from bone. He stooped with weariness.

Elric was surprised. "Rackhir! You command the Ilmioran coast. Why are you here?"

"We were driven back. The Theocrat launched not one fleet but two. The other came in from the Pale Sea and took us by surprise. Our defenses were crushed, Chaos swept in and we were forced to flee. The enemy has established itself less than a hundred miles from Bakshaan and marches across country—if march is the word, rather it *flows*. Presumably it expects to meet up with the army the Theocrat intends to land here."

"Aaahh, we are surely defeated . . ." Moonglum's voice was little more than a sigh.

"We must have that shield, Elric," Dyvim Slorm said.

Elric frowned, his heart sinking. "Any further steps we take against Chaos will be doomed unless we have its protection. You, Rackhir, will be the fourth man in the prophecy."

"What prophecy?"

"I'll explain later. Are you fit enough to ride back with us now?"

"Give me two hours to sleep and then I will be."

"Good. Two hours. Make your preparations, my friends, for we go to claim the sad giant's shield!"

* * *

From two sides now, Chaos enclosed the East and the four men left the Fortress of Evening knowing it was unlikely it would survive. They rode across the waters to the mainland to discover that garrisons were abandoned as men fled away from the dreadful threat of Chaos. It was not until a day later that they came upon the first survivors of the land fighting, many of them with bodies twisted into terrible shapes by Chaos, struggling along a white road leading towards Jadmar, a city still free. From them they learned that half Ilmiora, parts of Vilmir and the tiny independent kingdom of Org had all fallen. Chaos was closing in, its shadow spreading more and more swiftly as its conquests increased.

It was with relief that Elric and his companions finally reached Karlaak to find it still free from attack. But reports placed the Chaos army less than two hundred miles away and coming nearer.

Zarozinia greeted Elric with troubled joy. "There were rumours you were dead—killed in the sea battle."

"I cannot stay long. I have to go beyond the Sighing Desert."

"I know."

"You know? How?"

"Sepiriz was here. He left a gift in our stables for you. Four Nihrain horses."

"A useful gift. They will carry us far more swiftly than any other beasts. But will that be swift enough? I hesitate to leave you here with Chaos encroaching at such a rate."

"You must leave me, Elric. If all seems lost here, we shall flee to the Weeping Waste. Even Jagreen Lern can have scant interest in those barrens."

"Promise me that you will."

"I promise."

Feeling a little more relieved, Elric took her by the hand. "I spent the most restful period of my life in this palace," he said. "Let me spend this last night with you and perhaps we shall find a little of the old peace we once had—before I ride on to the sad giant's lair."

So they made love, but when they slept, their dreams were so full of dark portent that each wakened the other with their groans so that they lay side by side, clinging to one another until the dawn, when Elric rose, kissed her lightly, clasped her hand and then went to the stables where he found his friends waiting—around a fourth figure. It was Sepiriz.

"Sepiriz, thanks for your gift. They will probably make the difference between our being too late or not," Elric said sincerely. "But why are you here now?"

"Because I can perform another small service before your main journey begins," said the black seer. "All of you save Moonglum have retained weapons endowed with some special power. Elric and Dyvim Slorm have their runeblades, Rackhir, the Arrows of Law, which the sorcerer Lamsar gave him at the time of the Siege of Tanelorn—but Moonglum's weapon has nothing save the skill of its bearer."

"I think I prefer it thus," retorted Moonglum. "I've seen what a charmed blade can take from a man."

"I can give you nothing so strong—nor so evil—as Stormbringer," Sepiriz said. "But I have a charm for your sword, a slight one that my contact with the White Lords has enabled me to use. Give me your sword, Moonglum."

A trifle unwillingly, Moonglum unsheathed his curved steel blade and handed it to the Nihrain who took a small engraving tool from his robe and, whispering a rune, scratched several symbols on the sword near its hilt. Then he gave it back to the Eastlander.

"There. Now the sword has the blessing of Law and you will find it more able to withstand Law's enemies."

Elric said impatiently, "We must ride now, Sepiriz, for time grows desperately short."

"Ride, then. But be wary for patrolling bands of Jagreen Lern's warriors. I do not think they will be anywhere along your route when you journey there—but watch for them coming back."

They mounted the magical Nihrain steeds which had helped Elric more than once, and rode away from Karlaak by the Weeping Waste. Rode away perhaps for ever.

* * *

In a short while they had entered the Weeping Waste, for this was the quickest route to the Sighing Desert. Rackhir alone knew this country well, and he guided them.

The Nihrain steeds, treading the ground of their own strange plane, seemed literally to fly for it could be observed that their hoofs did not touch the damp grasses of the Weeping Waste. They moved at incredible speed and Rackhir, until he became used to the pace, gripped his reins tightly. In this place of eternal rain, the land was difficult to see far ahead, and the drizzle spread down their faces and into their eyes as they peered through it, trying to make out the high mountain range, which ran along the edge of the Weeping Waste, separating it from the Sighing Desert.

Then at last, after two days, they could observe tall crags and knew they were near the borders of the desert. Soon they were riding through the deep gorges and the rain ceased until, on the third day, the breeze became warm and then harsh and hot as they left the mountains and entered the desert. The sun blazed down and the wind soughed constantly over the barren sand and rocks, its continuous sighing giving the desert its name. They protected their faces, particularly their eyes, with their hoods as best they could, for the stinging sand was ever present.

Resting only for a few hours at a time, Rackhir directing them, they sped further and further into the depths of the vast desert, speaking little, for it was difficult to be heard over the wind.

Elric had long since fallen into what was virtually a mindless trance, letting the horse carry him over the desert. He had fought against his own churning thoughts and emotions, finding it hard, as he often did, to retain any objective impression of his predicament. His past had been too troubled, his background too morbid for him to do much now to see clearly.

He had always been a slave to his melancholic emotions, his physical failings and to the very blood flowing in his veins. He saw life not as a consistent pattern, but as a series of random events. Unlike others, he had fought all his life to assemble his thoughts and, if necessary, accept the chaotic nature of things, learn to live with it, but, except in moments of extreme personal crisis, had rarely managed to think coherently for any length of time. He was, perhaps, because of his outlawed life, his albinism, his very reliance on his runesword for strength, obsessed with the knowledge of his own doom.

What was thought, he asked himself, what was emotion? What was control and was it worth achieving? Better to live by instinct than to theorize and be wrong; better to remain the puppet, letting the gods move him at their pleasure, than to seek control of his own fate, clash with the will of the Higher Worlds and perish for his pains.

So he considered as he rode into the searing lash of the wind, already striving against natural hazard. And what was the difference between an earthly hazard and the hazard of uncontrolled thought and emotion? Both held something of the same qualities.

But his race, though they had ruled the world for ten thousand years, had lived under the dominance of a different star. They had been neither true men nor true members of the ancient races who had come before men. They were an intermediary type and Elric was half-consciously aware of this; aware that he was the last of an inbred line who had, without effort, used Chaos-given sorcery for convenience and for no other purpose. His race had been of Chaos, having no need of self-control or the self-restrictions of the new races who had emerged with the Age of the Young Kingdoms, and even these, according to the seer Sepiriz, were not the true men who would one day walk an Earth where order and progress might become the rule and Chaos rarely exert influence—if Elric triumphed, destroying the world he knew.

This thought added to his gloom, for he had no destiny but death, no purpose save what fate willed. Why fight against it, why bother to sharpen his wits or put his mind in order? He was little more than a sacrifice on the altar of destiny. He breathed deeply of the hot, dry air and expelled it from his stinging lungs, spitting out the clogging sand which had entered his mouth and nostrils.

Dyvim Slorm shared something of Elric's mood, though his feelings were not so strong. He had a more ordered life than had Elric, though they were of the same blood. Whereas Elric had questioned the custom of his folk, even renounced kingship that he might explore the new lands of the Young Kingdoms and compare their way of life with his own, Dyvim Slorm had never indulged in such questioning. He had suffered bitterness when through Elric's renegade activities, the Dreaming City of Imrryr, last stronghold of the old race of Melniboné, had been razed; shock, too, of a kind, when he and what remained of the Imrryrians had been forced out into the world, also, to make their living as mercenaries of those they considered upstart kings of lowly and contemptible peoples. Dyvim Slorm, who had never questioned, did not question now, though he was disturbed.

Moonglum was less self-absorbed. Since the time, many years before, when he and Elric had met and fought against the Dharzi together, he had felt a peculiar sympathy, even empathy, with his friend. When Elric sank into such moods as the one he was in now, Moonglum felt tormented only because he could not help him. Many times he had sought the means of pulling Elric out of his gloomy depression, but these days he had learned that it was impossible. By nature cheerful and optimistic, even he felt dominated by the doom which was on them.

Rackhir, too, who was of a calmer and more philosophical frame of mind than his fellows, did not feel capable of fully grasping the implications of their mission. He had thought to spend the rest of his days in contemplation and meditation in the peaceful city of Tanelorn, which exerted a strange calming influence on all who lived there. But this call to aid in the fight against Chaos had been impossible to ignore and he had unwillingly strapped on his quiver of Arrows of Law and taken up his bow again to ride from Tanelorn with a small party of those who wished to accompany him and offer their services to Elric.

Peering through the sand-filled air, he saw something looming ahead—a single mountain rising from the wastes of the desert as if placed there by unnatural means.

He called, pointing: "Elric! There! That must be Mordaga's castle!"

Elric roused himself and let his eyes follow Rackhir's pointing hand. "Aye," he sighed. "We are there. Let us rest here before we ride the final distance!"

They reined in their steeds and dismounted, easing their aching limbs and stretching their legs to allow the blood to flow freely again.

They raised their tent against the wind-blown sand and ate their meal in a mood of companionship, created by the knowledge that after they reached the mountain, they might never see one another alive again.

## Chapter Six

The steps wound up around the mountain. High above they could see the gleam of masonry and, just where the steps curved and disappeared for the first time, they saw an elder tree. It looked like any ordinary tree but it became a symbol for them—there was their initial antagonist. How would it fight? Elric placed a booted foot on the first step. It was high, built for the feet of a giant. He began to climb, the other three following behind him. Now, as he reached the tenth step, he unsheathed Stormbringer, felt it quiver and send energy into him. The climbing instantly became easier. As he came close to the elder, he heard it rustle, saw that there was an agitation in its branches. Yes, it was certainly sentient. He was only a few steps from the tree when he heard Dyvim Slorm shout: "Gods! *The leaves*—look at the leaves!"

The green leaves, their veins seeming to throb in the sunlight, were beginning to detach themselves from the branches and drift purposefully towards the group. One settled on Elric's bare hand. He attempted to brush it off, but it clung. Others began to settle on different parts of his body. They were coming in a green wave now and he felt a peculiar stinging sensation in his hand. With a curse he peeled it off and to his horror saw that tiny pin-pricks of blood were left where it had been. His body twitched in nausea and he ripped the rest from his face, slashing at others with his runesword. As they were touched by the blade, so they shriveled, but they were swiftly replaced. He knew instinctively that they were sucking not only blood from his veins, but the soul-force from his being.

With yells of terror, his companions discovered the same thing. These leaves were being directed and he knew where the direction came from—the tree itself. He clambered up the remaining steps, fighting off the leaves which swarmed like locusts around him. With grim intention he began hacking at the trunk which gave out an angry groaning and the branches sought to reach him. He slashed them away and then plunged Stormbringer deep into the tree. Sods of earth spattered upwards as the roots threshed. The tree screamed and began to heel over towards him as if, in death, it sought to kill him also. He wrenched at Stormbringer which sucked greedily at the sentient tree's lifestuff, failed to tug the sword out and leapt aside as the tree crashed down over the steps, barely missing him. One branch slashed his face and drew blood. He gasped and staggered, feeling the life draining from him.

He stumbled to the fallen tree and saw that the wood was suddenly dead and the remaining leaves brown and shriveled. "Quickly," he gasped as the three came up, "shift this thing. My sword's beneath and without it I'm dead!"

Swiftly they set to work and rolled the tree over so that Elric could weakly grasp the hilt of Stormbringer still imbedded therein. As he did so he almost screamed, experiencing a sensation of ecstatic power as the tree's energy filled him, pulsed through him so that he felt like a god himself. He laughed, as if possessed by a demon, and the others looked at him in astonishment. "Come, my friends, follow me. I can deal with a million such trees now!"

He leapt up the steps as another shoal of leaves came towards him. Ignoring their bites, he went straight for the second elder and drove his sword at its centre. Again, this tree screamed.

"Dyvim Slorm!" he shouted, drunk on its life-force. "Do as I do—let your sword drink a few such souls and we're invincible!"

"Such power is scarcely palatable," Rackhir said, brushing dead leaves from his body as Elric withdrew his sword again and ran towards the next. The elders grew thicker here and they bent their branches to reach him, looming over him, their branches like fingers seeking to pluck him apart.

Dyvim Slorm, a trifle less spontaneously, imitated Elric's method of dispatching the tree-creatures and soon he too became filled with the stolen souls of the demons imprisoned within the elders and his wild laugh joined Elric's as, like fiendish woodsmen, they attacked again and again, each victory lending them more strength so that Moonglum and Rackhir looked at each other in wonder and fear to see such a terrible change come over their friends.

But there was no denying that their methods were effective against the elders. Soon they looked back at a waste of fallen, blackened trees spreading down the mountain side.

All the old, unholy fervour of the dead kings of Melniboné was in the faces of the two kinsmen as they sang old battle-songs, their twin blades joining the harmony to send up a disturbing melody of doom and malevolence. His lips parted to reveal his white teeth, his red eyes blazing with dreadful fire, his milk-white hair streaming in the burning wind, Elric flung up his sword to the sky and turned to confront his companions.

"Now, friends, see how the ancient ones of Melniboné conquered man and demon to rule the world for ten thousand years!"

Moonglum thought that he merited the name of Wolf, gained in the West long since. All the chaos-force that was now within him had gained complete control over every other part of him. He realized that Elric was no longer split in his loyalties, there was no conflict in him now. His ancestors' blood dominated him and he appeared as they must have done ages since when all other races of mankind fled before them, fearing their magnificence, their malice and their evil. Dyvim Slorm seemed equally as possessed. Moonglum sent up a heartfelt prayer to whatever kindly gods remained in the universe that Elric was his ally and not his enemy.

They were close to the top now, Elric and his cousin springing ahead with superhuman bounds. The steps terminated at the mouth of a gloomy tunnel and into the darkness rushed the pair, laughing and calling to one another. Less speedily, Moonglum and Rackhir followed, the Red Archer nocking an arrow to his bow.

Elric peered into the gloom, his head swimming with the power that seemed to burst from every pore of his body. He heard the clatter of armoured feet coming towards him and, as they approached, he realized that these warriors were mere human beings. Though nearly a hundred and fifty, they did not daunt him. As the first group rushed at him, he blocked blows easily and struck them down, each soul taken making only a fraction of difference to the vitality already in him. Shoulder to shoulder stood the kinsmen, butchering the soldiers like so many unarmed children. It was dreadful to the eyes of Moonglum and Rackhir as they came up to witness the flood of blood which soon made the tunnel slippery. The stench of death in the close confines became too much as Elric and Dyvim Slorm moved past the first of the fallen and carried the attack to the rest.

Rackhir groaned: "Though they be enemies and the servants of those we fight, I cannot bear to witness such slaughter. We are not needed here, friend Moonglum. These are demons waging war, not men!"

"Aye," agreed Moonglum, disquieted. They broke out into sunlight again and saw the castle ahead, the remaining warriors reassembling as Elric and Dyvim Slorm advanced menacingly with malevolent joy towards them.

The air rang with the sounds of shouting and steel clashing. Rackhir aimed an arrow at one of the warriors and launched it to take the man in the left eye. "I'll see that a few of them get a cleaner death," he muttered, nocking another arrow to the string.

As Elric and his cousin disappeared into the enemy ranks, others, sensing perhaps that Rackhir and Moonglum were less of a danger, rushed at the two. Moonglum found himself engaging three warriors and discovered that his sword seemed extraordinarily light and gave off a sweet, clear tone as it met the warriors' weapons, turning them aside readily. The sword supplied him with no energy, but it did not blunt as it might have and the heavier swords could not force it down so easily. Rackhir had expended all his arrows in what had been an act of mercy. He engaged the enemy with his sword and killed two, taking Moonglum's third opponent from behind with an upward thrust into the man's side and through to his heart.

Then they went with little stomach into the main fray and saw that already the turf was littered with a great many corpses. Rackhir cried to Elric: "Stop! Elric—let *us* finish these. You have no need to take their souls. We can kill them with more natural methods!"

But Elric laughed and carried on his work. As he finished another warrior and there were no others in the immediate area, Rackhir seized him by the arm. "Elric—"

Stormbringer turned in Elric's hand, howling its satiated glee and clove down at Rackhir. Seeing his fate, the Red Archer sobbed and sought to avoid the blow. But it landed in his shoulder blade and sheared down to his breastbone. "Elric!" he cried. "Not *my* soul, too!"

And so died the hero Rackhir the Red Archer, famous in the Eastlands as the saviour of Tanelorn. Cloven by a treacherous blade. By the friend whose life he had saved, long ago when they had first met near the city of Ameeron.

And Elric laughed until realization came and he tugged his sword away though it was too late. The stolen energy still pulsed in him, but his great grief no longer gave it the same control over him. Tears streamed down Elric's tortured face and a great, racking groan came from him.

"Ah, Rackhir—will it ever cease?"

On opposite sides of the slain-strewed field, his two remaining companions stood regarding him. Dyvim Slorm had done with killing, but only because there was none left to kill. He gasped, staring around him half in bewilderment. Moonglum glared at Elric with horrified eyes which yet held a gleam of sympathy for his friend, for he knew well Elric's doom and knew that the life of one close to Elric was coveted by Stormbringer.

"There was no gentler hero than Rackhir," he said, "no man more desirous of peace and order than him." Then he shuddered.

Elric raised himself to his feet and turned to look at the huge castle of granite and bluestone which waited in enigmatic silence as if for his next action. On the battlements of the topmost turret he could make out a figure which could only be the giant.

"I swear by your stolen soul, Rackhir, that what you wished to come to pass *shall* come to pass, though I, a thing of Chaos, achieve it. Law will triumph and Chaos will be driven back! Armed with sword and shield of Chaos forging I shall do battle with every fiend of hell if needs be. Chaos was the indirect cause of your death. And Chaos will be punished for it. But first, we must take the shield."

Dyvim Slorm, not realizing quite what had happened, shouted in exultation to his kinsman. "Elric—let's visit the sad giant now!"

But Moonglum, coming up to gaze down on the ruined body of Rackhir, murmured: "Aye, Chaos is the cause, Elric. I'll join in your vengeance with a will so long as," he shuddered, "I'm spared from the attentions of your hellblade."

Together, three abreast, they marched through the open portal of Mordaga's castle and were immediately in a rich and barbarically furnished hall.

"Mordaga!" Elric cried. "We have come to fulfill a prophecy!"

They waited impatiently, until at last a bulky figure came through a great arch at the end of the vast hall. Mordaga was as tall as two men, but his back was bent. He had long, curling black hair and was clad in a deep blue smock belted at the waist. Upon his great feet were simple leather sandals. His black eyes were full of a sorrow such as Moonglum had only seen before in Elric's eyes.

Upon the sad giant's arm was a round shield which bore upon it the eight amber arrows of Chaos. It was of a silvery green colour and very beautiful. He had no other weapons.

"I know the prophecy," he said in a voice that was like a lonely, roaring wind. "But still I must seek to avert it. Will you take the shield and leave me in peace, human? I do not want death."

Elric felt a kind of sympathy for sad Mordaga and he knew something of what the fallen god must feel at this moment. "The prophecy says death," he said softly.

"Take the shield," Mordaga lifted it off his mighty arm and held it towards Elric. "Take the shield and change fate this once."

Elric nodded. "I will."

With a tremendous sigh, the giant deposited the Chaos Shield upon the floor.

"For thousands of years I have lived in the shadow of that prophecy," he said, straightening his back. "Now, though I die in old age, I shall die in peace and, though once I did not think so, I shall welcome such a death after all this time, I think."

"The whole world seems to sigh for death," Elric replied, "but you may not die naturally, for Chaos comes and will engulf you as it will engulf everything unless I can stop it. But at least, it seems, you'll be in a more philosophical frame of mind to meet it."

"Farewell and I thank you," said the giant, turning, and he plodded back towards the entrance through which he had come.

As Mordaga disappeared, Moonglum dashed forward on fleet feet and followed him through the entrance before either Elric or Dyvim Slorm could cry out or stop him.

Then they heard a single shriek that seemed to echo away into eternity, a crash which shook the hall and then the footfall returning.

Moonglum reappeared in the entrance, a bloody sword in his hand.

"It was murder," he said simply. "I admit it. I took him in the back before he was aware of it. It was a good, quick death and he died whilst happy. Moreover, it was a better death than any his minions tried to mete to us. It was murder, but it was necessary in my eyes."

"Why?" said Elric, still mystified.

Grimly, Moonglum continued: "He had to perish as Fate decreed. We are servants of Fate now, Elric, and to divert it in any small way is to hamper its aims. But more than that, it was the beginning of my own vengeance taking. If Mordaga had not surrounded himself with such a host, Rackhir would not have died."

Elric shook his head. "Blame me for that, Moonglum. The giant should not have perished for my own sword's crime."

"Someone had to perish," said Moonglum steadfastly, "and since the prophecy contained Mordaga's death, he was the one. Who else, here, could I kill, Elric?"

Elric turned away. "I wish it were I," he sighed. He looked down at the great, round shield with its shifting amber arrows and its mysterious silver-green colour. He picked it up easily enough and placed it on his arm. It virtually covered his body from chin to ankles.

"Let's make haste and leave this place of death and misery. The lands of Ilmiora and Vilmir await our aid—if they have not already wholly fallen to Chaos!"

## Chapter Seven

It was in the mountains separating the Sighing Desert from the Weeping Waste that they first learned of the fate of the last of the Young Kingdoms. They came upon a party of six tired warriors led by Lord Voashoon, Zarozinia's father.

"What has happened?" Elric asked anxiously. "Where is Zarozinia?"

"I know not if she's lost, dead or captured, Elric. Our continent has fallen to Chaos."

"Did you not seek for her?" Elric accused.

The old man shrugged. "My son, I have looked upon so much horror these past days that I am now bereft of emotion. I care for nothing but a quick release from all this. The day of mankind is over on the Earth. Go no further than here, for even the Weeping Waste is beginning to change before the crawling tide of Chaos. It is hopeless."

"Hopeless! No! We still live—perhaps Zarozinia still lives. Did you hear nothing of her fate?"

"Only a rumour that Jagreen Lern had taken her aboard the leading Chaos ship."

"She is on the seas?"

"No—those cursed craft sail land as well as sea, if it can be told apart these days. It was they who attacked Karlaak, with a vast horde of mounted men and infantry following behind. Confusion prevails—you'll find nothing but your death back there, my son."

"We shall see. I have some protection against Chaos at long last, plus my sword and my Nihrain steed." He turned in the saddle to address his companions. "Well, will you stay here with Lord Voashoon or accompany me into the heart of Chaos?"

"We'll come with you," Moonglum said quietly, speaking for them both. "We've followed you until now and our fates are linked with yours in any case. We can do nought else."

"Good. Farewell, Lord Voashoon. If you would do a service, ride over the Weeping Waste to Eshmir and the Unknown East where Moonglum's homeland lies. Tell them what to expect, though they're probably beyond rescue now."

"I will try," said Voashoon wearily, "and hope to arrive there before Chaos."

Then Elric and his companions rode away, towards the massed hordes of Chaos—three men against the unleashed forces of darkness. Three foolhardy men who had pursued their course so faithfully that it was inconceivable for them to flee now. The last acts must be played out whether howling night or calm day followed.

The first signs of Chaos were soon apparent as they saw the place where lush grassland once had been. It was now a yellow morass of molten rock that, though cool, rolled about with a purposeful air. The Nihrain horses, since they did not gallop on the plane of Earth, crossed it with comparative ease and here the Chaos Shield was first shown to work, for, as they passed, the yellow liquid rock changed and became grass again for a short time.

They met once a shambling thing that still had limbs of sorts and a mouth that could speak. From this poor creature they learned that Karlaak was no more, that it had been churned into broiling nothingness and where it had been the forces of Chaos, both human and supernatural, had set up their camp, their work done. The thing also spoke of something that was of particular interest to Elric. Rumour was that the Dragon Isle of Melniboné was the only place where Chaos had been unable to exert its influence.

"If, when our business is done, we can reach Melniboné," Elric said to his friends as they rode on, "we might be able to abide until such a time that the White Lords can help us. Also there are dragons slumbering in the caves—and these would be useful against Jagreen Lern if we could waken them."

"What use is it to fight them now?" Dyvim Slorm said defeatedly. "Jagreen Lern has won, Elric. We have not fulfilled our destiny. Our role is over and Chaos rules."

"Does it? But we have yet to fight it and test its strength against ours. Let us decide then what the outcome has been."

Dyvim Slorm looked dubious, but he said nothing.

* * *

And then, at last, they came to the Camp of Chaos.

No mortal nightmare could encompass such a terrible vision. The towering Ships of Hell dominated the place as they observed it from a distance, utterly horrified by the sight. Shooting flames of all colours seemed to flicker everywhere over the camp, fiends of all kinds mingled with the men, hell's evilly beautiful nobles conferred with the gaunt-faced kings who had allied themselves to Jagreen Lern and perhaps now regretted it. Every so often the ground heaved and erupted and any human beings unfortunate enough to be in the area were either engulfed and totally transformed, or else had their bodies warped in indescribable ways. The noise was a dreadful blending of human voices and roaring Chaos sounds, devils' wailing laughter and, quite often, the tortured shout of a human soul who had perhaps regretted his choice of loyalty and now suffered madness. The stench was disgusting, of corruption, of blood and of evil. The Ships of Hell moved slowly about through the horde which stretched for miles, dotted with great pavilions of kings, their silk banners fluttering; hollow pride compared to the might of Chaos. Many of the human beings could scarcely be told from the Chaos creatures, their forms were so changed under the influence of Chaos.

Elric muttered to his friends as they sat in their saddles watching. "It is obvious that the warping influence of Chaos grows even stronger among the human ranks. This will continue until even Jagreen Lern and the traitor kings will lose every semblance of humanity and become just a fraction of the churning stuff of Chaos. This will mean the end of the human race—mankind will pass away for ever, taken into the maw of Chaos.

"You look upon the last of mankind, my friends, save for ourselves. Soon it will be indistinguishable from anything else. All this unstable Earth is beneath the heel of the Lords of Chaos, and they are gradually absorbing it into their realm, into their own plane. They will first remould and then steal the Earth altogether; it will become just another lump of clay for them to mould into whatever grotesque shapes take their fancy."

"And we seek to stop *that*," Moonglum said hopelessly. "We cannot, Elric!"

"We must continue to strive, until we are conquered. I remember that Straasha the Sea-King said if Pyaray, commander of the Chaos fleet, is slain, the ships themselves will no longer be able to exist. I have a mind to put that to the test. Also, I have not forgotten that my wife may be prisoner aboard his ship, or that Jagreen Lern is there. I have three good reasons for venturing there."

"No, Elric! It would be more than suicide!"

"I do not ask you to accompany me."

"If you go, we shall come, but I like it not."

"If one man cannot succeed, neither can three. I shall go alone. Wait for me. If I do not return, then try to get to Melniboné."

"Elric—!" Moonglum cried and then watched as, his Chaos Shield pulsing, Elric spurred the Nihrain steed towards the camp.

Protected against the influence of Chaos, Elric was sighted by a detachment of warriors as he neared the ship which was his destination. They recognized him and rode towards him, shouting.

He laughed in their faces. "Just the fodder my blade needs before we banquet on yonder ship!" he cried as he slashed off the first man's head as if it were a buttercup. Secure behind his great round shield, he hewed about him with a will. Since Stormbringer had slain the demons imprisoned in the elder trees, the vitality which the sword passed into him was almost without limit, yet every soul that Elric stole from Jagreen Lern's warriors was another fraction of vengeance reaped. Against men, he was invincible. He split one heavily armoured warrior from head to crutch, sheared through the saddle and smashed the horse's backbone apart.

Then the remaining warriors dropped back suddenly and Elric felt his body tingle with peculiar sensations, knew he was in the area of influence exerted by the Chaos ship and knew also that he was being protected against them by his shield. He was now partially out of his own earthly plane and existed between his world and the world of Chaos. He dismounted from his Nihrain steed and ordered it to wait for him. There were ropes trailing from the huge sides of the foremost ship and

Elric saw with horror that other figures were climbing up them—and he recognized several as men he had known in Karlaak. But before he could reach the ship he was surrounded by all manner of horrifying shapes, things that flew at him cawing, with heads of men and beaks of birds, things that writhed from out of the seething ground and struck at him, things that groped and mewled and screamed, attempting to pull him down to join them. Frantically, he swung Stormbringer this way and that, cutting his way through the Chaos creatures, protected from becoming like them by the pulsing Chaos Shield on his left arm, until at length he joined the ghastly ranks of the dead and swarmed with them up the sides of the great, gleaming ship, grateful at least for the cover they gave him.

He reached the ship's rail and hauled himself over it, spitting bile from his throat as he entered a peculiar region of darkness and came to the first of a series of decks that rose like steps to the topmost one where he could see the occupants—a manlike figure and something like a huge, blood-red octopus. The first was probably Jagreen Lern, the second was obviously Pyaray, for this, Elric knew, was the guise he took when he manifested himself on Earth.

Contrasting with the ships seen from the distance, once aboard Elric became conscious of the dark, shadowy nature of the light, filled with moving threads, a network of dark reds, blues, yellows, greens and purples which, as he moved through it, gave and re-formed itself behind him. He was constantly being blundered against by the moving cadavers and he made a point of not looking at their faces too closely, for he had already recognized several of the sea-raiders whom he had abandoned, years before, during the escape from Imrryr.

Slowly he was gaining the top deck, noting that so far both Jagreen Lern and Lord Pyaray seemed unaware of his presence. Presumably they considered themselves entirely free from any kind of attack now they had conquered all the known world. He grinned maliciously to himself as he continued climbing, gripping the shield tightly, knowing that if once he lost hold of it, his body would become transformed either into some shambling alien shape or else flow away altogether to become absorbed into the Chaos stuff. By now Elric had forgotten everything but his main object, which was to destroy Lord Pyaray's earthly manifestation. He must gain the topmost deck and deal first with the Lord of Chaos. Then he would kill Jagreen Lern and, if she were really there, rescue Zarozinia and bear her to safety.

Up the dark decks, through the nets of strange colours, Elric went, his milk-white hair flowing in contrast to the moody darkness around him. As he came to the last deck but one, he felt a gentle touch on his shoulder and, looking in that direction, saw with heart-lurching horror that one of Pyaray's blood-red tentacles had found him. He stumbled back, putting up his shield.

The tentacle tip touched the shield and rebounded suddenly, the entire tentacle shriveling. From above, where the Chaos Lord's main bulk was, there came a terrible screaming and roaring.

"*What's this? What's this? What's this?*"

Elric shouted in impudent triumph at seeing his shield work with such effect: " 'Tis Elric of Melniboné, great lord. Come to destroy thee!"

Another tentacle dropped towards him, seeking to curl around the shield and seize him. Then another followed it and another. Elric hacked at one, severed its sensitive tip, saw another touch the shield, recoil and shrivel and then avoided the third in order to run round the deck and ascend, as swiftly as he could, the ladder leading to the deck above. Here he saw Jagreen Lern, his eyes wide. The Theocrat was clad in his familiar scarlet armour. On his arm was his buckler and in the same hand an axe, while his right hand held a broadsword. He glanced down at these weapons, obviously aware of their inadequacy against Elric's.

"You later, Theocrat," Elric promised.

"You're a fool, Elric! You're doomed now, whatever you do!"

It was probably true, but he did not care. "Aside, upstart," he said as, shield up, he moved warily towards the many-tentacled Lord of Chaos.

"You are the killer of many cousins of mine, Elric," the creature said in a low, whispering voice. "And you've banished several Dukes of

Chaos to their own domain so that they cannot reach Earth again. For that you must pay. I at least do not underestimate you, as, in likelihood, they did." A tentacle reared above him and tried to come down from over the shield's rim and seize his throat. He took a step backwards and blocked the attempt with the shield.

Then a whole web of tentacles began to come from all sides, each one curling around the shield, knowing its touch to be death. He skipped aside, avoiding them with difficulty, slicing about him with Stormbringer. As he fought, he remembered Straasha's last message: *Strike for the crystal atop his head. There is his life and his soul*. Elric saw the blue, radiating crystal which he had originally taken to be one of Lord Pyaray's several eyes. He moved in towards the roots of the tentacles, leaving his back poorly protected, but there was nothing else for it. As he did so, a huge maw gaped in the thing's head and tentacles began to draw him towards it. He extended his shield towards the maw until it touched the lips. Yellow, jellylike stuff spurted from the mouth as the Lord of Chaos screamed in pain. He got his foot on one tentacle stump and clambered up the slippery hide of the Chaos Lord, shuddering beneath his feet. Every time his shield touched Pyaray, it created some sort of wound so that the Chaos Lord began to thresh about dreadfully. Then he stood unsteadily over the glowing soul-crystal. For an instant he paused, then plunged Stormbringer point-first into the crystal!

There came a mighty throbbing from the heart of the entity's body. It gave vent to a monstrous shriek and then Elric yelled as Stormbringer took the soul of a Lord of Hell and channeled this surging vitality through to him. It was too much. He was hurled backwards. He lost his footing on the slippery back, stumbled off the deck itself and fell to another, nearly a hundred feet below. He landed with bone-cracking force, but, thanks to the stolen vitality, was completely unhurt. He got up, ready to clamber again towards Jagreen Lern. The Theocrat's anxious face peered down at him and he yelled: "You'll find a present for you in yonder cabin, Elric!"

Torn between pursuing the Theocrat and investigating the cabin, Elric turned and opened the door. From inside came a dreadful sobbing.

"Zarozinia!" He ducked into the dark place and there he saw her.

Chaos had warped her. Only her head, the same beautiful head was left.

But her lovely body was dreadfully changed. Now it resembled the body of a huge white worm.

"Did Jagreen Lern do this?"

"He and his ally."

"How have you retained your sanity?"

"By waiting for you. I have something to do that required me to keep my wits." The worm-body undulated towards him.

"No—stand back," he cried, disgusted against his will. He could hardly bear to look at her. But she did not heed him. The worm-body threshed forward and impaled itself on his sword. "There," cried her head. "Take my soul into you, Elric, for I am useless to myself and you now! Carry my soul with yours and we shall be forever together."

"No! You are wrong!" He tried to withdraw the thirsty runeblade, but it was impossible. And, unlike any other sensation he had ever received from it, this was almost gentle. Warm and pleasant, bringing with it her youth and innocence, his wife's soul flowed into his and he wept. "Oh, Zarozinia. Oh, my love!"

So she died, her soul blending with his as, years earlier, the soul of his first love, Cymoril, had been taken. He did not look at the grotesque worm-body, did not glance at her face, but walked slowly from the cabin.

Though he was moved to an aching sadness, his sword seemed to chuckle as he resheathed it.

As he left the cabin, it appeared to him that the deck was disintegrating, flowing apart. Straasha had been right. The destruction of Pyaray also meant the destruction of his ghastly fleet. Jagreen Lern had evidently made good his escape and Elric, in his present mood, did not feel ready to pursue him. He was only regretful that the fleet had achieved its purpose before he had been able to destroy it. Sword and shield both aiding him in their ways, he leapt from the ship to the pulsating ground and ran for the Nihrain steed which was rearing up and flailing with its hoofs to protect itself from a group of gibbering Chaos creatures. He drew his runesword again and drove into them, quickly dispersing them and mounting the Nihrain stallion. Then, the tears still flowing down his white face, he rode wildly from the Camp of Chaos, leaving the Ships of Hell breaking apart behind him. At least these would threaten the world no more and a blow had been struck against Chaos. Now only the horde itself remained to be dealt with—and the dealing would not be so easy.

Fighting off the warped things which clawed at him, he finally rejoined his friends, said nothing to them but wheeled his horse to lead the way over the shaking earth towards Melniboné, where the last stand against Chaos could be prepared, the last battle fought and his destiny completed.

And in his dark, tormented mind he seemed to hear Zarozinia's youthful voice whispering comfort as, still sobbing, he rode away from that Camp of Chaos.

*And then did the Forces of Chaos challenge Fate and the great Cosmic Balance and seek greater power on Earth through their human medium. And the Lords of Law were unable to gain entrance to the Earth and there was one man only, Elric who bore the Black Sword, and he was destined to be torn upon the rack of Time and his destiny was to destroy his world so that Law might mould it anew. Lower dipped the Balance as Chaos gained strength, weaker became Law, and only Elric who bore the Black Sword could right the Balance by his actions and the power of the Black Sword . . .*

*—The Chronicle of the Black Sword*
*SCIENCE FANTASY No. 64, April 1964*

## BOOK FOUR

# DOOMED LORD'S PASSING

*For the mind of Man alone is free to explore the lofty vastness of the cosmic infinite, to transcend ordinary consciousness, to roam the secret corridors of the brain where past and future melt into one . . . And universe and individual are linked, the one mirrored in the other, and each contains the other.*

*—The Chronicle of the Black Sword*

## Chapter One

THE DREAMING CITY no longer dreamed in splendour. The tattered towers of Imrryr were blackened husks, tumbled rags of masonry standing sharp and dark against a sullen sky. Once, Elric's vengeance had brought fire to the city, and the fire had brought ruin.

Streaks of cloud, like sooty smoke, whispered across the pulsing sun so that the shouting, red-stained waters beyond Imrryr were soiled by shadow, and they seemed to become quieter as if hushed by the black scars that rode across their ominous turbulence.

Upon a confusion of fallen masonry, a man stood watching the waves. A tall man, broad-shouldered, slender at hip, a man with slanting brows, pointed, lobeless ears, high cheekbones and crimson, moody eyes in a dead white ascetic face. He was dressed in black quilted doublet and heavy cloak, both high-collared, emphasizing the pallor of his albino skin. The wind, erratic and warm, played with his cloak, fingered it and passed mindlessly on to howl through the broken towers.

Elric heard the howling and his memory was filled by the sweet, the malicious and melancholy melodies of old Melniboné. He remembered, too, the other music his ancestors had created when they had elegantly tortured their slaves, choosing them for the pitch of their screams and forming them into the instruments of unholy symphonies. Lost in this nostalgia for a while, he found something close to forgetfulness and he wished that he had never doubted the code of Melniboné, wished that he had accepted it without question and thus left his mind unsundered. Bitterly, he smiled.

A figure appeared below him and climbed the tumbled stones to stand by his side. He was a small, red-haired man with a wide mouth and eyes that had once been bright and amused.

"You look to the East, Elric," Moonglum murmured. "You look back towards something irremediable."

Elric put his long-fingered hand on his friend's shoulder. "Where else is there to look, Moonglum, when the world lies beneath the heel of Chaos? What would you have me do? Look forward to days of hope and laughter, to an old age lived in peace, with children playing around my feet?" He laughed softly. It was not a laugh that Moonglum liked to hear.

"Sepiriz spoke of help from the White Lords. It must come soon.

We must wait patiently." Moonglum turned to squint into the glowering and motionless sun and then, his face set in an introspective look, cast his eyes down to the rubble on which he stood.

Elric was silent for a moment, watching the waves. Then he shrugged. "Why complain? It does me no good. I cannot act on my own volition. Whatever fate is before me cannot be changed. I pray that the men who follow us will make use of their ability to control their own destinies. I have no such ability." He touched his jawbone with his fingers and then looked at the hand, noting nails, knuckles, muscles and veins standing out on the pale skin. He ran this hand through the silky strands of his white hair, drew a long breath and let it out in a sigh. "Logic! The world cries for logic. I have none, yet here I am, formed as a man with mind, heart and vitals, yet formed by a chance coming together of certain elements. The world needs logic. Yet all the logic in the world is worth as much as one lucky guess. Men take pains to weave a web of careful thoughts—yet others thoughtlessly weave a random pattern and achieve the same result. So much for the thoughts of the sage."

"Ah," Moonglum winked with attempted levity, "thus speaks the wild adventurer, the cynic. But we are not all wild and cynical, Elric. Other men tread other paths—and reach other conclusions than yours."

"I tread one that's pre-ordained. Come, let's to the Dragon Caves and see what Dyvim Slorm has done to rouse our reptilian friends."

They stumbled together down the ruins and walked the shattered canyons that had once been the lovely streets of Imrryr, out of the city and along a grassy track that wound through the gorse, disturbing a flock of large ravens that fled into the air, cawing, all save one, the king, who balanced himself on a bush, his cloak of ruffled feathers drawn up in dignity, his black eyes regarding them with wary contempt.

Down through sharp rocks to the gaping entrance of the Dragon Caves, down the steep steps into torch-lit darkness with its damp warmth and smell of scaly reptilian bodies. Into the first cave where the great recumbent forms of the sleeping dragons lay, their folded leathery wings rising into the shadows, their green and black scales glowing faintly, their clawed feet folded and their slender snouts curled back, even in sleep, to display the long, ivory teeth that seemed like so many white stalactites. Their dilating red nostrils groaned in torpid slumber. The smell of their hides and their breath was unmistakable, rousing in Moonglum some memory inherited from his ancestors, some shadowy impression of a time when these dragons and their masters swept across a world they ruled, their inflammable venom dripping from their fangs and heedlessly setting fire to the countryside across which they flew. Elric, used to it, hardly noticed the smell, but passed on through the first cave and the second until he found Dyvim Slorm, striding about with a torch in one hand and a scroll in the other, swearing to himself.

He looked up as he heard their booted feet approach. He spread out his arms and shouted, his voice echoing through the caverns, "Nothing! Not a stir, not an eyelid flickering! There is no way of rousing them. They'll not wake until they have slept their necessary number of years. Oh, that we had not used them on the last two occasions, for we have greater need of them today!"

"Neither you nor I had the knowledge we have now. Regret is useless since it can achieve nothing." Elric stared around him at the huge, shadowy forms. Here, slightly apart from the rest, lay the leader-dragon, one he recognized and felt affection for: Flamefang, the eldest, who was five thousand years old and still young for a dragon. But Flamefang, like the rest, slept on.

He went up to the beast and stroked its metal-like scales, ran his hand down the ivory smoothness of its great front fangs, felt its warm breath on his body and smiled. Beside him, on his hip, he heard Stormbringer murmur. He patted the blade. "Here's one soul you cannot have. The dragons are indestructible. They will survive, even though all the world collapses into nothing."

Dyvim Slorm said from another part of the cavern: "I can't think of further action to take for the meantime, Elric. Let's go back to the Tower of D'a'rputna and refresh ourselves."

Elric nodded assent and, together, the three men returned through the caverns and ascended the steps into the sunlight.

"So," Dyvim Slorm remarked, "still no nightfall. The sun has remained in that position for thirteen days, ever since we left the Camp of Chaos and made our perilous way to Melniboné. How much power must Chaos wield if it can stop the sun in its course?"

"Chaos might not have done this for all we know," Moonglum pointed out. "Though it's likely, of course, that it did. Time has stopped. Time waits. But waits for what? More confusion, further disorder? Or the influence of the great Balance which will restore order and take vengeance against those forces who have gone against its will? Or does time wait for us—three mortal men adrift, cut off from what is happening to all other men, waiting on time as it waits on us?"

"Perhaps the sun waits on us," Elric agreed. "For is it not our destiny to prepare the world for its fresh course? It makes me feel a little more than a mere pawn if that's the case. What if we do nothing? Will the sun remain where it is for ever?"

They paused in their progress for a moment and stood staring up at the pulsating red disc which flooded the streets with scarlet light, at the black clouds which fled across the sky before it. Where were the clouds going? Where did they come from? They seemed instilled with purpose. It was possible that they were not even clouds at all, but spirits of Chaos bent on dark errands.

Elric grunted to himself, aware of the uselessness of such speculation. He led the way back to the Tower of D'a'rputna where years before he had sought his love, his cousin Cymoril, and later lost her to the ravening thirst of the blade by his side.

The tower had survived the flames, though the colours that had once adorned it were blackened by fire. Here he left his friends and went to his own room to fling himself, fully clad, upon the soft Melnibonéan bed and, almost immediately, fall asleep.

## Chapter Two

Elric slept and Elric dreamed and, though he was aware of the unreality of his visions, his attempts to rouse himself to wakefulness were entirely futile. Soon he ceased trying and merely let his dream form itself and draw him into its bright landscapes . . .

*He saw Imrryr as it had been many centuries ago. Imrryr, the same city he had known before he led the raid on it and caused its destruction. The same, yet with a different, brighter appearance as if it were newly built. As well, the colours of the surrounding countryside were richer, the sun darker orange, the sky deep blue and sultry. Since then, he realized, the very tints of the world had faded with the planet's aging . . .*

People and beasts moved in the shining streets; tall, eldritch Melnibonéans, men and women walking with grace, like proud tigers; hard-faced slaves with hopeless, stoic eyes, long-legged horses of a type now extinct, small mastodons drawing gaudy cars. Clearly on the breeze came the mysterious scents of the place, the muted sounds of activity—all hushed, for the Melnibonéans hated noise as much as they loved harmony. Heavy silk banners flapped from the scintillating towers of bluestone, jade, ivory, crystal and polished red granite. And Elric moved in his sleep and ached to be there amongst his own ancestors, the golden folk who had dominated the old world.

Monstrous galleys passed through the water-maze which led to Imrryr's inner harbour, bringing the best of the world's booty, tax gathered from all parts of the Bright Empire. And across the azure sky lazy dragons flapped their way towards the caves where thousands of the beasts were stabled, unlike the present where scarcely a hundred remained. In the tallest tower—the Tower of B'aal'nezbett, the Tower of Kings—his ancestors had studied sorcerous lore, conducted their malicious experiments, indulged their sensuous appetites—not decadently as men of the Young Kingdoms might behave, but according to their native instincts.

Elric knew that he looked upon the ghost of a now-dead city. And he seemed to pass beyond the tower's gleaming walls and see his emperor-ancestors indulging in drug-sharpened conversation, lazily sadistic, sporting with demon-women, torturing, investigating the peculiar metabolism and psychology of the enslaved races, delving into mystic lore, absorbing a knowledge which few men of the later period could experience without falling insane.

But it was clear that this must either be a dream or vision of a netherworld which the dead of all ages inhabited, for here were emperors of many different generations. Elric knew them from their portraits: Black-ringleted Rondar IV, twelfth emperor; sharp-eyed, imperious Elric I, eightieth emperor; horror-burdened Kahan VII, three-hundred-and-twenty-ninth emperor. A dozen or more of the mightiest and wisest of his four-hundred-and-twenty-seven ancestors, including Terhali, the Green Empress, who had ruled the Bright Empire from the year 8406 after its foundation until 9011. Her longevity and green-tinged skin and hair had marked her out. She had been a powerful sorceress, even by Melnibonéan standards. She was also reputed the daughter of a union between Emperor Iuntric X and a demon.

Elric, who saw all these as if from a darkened corner of the great main chamber, observed the shimmering door of black crystal open and a newcomer enter. He started and again attempted to wake himself, without success. The man was his father, Sadric the Eighty-Sixth, a tall man with heavy-lidded eyes and a misery in him. He passed through the throng as if it did not exist. He walked directly towards Elric and stopped two paces from him. He stood looking at him, the eyes peering upwards from beneath the heavy lids and prominent brow. He was a gaunt-faced man who had been disappointed in his albino son. He had a sharp, long nose, sweeping cheekbones and a slight stoop because of his unusual height. He fingered the thin, red velvet of his robe with his delicate, beringed hands. Then he spoke in a clear whisper which, Elric remembered, it had always been his habit to employ.

"My son, are you, too, dead? I thought I'd been here but a fleeting moment and yet I see you changed in years and with a burden on you that time and fate have placed there. How did you die? In reckless combat on some upstart's foreign blade? Or in this very tower in your ivory bed? And what of Imrryr now? Does she fare well or ill, dreaming in her decline of past splendour? The line continues, as it must—I will not ask you if that part of your trust was kept. A son, of course, born of Cymoril whom you loved, for which your cousin Yyrkoon hated you."

"Father—"

The old man raised a hand that was almost transparent with age. "There is another question I must ask of you. One that has troubled all who spend their immortality in the Forest of Souls, which surrounds this shade of a city. Some of us have noticed that the city itself fades at times and its colours dim, quivering as if about to vanish. Companions of ours have passed even beyond death and, perhaps, I shudder to contemplate it, into non-existence. Even here, in the timeless region of death, unprecedented changes manifest themselves and, those of us who've dared ask the question and also give its answer, fear that some tumultuous event has taken place in the world of the living. Some event, so great is it, that even here we feel our souls' extinction threatened. A legend says that until the Dreaming City dies, we ghosts may inhabit its earlier glory. Is that the news you bear to us? Is this your message? For I note on clearer observation that your body lives still and this is merely your astral body, released for a while to wander the realms of the dead."

"Father—" but already the vision was fading; already he was withdrawing back down the bellowing corridors of the cosmos, through planes of existence unknown to living men, away, away . . .

"Father!" he called, and his own voice echoed, but there was none there to make reply. And in some sense at least he was glad, for how could he answer the poor spirit and reveal to him the truth of his guesses, admit the crimes he himself was guilty of against his ancestral city, against the very blood of his forefathers? All was mist and groaning sorrow as his echoes boomed into his ears, seeming to take on their own independence and warp the word into weirder words: "F-a-a-ath-e-er-r-r . . . A-a-a-a-a-v-a-a-a . . . A-a-a-a-h-a-a-a-a-a . . . R-a-a-a . . . D-a-ra-va-ar-a-a . . . !"

Still, though he strove with all his being, he could not rouse himself from slumber, but felt his spirit drawn through other regions of smoky indeterminacy, through patterns of colour beyond his earthly spectrum, beyond his mind's conception.

A huge face began to take form in the mist.

"Sepiriz!" Elric recognized the face of his mentor. But the black Nihrainian, disembodied, did not appear to hear him. "Sepiriz—are *you* dead?"

The face faded, then reappeared almost at once upon the rest of the man's tall frame.

"Elric, I have discovered you at last, robed in your astral body, I see. Thank Fate, for I thought I had failed to summon you. Now we must make haste. A breach has been made in the defenses of Chaos and we go to confer with the Lords of Law!"

"Where are we?"

"Nowhere as yet. We travel to the Higher Worlds. Come, hurry, I'll be your guide."

Down, down, through pits of softest wool that engulfed and comforted, through canyons that were cut between blazing mountains of light which utterly dwarfed them, through caverns of infinite blackness wherein their bodies shone and Elric knew that the dark nothingness went away in all directions for ever.

And then they seemed to stand upon an horizonless plateau, perfectly flat with occasional green and blue geometric constructions rising from it. The iridescent air was alive with shimmering patterns of energy, weaving intricate shapes that seemed very formal. And there, too, were things in human form—things which had assumed such shape for the benefit of the men who now encountered them.

The White Lords of the Higher Worlds, enemies of Chaos, were marvelously beautiful, with bodies of such symmetry that they could not be earthly. Only Law could create such perfection and, Elric thought, such perfection defeated progress. That the twin forces complemented one another was now plainer than ever before, and for either to gain complete ascendancy over the other meant entropy or stagnation for the cosmos. Even though Law might dominate the Earth, Chaos *must* be present, and vice versa.

The Lords of Law were accoutred for war. They had made this apparent in their choice of Earthlike garb. Fine metals and silks—or their like on this plane—gleamed on their perfect bodies. Slender weapons were at their sides and their overpoweringly beautiful faces seemed to glow with purpose. The tallest stepped forward.

"So, Sepiriz, you have brought the one whose destiny it is to aid us. Greetings, Elric of Melniboné. Though spawn of Chaos you be, we have cause to welcome you. Do you recognize me? The one whom your earthly mythology calls Donblas the Justice Maker."

Immobile, Elric said: "I remember you, Lord Donblas. You are misnamed, I fear, for justice is nowhere present in the world."

"You speak of your realm as if it were all realms." Donblas smiled without rancour, though it appeared that he was unused to such impudence from a mortal. Elric remained insouciant. His ancestors had been opposed to Donblas and all his brethren, and it was still hard to consider the White Lord an ally. "I see now how you have managed to defy our opponents," Lord Donblas continued with approval. "And I grant you that justice cannot be found on Earth at this time. But I am named the Justice *Maker* and have still the will to make it when conditions change on your plane."

Elric did not look directly at Donblas, for the sight of his beauty was disturbing. "Then let's to work, my lord, and change the world as soon we may. Let's bring the novelty of justice to our sobbing realm."

"Haste, mortal, is impossible here!" It was another White Lord speaking, his pale yellow surcoat rippling over the clear steel of breastplate and greaves, the single Arrow of Law emblazoned on it.

"I'd thought the breach to Earth made," Elric frowned. "I'd thought this martial sight a sign that you prepared war against Chaos!"

"War *is* prepared—but not possible until the summons comes from your realm."

"From us! Has not Earth screamed for your aid? Have we not worked sorceries and incantations to bring you to us? What further summons do you need?"

"The ordained one," said Lord Donblas firmly.

"The ordained one? Gods! (You'll pardon me, my lords.) Is further work required of me, then?"

"One last great task, Elric," said Sepiriz softly. "As I have told you, Chaos blocks the attempts of the White Lords to gain access to our world. The Horn of Fate must be blown thrice before this business is fully terminated. The first blast will wake the Dragons of Imrryr, the second will allow the White Lords entrance to the earthly plane, the third—" he paused.

"Yes, the third?" Elric was impatient.

"The third will herald the death of our world!"

"Where lies this mighty horn?"

"In one of several realms," said Sepiriz. "A device of this kind cannot be made on our plane, therefore it has had to be constructed on a plane where logic rules over sorcery. You must journey there to locate the Horn of Fate."

"And how can I accomplish such a journey?"

Once again Lord Donblas spoke levelly. "We will give you the means. Equip yourself with sword and shield of Chaos, for they will be of some use to you, though not so powerful as in your world. Go you then to the highest point on the ruined Tower of B'aal'nezbett in Imrryr and step off into space. You will not fall—unless what little power we retain on Earth fails us."

"Comforting words, my Lord Donblas. Very well, I shall do as you decree, to satisfy my own curiosity if naught else."

Donblas shrugged. "This is only one of many worlds—almost as much a shadow as your own—but you may not approve of it. You will notice its sharpness, its clearness of outline—that will indicate that time has exerted no real influence upon it, that its structure has not been mellowed by many events. However, let me wish you safe passage, mortal, for I like you—and I have cause to thank you, too. Though you be of Chaos, you have within you several of the qualities we of Law admire. Go now—return to your mortal body and prepare yourself for the venture ahead of you."

Elric glanced at Sepiriz. The black Nihrainian stepped back

three paces and disappeared into the gleaming air. Elric followed him.

Once again their astral bodies ranged the myriad planes of the supernatural universe, experiencing sensations unfamiliar to the physical mind, before, quite without warning, Elric felt suddenly heavy and opened his eyes to discover that he was in his own bed in the Tower of D'a'rputna. Through the faint light filtering between chinks in the heavy curtain thrown over the window-slit, he saw the round Chaos Shield, its eight-arrowed symbol pulsing slowly as if in concert with the sun, and beside it his unholy runeblade, Stormbringer, lying against the wall as if already prepared for their journey into the might-be world of a possible future.

Then Elric slept again, more naturally, and was tormented, also, by more natural nightmares so that at last he screamed in his sleep and woke himself to find Moonglum standing by the bed. There was an expression of sad concern upon his narrow face. "What is it, Elric? What ails your slumber?"

He shuddered. "Nothing. Leave me, Moonglum, and I'll join you when I rise."

"There must be reason for such shouting. Some prophetic dream, perhaps?"

"Aye, prophetic sure enough. I thought I saw a vision of my thin blood spilt by a hand that was my own. What import has this dream, what moment? Answer that, my friend, and, if you can't, then leave me to my morbid bed until these thoughts are gone."

"Come, rouse yourself, Elric. Find forgetfulness in action. The candle of the fourteenth day burns low and Dyvim Slorm awaits your good advice."

The albino pulled himself upright and swung his trembling legs over the bed. He felt enfeebled, bereft of energy, Moonglum helped him rise. "Throw off this troubled mood and help us in our quandary," he said with a hollow levity that made his fears more plain.

"Aye," Elric straightened himself. "Hand me my sword. I need its stolen strength."

Unwillingly, Moonglum went to the wall where stood the evil

weapon, took the runeblade by its scabbard and lifted it with difficulty, for it was an over-heavy sword. He shuddered as it seemed to titter faintly at him, and he presented it hilt-first to his friend. Gratefully, Elric seized it, was about to pull it from the sheath when he paused. "Best leave the room before I free the blade."

Moonglum understood at once and left, not anxious to trust his life to the whim of the hellsword—or his friend.

When he was gone, Elric unsheathed the great sword and at once felt a faint tingle as its supernatural vitality began to stream into his nerves. Yet it was scarcely adequate and he knew that if the blade did not feed soon upon the lifestuff of another it would seek the souls of his two remaining friends. He replaced it thoughtfully in the scabbard, buckled it around his waist and strode to join Moonglum in the high-ceilinged corridor.

In silence, they proceeded down the twisting marble steps of the tower, until they reached the centre level where the main chamber was. Here, Dyvim Slorm was seated, a bottle of old Melnibonéan wine on the table before him, a large silver bowl in his hands. His sword Mournblade was on the table beside the bottle. They had found the store of wine in the secret cellars of the place, missed by the sea-reavers whom Elric had led upon Imrryr when he and his cousin had fought on opposite sides. The bowl was full of the congealed mixture of herbs, honey and barley which their ancestors had used to sustain themselves in times of need. Dyvim Slorm was brooding over it, but looked up when they came close and sat themselves on chairs opposite him. He smiled hopelessly.

"I fear, Elric, that I have done all I can to rouse our sleeping friends. No more is possible—and they still slumber."

Elric remembered the details of his vision and, half-afraid that it had been merely a figment of his own imaginings, supplying the fantasy of hope where, in reality, no hope was, said: "Forget the dragons, for a while at least. Last night I left my body, so I thought, and journeyed to places beyond the Earth, eventually to the White Lords' plane where they told me how I might rouse the dragons by blowing upon a horn. I intend to follow their directions and seek that horn."

Dyvim Slorm replaced his bowl upon the table. "We'll accompany you, of course."

"No need—and anyway impossible—I'll have to go alone. Wait for me until I return and if I do not—well, you must do what you decide, spending your remaining years imprisoned on this isle, or going to battle with Chaos."

"I have the idea that time has stopped in truth and if we stay here we shall live on for ever and shall be forced to face the resulting boredom," Moonglum put in. "If you don't return, I for one will ride into the conquered realms to take a few of our enemies with me to limbo."

"As you will," Elric said. "But wait for me until all your patience is ended, for I know not how long I'll be."

He stood up and they seemed a trifle startled, as if they had not until then understood the import of his words.

"Fare you well, then, my friend," said Moonglum.

"How well I fare depends on what I meet where I go," Elric smiled. "But thanks, Moonglum. Fare *you* well, good cousin, do not fret. Perhaps we'll wake the dragons yet!"

"Aye," Dyvim Slorm said with a sudden resurgence of vitality. "We shall, we shall! And their fiery venom will spread across the filth that Chaos brings, burning it clean! That day *must* come or I'm no prophet at all!"

Infected by this unexpected enthusiasm, Elric felt an increase of confidence, saluted his friends, smiled, and walked upright from the chamber, ascending the marble stairs to take the Chaos Shield from its place and go down to the gateway of the tower and pass through it, walking the jagged streets towards the magic-sundered ruin that had once been the scene of his dreadful vengeance and unwitting murder—the Tower of B'aal'nezbett.

## Chapter Three

Now, as Elric stood before the broken entrance of the tower, his mind was beset with bursting thoughts which fled about his skull, made overtures to his convictions and threatened to send him hopelessly to rejoin his companions. But he fought them, forced them down, forgot them, clung to his remembrance of the White Lord's assurance and passed into the shadowed shell which still had the smell of burned wood and fabric about its blackened interior.

This tower, which had formed a funeral pyre for the murdered corpse of his first love Cymoril and his warped cousin, her brother Yyrkoon, had been gutted of innards. Only the stone stairway remained and that, he noted, peering into the gloom through which rays of sunlight slanted, had collapsed before it reached the roof.

He dare not think, for thought might rob him of action. Instead, he placed a foot upon the first stair and began to climb. As he did so, a faint sound entered his ears, or it may have been that it came from within his mind. However it reached his consciousness, it sounded like a far-away orchestra tuning itself. As he climbed higher, the sound mounted, rhythmic yet discordant until, by the time he reached the final step still left intact, it thundered through his skull, pounded through his body producing a sensation of dull pain.

He paused and stared downward to the tower's floor far below. Fears beset him. He wondered whether Lord Donblas had intended him to climb to the highest point he could easily reach, or the actual point which was still some twenty feet above him. He decided it was best to take the White Lord literally and swinging the great Chaos Shield upon his back, reached above him and got his fingers into a crack in the wall, which now sloped gently inwards. He heaved himself up, his legs dangling and his feet seeking a hold. He had always been troubled by heights and disliked the sensation that came to him as he glanced down to the rubble-laden floor, eighty feet below, but he continued to climb and the climbing was made easier by the fissures in the tower's wall. Though he expected to fall, he did not, and at last reached the unsafe roof, easing himself through a hole and onto the sloping exterior. Bit by bit he climbed until he was on the highest part of the tower. Then, fearing hesitation still, he stepped outwards, over the festering streets of Imrryr far below.

The discordant music stopped. A roaring note replaced it. Swirling waves of red and black rushed towards him and then he had burst through them to find he was standing on firm turf beneath a small, pale sun, the smell of grass in his nostrils. He noted that, whereas the ancient world seen in his dream had seemed more colourful than his own, this world, in turn, contained even less colour, though it seemed to be cleaner in its outlines, in sharper focus. And the breeze that blew against his face was colder. He began to walk over the grass towards a thick forest of low, solid foliage which lay ahead. He reached the perimeter of the forest but did not enter, circumnavigating it until he came to a stream that went off into the distance, away from the forest.

He noticed with curiosity that the bright clear water appeared not to move. It was frozen, though not by any natural process that he recognized. It had all the attributes of a summer stream—yet it did not flow. Feeling that this phenomenon contrasted strangely with the rest of the scenery, he swung the round Chaos Shield onto his arm, drew his throbbing sword and began to follow the stream.

The grass gave way to gorse and rocks with the occasional clump of waving ferns of a variety he didn't recognize. Ahead, he thought he heard the tinkle of water, but here the stream was still frozen. As he passed a rock taller than the rest, he heard a voice above him.

"Elric!"

He looked up.

There, on the rock, stood a young dwarf with a long, brown beard that reached below his waist. He clutched a spear, his only weapon, and he was clad in russet breeks and jerkin with a green cap on his head and no shoes on his broad, naked feet. He had eyes like quartz that were at once hard, harsh and humorous.

"That's my name," Elric said quizzically. "Yet how is it you know me?"

"I am not of this world myself—at least, not exactly. I have no existence in time as you know it, but move here and there in the shadow worlds that the gods make. It is my nature to do so. In return for allowing me to exist, the gods sometimes use me as a messenger. My name is Jermays the Crooked, as unfinished as these worlds themselves." He clambered down the rock and stood looking up at Elric.

"What's your purpose here?" asked the albino.

"Methought you sought the Horn of Fate?"

"True. Know you where it lies?"

"Aye," smiled the young dwarf sardonically. "It's buried with the still-living corpse of a hero of this realm—a warrior they call Roland. Possibly yet another incarnation of the Champion Eternal."

"An outlandish name."

"No more than yours to other ears. Roland, save that his life was not so doom-beset, is your counterpart in his own realm. He met his death in a valley not far from here, trapped and betrayed by a fellow warrior. The horn was with him then and he blew it once before he died. Some say that the echoes still resound through the valley, and will resound for ever, though Roland perished many years ago. The horn's full purpose is unknown here—and was unknown even to Roland. It is called Olifant and, with his magic sword Durandana, was buried with him in the monstrous grave mound that you see yonder."

The dwarf pointed into the distance and Elric saw that he indicated something he had earlier taken to be a large hillock.

"And what must I do to gain this horn?" he asked.

The dwarf grinned with a hint of malice in his voice. "You must match that bodkin there 'gainst Roland's Durandana. His was consecrated by the Forces of Light whereas yours was forged by the Forces of Darkness. It should be an interesting conflict."

"You say he's dead—then how can he fight me?"

"He wears the horn by a thong about his neck. If you attempt to remove it, he will defend his ownership, waking from the deathless sleep that seems to be the lot of most heroes in this world."

Elric smiled. "It seems to me they must be short of heroes if they have to preserve them in that manner."

"Perhaps," the dwarf answered carelessly, "for there are a dozen or more who lie sleeping somewhere in this land alone. They are supposed to awaken only when a desperate need arises, yet I've known unpleasant things to happen and still they have slept. It could be they await the end of their world, which the gods may destroy if it proves unsuitable, in which case they will fight to prevent such a happening. It is merely a poorly conceived theory of my own and of little weight. Perhaps the legends arise from some dim knowledge of the fate of the Champion Eternal."

The dwarf bobbed a cynical bow and, hefting his spear, saluted Elric. "Farewell, Elric of Melniboné. When you wish to return I will be here to lead you—and return you must, whether alive or dead, for, as you are probably aware, your very presence, your physical appearance itself, contradicts this environment. Only one thing fits here . . ."

"What's that?"

"Your sword."

"My sword! Strange, I should have thought that would be the last thing." He shook a growing idea out of his mind. He did not have time to speculate. "I've no liking to be here," he commented as the dwarf clambered over the rocks. He glanced in the direction of the great burial mound and began to advance towards it. Beside him he saw that the stream was moving naturally and he had the impression that though Law influenced this world, it was to some extent still forced to deal with the disrupting influence of Chaos.

The grave barrow, he could now see, was fenced about with giant slabs of unadorned stone. Beyond the stones were olive trees that had dull jewels hanging from their branches, and beyond them, through the leafy apertures, Elric saw a tall, curved entrance blocked by gates of brass embossed with gold.

"Though strong, Stormbringer," he said to his sword, "I wonder if you'll be strong enough to war in this world as well as giving my body vitality. Let's test you."

He advanced to the gate and drawing back his arm delivered a mighty blow upon it with the runesword. The metal rang and a dent appeared. Again he struck, this time holding the sword with both hands, but then a voice cried from his right.

"What demon would disturb dead Roland's rest?"

"Who speaks the language of Melniboné?" Elric retorted boldly.

"I speak the language of demons, for I perceive that is what you are. I know of no Mulnebooney and am well-versed in the ancient mysteries."

"A proud boast," said Elric, who had not yet seen the speaker. She emerged, then, from around the barrow, and stood staring at him from out of her glowing green eyes. She had a long, beautiful face and was almost as pale as himself, though her hair was jet black. "What's your name?" he asked. "And are you a native of this world?"

"I am named Vivian, an enchantress, but earthly enough. Your Master knows the name of Vivian who once loved Roland, though he was too upright to indulge her, for she is immortal and a witch." She laughed good-humouredly. "Therefore I am familiar with demons of your like and do not fear you. Aroint thee! Aroint thee—or shall I call Bishop Turpin to exorcise thee?"

"Some of your words," said Elric courteously, "are unfamiliar and the speech of my folk much garbled. Are you some guardian of this hero's tomb?"

"Self-made guardian, aye. Now go!" She pointed towards the stone slabs.

"That is not possible. The corpse within has something of value to me. The Horn of Fate we call it, but you know it by another name."

"Olifant! But that's a blessed instrument. No demon would dare touch it. Even I . . ."

"I am no demon. I'm sufficiently human, I swear. Now stand aside. This cursed door resists my efforts too well."

"Aye," she said thoughtfully. "You could be a man—though an unlikely one. But the white face and hair, the red eyes, the tongue you speak . . ."

"Sorcerer I be, but no demon. Please—stand aside."

She looked carefully into his face and her look disturbed him. He took her by her shoulder. She felt real enough, yet somehow she had little real *presence*. It was as if she were far away rather than close to him. They stared at one another, both curious, both troubled. He whispered: "What knowledge could you have of my language? Is this world a dream of mine or of the gods? It seems scarcely tangible. Why?"

She heard him. "Say you so of us? What of your ghostly self? You seem an apparition from the dead past!"

"From the past! Aha—and *you* are of the future, as yet unformed. Perhaps that brings us to a conclusion?"

She did not pursue the topic but said suddenly: "Stranger, you will never break this door down. If you can touch Olifant, that speaks of you as mortal, despite your appearance. You must need the horn for an important task."

Elric smiled. "Aye—for if I do not take it back whence it came, you will never exist!"

She frowned. "Hints! Hints! I feel close to a discovery yet cannot grasp why, and that's unusual for Vivian. Here—" she took a big key from her gown and offered it to him—"this is the key to open Roland's tomb. It is the only one. I had to kill to get it, but oftimes I venture into the gloom of his grave to stare down at his face and pine that I might revive him and keep him living for ever on my island home. Take the horn! Rouse him—and when he has slain you, he will come to me and my warmth, my offer of everlasting life, rather than lie in that cold place again. Go—be slain by Roland!"

He took the key.

"Thanks, Lady Vivian. If it were possible to convince one who in truth did not yet exist, I would tell you that Roland's slaying of me would be worse for you than if I am successful."

He put the large key in the lock and it turned easily. The doors swung open and he saw that a long, low-roofed corridor twisted before him. Unhesitatingly, he advanced down it towards a flickering light that he could see through the cold and misty gloom. Yet, as he walked, it was as if he glided in a dream less real than that he had experienced the previous night. Now he entered the funeral chamber, illuminated by tall candles surrounding the bier of a man who lay upon it dressed in armour of a crude and unfamiliar design, a huge broadsword, almost as large as Stormbringer gripped to his chest and, upon the hilt, attached to his neck by a silver chain—the Horn of Fate, Olifant!

The man's face, seen in the candlelight, was strange; old and yet with a youthful appearance, the brow smooth and the features unlined.

Elric took Stormbringer in his left hand and reached out to grasp the horn. He made no attempt at caution, but wrenched it off Roland's neck.

A great roar came from the hero's throat. Immediately he had raised himself to a sitting position, the sword shifting into his two hands, his legs swinging off the bier. His eyes widened as he saw Elric with the horn in his hands, and he jumped at the albino, the sword Durandana whistling downwards towards Elric's head. He raised the shield and blocked the blow, slipped the horn into his jerkin and, backing away, returned Stormbringer to his right hand. Roland was now shouting something in a language completely unfamiliar to Elric. He did not bother trying to understand, since the angry tones were sufficient to tell him the knight was not suggesting a peaceful negotiation. He continued defending himself without once carrying the offensive to Roland, backing inch by inch down the long tunnel towards the barrow's mouth. Every time Durandana struck the Chaos Shield, both sword and shield gave out wild notes of great intensity. Implacably the hero continued to press Elric backwards, his broadsword whirling and striking the shield, sometimes the blade, with fantastic strength. Then they had broken into daylight and Roland seemed momentarily blinded. Elric glimpsed Vivian watching them eagerly for it appeared Roland was winning.

However, in daylight and with no chance of avoiding the angered knight, Elric retaliated with all the energy he had been saving until this moment. Shield high, sword swinging, he now took the attack, surprising Roland who was evidently unused to this behaviour on the part of an opponent. Stormbringer snarled as it bit into Roland's poorly forged armour of iron, riveted with big unsightly nails, painted on the front with a dull red cross that was a scarcely adequate insignia for so famous a hero. But there was no mistaking Durandana's powers for, though seemingly as crudely forged as the armour, it did not lose its edge and threatened to bite through the Chaos Shield with every stroke. Elric's left arm was numb from the blows and his right arm ached. Lord Donblas had not lied to him when he had said that the strength of his weapons would be diminished on this world.

Roland paused, shouting something, but Elric did not heed him, seized his opportunity and rushed in to crush his shield against Roland's body. The knight reeled and staggered, his sword giving off a keening note. Elric struck at a gap between Roland's helmet and gorget. The head sprang off the shoulders and rolled grotesquely away, but no blood pumped from the jugular. The eyes of the head remained open, staring at Elric.

Vivian screamed and shouted something in the same language which Roland had used. Elric stepped back, his face grim.

"Oh, his legend, his legend!" she cried. "The only hope the people have is that Roland will some day ride once more to their aid. Now you have slain him! Fiend!"

"Possessed I may be," he said quietly as she sobbed by the headless corpse, "but I was ordained by the gods to do this work. I'll take my leave of your drab world, now."

"Have you no sorrow for the crime you've done?"

"None, madam, for this is only one of many such acts which, I'm told, serve some greater purpose. That I sometimes doubt the truth of this consolation need not concern you. Know you this, though, I have been told that it is the fate of such as your Roland and myself never to die—always to be reborn. Farewell."

And he walked away from there; passed through the olive grove and the tall stones, the Horn of Fate cold against his heart.

He followed the river towards the high rock where he saw a small figure poised and, when he reached it, looked up at the young dwarf Jermays the Crooked, took the horn from his jerkin and displayed it.

Jermays chuckled. "So Roland is dead, and you, Elric, have left a fragment of a legend in this world, if it survives. Well, shall I escort you back to your own place?"

"Aye, and hurry."

Jermays skipped down the rocks and stood beside the tall albino. "Hmm," he mused, "that horn could prove troublesome to us. Best replace it in your jerkin and keep it covered by your shield."

Elric obeyed the dwarf and followed him down to the banks of the strangely frozen river. It looked as if it should have been moving, but it evidently was not. Jermays leapt into it and, incredibly, began to sink. "Quickly! Follow!"

Elric stepped in after him and for a moment stood on the frozen water before he, also, began to sink.

Though the stream was shallow, they continued to sink until all similarity to water was gone and they were passing down into rich darkness that became warm and heavy-scented. Jermays pulled at his sleeve. "This way!" And they shot off at right angles, darting from side to side, up and down, through a maze that apparently only Jermays could see. Against his chest, the horn seemed to heave and he pressed his shield to it. Then he blinked as he found himself in the light again, staring at the great red sun throbbing in the dark blue sky. His feet were on something solid. He looked and saw that it was the Tower of B'aal'nezbett. For a while longer the horn heaved as if alive, like a trapped bird but, after some moments, it became quiescent.

Elric lowered himself to the roof and began to edge down it until he came to the gap through which he had passed earlier.

Then suddenly he looked up as he heard a noise in the sky. There, his feet planted on air, stood grinning Jermays the Crooked. "I'll be passing on, for I like not this world at all." He chuckled. "It has been a pleasure to have had a part in this. Goodbye, Sir Champion. Remember me, the unfinished one, to the Lords of the Higher Worlds—and perhaps you could hint to them that the sooner they improve their memories or else their creative powers, the sooner I shall be happy."

Elric said: "Perhaps you'd best be content with your lot, Jermays. There are disadvantages to stability, too."

Jermays shrugged and vanished.

Slowly, all but spent, Elric descended the fractured wall and, with great relief, reached the first stair to stumble down the rest and run back to the Tower of D'a'rputna with the news of his success.

## Chapter Four

The three thoughtful men left the city and went down to the Dragon Caves. On a new silver chain, the Horn of Fate was slung around Elric's neck. He was dressed in black leather, with his head unprotected save for a golden circlet that kept his hair from his eyes. Stormbringer scabbarded at his side, the Chaos Shield on his back, he led his companions into the grottoes, to come eventually to the slumbering bulk of Flamefang the Dragon Leader. His lungs seemed to have insufficient capacity as he drew air into them and grasped the horn. Then he glanced at his friends, who regarded him expectantly, straddled his legs slightly and blew with all his strength into the horn.

The note sounded, deep and sonorous, and as it reverberated through the caverns, he felt all his vitality draining from him. Weaker and weaker he became until he sank to his knees, the horn still at his lips, the note failing, his vision dimming, his limbs shaking, and then he sprawled face down on the rock, the horn clattering beside him.

Moonglum dashed towards him and gasped as he saw the bulk of the leading dragon stir and one huge, unblinking eye, as cold as the Northern wastes, stare at him.

Dyvim Slorm yelled jubilantly: "Flamefang! Brother Flamefang, you wake!"

All about him he saw the other dragons stirring also, shaking their wings and straightening their slender necks, ruffling their horny crests. Moonglum felt smaller than usual as the dragons wakened. He began to feel nervous of the huge beasts, wondering how they would respond to the presence of one who was not a Dragon Master. Then he remembered the enervated albino and knelt beside Elric, touching his leathern-covered shoulder.

"Elric! D'you live?"

Elric groaned and tried to turn over onto his back. Moonglum helped him sit upright. "I'm weak, Moonglum—so weak I can't rise. The horn took all my energy!"

"Draw your sword—it will supply what you need."

Elric shook his head. "I'll take your advice, though I doubt whether you're right this time. That hero I slew must have been soulless, or else his soul was well-protected, for I gained nothing from him."

His hand fumbled towards his hip and grasped Stormbringer's hilt. With a tremendous effort, he drew it from the scabbard and felt a faint flowing leave it and enter him, but not enough to allow him any great exertion. He got up and staggered towards Flamefang. The monster recognized him and rustled its wings by way of welcome, its hard, solemn eyes seeming to warm slightly. As he moved round to pat its neck, he staggered and fell to one knee, rising with effort.

In earlier times there had been slaves to saddle the dragons but now they would have to saddle their beasts themselves. They went to the saddle-store and chose the saddles they needed, for each saddle was designed for an individual beast. Elric could scarcely bear the weight of Flamefang's elaborately carved saddle of wood, steel, jewels and precious metals. He was forced to drag it across the cavern floor. Not wishing to embarrass him with their glances, the other two ignored his impotent struggling and busied themselves with their own saddles. The dragons must have understood that Moonglum was a friend, for they did not demur when he cautiously approached to dress his dragon with its high wooden saddle with silver stirrups and sheathed, lance-like goad from which was draped the pennant of a noble family of Melniboné, now all dead.

When they had finished saddling their own beasts, they went to help Elric who was half-falling with weariness, his back leaning against Flamefang's scaly body. While they tied the girths, Dyvim Slorm said: "Will you have strength enough to lead us?"

Elric sighed. "Aye—enough, I think, for that. But I know I'll have none for the ensuing battle. There must be *some* means of gaining vitality."

"What of the herbs you once used?"

"Those I had have lost their properties, and there are no fresh ones to be found now that Chaos has warped plant, rock and ocean with its dreadful stamp."

Leaving Moonglum to finish Flamefang's saddling, Dyvim Slorm went away to return with a cup of liquid which he hoped would help revivify Elric. Elric drank it, gave the cup back to Dyvim Slorm and reached up to grasp the saddle-pommel, hauling himself into the high saddle. "Bring straps," he ordered.

"Straps?" Dyvim Slorm frowned.

"Aye. If I'm not secured in my saddle, I'll likely fall to the ground before we've flown a mile."

So he sat in the tall saddle and gripped the goad which bore his blue, green and silver pennant, gripped it in his gauntleted hand and waited until they came with the straps and bound him firmly into place. He gave a slight smile and shook the dragon's halter. "Forward, Flamefang, lead the way for your brothers and sisters."

With folded wings and lowered head, the dragon began to walk its slithering way to the exit. Behind it, on two dragons almost as large, sat Dyvim Slorm and Moonglum, their faces grimly concerned, watchful for Elric's safety. As Flamefang moved with rolling gait through the series of caverns, its fellow beasts fell in behind it until all of them had reached the great mouth of the last cave which overlooked the threshing sea. The sun was still in its position overhead, scarlet and swollen, seeming to swell in rhythm with the movement of the sea. Voicing a shout that was half-hiss, half-yell, Elric slapped at Flamefang's neck with his goad.

"Up, Flamefang! Up for Melniboné and vengeance!"

As if sensing the strangeness of the world, Flamefang paused on the brink of the ledge, shaking his head and snorting to himself. Then, as he launched into the air, his wings began to beat, their fantastic spread flapping with slow grace but bearing the beast along with marvelous speed.

Up, up, beneath the swollen sun, up into the hot, turbulent air, up towards the East where the camps of hell were waiting. And in Flamefang's wake came its two brother-dragons, bearing Moonglum and Dyvim Slorm who had a horn of his own, the one used to direct the dragons. Ninety-five other dragons, males and females, darkened the deep blue sky, all green, red and gold, scales clashing and flashing, wings beating and, in concert, sounding like the throbbing of a million drums as they flew over the unclean waters with gaping jaws and cold, cold eyes.

Though beneath him now Elric saw with blurring eyes many colours of immense richness, they were all dark and changing constantly, shifting from one extreme of a dark spectrum to the other. It was not water down there now—it was a fluid composed of materials both natural and supernatural, real and abstract. Pain, longing, misery and laughter could be seen as tangible fragments of the tossing tide, passions and frustrations lay in it also, as well as stuff made of living flesh that bubbled on occasions to the surface.

In his weakened condition, the sight of the fluid sickened Elric and he turned his red eyes upwards and towards the East as the dragons moved swiftly on their course.

Soon they were flying across what had once been the mainland of the Eastern Continent, the major Vilmirian peninsula. But now it was bereft of its earlier qualities and huge columns of dark mist rose into the air so that they were forced to guide their reptilian steeds among them. Lava streamed, bubbling, on the far-away ground, disgusting shapes flitted over land and air, monstrous beasts and the occasional group of weird riders on skeletal horses who looked up when they heard the beat of the dragon wings and rode in frantic fear towards their camps.

The world seemed a corpse, given life in corruption by virtue of the vermin which fed upon it.

Of mankind nothing was left, save for the three mounted on the dragons.

Elric knew that Jagreen Lern and his human allies had long since forsaken their humanity and could no longer claim kinship with the species their hordes had swept from the world. The leaders alone might retain their human shape, the Dark Lords don it, but their souls were warped just as the bodies of their followers had become warped into hell-shapes due to the transmuting influence of Chaos. All the dark powers of Chaos lay upon the world, yet deeper and deeper into its heart went the dragon flight, with Elric swaying in his saddle and only stopped from falling by the straps that bound his body. From the lands below there seemed to rise an aching shriek as tortured nature was defied and its components forced into alien forms.

Onward they sped, towards what had once been Karlaak by the Weeping Waste and which was now the Camp of Chaos. Then, from above, they heard a cawing yell and saw black shapes dropping down on them. Elric had not even strength to cry out, but weakly tapped Flamefang's neck and made the beast veer away from the danger. Moonglum and Dyvim Slorm followed his example and Dyvim Slorm sounded his horn, ordering the dragons not to engage the attackers, but some of the dragons in the rear were too late and were forced to turn and battle with the black phantoms.

Elric looked behind him and, for a few seconds, saw them outlined against the sky, rending things with the jaws of whales, locked in combat with the dragons that shot their flaming venom at them and tore at them with teeth and claws, wings flapping as they strove to hold their height, but then another wave of dark green mist spread across his field of vision and he did not see the fate that befell the dozen dragons.

Now Elric signaled Flamefang to fly low over a small army of riders fleeing through the tormented land, the eight-arrowed standard of Chaos flapping from their leader's encrusted lance. Down they went and loosed their venom, having the satisfaction of seeing the beasts and riders scream, burn and perish, their ashes absorbed into the shifting ground.

Here and there, now, they saw a gigantic castle, newly raised by sorcery, perhaps as a reward to some traitor king who had aided Jagreen Lern, perhaps as the keeps of the Captains of Chaos who, now that Chaos ruled, were establishing themselves on Earth. They swept down on them, released their venom and left them burning with unnatural fires, the gouting smoke blending with the shredding mist. And at last Elric saw the Camp of Chaos—a city but recently made in the same manner as the castles, the flaring Sign of Chaos hanging amber in the sky overheard. Yet he felt no elation, only despair that he was so weak he would not have the strength to meet his enemy Jagreen Lern in combat. What could he do? How could strength be found—for, even if he took no part in the fighting, he must have sufficient vitality to blow the horn a second time and summon the White Lords to Earth.

The city seemed peculiarly silent as if it waited or prepared for something. It had an ominous atmosphere and Elric, before Flamefang crossed the perimeter, made his dragon steed turn and circle.

Dyvim Slorm and Moonglum and the rest of the dragon flight followed his example and Dyvim Slorm called across the air to him. "What now, Elric? I had not expected a *city* to be here so soon!"

"Neither had I. But look—" he pointed with a trembling hand he could hardly lift, "there's Jagreen Lern's Merman standard. And there—" now he pointed to the left and right, "the standards of a score of the Dukes of Hell! Yet I see no other human standards."

Moonglum shouted: "Those castles we destroyed. I suspect that Jagreen Lern has already divided up these sundered lands and given them to his hirelings. How can we tell how much time has really passed—time in which all this could have been brought about?"

"True," Elric nodded, looking up at the still sun. He lurched forward in his saddle, half-swooning, pulled himself upright, breathing heavily. The Chaos Shield seemed like a huge weight on his arm, but he held it warily before him.

Then he acted on impulse and goaded Flamefang into speed so that the dragon rushed towards the city, diving down towards the castle of Jagreen Lern.

Nothing sought to stop him and he landed the beast among the turrets of the castle. Silence was dominant. He looked around, puzzled, but could see nothing save the towering buildings of dark stone that seemed to ooze beneath Flamefang's feet.

The straps stopped him from dismounting, but he saw enough to be sure the city was deserted. Where was the horde of hell? Where was Jagreen Lern?

Dyvim Slorm and Moonglum came to join him, while the rest of the dragons circled above. Claws scratched on rock, wings slashed the air and they settled, turning their mighty heads this way and that, ruffling their scales restlessly for, once aroused from their slumber, the dragons preferred the air to the land.

Dyvim Slorm stayed but long enough to mutter: "I'll scout the city," and then was flying away again, low amongst the castles until they heard him cry out and saw him swoop out of sight. There came a yell, but they could not see what caused it, a pause, and then Dyvim Slorm's dragon was flapping up again and they saw he had a writhing prisoner slung over the front of his saddle. He landed. The thing he had captured bore resemblance to a human being, but was misshapen and ugly with a jutting underlip, low forehead and no chin; huge, square, uneven teeth bristled in its mouth and its bare arms were covered in waving hairs.

"Where are your masters?" Dyvim Slorm demanded. The thing seemed to possess no fear, but chuckled: "They predicted your coming and, since the city limits movement, have assembled their armies on a plateau they have made five miles to the north-east." It turned its dilated eyes to Elric. "Jagreen Lern sent greetings and said he anticipated your foolish downfall."

Elric shrugged.

Dyvim Slorm drew his own runeblade and hacked the creature down. It cackled as it died, for its sanity had fled with its fear. He shivered as the thing's soul-stuff blended with his own and passed extra energy to him. Then he cursed and looked at Elric with pain in his eyes.

"I acted in haste—I should have given him to you."

Elric said nothing to this but whispered in his failing voice: "Let's to their battlefield. Hurry!"

Up to join their flight they went again, into the rushing, populated air and towards the north-east.

It was with astonishment that they sighted Jagreen Lern's horde, for they could not understand how it could have managed to regroup itself so swiftly. Every fiend and warrior on Earth seemed to have come to fight under the Theocrat's standard. It clung like a vile disease to the undulating plain. And around it, clouds grew darker, even though lightning, obviously of supernatural origin, blossomed and shouted, criss-crossing the plain.

Into this noisy agitation swept the dragon flight and they recognized the force commanded by Jagreen Lern himself for his banner flew above it. Other divisions were commanded by Dukes of Hell—Malohin, Zhortra, Xiombarg and others. Also Elric noted the three oldest and wisest Lords of Chaos, dwarfing the rest. Chardros the Reaper with his great head and his curving scythe, Mabelode the Faceless with his face always in shadow no matter which way you looked at it, and Slortar the Old, slim and beautiful, reputed the oldest of the gods. This was a force which a thousand powerful sorcerers would find it hard to defend against, and the thought of attacking them seemed folly.

Elric did not bother to consider this for he had embarked on his plan and was committed to carrying it through even though, in his present condition, he was bound to destroy himself if he continued.

They had the advantage of attacking from the air, but this would only be of value while the dragons' venom lasted. When it gave out, they must go in closer. At that moment Elric would need much energy—and he had none.

Down swept the dragons, shooting their incendiary venom into the ranks of Chaos.

Normally, no army could stand against such an attack but, protected by sorcery, Chaos was able to turn much of the fiery venom aside. The venom seemed to spread against an invisible shield and dissipate. Some of it struck its target, however, and hundreds of warriors were engulfed in flame and died blazing.

Again and again the dragons rose and dived upon their enemies, Elric swaying almost unconscious in his saddle, his awareness of what was going on diminishing with every attack.

His dimming vision was further encumbered by the stinking smoke that had begun to rise off the battlefield. From the horde, huge lances were rising with seeming slowness, lances of Chaos like streaks of amber lightning striking at the dragons so that the beasts hit bellowed and hurtled dead to the ground. Closer and closer Elric's steed bore him until he was flying over the division commanded by Jagreen Lern himself. He caught a misty glimpse of the Theocrat sitting a repulsive, hairless horse and waving his sword, convulsed with mocking mirth. He faintly heard his enemy's voice drift up to him.

"Farewell, Elric—this is our last encounter, for today you go to limbo!"

Elric turned Flamefang about and whispered into his ear: "That one, brother—that one!"

With a roar, Flamefang loosed his venom at the laughing Theocrat. It seemed to Elric that Jagreen Lern must surely be burned to ashes, but just as the venom seemed to touch him, it was hurled back and only a few drops struck some of the Theocrat's retainers, igniting their flesh and clothing.

Still Jagreen Lern laughed and now he released an amber spear which had appeared in his hand. Straight towards Elric it went and, with difficulty, the albino put up his Chaos Shield to deflect it.

So great was the force of the bolt striking his shield that he was hurled backwards in his saddle and one of the straps securing him snapped so that he fell to the left and was only saved by the other strap that had held. Now he crouched behind the shield's protection as it was battered with supernatural weapons. Flamefang, too, was encompassed by the shield's great power; but how long would even the Chaos Shield resist such an attack?

It seemed that he was forced to use the shield for an infinite time before Flamefang's wings cracked the air like a ship's sail and he was rushing high above the horde.

He was dying.

Minute by minute the vitality was leaving him as if he were an old man ready for death. "I cannot die," he muttered, "I must not die. Is there no escape from this dilemma?"

Flamefang seemed to hear him. The dragon descended towards the ground again and dropped until its scaly belly was scraping the lances of the horde. Then Flamefang had landed on the unstable ground and waited with folded wings as a group of warriors goaded their beasts towards him.

Elric gasped: "What have you done, Flamefang? Is nothing dependable? You have delivered me into the hands of the enemy!"

With great effort he drew his sword as the first lance struck his shield and the rider passed, grinning, sensing Elric's weakness. Others came on both sides. Weakly, he slashed at one and Stormbringer suddenly took control to make his aim true. The rider's arm was pierced and he was locked to the blade as it fed, greedily, upon his lifestuff. Immediately, Elric felt some slight return of strength and realized that between them dragon and sword were helping him gain the energy he needed. But the blade kept the most part to itself. There was a reason for this, as Elric found out at once, for the sword continued to direct his arm. Several more riders were slain in this manner and Elric grinned as he felt the vitality flowing back into his body. His vision cleared, his reactions became normal, his spirits rose. Now he carried the attack to the rest of the division, Flamefang moving over the ground with a speed belying his bulk. The warriors scattered and fled back to rejoin the main force, but Elric no longer cared, he had the souls of a dozen of them and it was enough. "Now up, Flamefang! Rise and let us seek out more powerful enemies!"

Obediently Flamefang spread his wings. They began to flap and bear him off the ground until he was gliding low over the horde.

In the midst of Lord Xiombarg's division, Elric landed again, dismounted from Flamefang and, possessed of his supernatural energy, rushed into the ranks of fiendish warriors, hewing about him, invulnerable to all but the strongest attack of Chaos. Vitality mounted and a kind of battle-madness with it. Further and further into the ranks he sliced his way, until he saw Lord Xiombarg in his earthly guise of a slender, dark-haired woman. Elric knew that the woman's shape was no indication of Xiombarg's mighty strength but, without fear, he leapt towards the Duke of Hell and stood before him, looking up at where he sat on his lion-headed, bull-bodied mount.

Xiombarg's girl's voice came sweetly to Elric's ears. "Mortal, you have defied many Dukes of Hell and banished others back to the Higher Worlds. They call you godslayer now, so I've heard. Can you slay me?"

"You know that no mortal can slay one of the Lords of the Higher Worlds whether they be of Law or Chaos, Xiombarg—but he can, if equipped with sufficient power, destroy their earthly semblance and send them back to their own plane, never to return!"

"Can you do this to me?"

"Let us see!" Elric flung himself towards the Dark Lord.

Xiombarg was armed with a long-shafted battle-axe that gave off a night-blue radiance. As his steed reared, he swung the axe down at Elric's unprotected head. The albino flung up his shield and the axe struck it. A kind of metallic shout came from the weapons and huge sparks flew away. Elric moved in close and hacked at one of Xiombarg's feminine legs. A light moved down from his hips and protected the leg so that Stormbringer was brought to a stop, jarring Elric's arm. Again the axe struck the shield with the same effect as before. Again Elric tried to pierce Xiombarg's unholy defense. And all the while he heard the Dark Lord's laughter, sweetly modulated, yet as horrible as a hag's.

"Your mockery of human shape and human beauty begins to fail, my lord!" cried Elric, standing back for a moment to gather his strength.

Already the girl's face was writhing and changing as, disconcerted by Elric's power, the Duke of Hell spurred his beast down on the albino.

Elric dodged aside and struck again. This time Stormbringer throbbed in his hand as it pierced Xiombarg's defense and the Dark Lord moaned, retaliating with another axe-blow which Elric barely succeeded in blocking. He turned his beast, the axe rushing about his head as he whirled it and flung it at Elric with the intention of striking him in the head.

Elric ducked and put up his shield, the axe clipping it and falling to the shifting ground. He ran after Xiombarg who was once again turning his steed. From nowhere he had produced another weapon, a huge double-handed broadsword, the breadth of its blade triple that of even Stormbringer's. It seemed incongruous in the small, delicate hands of the girl-shape. And its size, Elric guessed, told something of its power. He backed away warily, noting absently that one of the Dark Lord's legs was missing and replaced by an insect's claw. If he could only destroy the rest of Xiombarg's disguise, he would have succeeded in banishing him.

Now Xiombarg's laughter was no longer sweet, but had an unhinged note. The lion-head roared in unison with its master's voice as it rushed towards Elric. The monstrous sword went up and crashed upon the Chaos Shield. Elric fell on his back, feeling the ground itch and crawl beneath him, but the shield was still in one piece. He caught sight of the bull-hoofs pounding down on him, drew himself beneath the shield, leaving only his sword-arm free. As the beast thundered above, seeking to crush him with its hoofs, he thrust upwards into its belly. The sword was initially halted and then seemed to pierce through whatever obstructed it and draw out the life-force. The vitality of the unholy beast passed from sword to man and Elric was taken aback by its strange, insensate quality, for the soul-stuff of an animal was different from that of an intelligent protagonist. He rolled from under the beast's bulk and sprang to his feet as the lion-bull collapsed, hurling Xiombarg's still-earthly shape to the ground.

Instantly the Dark Lord was up, standing with a peculiarly unbalanced stance with one leg human and the other alien. It limped swiftly towards Elric, bringing the huge sword round in a sideways movement that would slice Elric in two. But Elric, full of the energy gained from Xiombarg's steed, leapt back from the blow and struck at the sword with Stormbringer. The two blades met, but neither gave. Stormbringer shrieked in anger for it was unused to resistance of this kind. Elric got the rim of his shield under the blade and forced it up. For an instant Xiombarg's guard was open and Elric used that instant with effect, driving Stormbringer into the Dark Lord's breast with all his strength.

Xiombarg whimpered and at once his earthly shape began to dissolve as Elric's sword sucked his energy into itself. Elric knew that this energy was only that fraction constituting Xiombarg's life-force on this plane, that the major part of the Dark Lord's soul was still in the Higher Worlds for not even the most powerful of these godlings could summon the power to transport all of himself to the Earth. If Elric had taken every scrap of Xiombarg's soul, his own body could not have retained it but would have burst. However, so much more powerful than any human soul was the force flowing into him from the wound he had made, that he was once again the vessel for a mighty energy.

Xiombarg changed. He became little more than a flickering coil of coloured light which began to drift away and finally vanish as Xiombarg was swept, raging, back to his own plane.

Elric looked upwards. He was horrified to see that only a few of the dragons survived. One was fluttering down now and it had a rider on its back. From that distance he could not see which of his friends it was.

He began to run towards the place where it fell.

He heard the crash as it came to ground, heard a weird wailing, a bubbling cry and then nothing.

He battled his way through the milling warriors of Chaos and none could withstand him, until he came at last to the fallen dragon. There was a broken body lying on the ground beside it, but of the runeblade there was no sign. It had vanished.

It was the body of Dyvim Slorm, last of his kinsmen.

There was no time for mourning. Elric and Moonglum and the bare score of remaining dragons could not possibly win against Jagreen Lern's strength, which had been hardly touched by the attack. Standing over the body of his cousin, he placed the Horn of Fate to his lips, took a huge breath and blew. The clear, melancholy note of the horn rang out over the battlefield and seemed to carry in all directions, through all the dimensions of the cosmos, through all the myriad planes and existences, through all eternity to the ends of the multiverse and the ends of time itself.

The note took long moments to fade and, when it had at last died away, there was an absolute hush over the world, the milling millions were still, there was an air of expectancy.

And then the White Lords came.

## Chapter Five

It was as if some enormous sun, thousands of times larger than Earth's, had sent a ray of light pulsing through the cosmos, defying the flimsy barriers of time and space, to strike upon that great black battlefield. And along it, appearing on the pathway that the horn's weird power had created for them, strode the majestic Lords of Law, their earthly forms so beautiful that they challenged Elric's sanity, for his mind could scarcely absorb the sight. They disdained to ride, like the Lords of Chaos, on bizarre beasts, but moved without steeds, a magnificent assembly with their mirror-clear armour and rippling surcoats bearing the single Arrow of Law.

Leading them came Donblas the Justice Maker, a smile upon his perfect lips. He carried a slender sword in his right hand, a sword that was straight and sharp and like a beam of light itself.

Elric moved swiftly then, rushed to where Flamefang awaited him and urged the great reptile into the moaning air.

Flamefang moved with less ease than earlier, but Elric did not know whether it was because the beast was tired or whether the influence of Law was weighing on the dragon which was, after all, a creation of Chaos.

But at last he flew beside Moonglum and, looking around, saw that the remaining dragons had turned and were flying back to the West. Only their own steeds remained. Perhaps the last of the dragons had sensed their part played and were returning to the Dragon Caves to sleep again.

Elric and Moonglum exchanged glances but said nothing, for the sight below was too awe-inspiring to speak of.

A light, white and dazzling, spread from the midst of the Lords of Law, the beam upon which they had come faded, and they began to move towards the spot where Chardros the Reaper, Mabelode the Faceless, and Slortar the Old and the lesser Lords of Chaos had assembled themselves, ready for the great fight.

As the White Lords passed through the other denizens of hell and the polluted men who were their comrades, these creatures backed away screaming, falling where the radiance touched them. The dross was being cleaned away without effort—but the real strength in the shape of the Dukes of Hell and Jagreen Lern was still to be encountered.

Though at this stage the Lords of Law were scarcely taller than the human beings, they seemed to dwarf them and even Elric, high above, felt as if he were a tiny figure, scarcely larger than a fly. It was not their *size* so much as the implication of vastness which they seemed to carry with them.

Flamefang's wings beat wearily as he circled over the scene. All around him the dark colours were now full of clouds of lighter, softer shades.

The Lords of Law reached the spot where their ancient enemies were assembled and Elric heard Lord Donblas's voice carry up to him.

"You of Chaos have defied the edict of the Cosmic Balance and sought complete dominance of this planet. Destiny denies you this—for the Earth's life is over and it must be resurrected in a new form where your influence will be weak."

A sweet, mocking voice came from the ranks of Chaos. It was the voice of Slortar the Old. "You presume too much, brother. The fate of the Earth has not yet been finally decided. Our meeting will result in that decision—nothing else. If we win, Chaos shall rule. If you succeed in banishing us, then paltry Law bereft of possibility will gain ascendancy. But we shall win—though Fate herself complains!"

"Then let this thing be settled," replied Lord Donblas, and Elric saw the shining Lords of Law advance towards their dark opponents.

The very sky shook as they clashed. The air cried out and the Earth appeared to tilt. Those lesser beings left alive scattered away from the conflict and a sound like a million throbbing harp-strings, each of a subtly different pitch, began to emanate from the warring gods.

Elric saw Jagreen Lern leave the ranks of the Dukes of Hell and ride in his flaming scarlet armour, away from them. He realized, perhaps, that his impertinence would be swiftly rewarded by death.

Elric sent Flamefang soaring down and he drew Stormbringer, yelling the Theocrat's name and shouting challenges.

Jagreen Lern looked up, but he did not laugh this time. He increased his speed until, as Elric had already noted, he saw towards what he was riding. Ahead, the earth had turned to black and purple gas that danced frenetically as if seeking to free itself from the rest of the atmosphere. Jagreen Lern halted his hairless horse and drew his war-axe from his belt. He raised his flame-red buckler which, like Elric's, was treated against sorcerous weapons.

The dragon hurtled downwards making Elric gasp with the speed of its descent. It flapped to earth a few yards from where Jagreen Lern sat his horrible horse, waiting, philosophically, for Elric to attack. Perhaps he sensed that their fight would mirror the larger fight going on around them, that the outcome of the one would be reflected in the outcome of the other. Whatever it was, he did not indulge in his usual braggadocio, but waited in silence.

Careless whether Jagreen Lern had the advantage or not, Elric dismounted and spoke to Flamefang in a purring murmur.

"Back, Flamefang, now. Back with your brothers. Whatever comes to pass, if I win or lose, your part is over." As Flamefang stirred and turned his huge head to look into Elric's face, another dragon descended and landed a short distance away. Moonglum, too, dismounted, beginning to advance through the black and purple mist. Elric shouted to him: "I want no help in this, Moonglum!"

"I'll give you none. But it will be my pleasure to see you take his life and soul!"

Elric looked at Jagreen Lern whose face was still impassive.

Flamefang's wings beat and he swept up into the sky and was soon gone, the other dragon following. He would not return.

Elric stalked towards the Theocrat, his shield high and his sword ready. Then, with astonishment, he saw Jagreen Lern dismount from his own grotesque mount and slap its hairless rump to send it galloping away. He stood waiting, slightly crouched in a position which emphasized his high-shouldered stance. His long, dark face was taut and his eyes fixed on Elric as the albino came closer. An unstable smile of anticipation quivered on the Theocrat's lips and his eyes flickered.

Elric paused just before he came within sword-reach of his enemy. "Jagreen Lern, are you ready to pay for the crimes you've committed against me and the world?"

"Pay? Crimes? You surprise me, Elric, for I see you have fully absorbed the carping attitude of your new allies. In my conquests I have found it necessary to eliminate a few of your friends who sought to stop me. But that was to be expected. I did what I had to and what I intended—if I have failed now, I have no regret, for regret is a fool's emotion and useless in any capacity. What happened to your wife was no direct fault of mine. Will you have triumph if you slay me?"

Elric shook his head. "My perspectives have, indeed, changed, Jagreen Lern. Yet we of Melniboné were ever a vengeful brood—and vengeance is what I claim!"

"Ah, now I understand you." Jagreen Lern changed his stance and he raised his axe to the defensive position. "I am ready."

Elric leapt at him, Stormbringer shrieking through the air to crash against the scarlet buckler and crash again. Three blows he delivered before Jagreen Lern's axe sought to wriggle through his defense and he halted it by a sideways movement of the Chaos Shield. The axe succeeded only in grazing his arm near the shoulder. Elric's shield clanged against Jagreen Lern's and Elric attempted to exert his weight and push the Theocrat backwards, meanwhile stabbing around the rims of the locked shields and trying to penetrate Jagreen Lern's guard.

For some moments they remained in this position while the music of the battle sounded around them and the ground seemed to fall from under them, columns of blossoming colours erupting, like magical plants, on all sides. Then Jagreen Lern jumped back, slashing at Elric. The albino rushed forward, ducked and struck at the Theocrat's leg near the knee—and missed. From above, the axe dashed down and he flung himself to one side to avoid it. Carried off-balance by the force of the blow, Jagreen Lern staggered and Elric leapt up and kicked at the small of the Theocrat's back. The man fell sprawling, losing his grip on both axe and shield as he tried to do many things at once and failed to do anything. Elric put his heel on the Theocrat's neck and held him there, Stormbringer hovering greedily over his prone enemy.

Jagreen Lern heaved his body round so that he looked up at Elric. He was suddenly pale and his eyes were fixed on the black hellblade when he spoke hoarsely to Elric. "Finish me now. There's no place for my soul in all eternity—not any more. I must go to limbo—so finish me!"

Elric was about to allow Stormbringer to plunge itself into the defeated Theocrat when he stayed the weapon, holding it back from its prey with difficulty. The runesword murmured in frustration and tugged in his hand.

"No," he said slowly, "I want nothing of yours, Jagreen Lern. I would not pollute my being by feeding off your soul. Moonglum!" His friend ran up. "Moonglum, hand me your blade."

Silently, the little Eastlander obeyed. Elric sheathed the resisting Stormbringer, saying to it: "There—that's the first time I've stopped you from feeding. What will you do now, I wonder?" Then he took Moonglum's blade and slashed it across Jagreen Lern's cheek, opening it up in a long, deep cut which began slowly to fill with blood.

The Theocrat screamed.

"No, Elric—kill me!"

With an absent smile, Elric slashed the other cheek. His bloody face contorted, Jagreen Lern shouted for death, but Elric continued to smile his vague, half-aware smile, and said softly: "You sought to imitate the Emperors of Melniboné, did you not? You mocked Elric of that line, you tortured him and you abducted his wife. You moulded her body into a hell-shape as you moulded the rest of the world. You slew Elric's friends and challenged him in your impertinence. But you are nothing—you are more of a pawn than Elric ever was. Now, little man, know how the folk of Melniboné toyed with such upstarts in the days when they ruled the world!"

* * *

Jagreen Lern took an hour to die and only then because Moonglum begged Elric to finish him swiftly.

Elric handed Moonglum's tainted sword back to him after wiping it on a shred of fabric that had been part of the Theocrat's robe. He looked down at the mutilated body and stirred it with his foot, then he looked away to where the Lords of the Higher Worlds were embattled.

He was badly weakened from the fight and also from the energy he had been forced to exert to return the resisting Stormbringer to its sheath, but this was forgotten as he stared in wonder at the gigantic battle.

Both the Lords of Law and those of Chaos had become huge and misty as their earthly mass diminished and they continued to fight in human shape. They were like half-real giants, fighting everywhere now—on the land and above it. Far away on the rim of the horizon, he saw Donblas the Justice Maker engaged with Chardros the Reaper, their outlines flickering and spreading, the slim sword darting and the great scythe sweeping.

Unable to participate, unsure which side was winning, Elric and Moonglum watched as the intensity of the battle increased and, with it, the slow dissolution of the gods' earthly manifestation. The fight was no longer merely on the Earth but seemed to be raging throughout all the planes of the cosmos and, as if in unison with this transformation, the Earth appeared to be losing its form, until Elric and Moonglum drifted in the mingled swirl of air, fire, earth and water.

The Earth dissolved—yet still the Lords of the Higher Worlds battled over it.

The stuff of the Earth alone remained, but unformed. Its components were still in existence, but their new shape was undecided. The fight continued. The victors would have the privilege of re-forming the Earth.

## Chapter Six

At last, though Elric did not know how, the turbulent dark gave way to light, and there came a noise—a cosmic roar of hate and frustration—and he knew that the Lords of Chaos had been defeated and banished. The Lords of Law victorious, Fate's plan had been achieved, though it still required the last note of the horn to bring it to its required conclusion.

And Elric realized he did not have the strength left to blow the horn the third time.

About the two friends, the world was taking on a distinct shape again. They found they were standing on a rocky plain and in the distance were the slender peaks of new-formed mountains, purple against a mellow sky.

Then the Earth began to move. Faster and faster it whirled, day giving way to night with incredible rapidity, and then it began to slow until the sun was again all but motionless in the sky, moving with something like its customary speed.

The change had taken place. Law ruled here now, yet the Lords of Law had departed without thanks.

And though Law ruled, it could not progress until the horn was blown for the last time.

"So it is over," Moonglum murmured. "All gone—Elwher, my birthplace, Karlaak by the Weeping Waste, Bakshaan, even the Dreaming City and the Isle of Melniboné. They no longer exist, they cannot be retrieved. And this is the new world formed by Law. It looks much the same as the old."

Elric, too, was filled with a sense of loss, knowing that all the places that were familiar to him, even the very continents were gone and replaced by different ones. It was like the loss of childhood and perhaps that was what it was—the passing of the Earth's childhood.

He shrugged away the thought and smiled. "I'm supposed to blow the horn for the final time if the Earth's new life is to begin. Yet I haven't the strength. Perhaps Fate is to be thwarted after all?"

Moonglum looked at him strangely. "I hope not, friend."

Elric sighed. "We are the last two left, Moonglum, you and I. It is fitting that even the mighty events that have taken place have not harmed our friendship, have not separated us. You are the only friend whose company has not worn on me, the only one I have trusted."

Moonglum grinned a shadow of his old, cocky grin. "And where we've shared adventures, I've usually profited if you have not. The partnership has been complementary. I shall never know why I chose to share your destiny. Perhaps it was no doing of mine, but Fate's, for there is one final act of friendship I can perform . . ."

Elric was about to question Moonglum when a quiet voice came from behind him.

"I bear two messages. One of thanks from the Lords of Law—and another from a more powerful entity."

"Sepiriz!" Elric turned to face his mentor. "Well, are you satisfied with my work?"

"Aye—greatly." Sepiriz's face was sad and he stared at Elric with a look of profound sympathy. "You have succeeded in everything but the last act which is to blow the Horn of Fate for the third time. Because of you the world shall know progression and its new people shall have the opportunity to advance by degrees to a new state of being."

"But what is the meaning of it all?" Elric said. "That I have never fully understood."

"Who can? Who can know why the Cosmic Balance exists, why Fate exists and the Lords of the Higher Worlds? Why there must always be a champion to fight such battles? There seems to be an infinity of space and time and possibilities. There may be an infinite number of beings, one above the other, who see the final purpose, though, in infinity, there can be no final purpose. Perhaps all is cyclic and this same event will occur again and again until the universe is run down and fades away as the world we knew has faded. Meaning, Elric? Do not seek that, for madness lies in such a course."

"No meaning, no pattern. Then why have I suffered all this?"

"Perhaps even the gods seek meaning and pattern and this is merely one attempt to find it. Look—" he waved his hands to indicate the newly formed Earth. "All this is fresh and moulded by logic. Perhaps the logic will control the newcomers, perhaps a factor will occur to destroy that logic. The gods experiment, the Cosmic Balance guides the destiny of the Earth, men struggle and credit the gods with knowing why they struggle—but do the gods know?"

"You disturb me further when I had hoped to be comforted," he sighed. "I have lost wife and world—and do not know why."

"I am sorry. I have come to wish you farewell, my friend. Do what you must."

"Aye. Shall I see you again?"

"No, for we are both truly dead. Our age has gone."

Sepiriz seemed to twist in the air and disappear.

A cold silence remained.

At length Elric's thoughts were interrupted by Moonglum. "You must blow the horn, Elric. Whether it means nothing or much—you must blow it and finish this business for ever!"

"How? I have scarcely enough strength to stand on my feet."

"I have decided what you must do. Slay me with Stormbringer. Take my soul and vitality into yourself—then you will have sufficient power to blow the last blast."

"Kill you, Moonglum! The only one left—my only true friend? You babble!"

"I mean it. You must, for there is nothing else to do. Further, we have no place here and must die soon at any rate. You told me how Zarozinia gave you her soul—well, take mine, too!"

"I cannot."

Moonglum paced towards him and reached down to grip Stormbringer's hilt, pulling it halfway from the sheath.

"*No*, Moonglum!"

But now the sword sprang from the sheath on its own volition. Elric struck Moonglum's hand away and gripped the hilt. He could not stop it. The sword rose up, dragging his arm with it, poised to deliver a blow.

Moonglum stood with his arms by his sides, his face expressionless, though Elric thought he glimpsed a flicker of fear in the eyes. He struggled to control the blade, but knew it was impossible.

"Let it do its work, Elric."

The blade plunged forward and pierced Moonglum's heart. His blood sprang out and covered it. His eyes blurred and filled with horror. "Ah, no—I—had—not—expected *this*!"

Petrified, Elric could not tug the sword from his friend's heart. Moonglum's energy began to flow up its length and course into his body, yet, even when all the little Eastlander's vitality was absorbed, Elric remained staring at the small corpse until the tears flowed from his crimson eyes and a great sob racked him. Then the blade came free.

He flung it away from him and it did not clatter on the rocky ground but landed as a body might land. Then it seemed to move towards him and stop and he had the suspicion that it was watching him.

He took the horn and put it to his lips. He blew the blast to herald in the night of the new Earth. The night that would precede the new dawn. And though the horn's note was triumphant, Elric was not. He stood full of infinite loneliness and infinite sorrow, his head tilted back as the sound rang on. And, when the note faded from triumph to a dying echo that expressed something of Elric's misery, a huge outline began to form in the sky above the Earth, as if summoned by the horn.

It was the outline of a gigantic hand holding a balance and, as he watched, the Balance began to right itself until each side was true.

And somehow this relieved Elric's sorrow as he released his grip on the Horn of Fate.

"There *is* something, at least," he said, "and if it's an illusion, then it's a reassuring one."

He turned his head to one side and saw the blade leave the ground, sweep into the air and then rush down on him.

"Stormbringer!" he cried, and then the hellsword struck his chest,

he felt the icy touch of the blade against his heart, reached out his fingers to clutch at it, felt his body constrict, felt it sucking his soul from the very depths of his being, felt his whole personality being drawn into the runesword. He knew, as his life faded to combine with the sword's, that it had always been his destiny to die in this manner. With the blade he had killed friends and lovers, stolen their souls to feed his own waning strength. It was as if the sword had always used him to this end, as if he was merely a manifestation of Stormbringer and was now being taken back into the body of the blade which had never been a true sword. And, as he died, he wept again, for he knew that the fraction of the sword's soul which was his would never know rest but was doomed to immortality, to eternal struggle.

Elric of Melniboné, last of the Bright Emperors, cried out, and then his body collapsed, a sprawled husk beside its comrade, and he lay beneath the mighty balance that still hung in the sky.

Then Stormbringer's shape began to change, writhing and curling above the body of the albino, finally to stand astraddle it.

The entity that was Stormbringer, last manifestation of Chaos which would remain with this new world as it grew, looked down on the corpse of Elric of Melniboné and smiled.

"Farewell, friend. I was a thousand times more evil than thou!"

And then it leapt from the Earth and went spearing upwards, its wild voice laughing mockery at the Cosmic Balance; filling the universe with its unholy joy.

# LETTERS AND MISCELLANY

# ELRIC
(1963)

VERY NICE OF you to devote so much time to Elric—though he doesn't altogether merit it! I'd disagree with the writer when he says, "I expect the 'sword and sorcery' stories are by far the most popular type . . . etc." I think those who like them receive them enthusiastically, but it's a fairly small minority compared with those who like, for instance, "science fantasy" of *The Dragon Masters* variety and the stuff Kuttner, Brackett and others used to turn out for *Startling, Super Science*, etc. These days people seem to want information of some kind with their escapism—and sword and sorcery doesn't strictly supply information of the type required. (The appeal of James Bond appears to be based primarily on the lumps of pseudo-data inserted every so often in the narrative.) The only sword-and-sorcery stuff I personally enjoy reading is Leiber's. Don't go much for Tolkien, Dunsany, Smith, Howard—or Edgar Rice Burroughs in spite of what some critics have said of my books recently.

Though I didn't know *Science Fantasy* was due to fold when I wrote it, I wound up the Elric series just in time to catch the last issue quite by coincidence. I had intended to kill off Elric (as is probably plain from the second story in the currently appearing quartet, "Black Sword's Brothers") and his world, so it is just as well. A story set in a world which so closely borders Elric's that some of the place names are the same will be appearing in *Fantastic* some time this year. This was originally called "Earl Aubec and the Golem" but the title has been changed to "Master of Chaos" (the cosmology is identical with the Elric stories' cosmology) and will be, if Cele Goldsmith likes the next one

I'm planning, the first of a series showing the development of the Earth from a rather unusual start. It is vaguely possible that Elric will appear in future stories and some of his background not filled in in the concluding stories ("Sad Giant's Shield" in *Science Fantasy* No. 63 and "Doomed Lord's Passing" in *Science Fantasy* 64) will be filled in there. But this depends on how the series develops and what Cele Goldsmith thinks of the stories. "Master of Chaos" is, I think, in many ways my best S&S tale.

It is a great disappointment, however, that *Science Fantasy* has folded. Not simply because stories sold to it paid my rent, but because for me and many other writers in this country (particularly, like me, the younger ones) it was an outlet for the kind of story that is very difficult to sell in America—even to Cele Goldsmith who appears to be the most open-minded of the U.S. editors. Particularly this went for the short novel of the "Earth Is but a Star" length and the recent 37,000-word "Skeleton Crew" by Aldiss. The slow-developing, borderline-mainstream story of the kind Ballard does so well will find more difficulty selling in the States too, though Ballard's "Question of Re-entry" was of this kind and published in *Fantastic*. It seems a pity that English SF has reached, in people like Ballard and Aldiss, an exceptionally high standard and a strongly English flavour, and now it has no markets here.

The landscapes of my stories are metaphysical, not physical. As a faltering atheist with a deep irradicable religious sense (I was brought up on an offbeat brand of Christian mysticism) I tended, particularly in early stories like "While the Gods Laugh," to work out my own problems through Elric's adventures. Needless to say, I never reached any conclusions, merely brought these problems closer to the surface. I was writing not particularly well, but from the "soul." I wasn't just telling a story, I was telling *my* story. I don't think of myself as a fantasy writer in the strict sense—but the possibilities of fantasy attract me. For some sort of guide to what I see as worth exploiting in the fantasy form, I'd suggest you bear this in mind when you read "The Deep Fix" which will appear in the last issue of *Science Fantasy* along with "Doomed Lord's Passing," the last Elric story . . . which might also provide a clue. "The Deep Fix" will be under a pseudonym [the late James Colvin, ed.].

I am not a logical thinker. I am, if anything, an intuitive thinker. Most facts bore me. Some inspire me. Nuclear physics, for instance, though I know scarcely anything about the field, excites me, particularly when watching a nuclear physicist explaining his theories on TV. My only interest in any field of knowledge is literary. This is probably a narrow interest, but I'm a writer and want to be a good one. I have only written two fantasy stories in my life which were deliberately commercial (sorry, three—one hasn't been published). These were "Going Home" in *Science Fiction Adventures* and "Kings in Darkness" in *Science Fantasy*. The rest, for better or worse, were written from inside. Briefly, physics doesn't interest me—metaphysics does. The only writer of SF I enjoy is J. G. Ballard. The only writer of fantasy currently working in the magazines I like is Leiber. The three works of fantasy I can still reread and enjoy, apart from those, are Anderson's *The Broken Sword*, Peake's Titus Groan trilogy, and Cabell's *Jurgen*. Anderson has done nothing better than *The Broken Sword*, in my opinion, and I sometimes feel that his talent has since been diverted, even lessened. I feel that writing SF can ruin and bleed dry a writer's talent. The best he can do in this field is improve his technique—at the expense of his art. I think of myself as a bad writer with big ideas, but I'd rather be that than a big writer with bad ideas—or ideas that have gone bad. I tend to think of the SF magazine field as a field in which it is possible to experiment—and sell one's mistakes; but the impulse to sell tends to dominate the impulse to experiment the longer one stays in the field.

And fear of death, incidentally, is probably another source of inspiration in the Elric stories. I don't believe in life after death and I don't want to die. I hope I shan't. Maybe I'll be the exception that proves the rule . . .

Now for some specific remarks about the Elric material in *Niekas*. Firstly, a few carping points on the spelling. As you'll see from the book *Stealer of Souls*, which I had an opportunity to get at before it was printed, there is an accented é in the spelling of Melniboné. Melnibonay—this accent was, of course, left out of all but the first story.

Imrryr is spelled thus. Count Smiorgan Baldhead—not *of* Baldhead (his head was hairless).

A point about the end of "The Dreaming City": Elric used the wind to save himself, abandoning his comrades to the dragons. This, and Cymoril's death, is on his conscience.

I don't know whether the Imrryrians would have *despised* Elric (second story synopsis, line 1). I think of them as accepting his treachery fairly calmly, and yet bound to do something about it if they caught up with him.

When I wrote this story I was thinking of Stormbringer as a symbol—partly, anyway—of Man's reliance on mental and physical crutches he'd be better off without. It seems a bit pretentious, now. I suppose you could call the Dharzi zombie men, but really I didn't think of them as men at all, in the strict sense. The sea is, of course, an underground sea—and also not "natural" as Elric discovered. The hill, castle, etc.—all the bits and pieces in this episode—are all underground. There was the intention here to give the whole episode the aspect of taking place within a womb. The Book is a similar symbol to the Sword in this story. Again, in the end of this story, he leaves Shaarilla to her fate—abandoning her. At this period of my writing women either got killed or had some other dirty trick played on them. The only female character who survived was my own La Belle Dame sans Merci—Yishana. I won't explain that here—too personal. . . .

"The exact nature of the feud is a mystery" ("Theleb K'aarna," line 6): Maybe I wasn't clear enough here—but I have the idea that I explained somewhere how Theleb K'aarna had devised a means of sending Elric on a wild goose chase by loosing some supernatural force or other against him. This was why Elric wanted blood. That story by the way was the most popular of the first three. I guess a Freudian psychologist would know why. . . .

"Kings in Darkness" I'd rather not deal with, since it was the worst of the series and, as I mentioned, written commercially. Therefore there is little of it which fits in with what I like to think of as the *real* content of the Elric series.

No comments, either, on "The Flame Bringers"—although I enjoyed writing the Meerclar bit and the last sequence with Elric on the back of the dragon. This, I think, is nothing much more than an adventure story, though it serves to show up Elric's weakness in that the moment things get tough he's seeking his sword again. Also the last bit where the sword returns is a hint of the sword's "true" nature.

In the book version of the last quartet (of which "Black Sword's Brothers" is the first part) I've revised the opening a bit. It was—and C. R. Kearns pointed this out and I agreed with him—what you might call a confused start. In the final revision of the short story version I changed it fairly considerably from the original and one or two inconsistencies crept through—I was working hard at the time and was very tired.

I would rather you had left this story out or waited until all four had been published before synopsizing it since this is the first part of a novel and many issues are not clarified until the end. I'm not happy with any of the magazine stories as they stand and have made, in places, quite heavy revisions. The last story to be written is, I feel, the best though. A final word—the Lords of Chaos hated Tanelorn not because it was a utopia, but because nearly all those in the city had once owed them, the Lords, allegiance and had forsworn it when they came to Tanelorn (or so the story goes). This is probably the most overtly philosophical or mystical of the Young Kingdom tales, as you say, and took much longer to write than the rest. It could be improved, I feel, by more play on the actual characters involved.

The writer feels that "Black Sword's Brothers" was the dullest Elric story. It was certainly, as explained above, one of the most patchy from the point of view of construction. It's true, in one sense, that I was losing interest in the Elric series—or rather that I had reached a point before it was written where I had run out of inspiration. But the interest picked up as I began to write and, by the time I'd got into the second part, I was enjoying the writing again. I think it's possible to look at the Elric stories as a sort of presentation of the crude materials which I hope to fashion into better stories later. Being non-logical, I have to produce a great deal of stuff in order to find the bits of it I really want. My ideas about Law and Chaos and the rest became clearer as I wrote.

Of the four, "Black Sword's Brothers" and "Sad Giant's Shield" (the most recently published) are the weakest in my opinion. Both were revised (something I do not usually do with the Elric stories) and both suffered from this revision, I think. My mind was at its clearest (not very clear by normal standards) when I wrote "Doomed Lord's Passing." I've found that I can only really learn from my mistakes after they've been published, which is hard on the reader.

Ted Carnell, who handles my other work as well, said that he felt "Earl Aubec and the Golem" (or "Master of Chaos") was a sort of crystallization of everything I'd been working on in the Elric series. Maybe not everything, but I think he's right. "Earl Aubec" is more a kind of sword-and-philosophy tale than an outright sword-and-sorcery. Elric tales—or the best of them—were conceived similarly.

The writer thinks that John Rackham's fantasies (or properly "Occult-thrillers") will outlast my stories. I don't think either will last for long, but I might as well admit that I was slightly hurt by this remark, for Rackham's stories that I have read struck me as being rather barren, stereotyped tales with no "true" sense of the occult at all (whatever a true sense of the occult is). Moreover I know John doesn't believe in his stuff for a second (at least not in any supernatural sense), whereas I believe whole-heartedly in mine, as I've pointed out. It's silly to take up someone's remark like this, especially since it is fair criticism and just a statement of someone's individual taste, but I suppose I'm still young enough to feel defensive about my stories—especially my Elric stories for which I have an odd mixture of love and hate. They are so closely linked to my own obsessions and problems that I find it hard to ignore any criticisms of them and tend momentarily to leap to their defense.

As I said earlier, and Cele Goldsmith said in a supplement to *AMRA*, sword and sorcery seems to appeal to an enthusiastic minority and may receive a large volume of praise from a fairly small section of readers.

When Carnell asked me to think up a sword-and-sorcery series, I tried to make it as different as possible from any other I'd read. I'd hesitate to agree that the two best known magic swords are Excalibur and Prince Valiant's Singing Blade—Excalibur, certainly, and probably

Roland's Durandana. The idea of the magic sword came, of course, from legend, but I willingly admit to Anderson's influence, too. The idea of an albino hero had a more obscure source. As a boy I collected a pre-War magazine called *Union Jack*. This was Sexton Blake's Own Paper—Blake was the British version of your Nick Carter, I should imagine, and *Union Jack* was the equivalent of your dime novels. One of Blake's most memorable opponents was a character named M. Zenith—or Zenith the Albino, a Byronic hero-villain who aroused more sympathy in the reader than did the intrepid detective. Anyway, the Byronic h-v had always appealed; I liked the idea of an albino, which suited my purpose, and so Elric was born—an albino. Influences include various Gothic novels, also. Elric is not a new hero to fantasy—although he's new, I suppose, to S&S.

I cannot altogether agree that Elric remains an essentially simple character. I think of him as complex but inarticulate when he tries to explain his predicament. His taste for revenge seems to be a sort of extension of his search for peace and purpose—he finds, to coin a phrase, forgetfulness in action. Elric's guilt over the slaying of Nikorn was guilt for the *slaying* itself, not because he'd killed a particular man.

I don't know whether I could have left Moonglum out and still kept the stories the same. Moonglum is, apart from everything else, to some extent a close, valued friend of mine who has been a lot of help in various ways over the last few years. If Elric is my fantasy self, then Moonglum is this friend's fantasy self (as I see him at any rate). I am not particularly gloomy by nature. I put Moonglum in to make remarks about Elric when he gets too self-absorbed or too absorbed in self-pity, etc.

A little more of Elric's background and some clue as to why he is what he is will be found in "Doomed Lord's Passing." I've been aware of this absence and have tried to rectify it a bit here.

I was pleased that you have used the Gray Mouser as a comparison since, as must now be evident, I'm a great fan of the Mouser's. Perhaps Moonglum also owes a little to the Mouser. As for Elric being an idealist rather than a materialist, this is probably because I'm often told I'm a materialist rather than an idealist. I don't like to be told this, but it could be true.

Elric's disregard for danger is of the nature of panic rather than courage, maybe. The Mouser, on the other hand, seems not to disregard danger—he evaluates it and then acts. Conan—well . . .

The cosmology of the Elric stories probably owes its original inspiration to two things—Zoroastrianism (which I admire) and Anderson's *Three Hearts and Three Lions*. It was developed from there, of course. This set-up simply is:

COSMIC HAND<br>
"<br>
"<br>
"<br>
"<br>
"<br>
"<br>
balance<br>
/ \\<br>
Law Chaos<br>
Grey Lords<br>
Elementals<br>
Men<br>
Law Sorcerers Chaos Sorcerers<br>
Beasts<br>
Men pledged to Law Men pledged to Chaos<br>
etc.<br>
etc.

I have a more complex chart. The sixth story is the one where the cosmology becomes clearer and the reader should realize the rest as he reads the last stories.

I have probably helped anyone who wants to assess the Elric stories on a slightly different level. Who wants to?

# THE SECRET LIFE OF ELRIC OF MELNIBONÉ
(1964)

SOME YEARS AGO, when I was about eighteen, I wrote a novel called *The Golden Barge*. This was an allegorical fantasy about a little man, completely without self-knowledge and with little of any other kind, going down a seemingly endless river, following a great Golden Barge which, he felt, if he caught it would contain all truth, all secrets, all the solutions to his problems. On the journey he met various groups of people, had a love affair, and so on. Yet every action he took in order to reach the Golden Barge seemed to keep him farther away from it. The river represented Time, the barge was what mankind is always seeking outside itself, when it can be found inside itself, etc., etc. The novel had a sad ending, as such novels do. Also, as was clear when I'd finished it, my handling of many of the scenes was clumsy and immature. So I scrapped it and decided that in future my allegories would be intrinsic within a conventional narrative—that the best symbols were the symbols found in familiar objects. Like swords for instance.

Up until I was twenty or so, I had a keen interest in fantasy fiction, particularly sword-and-sorcery stories of the kind written by Robert E. Howard, Clark Ashton Smith and the like, but this interest began to wane as I became more interested in less directly sensational forms of literature, just as earlier my interest in Edgar Rice Burroughs's tales had waned. I could still enjoy one or two sword-and-sorcery tales, particularly Poul Anderson's *The Broken Sword* and Fritz Leiber's Gray Mouser stories. A bit before this casting off of old loyalties, I had been in touch with Sprague de Camp and Hans Santesson of *Fantastic Universe* about doing a new series of Conan tales.

I think it was in the autumn of 1960, when I was working for Sexton Blake Library and reading SF for *Suspense* (the short-lived companion to *Argosy*) that I bumped into a colleague at Fleetway Publications, Andy Vincent, who was an old friend of Harry Harrison's (who had also free-lanced for Fleetway for some time). Andy told me he was meeting Harry and Ted Carnell in the Fleetway foyer and suggested I come along. As I remember, that was where I first met Harry. Previously, I'd sold a couple of stories to Ted, one in collaboration with Barry Bayley, and had had more bounced than bought. Later on in a pub, Ted and I were talking about Robert E. Howard and Ted said he'd been thinking of running some Conan-type stuff in *Science Fantasy*. I told him of the *Fantastic Universe* idea which had fallen through when *Fantastic Universe* folded, and said I still had the stuff I'd done and would he like to see it. He said he would. A couple of days later I sent him the first chapter and outline of a Conan story. To tell you the truth, writing in Howard's style had its limitations, as did his hero as far as I was concerned, and I wasn't looking forward to producing another 10,000 words of the story if Ted liked it.

Ted liked it—or at least he liked the writing, but there had been a misunderstanding. He hadn't wanted Conan—he had wanted something on the same lines.

This suited me much better. I decided that I would think up a hero as different as possible from the usual run of S&S heroes, and use the narrative as a vehicle for my own "serious" ideas. Many of these ideas, I realize now, were somewhat romantic and coloured by a long-drawn-out and, to me at the time, tragic love affair which hadn't quite finished its course and which was confusing and darkening my outlook. I was writing floods of hack work for Fleetway and was getting sometimes £70 or £80 a week which was going on drink, mainly, and, as I remember, involved rather a lot of broken glass of one description or another. I do remember, with great pride, my main achievement of the winter of 1960 or 1961, which was to smash entirely an unbreakable plate glass door in a well-known restaurant near Piccadilly. And the management apologized . . .

I mention this, to give a picture of my mood at the time of Elric's creation. If you've read the early Elric stories in particular, you'll see that Elric's outlook was rather similar to mine. My point is that Elric *was* me (the me of 1960/61 anyway) and the mingled qualities of betrayer and betrayed, the bewilderment about life in general, the search for some solution to it all, the expression of this bewilderment in terms of violence, cynicism and the need for revenge were all characteristic of mine. So when I got the chance to write "The Dreaming City," I was identifying very closely with my hero-villain. I thought myself something of an outcast (another romantic notion largely unsubstantiated now I look back) and emphasized Elric's physical differences accordingly:

> His bizarre dress was tasteless and gaudy, and did not match his sensitive face and long-fingered, almost delicate hands, yet he flaunted it since it emphasized that he did not belong in any company—that he was an outsider and an outcast. But, in reality, he had little need to wear such outlandish gear—for . . . [he] was a pure albino who drew his power from a secret and terrible source.
>
> (*The Stealer of Souls*, page 13)

The story was packed with personal symbols (as are all the stories, bar a couple). The "secret and terrible source" was the sword Stormbringer, which symbolized my own and others' tendency to rely on mental and physical crutches rather than cure the weakness at source. To go further, Elric, for me, symbolized the ambivalence of mankind in general, with its love-hates, its mean-generosity, its confident-bewilderment act. Elric is a thief who believes *himself* robbed, a lover who hates love. In short, he cannot be sure of the truth of anything, not even of his own emotions or ambitions. This is made much clearer in a story containing even more direct allegory, the second in the series, "While the Gods Laugh." Unfortunately, Ted left out the verse from which the title was taken:

> I, while the gods laugh, the world's vortex am;
> Maelstrom of passions in that hidden sea
> Whose waves of all-time lap the coasts of me,
> And in small compass the dark waters cram.
>
> Mervyn Peake, "Shapes and Sounds"

This, I think, gave more meaning to both title and story which involved a long quest after the Dead Gods' Book—a mythical work alleged to contain all the knowledge of the universe, in which Elric feels he will at last find the true meaning of life. He expresses this need in a somewhat rhetorical way. When the wingless woman Shaarilla asks him why he wants the book he replies [in the magazine version]:

> "I desire, if you like, to know one of [misprinted as *or* in magazine version] two things. Does an ultimate God exist—or not. Does Law or Chaos govern our lives? Men need a God, so the philosophers tell us. Have they made one—or did one make them?" etc., etc.

Here, as in other passages, the bewilderment is expressed in metaphysical terms, for at that time, due mainly to my education, I was very involved with mysticism. Also, the metaphysical terms suited the description of a sword-and-sorcery hero and his magical, low-technology world.

It may seem odd that I use such phrases as "at that time" and so on, as if I'm referring to the remote past, but in many ways, being a trifle more mature, perhaps, happily married with a better sense of direction, etc., all this *does* seem to have taken place in the remote past.

The Dead Gods' Book is eventually located in a vast underground world which I had intended as a womb-symbol, and after a philosophical conversation with the book's Keeper, Elric discovers it. This passage is, to me now, rather overwritten, but, for better or worse:

> It was a huge book—the Dead Gods' Book, its covers encrusted with alien gems from which the light sprang. It gleamed, it *throbbed* with light and brilliant colour.
>
> "At last," Elric breathed. "At last—the Truth!"
>
> He stumbled forward like a man made stupid with drink, his pale hands reaching for the thing he had sought with such savage bitterness. His hands touched the pulsating cover of the Book and, trembling, turned it back . . . With a crash, the cover fell to the floor, sending the bright gems skipping and dancing over the paving stones. *Beneath Elric's . . . hands lay nothing but a pile of yellowish dust.*

The Dead Gods' Book and the Golden Barge are one and the same. They have no real existence, save in the wishful imagination of mankind. There is, the story says, no Holy Grail which will transform a man overnight from bewildered ignorance to complete knowledge—the answer already is within him, if he cares to train himself to find it. A rather over-emphasized fact, throughout history, but one generally ignored all the same.

"The Stealer of Souls," the third story, continues this theme, but brought in rather different kinds of symbols. Coupled with the Jungian symbols already inherent in any tale using direct mythic material, I used Freudian symbols, too. This was a cynical attempt and a rather vulgar attempt to make the series popular. It appeared to work. "The Stealer of Souls," whatever else it may be, is one of the most pornographic stories I have ever written. In Freudian terms it is the description of, if you like, a night's love-making.

Which brings me to another point. Although there is comparatively little direct description of sexual encounters in the stories, and what there are are largely romanticized, the whole Elric saga has, in its choice of situations and symbols, very heavy sexual undertones. This is true of most sword-and-sorcery stories, but I have an idea that I may be the first such author to understand his material to this extent, to know what he's using. If I hadn't been a bit fed-up by the big response received by "The Stealer of Souls" (magazine story, not the book), I could have made even greater use of what I discovered.

Other critics have pointed out the close relationship the horror story (and often the SF story for that matter) has with the pornographic story, so there's no need to go any deeper into it here.

The pornographic content of the Elric saga doesn't interest me much, but I have hinted at the relationship between sex and violence in several stories, and, indeed, there are a dozen syndromes to be found in the stories, particularly if you bear in mind my own involvement with sexual love, expression in violence, etc., at the time the stories were first conceived. Even my own interpretation of what I was doing is open to interpretation, in this case!

The allegory goes through all ten stories (including "To Rescue Tanelorn . . . " which did not feature Elric) in *Science Fantasy*, but it tends to change its emphasis as my own ideas take better shape and my emotions mature. When, in the last Elric story of all, the sword, his crutch, Stormbringer turns and slays Elric, it is meant to represent, on one level, how mankind's wish-fantasies can often bring about the destruction of (till now at least) part of mankind. Hitler, for instance, founded his whole so-called political creed on a series of wish-fantasies (this is detailed in that odd book *Dawn of Magic*, recently published here). Again this is an old question, a bit trite from being asked too often, maybe, but how much of what we believe *is* true and how much is what we *wish* were true? Hitler dreamed of his Thousand Year Reich, Chamberlain said There Will Be No War. Both were convinced—both ignored plain fact to a frightening extent, just as many people (not just politicians whose public statements are not always what they really believe) ignore plain facts today. This is no new discovery of mine. It is probably one of the oldest discoveries in the world. But, in part, this is what nearly all my published work points out. Working, as I did once, as editor of a party journal (allegedly an information magazine for party candidates) this conviction was strengthened. The build-up of a fantasy is an odd process and sometimes happens, to digress a bit, like this.

The facts are gathered, related, a picture emerges. The picture, though slightly coloured by the personalities of the fact-relaters, is fairly true. The picture is given to the politician. If the politician is a man of integrity he will not deliberately warp the facts, but he will present them in a simplified version which will be understood by the general public (he thinks). This involves a selection, which can change a picture out of all recognition, though the politician didn't deliberately intend to warp the facts. The other kind of politician almost automatically selects and warps in order to prove a point he, or his party, is trying to make. So the fantasy begins. Soon the real picture is almost irrevocably lost.

Therefore this reliance on pseudo-knowledge, which seems to prove something we wish were true, is a dangerous thing to do.

This is one of the main messages of the Elric series, though there are several others on different levels.

Don't think I'm asking you to go back over the stories looking for these allegories and symbols. The reason I abandoned *The Golden Barge* was because among other things it wasn't entertaining. The Elric stories are meant to entertain as much as anything else, but if anyone cares to look for substance beyond the entertainment level, they might find it.

One of the main reasons, though, for taking this angle when Alan [Dodd] asked me to write a piece on Elric, was because I have been a little disappointed at the first book being dismissed by some professional critics (who evidently didn't bother to read it closely, if at all) as an imitation of Conan. When you put thought and feeling into a story—thought and feeling which is yours—you don't much care for being called an imitator or a plagiarist however good or bad the story. Probably the millionth novel about a young advertising executive in love with a deb and involved with a married woman has just been published, yet the author won't be accused of imitating anyone or plagiarizing anyone. It is the use to which one puts one's chosen material, not that material, which matters.

*This is the first lengthy review of* Stormbringer *published, as it happened, in* New Worlds. *Perhaps I should not have let it be reviewed in my own magazine, but Alan Forrest the writer was at the time literary editor of a national newspaper and I thought the book might best be reviewed by someone who had no intimate knowledge of SF and fantasy. Also I didn't want the book reviewed by someone who might be hoping to sell me a story. Forrest does give a flavour, I think, of how strange and* sui generis *such fiction seemed to readers in 1965.*

## FINAL JUDGEMENT

by Alan Forrest (1965)

STORMBRINGER IS A magic sword, a great, evil blade with a life of its own. It sucks souls like a vampire sucks his victims' blood. It is the real hero-villain of Michael Moorcock's strange new novel set in a blood-soaked and bewitched world, anti-time and anti-history, in which nightmare armies battle, statues scream and heroines can be turned into big white worms at the drop of a warlock's hat.

Mr. Moorcock stirs up this hell-brew with an inventiveness that leaves one gasping. His is the territory that has always been dear to a certain kind of English writer, the genuine exotic, who exists to remind us that we're really a most exotic race.

I'm thinking of people like Mervyn Peake and, in the last few years, Jane Gaskell. *Stormbringer* (Herbert Jenkins, 12/6d.) has, for me, the same kind of offbeat integrity and complete involvement with a dream-world that impressed me in *The Serpent*, Miss Gaskell's novel about Atlantis.

Mr. Moorcock's Bright Empire of Melniboné existed "ten thousand years before history was recorded—or ten thousand years after history had ceased to be chronicled, reckon it how you will." It is far from easy to describe, but it is a kind of primitive myth-land with touches of Victorian Gothick, Wagnerian darkness and even undertones of the Book of Revelations.

The plot is about the battle between the Forces of Law and Chaos for nothing less than the future of the universe. The characters have a kind of human form, but we're told they are less than men, ghostly epic-types who live only to intrigue and slaughter to settle the shape of quality of the world of real men which is to follow them.

So *Stormbringer* is an exciting fantasy about the eternal struggle of Good and Evil. The forces of Order are led by Elric, the last ruler of Melniboné, a red-eyed albino who has little real physical strength, but draws it from the soul-sucking sword. With Stormbringer in his hand, he is ten feet tall and a match for any Theocrat called Jagreen Lern, his warrior-priests and the Lords of Hell. Without the sword, he couldn't take on a reasonably skilled light weight.

Elric is an excellent character, pretty well-rounded and convincing for a myth-figure. He could have been the familiar strong, but lily-white hero. Mr. Moorcock doesn't make him any such thing.

Elric and Stormbringer—between whom there's a skillfully established love-hate relationship; neither can do without the other—take the field in a world ruled by chance, destiny, sorcery, all the supernatural forces that strangle men's free will. The atmosphere is chilly and oppressive and that's, perhaps, my only quibble at Mr. Moorcock's fascinating novel.

I don't ask for sweetness and light from science fiction, fantasy and its associated literatures, but I wish more young writers like Michael Moorcock would show us characters who are real masters of their fate and not just dancing on a cosmic puppet-master's strings.

But I wouldn't have missed *Stormbringer* for anything. The excitement and blood-letting never lets up, from the moment Jagreen Lern kidnaps Elric's wife and Elric and his buddies set hot-foot across the Sighing Desert and the Pale Sea to dish the villains of Pan Tang.

Elric himself is no goody-goody, his crimson eyes burning with hate as phantom horsemen bear down on him. "He was capable of cruelty and malevolent sorcery, had little pity, but could love and hate more violently than ever his ancestors." He'll lop a man's head off for sheer expediency and ask questions afterwards.

But slowly he emerges as a lone goodish man in a landscape that drips with blood and hate. And Mr. Moorcock's landscapes are compelling.

There are dark battlefields where bloody men come screaming out of the night, black-cowled midnight horrors with fixed grins, ghastly wailing winged women running amok with their wings clipped, doom-laden seas where black, rat-infested warships fill the air with fireballs.

Elric fights an army of vampire trees with his vampire sword as they try to tear him apart using branches like superhuman fingers. He takes a journey in time to fight that dead hero of another age, Roland, to get his magic horn.

Is there too much blood? I said the weird inventiveness of it all leaves one gasping. Does it tend to drain one dry? Is there a danger of Mr. Moorcock's work becoming a parody of itself as this kind of literature often does? On the strength of this one book, he avoids it by a hair's-breadth and I can recommend *Stormbringer*. In a tight corner I would rather have Elric's sword than Arthur's Excalibur for all its malevolent habit of doing what it likes and standing there, alive, sinister and smiling when nearly every other character has had his chips in some way.

Most of all, I feel that Mr. Moorcock's battle between good and evil is a sad story. If it did happen in some early world of supernatural twilight, a lot of men died in vain.

Elric fought for a decent world of the future, one that he would never enjoy. What did we get? Buchenwald, the atom bomb and brainwashing. Perhaps Mr. Moorcock's world has something? Could the sorcerers have done much worse than that?

# THE ZENITH LETTER

by Anthony Skene (1924)

"Woodlands"
Oakhill Gdns
Woodford Green
Essex

2.7.24

Dear Mr. Young,

Many thanks!

The Editor of the *Union Jack* of course receives letters from readers galore as to his yarns and most of them have something to say about Zenith.

They are not all complimentary, some are very much the reverse; but the Albino is usually liked (or disliked) very much indeed.

That shows, I think, that to them, as to you—and me, Zenith is a living man. It is impossible to feel strongly about a phantasm.

One likes appreciation naturally. Literary art, so far as I understand it, is translation, by means of words, from the mind of the writer to the mind of the reader, of certain interests and emotions. When I read that for you Zenith *lived*, I was delighted to perceive that, so far as you were concerned, I had succeeded.

In 1913, I encountered, in the West End, a true albino, a man of about fifty-five.

He was a slovenly fellow: fingers stained with tobacco, clothes soiled by dropped food. Yet he was dressed expensively, and had about him a look of adequacy.

I should have forgotten him in a day or so; but when, an hour afterwards and five miles away, I sat down to have my lunch, he walked in to the restaurant and sat himself within a few feet of me.

This coincidence made an impression upon my mind, and when I needed a central figure not quite so banal as Blake for the *U.J.* stories, I re-created this albino fellow "moulded nearer to the heart's desire."

As I expect you will agree, Mr. Young, the lordly crook exists in most of us, only he is shackled by conventions and virtues. The Jekyll-and-Hyde trick of setting him free is, of course, a trick of the writer's trade. One cannot, alas, have the excitement of a crook's brief life in actuality; but one can, vicariously, with arm-chair and cigarette, experience not only the actions thereof, but the re-actions also. I am telling you what you have already divined.

Regarding my novels, I regret to inform you that I have written none. The disgusting truth is that novel-writing does not pay. I have planned a novel, and soon I shall write it. I think it will be good, but I do not expect to make more than £50 out of it. That's that. I have to live, Mr. Young. Novel-writing is an expensive hobby.

Otherwise, you appear to have read all my long stories. In my opinion (which is probably unreliable on the subject) the best chapters I ever wrote were the first one of two in "The Case of the Crystal Gazer" and the best yarn "The Tenth Case" (published immediately after "A Duel to the Death," in 1918). The Editor liked "The Curse of the Crimson Curtain" (published recently).

In addition to these *Union Jack*, etc., yarns I have written nothing but newspaper articles, and one or two "shorts" not worth mentioning. I have a single copy of most of my Zenith yarns, but I need these frequently for reference, and further copies are, I fear, largely out of print.

I am now writing an S.B. Library story of which, when it is published, I should like to send you a copy.

That I have awakened so strong an interest in one who is, obviously, intellectually superior to the average reader of the *Union Jack*, I find both flattering and stimulating.

Sincerely yours,
Anthony Skene

ACKNOWLEDGMENTS

Very special thanks to The Savoyards (David Britton, Michael Butterworth, John Coulthart), to John Davey and to the residents of Sporting Club Square for all their considerable help in locating lost or forgotten material relating to the Elric stories. They are the real creators of this edition. My thanks, also, to the late John Carnell, editor of *Science Fantasy* magazine, who commissioned the first Elric stories. To Jimmy Ballard and Barry Bayley, whose enthusiasm encouraged me to write these, and to the late Sprague de Camp, who first persuaded me to write epic fantasy. To the late Hans Stefan Santesson, who almost commissioned the first fantasy story. To Jack Vance and the late Poul Anderson, who inspired me, and in affectionate memory of Fritz Leiber, who became a friend.

And, of course, I must thank my wife, Linda, for all her ongoing help and as a proper, old-fashioned muse, praising what she likes and spurning with contempt that which she doesn't. Some of these stories were appearing at about the same time my daughters, Sophie and Katie, were also making their first public appearances, so I must thank them and the great spoon Formulamixer for their involvement. I could say a great deal about Ron Bennett, Alan Dodd, Eric Bentcliffe, Arthur Thompson, Vince Clarke, Syd Bounds and a host of others who filled the Globe in Hatton Garden when I was a boy editor and whose fanzines were so funny, literate and had almost nothing whatsoever to do with SF or fantasy but who commissioned the odd piece from me anyway, helping me get my spurs long before the time it was seemly to be published. For John Picacio and an association that now enters its second decade. And, lastly, I'd like to thank Betsy Mitchell of Del Rey books for her commitment to making these new editions the best they could be.

For further information about Michael Moorcock and his work, please send a stamped, self-addressed envelope to:

**The Nomads of the Time Streams**
**P.O. Box 15910**
**Seattle, WA 98115-0910**

## ABOUT THE AUTHOR

Michael John Moorcock is the author of a number of science fiction, fantasy, and literary novels, including the Elric novels, the Cornelius Quartet, *Gloriana, King of the City,* and many more. As editor of the controversial British science fiction magazine *New Worlds,* Moorcock fostered the development of the New Wave in the U.K. and indirectly in the U.S. He won the Nebula Award for his novella *Behold the Man.* He has also won the World Fantasy Award, the British Fantasy Award, and many others.

## ABOUT THE ILLUSTRATOR

John Picacio has illustrated covers for books by Harlan Ellison, Robert Silverberg, Frederik Pohl, Jeffrey Ford, Charles Stross, and Joe R. Lansdale, amongst others, but his very first book cover assignment was for a Michael Moorcock work. Picacio not only illustrated the cover of the Thirtieth Anniversary edition of *Behold the Man* (Mojo Press, 1996), he also contributed interior illustrations and designed the entire book. Moorcock's early support and encouragement provided the right nudge at the right time, and that job energized Picacio to pursue a career as a book cover artist. In spring 2001, he left his day job in the world of architecture and has been a full-time professional illustrator ever since. He's produced cover art for major franchises, such as *Star Trek* and *The X-Men* amongst others. A three-time Hugo Award nominee for Best Professional Artist, he has won the Locus Award, two International Horror Guild Awards, the Chesley Award, and the much-coveted World Fantasy Award—all in the artist category. A little more than a decade after that first gig with Moorcock's *Behold the Man,* Picacio couldn't be prouder to help initiate this sparkling new Del Rey series of Elric editions. He lives in San Antonio, Texas, with his wife, Traci. For more info, please visit www.johnpicacio.com.